THE MEZENTIAN
GATE

Also by E. R. Eddison

THE MEZENTIAN GATE

by

E. R. Eddison

Edited and Introduced by
Paul Edmund Thomas

HarperCollins*Publishers*

HarperCollins*Publishers*
77-85 Fulham Palace Road
Hammersmith, London W6 8JB
www.harpercollins.co.uk

This edition 2014
1

ISBN 978-0-00-757817-7

Typeset by Palimpsest Book Production Ltd, Falkirk, Stirlingshire

Find out more about HarperCollins and the environment at
www.harpercollins.co.uk/green

CONTENTS

INTRODUCTION

BY PAUL EDMUND THOMAS

THE twelfth chapter of E. R. Eddison's first novel, *The Worm Ouroboros*, contains a curious episode extraneous to the main plot. Having spent nearly all their strength in climbing Koshtra Pivrarcha, the highest mountain pinnacle on waterish Mercury, the Lords Juss and Brandoch Daha stand idly enjoying the glory of their singular achievement atop the frozen wind-whipped summit, and they gaze away southward into a mysterious land never before seen:

> Juss looked southward where the blue land stretched in fold upon fold of rolling country, soft and misty, till it melted in the sky. 'Thou and I,' said he, 'first of the children of men, now behold with living eyes the fabled land of Zimiamvia. Is that true, thinkest thou, which philosophers tell us of that fortunate land: that no mortal foot may tread it, but the blessed souls do inhabit it of the dead that be departed, even they that were great upon earth and did great deeds when they were living, that scorned not earth and the delights and the glories thereof, and yet did justly and were not dastards nor yet oppressors?'
>
> 'Who knoweth?' said Brandoch Daha, resting his chin in his hand and gazing south as in a dream. 'Who shall say he knoweth?'

The land of Zimiamvia probably held only a fleeting and evanescent place in the minds of Eddison's readers in 1922, because this, the first and last mentioning of Zimiamvia in *Ouroboros,* flits quickly past the reader, and though it has a local habitation and a name, it does not have a place in the story. Yet in the author's mind, the name rooted itself so deeply that its engendering and growth cannot be clearly traced. Where did this name and this land come from? How and when was Zimiamvia born? How, while writing *Ouroboros* in 1921, did Eddison come to think of including this extraneous description of a land inconsequential to the story? Why did he include it?

Who knows? Who shall say he knows? No living person can answer these questions with certainty. What is certain is that Zimiamvia existed in Eddison's imagination for at least twenty-three years and that he spent much of the rare leisure time of his last fifteen years writing three novels to give tangible shape to that misty land whose existence the Lords Juss and Brandoch Daha ponder and question in those moments on the ice-clad jagged peak of Koshtra Pivrarcha.

When he finished *Ouroboros* in 1922, Eddison did not ride the hippogriff-chariot through the heavens to Zimiamvian shores directly. Instead he remained firmly earth-bound and wrote *Styrbiorn the Strong,* a historical romance based on the life of the Swedish prince Styrbiorn Starki, the son of King Olaf, who died in 983 in an attempt to usurp the kingdom from his uncle, King Eric the Victorious. Eddison finished this novel in December 1925, and on 3 January 1926, during a vacation to Devonshire, he found himself desiring to pay homage to the Icelandic sagas that had inspired so many aspects of *Ouroboros* and *Styrbiorn the Strong:* 'Walking in a gale over High Peak Sidmouth . . . I thought suddenly that my next job should be a big saga translation, and that should be *Egil.*' After noting his decision, he justified it: 'This may pay back some of my debt to the sagas, to which I owe more than can ever be counted.' Resolved on this project, he steeped himself for five years in the literary and historical scholarship requisite for translating a thirteenth-century Icelandic text into English. It was

not until 1930, after *Egil's Saga* had been finished and dispatched
to the Cambridge University Press, that Eddison focused his attention on the new world that had lain nearly dormant in his mind
since at least 1921. Eddison finished the first Zimiamvian novel,
Mistress of Mistresses, in 1935. Faber & Faber published it in
England; E. P. Dutton published it in America. Eddison says
Mistress of Mistresses did not explore 'the relations between that
other world and our present here and now', and so his ideas of
those relations propelled him to write a second novel setting some
scenes in Zimiamvia and others in modern Europe. Eddison finished
this second novel, *A Fish Dinner in Memison,* in 1940, but the
wartime paper shortage prevented Faber & Faber from publishing
it, yet E. P. Dutton published it for American readers in 1941.
Eddison says that writing this second novel made him 'fall in love
with Zimiamvia', and since 'love has a searching curiosity which
can never be wholly satisfied', the new ideas sprouting from his
love grew into *The Mezentian Gate.*

Eddison never finished this third Zimiamvian novel, for he died
from a massive stroke in 1945. He intended *The Mezentian Gate*
to have thirty-nine chapters. Between 1941 and 1945, he wrote the
first seven, the last four, and Chapters XXVIII and XXIX. Like
many others, Eddison feared a German invasion of England, and
he worried that events beyond his control would prevent his
finishing *The Mezentian Gate.* So before November 1944, he wrote
an Argument with Dates, a complete and detailed plot synopsis of
all of the unwritten chapters. After completing the Argument and
thus assuring himself that his novel's story, at least, could be
published as a whole even if something happened to him, Eddison
went on to write drafts for several more chapters during his last
year of life. In 1958 his brother Colin Eddison, his friend Sir George
Rostrevor Hamilton and Sir Francis Meynell (the founder of the
Nonesuch Press and son of the poet Alice Meynell) privately
published this fragmentary novel at the Curwen Press in Plaistow,
West Sussex. The Curwen edition included only the finished chapters
and the Argument; it did not include the substantial number of
preliminary drafts for unfinished chapters that Eddison composed

between January and August 1945. These drafts, extant in hand-written leaves, have lain in the darkness of manuscript boxes in the underground stacks of the Bodleian Library in Oxford, and they have been read by few since Eddison's death.

In Dell's 1992 edition, Eddison's neglected manuscript drafts for *The Mezentian Gate* were finally brought into the light of print, and for the first time the three Zimiamvian novels were pressed within the covers of one volume and united under the title *Zimiamvia*.

The Writing of *The Mezentian Gate*

On 25 July 1941, E. R. Eddison wrote to George Rostrevor Hamilton and told of the birth of *The Mezentian Gate*: 'After laborious lists of dates and episodes and so on, extending over many weeks, I really think the scheme for the new Zimiamvian book crystallized suddenly at 9 p.m. last night.' On 2 September Eddison was still excited about his progress and wrote to Hamilton again: 'You will be glad to know that about 1500 words of the (still nameless) new Zimiamvian book are already written.' The opening sections, the Praeludium, which he first called 'Praeludium in Excelsis' (literally, 'a preface set in a high place'), and 'Foundations in Rerek' alternately filled the sails of his imagination, but he decided to finish the voyage to Rerek before turning his prow toward Mount Olympus, the original setting for the Praeludium. Seven months later, on 2 April 1942, another letter to Hamilton shows that Eddison's initial swift sailing had quickly carried his imagination into the doldrums:

> I am still struggling with the opening of the new book. The 'Praeludium in Excelsis' which I had written dissatisfies me: seems to be ornamental rather than profound. So I'm changing the *mise en scene* from Olympus to Lofoten, and think it will create the atmosphere I'm sniffing for. But, Lord, it comes out unwillingly and painfully.

Evidently, Eddison abandoned his resolve to finish 'Foundations in Rerek' first, and his imagination tacked toward Rerek and Olympus in turns, but without gaining much momentum toward either destination. Eddison eventually completed the Praeludium in July and sent it to Hamilton for a critical reading with this qualifying statement attached: 'it has given me infinite trouble.' He did not complete 'Foundations in Rerek' until 1 October 1942, fourteen months after he began it.

The two opening sections add up to about ten thousand words, and Eddison spent about 420 days composing them. On a strictly mathematical level, Eddison's average daily rate of composition was about twenty-five words. Surely a turtle's pace across the page. Such meticulous slowness seems to mark Eddison's composition: he once told Edward Abbe Niles, his consulting lawyer in America, that the ten thousand words of the thickly philosophical Chapters XV and XVI of *A Fish Dinner in Memison* took him ten months of 1937. Yet in 1937, Eddison had little free time for writing because he was fully occupied with civil service as the Head of Empire Trades and Head of the Economic Division in the Department of Overseas Trade. One would expect that in 1942, three years into retired life, Eddison would be composing at a faster rate than during his working life, simply because he had more time for writing, but that is not the case. The explanation lies in our understanding the intrusion of World War II upon Eddison's life and the response of his dutiful nature to the home effort in the war.

On 10 September 1939, one week after Britain and France had declared war on Germany, Eddison speaks of his domestic preparations for wartime:

> ARP curtains, 'Nox' lights, and so on have occupied most of my waking hours since the trouble began. We are well blacked out – but what a bore it is, night and morning.'

The annoyed tone of the last sentence is notable. Eddison's 'motto' as he declared it in one letter, was 'anything for a quiet life.' After spending most of his years in London, Eddison moved to the countryside near Marlborough to live this desired quiet life in which the breezy hours of sunshine and birdsong could be devoted to writing and reading and happy companionship with his wife and family. To have the bright hope for this life, in its first months, tangibly darkened by blackout curtains, and intangibly darkened by the fear of bombing or invasion, must have been bitterly discouraging. Time was out of joint for Eddison's retired life.

Some people in Eddison's position would have ignored the home effort in the war. Eddison could not do this: his long career in government, his interest in history and politics, his patriotism, and his keen sense of responsibility would not allow this in him. In the same letter in which he speaks of hanging the blackout curtains, Eddison tells Hamilton of his volunteering for war service:

> I've offered my services in general for any local work here that I can tackle: nothing doing so far, but that is hardly surprising. I was going to stage a 'comeback' in Whitehall if war burst out a year ago; but fear it would quickly end me were I to attempt it, and that would help nobody. So, I propose to carry on to the best of my ability till a bomb drops on me, or some other form of destruction overtakes me, or till the war comes to an end.

Here is a man fifty-seven and well beyond the age parameters of active military duty, a man recently retired from public life and settled into a new house, a man who retired to devote himself to his personal literary goals, a man not in his best state of health: this man volunteers for war service during the first days of the war. Surely his action reveals a mind instinct with duty.

Only those who lived through the war years in England can truly speak about the anxieties and frustrations of carrying on daily life under the constant danger of the air raids. Living in London, Hamilton felt the German threat closely. On September 13, 1940, he wrote to say that his wife's mother had come to live at his house, for bombs had fallen perilously near to hers. Plus, Hamilton had gone to work that morning and found the floor of his office covered with shards of window glass shattered by a bomb's concussion during the previous night. Because he and his family lived in Wiltshire, Eddison did not feel the threat so imminently, and he told Hamilton on September 15, 1940, that although several bombs had fallen in the countryside and one in Marlborough itself, the 'total casualties and material damage is so far precisely three rabbits!'

Even though the danger was not as grave in Marlborough as it was in London, Eddison's work as an air raid patrol warden continually interrupted his consciously regular life, a retired life that nevertheless maintained the structure of his working life. On 27 October 1940, Eddison told Hamilton of one incident that exemplifies these interruptions:

> I had a complete *nuit blanche* last Sunday: siren went off and woke me from my first sleep [at] 11.15 p.m.: dressed in five minutes, got here 11.25, and here we were stuck – 3 men and two girls – till 5.50 a.m. Monday, when the siren sounded 'raiders passed'. No incidents for us to deal with, but they had it in Swindon I gather. Home to bed for ¼ hour, and up, as usual, at 6.30. But, by 9.30 a.m. I was so dead stupid I went to bed and slept till 12.00 and even so pretty washed out for the rest of the day. I don't know how you folks stick it night after night: I suppose the adaptability of the human frame comes blessedly into play.

Eddison's coming home to sleep for fifteen minutes and then rising 'as usual' at 6.30 seems silly. He was living in retirement without professional responsibilities, and the scheduled hour of his rising from sleep was a demand self-imposed. The consequence of maintaining such rigid regularity on this occasion produced only weariness and inefficiency in the morning. And yet the disciplined Eddison surrendered to the needs of his body reluctantly, for he did not return to bed until three hours later.

Eddison's ARP work affected the whole of his six years of retired life, but although it was wearying and annoying to him, the ARP work was not the most demanding of the daily tasks that kept him from his writing desk. He begins the 27 October *'nuit blanche'* letter with a paragraph about gardening:

> I'm writing this in the ARP control room: my Sunday morning turn of duty. I boil my egg and have my breakfast about 7 a.m., and get down here by 7.45 and take charge until 11. I like it, because after that my day is free to garden; which at the moment, is a pressing occupation. I'm cleaning the herbaceous border of bindweed, a most pernicious and elusive pest: it takes about 2 hours of hard digging and sorting to do a one foot run, and there are sixty feet to do. And the things are heeled in elsewhere and waiting to be planted when my deinfestation is complete.

For Eddison, gardening was not welcome physical exercise after stiff-backed hours of concentration at the writing table. Rather, gardening was his major occupation during these years; it was the work of duty that had to be done before the work of his heart's desire. Gardening is, of course, a seasonal work, and the hours Eddison spent at it surely fluctuated, but during the autumnal harvest it took up many hours every day. Eddison told Gerald Hayes in the autumn of 1943 that gardening took 42 hours per week, ARP work took 10 or 11 hours, and that he was also trying to work on *The Mezentian Gate* every day even if he could only give it one half-hour.

Eddison devoted himself to gardening because the wartime food rationing in England created discomforting shortages, and Eddison wanted to be as self-sufficient as possible so that the rations could be supplemented without having to be relied on. Gardening became more important after the birth of Eddison's granddaughter Anne in November 1940, because then Eddison had another person to feed besides his wife, Winifred, his daughter Jean, his mother, Helen, when she came to visit, and himself. For Christmas in 1941,

Edward Abbe Niles sent the Eddisons food parcels from New York, and on 18 December, Eddison thanked him in a letter: 'On the whole we don't do too badly for food . . . One gets used (though I won't say reconciled) to short commons in things like bacon and sugar: eggs would be a severe deprivation if one had to depend on a ration, but we have six hens who keep us going with their contributions, and very lucky we are, and wise, to have started keeping them last summer.' Eddison's strenuous efforts in the garden, and the clucking efforts of the hens, seem to have been successful in allowing the family to live comfortably. However, Eddison's daughter Jean says that it was eventually necessary to eat all of the hens, even the ones they had become attached to as household pets.

Although Eddison's many hours of gardening and ARP work filled his days and sometimes his nights, his letters from the first year and a half of the war do not have a strong tone of frustration over his lack of time for writing. Perhaps the reason is that he was between books during these months. He was busy with matters relating to *A Fish Dinner in Memison*: rewriting the cricket scene in Chapter III for an American audience unfamiliar with the game, and sending many letters to Niles in regard to the contract with Dutton. These things occupied his writing hours well into the first months of 1941. Also, perhaps he was not frustrated because he was enjoying the sweetness of having finished a work that pleased him well, and he was happily anticipating the publication of *A Fish Dinner in Memison* in May 1941.

But Eddison was never a dawdler, especially when new ideas arose like breezes to fill the sails of his imagination: only three months after *A Fish Dinner in Memison* was published, he began working on *The Mezentian Gate*. A cluster of letters from late in 1941, the period in which Eddison was working on the opening sections, shows his careworn tone and his frustration with the ability of these mundane tasks to balk his efforts to have time for writing. The two most potent letters are enough to show this wearied tone. On 27 November 1941, Eddison wrote to his Welsh friend Lewellyn Griffith:

I too am the sport and shuttlecock of potatoes, onions, carrots, beets, turnips, and – for weeks on end – after these are laid to rest – of autumn diggings and sudden arithmetical calculations aiming at a three year rotation of crops scheme for our kitchen garden, to enable me to get on with these jobs without further thought, and learn perhaps to garden as an automaton while my mind works on the tortuous politics of the three kingdoms and the inward beings and outward actors in that play, over a period of eighty years.

The second letter is to Eddison's American friend Professor Henry Lappin and was written one month after the first:

Forgive a brief letter. I have no leisure for writing – either my next book or the letters I badly owe. For I am already whole time kitchen gardener, coal heaver, and so on, and look likely to become part time cook and housemaid into the bargain, this in addition to my part-time war work; and these daily jobs connected with keeping oneself and family clean, warm, and nourished, leave little enough time for the higher activities. Perhaps this is good for one, for a time; anyway it is part of the price we all have to pay if we want to win this war.

Eddison is tired of his domestic tasks, and in both letters he stresses the time they take up. He also makes a clear separation between these chores and his writing by calling his writing a 'higher activity' in the second letter and by stating his mental detachment from gardening in the first letter.

Part of Eddison's frustration must have stemmed from the sheer size of *The Mezentian Gate*. The plot of *Mistress of Mistresses* covers fifteen months; that of *A Fish Dinner in Memison*, one month. Had he completed the sagalike *Mezentian Gate*, the plot would have extended over seventy-two years. Considering the number of episodes alone, Eddison's working on the 'tortuous politics of the three kingdoms' over a period of seven decades was the most ambitious goal of imaginative contriving he ever attempted.

Eddison's progress on *The Mezentian Gate* crawled doggedly through 1942 and through most of 1943. On 6 November 1943, Eddison wrote to his new friend C. S. Lewis and said that he was feeling joyful about the new progress he was making on the novel. This letter signals the beginning of a nine-month period of fruitful productivity. Though he had been at work on Chapter II, 'Foundations in Fingiswold', since he had finished 'Foundations in Rerek' in October 1942, Eddison completed Chapters II–VI between December 1943 and 14 February 1944.

Eddison's constant rule of composition was that he worked on whatever part of the novel made his imagination sail most confidently; he did not hold himself to a course bearing determined by the plot's chronology. In early 1944, Eddison decided to work on the end of the novel, and he wrote to Gerald Hayes on 22 February about his intention:

> I am getting on with *The Mezentian Gate,* being now about to write the last five chapters which in the last two weeks I have roughed out on paper in scenario form, or synopsis, or by whatever absurd name it should be called. When they are written there will be in existence at least the head and tail. That is a stage I shall be glad to have reached and passed; not only because there will then be cardinal points fixed, by which to build the body of the book, but also because if I were then to be snuffed out there would remain a publishable fragment able to convey some suggestion of what the finished opus was to have been.

The clause 'because if I were then to be snuffed out' is a curious one because it most obviously refers to the threat of the German bombings, but it could also refer to the questionable state of Eddison's health, a matter that he held in close privacy. In any case, the sentence helps to explain why Eddison, several months later, composed such a meticulously complete synopsis of the middle twenty-six chapters.

Writing steadily over the spring and summer of 1944, Eddison completed the four final chapters and Chapter XXXIV, nearly 31,000 words, in six months. He was especially proud of the climactic chapter, 'Omega and Alpha in Sestola.' Eddison told Hamilton that he had spent 290 hours upon the chapter, and that it had cost him more energy than anything he had written previously. By late January 1945, Eddison had completed Chapters XXVIII and XXIX, which concern Fiorinda's first appearance on the Zimiamvian stage and her ill-fated marriage to Baias. Then Eddison worked extensively on Chapter XXX, which he designed to show Fiorinda's entrance into society after the death of Baias, and especially to show the responses of the other characters to her and her somewhat tainted reputation. Many of Eddison's unfinished pieces for the chapter have a light-hearted humorous tone which is refreshing after so much Zimiamvian solemnity. The chapter's best scene shows Zapheles falling in adoration at Fiorinda's feet only to become a plaything for her amusement. In Beroald's words: 'it is but one more pair of wings at the candle flame: they come and go till they be singed'. Eddison never completed the chapter, and it is the last part of the book that he worked on. It is a sad thing to read the unfinished pieces of this chapter, for they are confidently and sometimes exquisitely written, yet some of them date to within two weeks of his sudden death.

Another sad thing is that just before his death, Eddison was discovering a basis for a new Zimiamvian book. 'I foresee the 4th beginning to shape itself,' he wrote to his friend Christopher Sandford in May 1945. 'I think if it materializes it will really be the fourth – an exception to my habit of writing history backwards.' But the book would never get its chance, for the end came quickly and unexpectedly on 18 August. Winifred Eddison tells the story to George Hamilton:

> I cannot be anything but thankful that he went so quickly. He and I had been sitting outside after tea last Friday, talking most happily. I felt so strongly at the time how happy he seemed. We fed the hens together and those of our neighbours, who are away. At about 6:30 I came in to prepare supper and

at 7:00 p.m. gave the usual whistle that all was ready. There was no answer, but often the whistle didn't carry. On searching for him, I found him lying unconscious and breathing heavily-Jean came almost at once and has been the greatest help and support. The doctor said it was 'a sudden and complete blackout' for him. He could have felt nothing and that is what makes me so glad. He never regained consciousness.

The suddenness of the fatal stroke makes me wonder whether it was caused by a gradual period of declining health or by the strenuous work impressed upon Eddison by the war. If his war work brought him to his unfortunate and untimely end, he would not have changed events if he could have. He declared his views on his war service on 24 November 1942, in a letter to an American writer named William Hurd Hillyer:

When the civilized world is agonized by a Ragnarok struggle between good and evil; when everything that can be shaken is shaken, and the only comfort for wise men is in the certitude that the things that cannot be shaken will stand; poets and artists are faced squarely with the question whether they are doing any good producing works of art: whether they had not better put it by and get on with something more useful. That is not a question that can with any honour be evaded. Nor can any man answer it for others.

This philosophically minded man was dutiful and responsible; he placed the interests of his family and his community above his own. Eddison exhausted himself in the garden to ensure that his family had enough to eat. In doing this, one could say, Eddison was doing only what was necessary and what he was obliged to do as the head of the household. True, and yet the ARP work was neither necessary nor obligatory: he volunteered for it, it seems, as an alternative form of service when his doctor forbade his joining the Home Guard. His sense of duty made the service obligatory.

Looking at the whole of his retired years, I wonder whether Eddison took too much upon himself. He viewed his wartime tasks as work that could not be evaded without dishonour. But writing was his real work. He would have written more, and he would have lived less strenuously had there been no national crisis impinging on his retired life. Perhaps he would have lived longer, too. Part of me wants to see him as a victim, but I know that he would not want to be thought of in that way; his Scandinavian heritage was too ingrained in him for that. I think he would rather it be said that he thought of death as did Prince Styrbiorn, the hero of his historical novel *Styrbiorn the Strong:* when the Earl Strut-Harald predicts that Styrbiorn will live a short life, Styrbiorn replies, 'I reck not the number of my days, so they be good.'

PAUL EDMUND THOMAS
July 1991

PREFATORY NOTE

BY COLIN RÜCKER EDDISON

My brother Eric died on 18 August 1945. He had written the following note in November 1944:

Of this book, *The Mezentian Gate*, the opening chapters (including the *Praeludium*) and the final hundred pages or so which form the climax are now completed. Two thirds of it are yet to write. The following 'Argument with Dates' summarizes in broad outline the subject matter of these unwritten chapters. The dates are 'Anno Zayanae Conditae': from the founding of the city of Zayana.

The book at this stage is thus a full-length portrait in oils of which the face has been painted in but the rest of the picture no more than roughly sketched in charcoal, As such, it has enough unity and finality to stand as something more than a fragment. Indeed it seems to me, even in its present state, to contain my best work.

If through misfortune I were to be prevented from finishing this book, I should wish it to be published as it stands, together with the 'Argument' to represent the unwritten parts.

E. R. E.
7th November, 1944

Between November 1943 and August 1945 two further chapters, XXVIII and XXIX, were completed in draft and take their place in the text.

A letter written in January 1945 indicates that in the writing of Books Two to Five my brother might perhaps have 'unloaded' some of the detail comprised in the Argument with Dates. In substance, however, there can be no doubt that he would have followed the argument closely.

My brother had it in mind to use a photograph of the El Greco painting of which he writes at the end of his letter of introduction. I am sure that he would have preferred and welcomed the drawing by Keith Henderson which appears as a frontispiece. The photograph has been used, by courtesy of the Hispanic Society of America, as a basis for the drawing.

We are deeply grateful to my brother's old friend Sir George Rostrevor Hamilton for his unstinted help and counsel in the preparation of *The Mezentian Gate* for publication. We also warmly appreciate the generous assistance given by Sir Francis Meynell in designing the form and typographical layout for the book. The maps were originally prepared by the late Gerald Hayes for the other volumes of the trilogy of which *The Mezentian Gate* is a part.

COLIN RÜCKER EDDISON
1958

To *you, madonna mia,*
WINIFRED GRACE EDDISON
and to my mother,
HELEN LOUISA EDDISON
and to my friends,
JOHN AND ALICE REYNOLDS
and to
HARRY PIRIE-GORDON
*a fellow explorer in whom (as in Lessingham)
I find that rare mixture of man of action and
connoisseur of strangeness and beauty in their
protean manifestations, who laughs where I laugh
and likes the salt that I like, and to whom I owe
my acquaintance (through the* Orkneyinga Saga*)
with the earthly ancestress
of my Lady Rosma Parry*
I dedicate this book.

E. R. E.

Proper names the reader will no doubt pronounce as he chooses. But perhaps, to please me, he will keep the *i*'s short in *Zimiamvia* and accent the third syllable: accent the second syllable in *Zayana*, give it a broad *a* (as in 'Guiana'), and pronouce the *ay* in the first syllable – and the *ai* in *Laimak, Kaima,* etc., and the *ay* in *Krestenaya* – like the *ai* in 'aisle'; keep the *g* soft in *Fingiswold*: let *Memison* echo 'denizen' except for the *m*: accent the first syllable in *Rerek* and make it rhyme with 'year': pronounce the first syllable of *Reisma* 'rays'; remember that *Fiorinda* is in origin an Italian name, *Amaury*, *Amalie*, and *Beroald* French, and *Antiope*, *Zenianthe*, and a good many others, Greek: last, regard the *sz* in *Meszria* as ornamental, and not be deterred from pronouncing it as plain 'Mezria'.

Let me not to the marriage of true mindes
Admit impediments, love is not love
Which alters when it alteration findes,
Or bends with the remover to remove:
O no, it is an ever fixed marke
That lookes on tempests, and is never shaken;
It is the star to every wandring barke,
Whose worths unknowns, although his higth be taken.
Love's not Times foole, though rosie lips and cheeks
Within his bending sickles compasse come,
Love alters not with his breefe houres and weekes,
But beares it out even to the edge of doome:
If this be error, and upon me proved,
I never writ, nor no man ever loved.

SHAKESPEARE

And ride in triumph through Persepolis!
Is it not brave to be a King, Techelles?
Usumcasane and Theridamas,
Is it not passing brave to be a King,
And ride in triumph through Persepolis?

MARLOWE

I cannot conceive any beginning of such love as I have for
you but Beauty. There may be a sort of love for which,
without the least sneer at it, I have the highest respect and
can admire it in others: but it has not the richness, the bloom,
the full form, the enchantment of love after my own heart.

KEATS

LETTER OF INTRODUCTION

To My Brother Colin

Dear Brother:

Not by design, but because it so developed, my Zimiamvian trilogy has been written backwards. *Mistress of Mistresses*, the first of these books, deals with the two years beginning 'ten months after the death, in the fifty-fourth year of his age, in his island fortress of Sestola in Meszria, of the great King Mezentius, tyrant of Fingiswold, Meszria, and Rerek'. *A Fish Dinner in Memison*, the second book, belongs in its Zimiamvian parts to a period of five weeks ending nearly a year before the King's death. This third book, *The Mezentian Gate*, begins twenty years before the King was born, and ends with his death. Each of the three is a drama complete in itself; but, read together (beginning with *The Mezentian Gate*, and ending with *Mistress of Mistresses*), they give a consecutive history, covering more than seventy years in a special world devised for Her Lover by Aphrodite, for whom (as the reader must suspend unbelief and suppose) all worlds are made.

The trilogy will, as I now foresee, turn to a tetralogy; and the tetralogy probably then (as an oak puts on girth and height with the years) lead to further growth. For, certain as it is that the treatment of the theme comes short of what I would, the theme itself is inexhaustible. Clearly so, if we sum it in the words of a philosopher who is besides (as few philosophers are) a poet in bent of mind and a master of art, George Santayana: 'The divine beauty is evident, fugitive, impalpable, and homeless in a world of material fact; yet it is unmistakably individual and sufficient unto itself, and although perhaps soon eclipsed is never really extinguished: for it visits time and belongs to eternity.' Those words I chanced upon while I was writing the *Fish Dinner*, and liked the more because they came as a catalyst to crystallize thoughts that had long been in suspension in my mind.

In this world of Zimiamvia, Aphrodite puts on, as though they were dresses, separate and simultaneous incarnations, with a different personality, a different *soul*, for each dress. As the Duchess of Memison, for example, She walks as it were in Her sleep, humble, innocent, forgetful of Her Olympian home; and in that dress She can (little guessing the extraordinary truth) see and speak with her own Self that, awake and aware and well able to enjoy and use Her divine prerogatives, stands beside Her in the person of her lady of the bedchamber.

A very unearthly character of Zimiamvia lies in the fact that nobody wants to change it. Nobody, that is to say, apart from a few weak natures who fail on their probation and (as, in your belief and mine, all ultimate evil must) put off at last even their illusory semblance of being, and fall away to the limbo of nothingness. Zimiamvia is, in this, like the saga-time; there is no malaise of the soul. In that world, well fitted to their faculties and dispositions, men and women of all estates enjoy beatitude in the Aristotelian sense of ενέργεια κατ᾽ αρετήν ἀρίσγήν (activity according to their highest virtue). Gabriel Flores, for instance, has no ambition to be Vicar of Rerek: it suffices his lust for power that he serves a master who commands his dog-like devotion.

It may be thought that such dark and predatory personages as the Vicar, or his uncle Lord Emmius Parry, or Emmius's daughter Rosma, are strangely accommodated in these meads of asphodel where Beauty's self, in warm actuality of flesh and blood, reigns as Mistress. But the answer surely is (and it is an old answer) that 'God's adversaries are some way his owne'. This ownness is easier to accept and credit in an ideal world like Zimiamvia than in our training-ground or testing-place where womanish and fearful mankind, individually so often gallant and lovable, in the mass so foolish and unremarkable, mysteriously inhabit, labouring through bog that takes us to the knees, yet sometimes momentarily giving an eye to the lone splendour of the stars. When lions, eagles, and she-wolves are let loose among such weak sheep as for the most part we be, we rightly, for sake of our continuance, attend rather to their claws, maws, and talons than stay to contemplate their magnificences. We forget, in our necessity lest our flesh become their meat, that they too, ideally and *sub specie aeternitatis*, have their places (higher or lower in proportion to their integrity and to the mere consciencelessness and purity of their mischief) in the hierarchy of true values. This world of ours, we may reasonably hold, is no place for them, and they no fit citizens for it; but a tedious life, surely, in the heavenly mansions, and small scope for Omnipotence to stretch its powers, were all such great eminent self-pleasuring tyrants to be banned from 'yonder starry gallery' and lodged in 'the cursed dungeon'.

The Mezentian Gate, last in order of composition, is by that very fact first in order of ripeness. It in no respect supersedes or amends the earlier books, but does I think illuminate them. *Mistress of Mistresses*, leaving unexplored the relations between that other world and our present here and now, led to the writing of the *Fish Dinner*; which book in turn, at its climax, raised the question whether what took place at that singular supper party may not have had yet vaster and more cosmic reactions, quite overshadowing those affecting the fate of this planet. I was besides, by then, fallen in love with Zimiamvia and my persons; and love has a searching curiosity which can never be wholly satisfied (and well that it cannot, or mankind might die of boredom). Also I wanted to find out how it came that the great King, while still at the height of his powers, met his death in Sestola; and why, so leaving the Three Kingdoms, he left them in a mess. These riddles begot *The Mezentian Gate*.

With our current distractions, political, social and economic, this story (in common with its predecessors) is as utterly unconcerned as it is with Stock Exchange procedure, the technicalities of aerodynamics, or the Theory of Vectors. Nor is it an allegory. Allegory, if its persons have life, is a prostitution of their personalities, forcing them for an end other than their own. If they have not life, it is but a dressing up of argument in a puppetry of frigid make-believe. To me, the persons are the argument. And for the argument I am not fool enough to claim responsibility; for, stripped to its essentials, it is a great eternal commonplace, beside which, I am sometimes apt to think, nothing else really matters.

The book, then, is a serious book: not a fairy-story, and not a book for babes and sucklings; but (it needs not to tell you, who know my temper) not solemn. For is not Aphrodite φιλομμειδής – 'laughter-loving'? But She is also αιδοίη – 'an awful' Goddess. And She is ελικοβλέφαρος – 'with flickering eyelids', and γλυκυμείλιχος – 'honey-sweet'; and She is Goddess of Love, which itself is γλυκύπικρον αμάχανον όρπετον – 'Bitter-sweet, an unmanageable Laidly Worm': as Barganax knows. These attributes are no modern inventions of mine: they stand on evidence of Homer and of Sappho, great poets. And in what great poets tell us about the Gods there is always a vein of truth. There is an aphorism of my learned Doctor Vandermast's (a particular friend of yours), which he took from Spinoza: *Per realitatem et perfectionem idem intelligo*: 'By Reality and Perfection I understand the same thing.' And Keats says, in a letter: 'Axioms in philosophy are not axioms until they are proved upon our pulses.'

Fiorinda I met, and studied, more than fifteen years ago: not by any means her entire self, but a good enough shadow to help me to set down, in *Mistress of Mistresses* and these two later books, the quality and play of her features, her voice, and her bearing. The miniature, a photograph of which appears as frontispiece, belongs to the Hispanic Society of America, New York: it was painted *circa* 1596 by El Greco, from a sitter who has not, so far as I know, been identified. But I think it was painted also in Memison: early July, A.Z.C. 775, of Fiorinda (*aet.* 19), in her state, as lady of honour: the first of Barganax's many portraits of her. A comparison with *Mistress of Mistresses* (Chapter II especially, and – for the eyes – last paragraph but one in Chapter VIII) shows close correspondence between this El Greco miniature and descriptions of Fiorinda written and published more than ten years before I first became acquainted with it (which was late in 1944): so close as to make me hope the photograph may quicken the reader's imagination as it does mine. I record here my acknowledgements and thanks to the Hispanic Society of America for generously giving me permission to reproduce the photograph now used, by courtesy of the Hispanic Society of America, as a basis for the drawing which appears as a frontispiece.

So here is my book: call it novel if you like; poem if you prefer. Under whatever label—

I limb'd this night-peece and it was my best.

Your loving brother,
E. R. E.

Dark Lane,
Marlborough,
Wiltshire.

Praeludium

LESSINGHAM ON THE RAFTSUND

It was mid July, and three o'clock in the morning. The sun, which at this time of year in Lofoten never stays more than an hour or two below the horizon, was well up, fingering to gold with the unbelievably slowed deliberation of an Arctic dawn first the two-eared peak itself and then, in a gradual creeping downward, the enormous up-thrusts of precipice that underpin that weight and bulk, of Rulten across the Raftsund. Out of the waters of that sea-strait upon its westerly side the mountains of naked stone stood up like a wall, Rulten and his cubs and, more to the north, the Troldtinder which began now, with the swinging round of the sun, to take the gold in the jags of their violent sky-line. The waters mirrored them as in a floor of smoke-coloured crystal: quiet waters, running still, running deep, and having the shadow of night yet upon them, like something irremeable, like the waters of Styx.

That shadow lingered (even, as the sun drew round, seemed to brood heavier) upon this hither shore, where Digermulen castle, high in the cliffs, faced towards Rulten and the Troldfjord. The castle was of the stone of the crags on whose knees it rested, like-hued, like-framed, in its stretches of blind wall and megalithic gauntnesses of glacis and tower and long outer parapet overhanging the sea. To and fro, the full length of the parapet, a man was walking: as for his body, always in that remaining and untimely thickening dusk of night, yet, whenever he turned at this end and that, looking across the sound to morning.

It would have been a hard guess to tell the age of him. Now and again, under certain effects of the light, deep old age seemed suddenly to glance out of his swift eagly eyes: a thing incongruous with that elasticity of youth which lived in his every movement as he paced, turned, or paused: incongruous with his thick black hair, clipped short but not so short as to hide the curliness of it which goes most with a gay superfluity of vigour of both body and mind that seldom outlasts the prime, and great coal-black beard. Next instant, what had shown as the ravages of the years, would seem but traces of wind and tempest, as in a man customed all his life to open weather at sea or on mountain ridges and all desolate sun-smitten places about the world. He was taller than most tall men: patently an Englishman, yet with that facial angle that belongs to old Greece. There was in him a magnificence not kingly as in ordinary experience that term fits, but deeper in grain, ignoring itself, as common men their natural motions of breathing or heart-beat: some inward integrity emerging in outward shape and action, as when a solitary oak takes the storm, or as the lion walks in grandeur not from study nor as concerned to command eyes, but from ancestral use and because he can no other.

He said, to himself: 'Checkmate. And by a bunch of pawns. Well, there's some comfort in that: not to be beaten by men, but the dead weight of the machine. I can rule men: have, all my life ruled them: seen true ends, and had the knack to make them see my ends as their own. Look at them here: a generation bred up in these five-and-twenty years like-minded with me as if I had spit 'em. Liker minded than if they had been sprung from my loins. And now?—

> the bright day is done,
> And we are for the dark.

What can a few thousand, against millions? Even if the millions are fools. It is the old drift of the world, to drabness and

sameness: water, always tending by its very nature to a dead level.'
He folded his arms and stood looking seaward over the parapet.
So, perhaps, Leonidas stood for a minute when the Persians began
to close in upon the Pass.

Then he turned: at a known step, perhaps: at a known perfume,
like the delicate scent of the black magnolia, sharpened with
spindrift and sea-foam and wafted on some air far unlike this cool
northern breath of the Raftsund. He greeted her with a kind of
laugh of the eyes.

'You slept?'

'At last, yes. I slept. And you, *mon ami*?'

'No. And yet, as good as slept: looking at you, feeding on you,
reliving you. Who are you, I wonder, that it is the mere patent of
immortality, after such a night, only to gaze upon your dear beauties asleep? And that all wisdom since life came up upon earth,
and all the treasure of old time past and of eternity to come, can
lie charmed within the curve of each particular hair?' Then, like
the crack of a whip: 'I shall send them no answer.'

Something moved in her green eyes that was like the light
beyond the sound 'No? What will you do, then?'

'Nothing. For the first time in my life I am come to this, that
there is nothing I can do.'

'That,' said she, 'is the impassable which little men are faced
with, every day of their lives. It awaits even the greatest at last.
You are above other men in this age of the world as men are
above monkeys, and have so acted; but circumstance weighs at
last too heavy even for you. You are trapped. In the tiger-hunts
in old Java, the tiger has no choice left at last but to leap upon
the spears.'

'I could have told you last night,' he said '(but we were engrossed
with things worthier our attention), I've everything ready here: for
that leap.' After a pause: 'They will not move till time's up: noon
tomorrow. After that, with this new Government, bombers no
doubt. I have made up my mind to meet them in the air: give
them a keepsake to remember me by. I will have you go today.
The yacht's ready. She can take you to England, or wherever you

wish. You must take her as a good-bye gift from me: until we meet – at Philippi.'

She made no sign of assent or dissent, only stood still as death beside him, looking across at Rulten. Presently his hand found hers where it hung at her side: lifted it and studied it a minute in silence. It lay warm in his, motionless, relaxed, abandoned, uncommunicative, like a hand asleep. 'Better this way than the world's way, the way of that yonder,' he said, looking now where she looked; 'which is dying by inches. A pretty irony, when you think of it: lifted out of primaeval seas not a mountain but a 'considerable protuberance'; then the frosts and the rains, all the infinitely slow, infinitely repeated, influences of innumerable little things, getting to work on it, chiselling it to this perfection of its maturity: better than I could have done it, or Michael Angelo, or Pheidias. And to what end? Not to stay perfect: no, for the chisel that brought it to this will bring it down again, to the degradation of a second childhood. And after that? What matter, after that? Unless indeed, the chisel gets tired of it.' Looking suddenly in her eyes again: 'As I am tired of it,' he said.

'Of life?'

He laughed. 'Good heavens, no! Tired of death.'

They walked a turn or two. After a while, she spoke again. 'I was thinking of Brachiano:

> On paine of death, let no man name death to me,
> It is a word infinitely terrible—'

'I cannot remember,' he said in a detached thoughtful simplicity, 'ever to have been afraid of death. I can't honestly remember, for that matter, being actually afraid of anything.'

'That is true, I am very well certain. But in this you are singular, as in other things besides.'

'Death, at any rate,' he said, 'is nothing: nil, an estate of not-being. Or else, new beginning. Whichever way, what is there to fear?'

'Unless this, perhaps?—

> Save that to dye, I leave my love alone.'

'The last bait on the Devil's hook. I'll not entertain it.'

'Yet it should be the king of terrors.'

'I'll not entertain it,' he said. 'I admit, though,' – they had stopped. She was standing a pace or two away from him, dark against the dawn-light on mountain and tide-way, questionable, maybe as the Sphinx is questionable. As with a faint perfume of dittany afloat in some English garden at evening, the air about her seemed to shudder into images of heat and darkness: up-curved delicate tendrils exhaling an elusive sweetness: milk-smooth petals that disclosed and enfolded a secret heart of night, pantherine, furred in mystery. – 'I admit this: suppose I could entertain it, that might terrify me.'

'How can we know?' she said. 'What firm assurance have we against that everlasting loneliness?'

'I will enter into no guesses as to how you may know. For my own part, my assurance rests on direct knowledge of the senses: eye, ear, nostrils, tongue, hand, the ultimate carnal knowing.'

'As it should rightly be always, I suppose; seeing that, with lovers, the senses are the organs of the spirit. And yet – I am a woman. There is no part in me, no breath, gait, turn, or motion, but flatters your eye with beauty. With my voice, with the mere rustle of my skirt, I can wake you wild musics potent in your mind and blood. I am sweet to smell, sweet to taste. Between my breasts you have in imagination voyaged to Kythera, or even to that herdsman's hut upon many-fountained Ida where Anchises, by will and ordainment of the Gods, lay (as Homer says) with an immortal Goddess: a mortal, not clearly knowing. But under my skin, what am I? A *memento mori* too horrible for the slab in a butcher's shop; or the floor of a slaughter-house; a clockwork of muscle; and sinew, vein and nerve and membrane, shining – blue, grey, scarlet – to all colours of corruption; a sack of offals, to make you stop your nose at it. And underneath (when you have purged away these loathsomeness of the flesh) – the scrannel piteous residue: the stripped bone, grinning, hair-less, and sexless, which even the digestions of worms and

devouring fire rebel against: the dumb argument that puts to
silence all were's, maybe's, and might-have-beens.'

His face, listening, was that of a man who holds a wolf by the
ears; but motionless: the poise of his head Olympian, a head of
Zeus carved in stone. 'What name did you give when you
announced yourself to my servants yesterday evening?'

'Indeed,' she answered, 'I have given so many. Can you remember
what name they used to you, announcing my arrival?'

'The Señorita del Rio Amargo.'

'Yes. I remember now. It was that.'

'"Of the Bitter River." As though you had known my decisions
in advance. Perhaps you did?'

'How could I?'

'It is my belief,' he said, 'that you know more than I know. I
think you know too, in advance, my answer to this discourse with
which you were just now exploring me as a surgeon explores a
wound.'

She shook her head. 'If I knew your answer before you gave it,
that would make it not your answer but mine.'

'Well,' he said, 'you shall be answered. I have lived upon this earth
far into the third generation. Through a long life, you have been my
book (poison one way, pleasure another), reading in which I have
learnt all I know: and this principally, to distinguish in this world's
welter the abiding from the fading, real things from phantoms.'

'Real things or phantoms? And you can credit seeing, hearing,
handling, to resolve you which is which?'

'So the spirit be on its throne, I can; and answer you so out of
your own mouth, madonna. But I grant you, that twirk in the
corner of your lips casts all in doubt again and shatters to confusion all answers. I have named you, last night, Goddess, Paphian
Aphrodite. Was that a figure of speech? a cheap poetaster's compliment to his mistress in bed? or was it plain daylight, as I discern
it? Come, what do you think? Did I ever call you that before?'

'Never in so many words,' she said, very low. 'But I sometimes
scented in you, great man of action you are in the world's eyes,
a strange capacity to incredibilities.'

'Let me remind you, then, of facts you seem to affect have forgotten. You came to me – once in my youth, once in my middle age – in Verona. In the interval, I lived with you, in our own house of Nether Wastdale, lifted up and down the world, fifteen years, flesh of my heart, heart of my heart. To end that, I saw you dead in the Morgue at Paris: a sight beside which your dissecting-table villainy a few minutes since is innocent nursery prattle. That was fifty years ago, next October. And now you are come again, but in your black dress, as in Verona. For the good-bye.' She averted her face, not to be seen. 'This is wild unsizeable talk. Fifty years!'

'Whether it be good sense or madhouse talk I am likely to know,' he said, 'before tomorrow night; or, in the alternative, to know nothing and to be nothing. If that be the alternative, so be it. But I hold it an alternative little worthy to be believed.'

They were walking again, and came to a bench of stone. 'O, you have your dresses,' he said, taking his seat beside her. His voice had the notes the deeps and the power of a man's in the acme of his days. 'You have your dresses: Red Queen, Queen of Hearts, *rosa mundi*; here and now, Black Queen of the sweet deep-curled lily-flower, and winged wind-rushing darknesses of hearts' desires. I envy both. Being myself, to my great inconvenience, two men in a single skin instead of (as should be) one in two. Call them rather two Devils in a bag, when they pull against one another or bite one other. Nor can I ever even incline to take sides with either, without I begin to wish t'other may win.'

'The fighter and the dreamer,' she said: 'the doer, the enjoyer.' Then, with new under-songs of an appassionate tenderness in her voice: 'What gift would you have me give you, O my friend, were I in sober truth what you named me? What heaven or Elysium, what persons and shapes, would we choose to live in, beyond the hateful River?'

His gaze rested on her a minute in silence, as if to take a fresh draft of her: the beauty that pierced her dress as the lantern-light the doors of a lantern: the parting of her hair, not crimped but drawn in its native habit of soft lazy waves, as of some unlighted sea, graciously back on either side over the tips of her ears: the

windy light in her eyes. 'This is the old story over again,' he said.
'There is but one condition for all the infinity of possible heavens:
that you should give me yourself, and a world that is wholly of
itself a dress of yours.'

'This world again, then, that we live in? Is that not mine?'

'In some ways it is. In many ways. In every respect, up to a
point. But damnably, when that point is reached, always and in
every respect this world fails of you. Soon as a bud is ready to
open, we find the canker has crept in. Is it yours, all of it, even
to this? I think it is. Otherwise, why have I sucked the orange of
this world all my life with so much satisfaction, savoured it in
every caprice of fortune, waded waist-deep in this world's violences,
groped in its clueless labyrinths of darkness, fought it, made treaty
with it, played with it, scorned it, pitied it, laughed with it, been
fawned on by it and tricked by it and be-laurelled by it; and all
with so much zest? And now at last, brought to bay by it; and,
even so, constrained by something in my very veins and heart-roots
to a kind of love for it? For all that, it is not a world I would
have you in again, if I have any finger in the plan. It is no fit habit
for you, when not the evening star, unnailed and fetched down
from heaven, were fair enough jewel for your neck. If this is, as
I am apt to suspect, a world of yours, I cannot wholly commend
your handiwork.'

'Handiwork? Will you think I am the Demiurge: builder of
worlds?'

'I think you are not. But chooser, and giver of worlds: that I
am well able to believe. And I think you were in a bad mood
when you commissioned this one. The best I can suppose of it is
that it may be some good as training-ground for our next. And
for our next, I hope you will think of a real one.'

While they talked she had made no sign, except that some scarce
discernible relaxing of the poise of her sitting there brought her
a little closer. Then in the silence, his right hand palm upwards
lightly brushing her knee, her own hand caught it into her lap,
and there, compulsive as a brooding bird, pressed it blindly down.

Very still they sat, without speaking, without stirring: ten minutes perhaps. When at length she turned to look at him with eyes which (whether for some trick of light or for some less acceptable but more groundable reason) seemed now to be the eyes of a person not of this earth, his lids were closed as in sleep. Not far otherwise might the Father of Gods and men appear, sleeping between the Worlds.

Suddenly, even while she looked, he had ceased breathing. She moved his hand, softly laying it to rest beside him on the bench. 'These counterfeit worlds!' she said. 'They stick sometimes, like a plaster, past use and past convenience. Wait for me, in that real one, also of Your making, which, in this world here, You but part remembered, I think, and will there no doubt mainly forget this; as I, in my other dress, part remembered and part forgot. For forgetfulness is both a sink for worthless things and a storeroom for those which are good, to renew their morning freshness when, with the secular processions of sleeping and waking, We bring them out as new. And indeed, shall not all things in their turn be forgotten, but the things of You and Me?'

BOOK ONE

FOUNDATIONS

I

FOUNDATIONS IN REREK

PERTISCUS Parry dwelt in the great moated house beside
Thundermere in Latterdale. Mynius Parry, his twin brother, was
lord of Laimak. Sidonius Parry, the youngest of them, dwelt at
Upmire under the Forn.

To Pertiscus it had long seemed against reason, and a thing not
forever to be endured, that not he but his brother Mynius must
have Laimak; which, seated upon a rock by strength inexpugnable,
had through more than twenty-five generations been to that family
the fulcrum of their power, making men regard them, and not
lightly undertake anything that ran not with their policy. In those
days, as from of old, no private man might live quiet in Rerek,
for the envies, counterplottings, and open furies of the great houses,
each against each: the house of Parry, sometimes by plain violence,
other times using under show of comity and friendship a more
mole-like policy, working ever to new handholds, new stances, on
the way up towards absolute dominion; while, upon the adverse
side, the princely lines of Eldir and Kaima and Bagort in the north
laboured by all means, even to the sinking now and then of their
mutual jealousies, to defeat these threats to their safeties and very
continuance. Discontents in the Zenner marches: emulations among
lesser lords, and soldiers of fortune: growing-pains of the free
towns, principally in the northern parts: all these were wound by
one party and the other to their turn. And always, north and

south, wings shadowed these things from the outlands: eagles in the air, whose stoops none might securely foretell: Meszria in the south, and (of nearer menace, because action is of the north but the south apter to love ease and to repose upon its own) the great uneasy power of the King of Fingiswold.

So it was that the Lord Pertiscus Parry, upon the thirty-eighth birthday of him and Mynius, which fell about winter-nights, took at last this way to amend his matter: bade his brother to a birthday feast at Thundermere, and the same night, when men were bemused with wine and Mynius by furious drinking quite bereft of his senses, put him to bed to a bear brought thither on purpose, and left this to work till morning. Himself, up betimes, and making haste with a good guard to Laimak swiftlier than tidings could overtake him, was let in by Mynius's men unsuspecting; and so, without inconvenience or shedding of blood made himself master of the place. He put it about that it was the Devil had eat his brother's head off, coming in the likeness of a red bear with wings. Simple men believed it. They that thought they knew better, held their tongues.

After this, Pertiscus Parry took power in Laimak. His wife was a lady from the Zenner; their children were Emmius, Gargarus, Lugia, Lupescus, and Supervius.

Emmius, being come of age, he set in lordship at Sleaby in Susdale. Lugia he gave in marriage to Count Yelen of Leveringay in north Rerek. Gargarus, for his part simple and of small understanding, grew to be a man of such unthrifty lewd and abominable living that he made it not scrupulous to lay hand on men's daughters and lawful wives, keep them so long as suited the palate of his appetite, then pack them home again. Because of these villainies, to break his gall and in hope to soften the spite of those that had suffered by him, his father forced him to pine and rot for a year in the dungeons under Laimak. But there was no mending of his fault: within a month after his letting out of prison he was killed in a duello with the husband of a lady he had took by force in the highway between Swinedale and Mornagay. Lupescus grew up a very silent man. He lived much shut up from the world at Thundermere.

Of all Pertiscus's children the youngest, Supervius, was most to his mind, and he kept him still at his side in Laimak.

He kept there also for years, under his hand, his nephew Rasmus Parry, Mynius's only son. Rasmus had been already full grown to manhood when he had sight of his father's corpse, headless and its bowels ploughed up and the bear dead of her wounds beside it (for Mynius was a man of huge bodily strength) in that inhospitable guest-chamber at Thundermere; yet these horrid objects so much inflamed his mind that nought would he do thenceforth, day or night, save rail and lament, wishing a curse to his soul, and drink drunk. Pertiscus scorned him for a milksop, but let him be, whether out of pity or for fear lest his taking off might be thought to argue too un-manlike a cruelty. In the end, he found him house and land at Lonewood in Bardardale, and there, no great while afterwards, Rasmus, being in his drunken stupor, fell into a great vat of mead and thus, drowned like a mouse, ended his life-days.

Seventeen years Pertiscus sat secure in Laimak, begraced and belorded. Few loved him. Far fewer were those, how high soever their estate, that stood not in prudent awe of him. He became in his older years monstrously corpulent, out-bellied and bulked like a toad. This men laid to the reproach of his gluttony and gormandizing, which indeed turned at last to his undoing; for, upon a night when he was now in his fifty-sixth year, after a surfeit he had taken of a great haggis garnished with that fish called the sea-grape putrefied in wine, a greasy meat and perilous to man's body, which yet he affected beyond all other, he fell down upon the table and was suddenly dead. This was in the seven hundred and twenty-first year after the founding of the city of Zayana. In the same year died King Harpagus in Rialmar of Fingiswold, to whom succeeded his son Mardanus; and it was two years before the birth of Mezentius, son of King Mardanus, in Fingiswold.

Supervius was at this time twenty-five years of age: in common esteem a right Parry, favouring his father in cast of feature and frame of mind, but taller and without superfluity of flesh: all hardness and sinew. Save that his ears stood out like two funguses, he was a man fair to look upon: piercing pale eyes set near together, like a gannet's: red hair, early bald in front: great of jaw, and with a fiery red beard thick and curly, which he oiled and perfumed, reaching to his belt. He was of a most haughty overweeningness of bearing: hard-necked and unswayable in policy, albeit he could look and speak full smoothly: of a sure memory for things misdone against him, but as well too for benefits received. He was held for a just man where his proper interest was not too nearly engaged, and a protector of little men: open-handed, and a great waster in spending: by vulgar repute a lycanthrope: an uneasy friend, undivinable, not always to be trusted; but as unfriend, always to be feared. He took to wife, about this time, his cousin Rhodanthe of Upmire, daughter of Sidonius Parry.

Men judged it a strange thing that Supervius, being that he was the youngest born, should now sit himself down in his father's seat as though head of that house unquestioned. Prince Keriones of Eldir, who at this time had to wife Mynius's daughter Morsilla, and had therefore small cause to love Pertiscus and was glad of any disagreeings in that branch of the family, wrote to Emmius to condole his loss, styling him in the superscription *Lord of Laimak*, as with intent by that to stir up his bile against his young brother that had baulked him of his inheritance. Emmius returned a cold answer, paying no regard to this, save that he dated his letter from Argyanna. The Prince, noting it, smelt in it (what soon became generally opinioned and believed) that Supervius had prudently beforehand hatched up an agreement with his eldest brother about the heirship, and that Emmius's price for waiving his right to Laimak had been that strong key to the Meszrian marchlands: according to the old Rerek saying:

> A brace of buttocks in Argyanna
> Can swing the scales upon the Zenner.

This Lord Emmius Parry, six years older than Supervius, was of all that family likest to his mother: handsomer and finelier-moulded of feature than any else of his kindred: lean, loose-limbed, big-boned, black of hair, palish of skin, and melancholic: wanting their fire and bestial itch to action, but not therefore a man with impunity to be plucked by the beard. He was taciturn, with an ordered tongue, not a swearer nor an unreverent user of his mouth: men learned to weigh his words, but none found a lamp to pierce the profoundness of his spirit. He was a shrewd ensearcher of the minds and intents of other men: of a saturnine ironic humour that judged by deed sooner than by speech, not pondering great all that may be estimate great: saw where the factions drew, and kept himself unconcerned. No hovering temporizer, nor one that will strain out a gnat and swallow a camel, neither yet, save upon carefully weighed necessity, a meddler in such designs as can hale men on to bloody stratagems: but a patient long-sighted politician with his mind where (as men judged) his heart was, namely south in Meszria. His wife, the Lady Deïaneira, was Meszrian born, daughter to Mesanges of Daish. He loved her well, and was faithful to her, and had by her two children: Rosma the first-born, at that time a little maid seven winters old, and a son aged four, Hybrastus. Emmius Parry lived, both before at Sleaby and henceforward in Argyanna, in the greatest splendour of any nobleman in Rerek. He was good to artists of all kind, poets, painters, workers in bronze and marble and precious stones, and all manner of learned men, and would have them ever about him and pleasure himself with their works and with their discourse, whereas the most of his kin set not by such things one bean. There was good friendship between him and his brother Supervius so long as they were both alive. Men thought it beyond imagination strange how the Lord Emmius quietly put up his brother's injuries against him, even to the usurping of his place in Laimak: things which, enterprised by any other man bom, he would have paid home, and with interest.

For a pair of years after Supervius's taking of heirship, nought befell to mind men of the change. Then the lord of Kessarey died heirless, and Supervius, claiming succession for himself upon some patched-up rotten arguments with more trickery than law in them, when the fruit did not fall immediately into his mouth appeared suddenly with a strength of armed men before the place and began to lay siege to it. They within (masterless, their lord being dead and all affairs in commission), were cowed by the mere name of Parry. After a day or two, they gave over all resistance and yielded up to him Kessarey, tower, town, harbour and all; being the strongest place of a coast-town between Kaima and the Zenner. Thus did he pay himself back somewhat for loss of Argyanna that he had perforce given away to his brother.

Next he drew under him Telia, a strong town in the batable lands where the territories of Kaima marched upon those subject to Prince Keriones: this professedly by free election of a creature of his as captal of Telia, but it raised a wind that blew in Eldir and in Kaima: made those two princes lay heads together. Howsoever, to consort them in one, it needed a solider danger than this of Telia which, after a few months, came to seem no great matter and was as good as forgot until, the next year, the affair of Lailma, being added to it, brought them together in good earnest.

Lailma was then but a small town, as it yet remains, but strongly seated and walled. Caunas has formerly been lord of it, holding it to the interest of Mynius Parry whose daughter Morsilla he had to wife: but some five years before the death of Pertiscus Parry, they of Lailma rose against Caunas and slew him: proclaimed themselves a free city: then, afraid of what they had done, sought protection of Eldir. Keriones made answer, he would protect them as a free commonalty: let them choose them a captain. So all of one accord assembled together and put it to voices, and their voices rested on Keriones; and so, year by year, for eight years. The Lady Morsilla, Caunas's widow, was shortly after the uproar matched to Prince Keriones; but the son of her and Caunas, Mereus by name, being at Upmire with his great-uncle Sidonius Parry and then about twelve years of age, Pertiscus got into his claws and kept him in Laimak treating him kindly and making much of him, as a young hound that he might someday find a use for. This Mereus, being grown to manhood, Supervius (practising with the electors in Lailma) now at length in the ninth year suborned as competitor of Keriones to the captainship. Faction ran high in the town, and with some blood-letting. In the end, the voices went on the side of Mereus. Thereupon the hubble-bubble began anew, and many light and unstable persons of the Parry faction running together to the signiory forced the door, came riotously into the council chamber, and there encountering three of the prince's officers, with saucy words and revilings bade them void the chamber; who standing their ground and answering threat for threat, were first jostled, next struck, next overpowered, seized, their breeches torn off, and in that pickle beaten soundly and thrown out of the window.

Keriones, upon news of this outrage, sent speedy word to his neighbour princes, Alvard of Kaima and Kresander of Bagort. The three of them, after council taken in Eldir, sent envoys to both Laimak and Argyanna, to make known that they counted the election void because of intermeddling by paid agents of Supervius Parry (acting, the princes doubted not, beyond their commission). In measured terms the envoys rehearsed the facts, and prayed the Lords Emmius and Supervius, for keeping of the peace, to join with the princes in sending of sufficient soldiers into Lailma to secure the holding of new elections soberly, so as folk might quietly and without fear of duress exercise their choice of a captain.

In both places the envoys got noble entertainment and good words; but as for satisfaction, they came bare and were sent bare away. Supervius rejected, as a just man wrongfully accused, the charges of coercion. As touching their particularities of violence done by fools, frantics and so forth, if Prince Keriones misliked it, so too did he. But 'twas no new or unheard of thing. He could rake up a dozen injuries to match it, suffered by his friends in the same town within these nine years, and upon smaller provocation; they must have respect also that many still believed (as he had heard tell) that it was not without pulling of strings from Eldir that Caunas, his kinsman-in-law, got his death. But all such things, for peace sake, it were now unproper and unprofitable to pursue, and he had very charitably passed them by. For his own part (stroking his beard), enough to say that he upheld free institutions in the free cities of the north: would uphold them by force, too, if need were.

Emmius, standing firm and unaffable in support of his brother, left the envoys in no doubt that, in case attempt were made to meddle with Lailma, he would immediately aid Mereus by force of arms. So far in audience; and this upon taking leave: 'If the princes desire peace and amity, as I think they do and as we do, let's meet in some place convenient, not under either side's dominion, and hammer the thing to agreement. Tell them, if they will, I'll come and see them in Mornagay.' With that, he gave them a letter to Supervius, that in their way home they might deliver it to him and (if he were of like mind) join him in this offer.

The princes sat in Eldir, last week of June, to consider of their envoys' report. Judging the business, upon examination, to be a chestnut not easy to unhusk, or with unpricked fingers, they thought fittest to accept the proffer of parley. Accordingly, after delays which all had show of reason but had origin, most of them, in Argyanna or Laimak, upon the twenty-fifth of August, in the wayside inn at Mornagay, both sides met.

The Lord Emmius Parry, arm in arm with his brother upon the stairs in their way up to the chamber where their conference should be, stayed him a moment (the others being gone before). 'You took all means that the answer, on that matter of yours, should be brought hither? Not miss you by going past us to Laimak?'

'All means. I am not a fool.'

'I like it not, seeing, by our last intelligence 'twas directly said the letter but waited signature and should be sent you by speedy hand within twenty-four hours from them. This, in Laimak yesterday afore breakfast. A master card to deal unto them today, held we but that in our hand.'

'I've plied every mean to hasten it, this two months past,' said Supervius. 'Much against my own nature, too: Satan sain them, sire and filly both. Ay, and I do begin to think I did ill to follow your counsel there, brother.'

Emmius laughed. 'I may come upon you for this hereafter.'

'To cap and knee them, like some rascally suitor for a chipping; and so be thus trained. Even to putting away of my wife, too, not to miss of this golden chance, and she at the long last with child; and nought but black looks so from my uncle Sidonius, for that slight upon his daughter. 'Twas ill done. Would it were undone.'

'Go, I would have you resolute and patient: not as thus, full of vertibility. Nothing was lost for asking, and this an addition most worth your waiting for.'

Being set, they now fell to business. The princes, using mediocrity and eschewing all kind of provocation, first argued their case. Supervius, in answer, spoke much, full of compliment indeed but with small show of compliancy: later, when, leaving generalities, they fell to disputing of particular facts, he spoke little: Emmius, here a word and there a word. When they had thus spent near two hours but to tiffle about the matter, Prince Keriones, as a man wearied past bearing of these jugglings and equivocations, laid the question plump and fair: Were the Parry resolved to content them with nought less than leave things where they stood: Mereus in Lailma?

There was no answer. Supervius looked at the ceiling. 'You are a harsh stepfather, when his own people would have him back, to wish to put him out again; and with our help, God save the mark!' Emmius raised an eyebrow, then fell to tracing with his pen-point little jags and stars on the paper before him. Keriones repeated his question. 'Briefly so,' said Supervius, and thrust out his jaw.

'Will you stand upon that, my Lord Emmius Parry?' said the prince. And, upon Emmius's shrugging his shoulders and saying, 'At least it conveniently brings us back to a base on which we can, maybe, by further debate frame some mean toward agreement', 'Then,' said the prince, gathering up his papers, 'our work is but waste work, for we will not for our part any longer endure this thing.'

Supervius opened his mouth for some damageful rejoinder, but his brother, checking him with a hand upon his arm, made for both: 'I pray you yet have patience awhile. Nor I nor my brother desire troubles in the land. But if, spite of that, troubles be raised, we are not unprepared; men may wisely beware how they stamp upon our peaceful stockinged feet, be it in the north there or nigher home.'

'You think to cow us,' said Keriones violently, 'with threats of war? seeing that by fraud, art and guile you can no further? But you shall find that neither are we unprepared. Neither are we without friends to fight beside us, if needs must, in our just quarrel. Yea, friends right high and doubtable: out of Fingiswold, if you goad us to that. We will call in King Mardanus to aid us.'

There was a silence. One or two startled as if a rock had fallen from the sky. The Lord Emmius smiled, drumming delicately on the table with his fingers. 'Our words, of both sides,' he said at last, 'out-gallop our thoughts: sign we are hungry. These be not matters to be swept up in a rage, as boys end a game of marbles. Let's dine and forget 'em awhile. Then, with minds refreshed, chance our invention may devise a picture shall please us all.'

Kresander said beneath his breath, but Supervius, as catching the sense of it, reddened to the ears, 'He that shaketh hands with a Parry, let him count the fingers a receiveth back again.'

But Keriones, his brow clearing (as though that rude discourtesy, contrariwise to its sense and purpose, wrought in him but to second Emmius's pleasant words and with potenter force than theirs), said to Emmius, 'You have counselled well, my lord. Truly, he that will argue matters of state on an empty belly hath his guts in his brains.'

While they waited for dinner, there were brought in spice-plates and wines. Emmius said, 'I pray you do me that favour as to taste this wine. I brought it north on purpose for our entertainment. It is of Meszria, of their famousest vintage: a golden wine of Armash.' With his own hand he filled round the goblets from the jewelled silver flagon. 'Prince Kresander, I'll pledge you first: I know not why, unless 'tis because you and I have, of all of us, journeyed farthest to this meeting-place.' With that, he drained his cup: 'To our soon agreement.' Kresander, flushing in the face with an awkward look, drained his. And now, carousing deep healths, the whole company pledged one another.

They dined lightly on what the inn afforded: capon, neats' tongues, bacon pies, sallets, and round white cheeses pressed in the hill-farms above Killary. These things, with much quaffing down of wine, soon warmed them to quips and merriment, so that, dinner being done, they came again, with minds cleared and blood cooled, to their chief matter subject.

'Ere we begin,' said Emmius, 'I would say but this. With what intent came we to this place, if not to seek agreement? Yet we spent the morning upon a dozen prickly questions, most of them not worth the reward paid to a courtesan for a night's lodging, and yet each enough by itself to stir up the gall of some or other of us and set us by the ears. How were it now if we set about it another way: talk first on those matters whereon we are at one? And, most worth of all, this: that we will have no foreign hand meddling in Rerek. That is an old tried maxim, profitably observed by us in all our private differences whatsoever, and by our fathers, and fathers' fathers.'

'Your lordship has well and truly said,' said Kresander; 'as myself, most of all, should feel the mischief, were outlanders to come in upon us from that quarter. So much the more, then, behoveth some not to bring things to that pass that others may think it a less evil to fetch in help from without than to abide the injustices put upon them within the land.'

Emmius said, 'Our private differences it is for us to untangle and set in order as we have had wont to: not by war, nor by threat of war, but by wise policy, giving a little back when need be, between ourselves. They cannot, unless we have ta'en leave of our sober wits, to be let hunt counter to that cardinal trending of our politic.'

'What of Kessarey?' said Keriones. 'Was not that by war-stirring or war-threat? What of Telia? Nay, I cry you mercy, finish your say, my lord. I desire our agreement as much as you desire it.'

'As much as that?' Alvard said, behind his hand. 'Mich 'em God dich 'em! Fine agreement there, then!'

'Kessarey,' replied Emmius Parry, 'was anciently of Laimak; we but fetched it back where it belonged. Telia, by full franchise and liberties, chose their governor. We are here not to treat of things over and done with, but of this late unhappy accident in Lailma.'

'Good,' said Prince Keriones. 'There's yet comfort, if you say that. Afore dinner, it seemed you would have but one way in Lailma, and that your own way.'

'No, no. I never said so. I never thought so.'

'My Lord Supervius said it.'

Supervius shook his head. 'I would not be taken altogether thus. Some way, there's ne'er a doubt, we shall patch matters together.'

'As for Lailma,' said Emmius, 'we shall be easily set at one, so we but hold by that overruling maxim of *no foreign finger*. If we are to treat, it must be upon that as our platform. We can affirm that, my lords? that, come what may, we will have no foreign finger in Rerek?'

'I have been waiting these many minutes,' said Supervius, looking across the table with a cold outfacing stare, 'to hear Prince Keriones say yea to that principle.'

The prince frowned: first time since dinner. 'It is a principle I have resolutely stood upon,' he said, 'since first I had say in the affairs of this land. And that's since I first had a beard to my chin; at which time my Lord Supervius Parry was but a year or two out of's swaddling-clothes. And will you thus ridiculously pretend that I and my friends would go about to undo this wholesome rule and practice? When in truth it is you who, seeking to perturbate these towns in our detriment and to under-creep my might and title in Lailma, hope so to drive us into a corner where we have the choice but of two things: either to give way to you at every turn and so be made at last your under-men in Rerek, either else (if we will maintain our right) to take a course which you may cry out against as violating the very principle we ourselves have made our policy and have urged upon you.'

Emmius said, 'Nay, pray you, my lords, let's stick to our tacklings. Mutual imputations of working underhand do but put true matters aback. Let's pledge ourselves to Prince Keriones's policy: this knotty question of Lailma we shall then easily undo. Are we accorded so far?'

'No,' answered Keriones. 'And, in frank plainness, for this reason. You have levies of armed men (we know this by our espials) in a readiness to march north and set upon us. I say not we are afeared of what you may do to us, but we mean not to tie our own hands and so fall in your hazard. Let's talk, if you please, of Lailma. But if in that obstinacy my Lord Supervius remains, then we sit out. And then will we assuredly bring in Fingiswold to help us, and the rebuke and damage of that will be yours, not ours.'

'It will be your very deed,' said Supervius, 'sprung from your own fury, howsoever you colour it.'

'O, no hot respectless speeches, brother,' said Emmius. 'These matters must be handled with clear eyes, not in a swimming of the brain.

'Prince Keriones,' he said then, sharpening his eyes upon him, 'this is a very peremptory sentence plumped down of you. Well, I also will speak plain, and without offence. We have offered to treat with you upon your own avouched basis of *no foreign finger*. You will not engage yourselves so far. Upon this, then, we set up our rest, I and my brother. We accept that basis. More, we are minded to enforce it. The fortress of Megra, lying upon your (and our) northern border, and longing to Fingiswold, is threat enough. It is (with all humility) for you princes to govern well your realms and give example to the cities upon your confines: so do we with ours. I have friends and affines in the southland, but I would think scorn to call upon King Kallias to prop me. If you call upon King Mardanus, I will march with my brother to defend that northern frontier thus betrayed by you. And I think we can be upon you, and deal with you, before you have time to bring in your foreign succours; as in common prudence indeed we must, since you have so threatened us, unless you give us security of peace. That is to say, material pledges: fair words, spoken or written, can by no means suffice us now.

'So much, since I would be honest, you left me no choice but to say. But surely it is not a thing unpossible or unlikely, that'—

Here Kresander could contain no longer. 'We had better never have come hither,' he shouted, and smote the table with his fist. 'This meeting was but to mock us and dally the matter off while they sharpened their swords against us. I'm for home.' He pushed back his chair and was half risen, but Kariones pulled him down again, saying, 'Wait. We will hear this out.'

Supervius, while his brother had been speaking, had broke the seal of a letter brought hastily in by his secretary. Keriones and Alvard watched him read it, as if themselves would read in his face something of its purport. But his face, haughty and imperturbable, showed not so much as a hairsbreadth movement of nostril or eyelid as he scanned the letter, neither at Kresander's outburst.

'Tongues can outbrawl swords,' said Emmius, chilling cold of voice; 'but that is for rude beasts, not for men that be reasonable. I pray you, let me finish my say. And first, by your leave,' as Supervius put the letter into his hands. He read it, folded it again thoughtfully, gave it back: his face like his brother's, not to be unciphered. 'Let us,' he said, 'as great statesmen, hold fast by our common good, of all of us, which is peace in Rerek. History hath remembered the ruins of many estates and powers which have gone down in civil strife or, albeit victorious, got in the end but a handful of smoke to the bargain. Let us live as friends. I unfeignedly wish it: so do my brothers and all that adhere to our interest. But others must do their part. This is my counsel: that we, of both sides, agree to go home, keep truce for a month, then meet again and, as I hope, determine of some new assured basis for our unluckily shaken friendship. Where shall we meet?' he said, turning to his brother.

'Why, if it shall please your excellencies to kill two birds with one stone and add merry-making to crown our peace-making,' said Supervius, 'what happier meeting-place than Megra? upon the twentieth day of September, which is appointed there for the feast of my betrothal' – he paused, gathering their eyes – 'to the Princess Marescia of Fingiswold. Nay, read it if you please: I had it but five minutes since.' And with a wolvish look he tossed the letter upon the table.

II

FOUNDATIONS IN FINGISWOLD

IT was eight months after that meeting in Mornagay: mid-March, and mid-afternoon. Over-early spring was busy upon all that grew or breathed in the lower reaches of the Revarm. Both banks, where the river winds wide between water-meadows, were edged with daffodils; and every fold of the rising ground, where there was shelter from north and east for the airs to dally in and take warmth from the sunshine, held a mistiness of faint rose-colour: crimp-petalled blossoms, with the leaf-buds scarcely as yet beginning to open, of the early northern plum. Higher in the hillsides pasque-flowers spread their tracery of soft purple petal and golden centre. A little downstream, on a stretch of shingle that lay out from this right bank into the river, a merganser drake and his wife stood preening themselves, beautiful in their whites and bays and iridescent greens. It was here about the high limit of the tides, and from all the marshland with its slowly emptying creeks and slowly enlarging flats (for the ebb was well on its way) of mud and ooze, came the bubbling cascade of notes as curlew answered curlew amid cries innumerable of lesser shore-birds; plover and sandpiper, turnstone and spoonbill and knot and fussy redshank, fainter and fainter down the meanderings of the river to where, high upon crags which rose sudden from water-level to shut out the prospect southwards, two-horned Rialmar sat throned.

Anthea spoke: 'I have examined it, honoured sir: scented it, as you bade me, from every airt.'

Doctor Vandermast was sat a little above her on the rib of rock which, grown over with close-lying twigs and leaf-whorls of the evergreen creeping daphne, made for these two a dry and a cushioned resting-place. His left hand, palm-upward in white beard, propped his chin. His gaze was south, in a contemplation which seemed to look through and behind the immediate things of earth and sky, as through windows giving upon less alterable matters. Nothing moved, save when here and there, in a sparkle of black and white, a flock of shy golden-eye took wing, upstream or downstream, or a butterfly flight of terns rose and fell, drifting on air toward the unseen headwaters of the Midland Sea.

'Rialmar town?' said the doctor, at last, without shifting his gaze.

'No. This whole new world. I have quartered it over, pole to pole, so as I could (if you desired me) give you an inventory. And all since day dawning.'

'What make you of it? In a word?'

'Something fair and free,' she answered. 'Something immeasurably old. As old as myself.'

'Or as young?'

'Or as young.'

'But a minute ago you called it new?' He looked down now, into this girl's staring yellow eyes: eyes whose pupils were upright slits that opened upon some inward quivering of incandescence, as of iron fired beyond redness; and his gaze grew gentle. 'And you are becharmed by it: like a bee of the new brood come out to dance before the hive on a still sunshiny evening and taste open air for the first time and find your landmarks.'

Anthea laughed: a momentary disclosing of pointed teeth that transshaped, as with leap and vanishing again of lightning, the classic quietude of her features. 'I knew it all before,' she said. 'Yet for all that, it is as new and unexperimented as last night's snowfall on my high glaciers of Ramosh Arkab. A newness that makes my heckles rise. Does it not yours?'

He shook his head: 'I am not a beast of prey.'

'What are you, then?' she said, but without waiting for an answer. 'There is a biting taste to it: a scent, a stirring: and up there, especially. In the Teremnene palace.' She lifted her nose towards the royal seat-town upon its solitary heights, as if even down wind her eager sense tasted its quality.

Vandermast said, 'There is a child there. You saw it no doubt? A boy.'

'Yes. But no past ordinary novelty in that. Unless perhaps that when, changing my smooth skin for my furred, I slunk in and made teeth at it behind the nurse's back, it was not scared but gave me a look, so that I went out and glad to be gone. And, now I think on it, 'twas that first set me scenting this newness at every corner. Beyond all, in the Queen.' She looked at him, paused, then asked suddenly. 'This Queen. Who in truth is she?'

He made no reply.

'Tell me, dear master,' she said, drawing herself closer by a most unhuman self-elongating of body and limbs and rubbing her cheek, as might some cattish creature, against his knee.

He said, 'You must not ask questions when you know the answer.'

Anthea sat back on her heels and laughed. Upon the motion, her hair, loosely bound up with a string of clouded zircon stones of that translucent blue which is in the lip of an ice-cave looked up to from within, fell, in tumbled cataracts as of very sunlight, down about her shoulders and, in one of its uncoiling fulvid streams, over her breast. 'She Herself does not know the answer. I suppose, in this present dress of Hers, She is asleep?'

'In this present dress,' said the ancient doctor, 'She is turned outward from Herself. You may, if you choose, conceive it as a kind of sleep: a kind of forgetting. As the sunshine were to forget itself in the thing it shines on.'

'In that lion-cub of hers? I cannot understand such a forgetting in Her.'

'No, my oread. Nor I would not wish you able to understand it, for that were to maculate the purity of your own proper nature.'

'And you would wish me be as I am?'

'Yes,' answered he. 'You, and all true beings else.'

The girl, silent, putting up her hair, met his look unsmilingly with her unquiet, feline, burning eyes.

'We will go on,' said the doctor, rising from his seat.

Anthea with a lithe and sinuous grace rose to follow him.

'Whither?' she asked as they came southward.

'Up to Teremne. We will look upon these festivities.'

In the old Teremnene palace which, like an eagle's nest, crowns the summit ridge of the south-eastern and loftier of the twin steep rock bastions called Teremne and Mehisbon, on and about which has grown up as by accretion of ages Rialmar town, is a little secret garden pleasaunce. It lies square between walls and the living rock, in good shelter from the unkinder winds but open to the sun, this side or that, from fore-noon till late evening. No prying windows overlook it: no intrusive noises visit it of the world's stir without: a very formal garden artificially devised with paved walks of granite trod smooth by the use of centuries, and with flights of steps going down at either side and at either end to an oval pond in the midst, and upon a pedestal in the midst of that pond a chryselephantine statue of Aphrodite as rising from the sea. At set paces there were parterres of tiny mountain plants: stonecrop, houseleek, rock madwort, mountain dryas, trefoils, and the little yellow mountain poppy; and with these that creeping evening primrose, which lifts up wavy-edged four-lobed saucers of a spectral whiteness, new every night at night-fall, to bloom through the hours of dark and fill the garden with an overmastering sharp sweetness. And at full morning they droop and begin to furl their petals, suffused now with pink colour which were white as a snowdrop's, and lose all their scent, and the thing waits lifeless and inert till night shall return again and wake it to virgin-new delicacy and deliciousness. This was Queen Stateira's garden, furnished out anew for her sake seven years ago by Mardanus her lord, who in those days made little store of gardens, but much of his young new-wedded wife.

Shadows were lengthening now, as afternoon drew towards evening. In one of the deep embrasures of the east wall which look down the precipice sheer eight hundred feet, to the river mouth and the harbour and so through skyey distances to the great mountain chains, so blanketed at this hour with cloud that hard it was to discern snowfield from cloudbank, leaned King Mardanus in close talk with two or three about him. No wind stirred in the garden, and the spring sunshine rested warm on their shoulders.

Away from them at some twenty yards' remove, by the waterside, upon a bench of lapis lazuli and mother-of-pearl, sat the Queen. The brightness of the sun shining from behind her obscured her features under a veiling mystery, but not to conceal an ambiency of beauty that lived in her whole frame and posture, an easefulness and reposefulness of unselfregarding grace. The light kindled to flame the native fire-colours in her hair, and the thrown shadow of that statue touched the furred hem of her skirt and the gold-woven lace-work on her shoe.

Over against her on the same bench the Lady Marescia Parry, only child of Prince Garman of Fingiswold, and so cousin german to the King, faced the sun. She was at this time in the twenty-fourth year of her age: of a dazzling whiteness of skin: her eyes, busy, bold and eager, of a hot chestnut brown: her nose a falcon's, her yellow hair, strained back from her high forehead by a thin silver circlet garnished with stone and pearls, fell loose and untressed about her back and powerful shoulders, in fashion of a bride's.

The Queen spoke: 'Well, cousin, you are wedded.'

'Well wedded, but not yet bedded.'

''Las, when mean you to give over that ill custom of yours?'

'Ill custom?'

'Ever to speak broad.'

'O, between kinsfolk. Tell me unfeignedly, what thinks your highness of my Supervius? Is a not a proper man?'

'He belieth not his picture. And since 'twas his picture you fell in love with, and he with yours, I dare say you have gotten the husband of your choice.'

The Princess smiled with her lips: cherry-red lips, lickerous, and masterful. 'And by right of conquest,' she said. 'That sauceth my dish: most prickingly.'

'Yet remember,' said the Queen, 'we wives are seldom conquerors beyond first se'nnight.'

'I'll talk to your highness of that hereafter. But I spake not of conquest upon him. My blood tells me there's fire enough in the pair of us to outburn such cold-hearth rivalries as that. Dear Gods forfend I should e'er yield myself chattel to the man I wed: but neither could I be fool enough to wed with such a man as I could bring down to be chattel of mine. Nay, I spoke of my parents; ay, and (with respect) of yourself, and of the King.'

'Your conquest there,' replied the Queen, 'is measure of our love of you.'

'Doubtless. But measure, besides, of mine own self will. Without that,' here she glanced over her shoulder and leaned a little nearer, 'I am apt to think your love of me (the King's, at least) had played second fiddle to more deeper policies.'

The Queen said, 'Well, fret not for that. You have had your way.'

Marescia lifted her superb white chin and her mouth smiled. 'Truly, cousin,' she said, managing her voice almost to a whisper, 'I think you are to thank me, all of you. Put case I had fallen in with your fine design to match me to yonder outed Prince of Akkama. The man is well enough: personable, I grant: qualified out of all ho, I'd swear, to please a woman: but of what avail? With's father dead, and himself, driven away by the usurper, a landless exile still sitting on your door-step here. How shall such an one be ever a king, or lord of aught save's own empty imaginings and discontents? I swear the King (Gods send he live for ever) may get better purchase by this that, following my own natural lust o' the eye, I have brought him, than by Aktor, be he ten times prince indeed. And Rerek, far nearer us in blood and custom. Wed with yonder foreign lick-dish! God's dignity, I'd sleep in the byre sooner and breed minotaurs.'

Queen Stateira laughed: honest lovely laughter, bred of sweet blood and the life-breath fancy free; 'Come, you're too bitter.'

'Aktor is in your highness's books, I think.'

'Why think that?'

'Strange else, professing so much cousinly love to me, you should a wished me give my hand there.'

The Queen looked away. 'To tell you true, dear Marescia, 'twas the King's wish, and but therefore mine, as being my duty.'

'Duty?' said the Princess: 'to be led blindfold by your husband? Go, they'll ne'er call me perfect wife a those terms.'

There was a pause. Then Marescia, sitting back again, her voice now at its ordinary strength and pitch: 'What is this prognosticator by the stars, this soothsayer, your highness keeps i' the palace?'

'What do you mean? I keep none such.'

'O yes: a greybeard signior: long gaberdine, and capped *magister artium*: some compliment-monger, I would wager. Comes to me as I passed among the throng of guests not half an hour since on my Lord Supervius's arm, gives me a stare o' the eye turned all my backside to gooseflesh, and crieth out that I shall bear Supervius a son shall be greater than his father.'

'Heaven hold fast the omen,'

'And then to my Lord Emmius, whom I must now call brother-in-law: crieth out and saith that of the seed of Emmius Parry shall come both a queen of earth and a queen of heaven.'

'And what will he cry out at me, think you?' said the Queen.

'Please you enter the hall of the Sea Horses, I can show him to you, and you may examine him.'

'Dear my Lord,' said Stateira, as the King and those about him, their business being it seemed concluded, approached her, 'here's diversion for you,' and told him what Marescia had said. The King bluffly humouring it as child's talk, assented.

'Yonder standeth the old man: there, that tall, lanky one,' Marescia said in the Queen's ear, from behind, as they descended the great staircase into that vast hall and paused upon the last steps between the two sea-horses of dark blue rock-crystal well the height of a man's shoulder, there to take their stand and survey the company that, upon sounding of trumpets to a sennet to proclaim the King's presence, abode all motionless now and with all faces turned that way: 'and the girl with beastly eyes,' she said, 'who is, I suppose his granddaughter. Or, may hap, his bona roba, if such a jack pudding have use or custom of such commodities.'

Supervius eyed his princess with the deepening satisfaction of a skilled rider who begins to know the paces of a new high-blooded but untried mare. 'Speak within door, Marescia,' said her father. The King sent a little page of his of six year old that was named Jeronimy, to bring the doctor before him.

When that was done, and Vandermast made his obeisance, the King surveyed him a while in silence: then said, 'Who are you, old sir? Of my folk or an outlander?'

'I am,' answered he, 'your serene highness's life-long loyal faithful subject: my habitation many journeys from this, south on the Wold: my practice, that of a doctor in philosophy.'

'And what make you here i' the court?'

'To pay my humble duty where most I do owe it, and to behold with mine eyes at last this place and the glory thereof.'

'And to seek a pension?'

'No, Lord. Being entered now upon my ninth ten years I do find my lean patrimony sufficient to my livelihood, and in meditation of the metaphysicals food sufficient to sustain my mind. Over and above these things, I have no needs.'

'A wise man,' gently said the Queen, 'by what he saith. For, to speak true, here is freedom indeed.'

'I ne'er heard philosophy filled a man's belly,' said the King, with a piercing look still regarding him. 'You are bruited to me, you, to have uttered here, this instant afternoon, prognosticks and probabilities (some would call 'em improbabilities, but let that pass) touching certain noble persons, guests at our wedding feast.'

Vandermast said, 'I did so, my Lord and King, but in answer to interrogatives proposed to me by the persons in question.'

The King raised an eyebrow at Marescia. 'O yes,' said she: 'we did ask him.'

'I gave but voice to my thoughts that came me in mind,' said Vandermast. 'Neither spake I unconsiderately, but such things only as upon examination with mine inward judgement seemed likely and reasonable.'

The King was fallen silent a minute, glaring with his eyes into the eyes, steadfast and tranquil, of that learned doctor beneath their snow-thatched eaves, as though he would plumb some unsoundable darkness that underlay their shining and candid outward. Shifting his gaze at last, 'You shall not be blamed for that,' he said: then privately, to Prince Aktor, who was stood close on his right, 'Here is a man I like: is able to look me in the eye without brave nor slavishness. Kings seldom have to deal but with the one or t'other.'

'Your serene highness hath never, I think,' replied Aktor, 'had to deal with the first.' He glanced across to Queen Stateira who, upon the King's left hand, wide-eyed and with lovely lips half parted, was watching Doctor Vandermast with the intent and pleasure and wonder of a child. She caught the glance and looked away.

'You have answered well,' said the King to Vandermast. 'These be days of mirth and rejoicing, and fitting it is folk show themselves open-handed on high holiday, to give somewhat of alms to poor needy persons, most of all when such do utter good words or in what other way soever do seem to merit it. Wear this from me,' he said, taking a ring from his finger. 'My grandfather's it was, King Anthyllus's upon whom be peace. 'Tis thought there be virtue in the stone, and I would not bestow it save on one in whom I seemed to smell some deserts answerable to its worth. But forget not, the law lieth very deadly against whoso shall make bold to prophesy concerning the King's person. Aim not therefore at me in your conjectures, old man, bode they good or ill, lest a worse thing overtake you.'

'My Lord the King,' said Vandermast, 'you have commanded, and your command shall with exactness be obeyed. I have told your serenity that few and little are my possessions, and yet that there is nought whereof I do stand in want, nor will I be a taker of rewards. For it is a property universal of rewards that they can corrupt action, propounding to the actor (if the action be bad) a reason beyond the action's self, without which reason the action must have remained unacted. Because badness of itself is no reason. Contrariwise, be the action good, then the mere fact that it was acted for sake of reward can beget this bad habit in a man: to have respect to cheap, decaying, extern rewards; which enureth in the end so to debauch his inmost understanding that he becometh unable to taste or to desire the true only costly everlasting and ever satisfying reward, which hath its seat in the good action itself. But this,' he said, drawing onto his finger the King's ring, 'cometh not as a reward but as a gift royal, even as great Kings have from the antique times been renowned and honoured as ring-scatterers: a noble example which I find your serene highness do make your own.'

'Be such as I think you to be,' said the King, 'and my friendship followeth the gift.'

The doctor, that audience being done, came and went for a while his leisurely to and fro, within door and without, and always upon the fringes of the company, not as member thereof so much as looker on rather and listener, remarking whatsoever in any person appeared of remarkable: carriages, aspects, moods, manners, silences, little subtleties of eye, nostril, lip. And about and above him, at every succeeding step of his progress through this palace upon the southern horn of Rialmar, the greatness and the ancientness of the place hung heavier. Even as, to a climber, the mere vastness of the mountain becomes, as he goes higher, a presence, unite and palpable, built up of successive vastness of slabbed rock-face, vertiginous ice-cliff, eye-dazzling expanse of snow-field, up-soaring ultimate cornice chiselled by the wind to a sculptured perfection of line, sun-bright and remote against an infinite remoteness of blue heaven above it, so here was all gathered to an immobility of time-worn and storied magnificence: cyclopaean walls and gateways; flights of stairs six riders abreast might ride down on horseback and not touch knees; galleries, alcoves and clerestories cut from the rock; perspectives flattening the eye down distances

of corbel and frieze and deep-mullioned windows six times the
height of a man; colonnades with doric capitals curiously carved,
supporting huge-timbered vaulted roofs; and domed roofs that
seemed wide as the arch of day. All of which, apprehended in its
wholeness, might cast a wise mind into oblivion not of its own
self only and of all mankind but even of the everlasting mountains
themselves; in the sudden apprehension that this Rialmar might
be the nursery or breeding-place of a majesty and a loneliness
older-rooted than theirs.

Closed in these meditations, he came once more into that
presence-chamber, with its sea-horse staircase, and here was one
of the Queen's chamberlains with her highness's bidding that
Doctor Vandermast should attend her in the privy garden. The
doctor followed him; and, passing on their way through a vaulted
corridor hewn in the rock and brightly lighted with hanging lamps,
they were met with a nurse leading in her hand a child yet in his
side-coats, of two or three years old. The doctor viewed the boy
narrowly, and the boy him. 'What child was that?' he asked, when
they were gone by. The chamberlain, with a skewing of his eye at
him as of one smally trusting old vagrant men that were likely
sprung of a stone and certainly best told nothing, as soonest
mended, answered that it was one of the children of the palace,
he knew not for sure which. Which answer the learned doctor let
go without further remark.

'It is her highness's pleasure,' said the chamberlain, at the garden
gate, 'to receive you in private. Be pleased to walk on': so
Vandermast entered in alone and stood before Queen Stateira.

She was sitting sideways now on the jewelled bench, her feet
up, sewing a kirtle of white satin embroidered with flowers of
silver. Upon the doctor's coming she but glanced up and so back
to her needlework. It was yet bright sunshine, but with the wearing
of the afternoon the shadow of that gold and ivory statue of our
Lady of Paphos no longer touched the Queen where she sat. The
air was colder, and she had a high-collared cloak about her shoulders of rich brown velvet, coloured of the pine-marten's skin in
summer and lined with vair. He waited, watching her, while she

with down-bended eyes plied her needle. Nought else stirred, except now and then a blazing of hot colour where her hair caught the sun, and except, where the pleated neck-ruff of her gown ran lowest, the gentle fall and swell of her breathing. After a little, she raised her eyes. 'Can you guess, reverend sir, why I have sent for you?' The sun was behind her, and her countenance not to be read.

He answered, 'I will not guess, for I know.'

'Then tell me. For, in good sadness, I know not why I did it. Answer freely: you see we are alone.'

'Because,' answered he, after a moment's silence, 'your highness is fugitive and homeless, therefore you did do it; vainly expecting that the will-o'-the-wisp of an old man's fallible counsel should be a lamp to light you home.'

'These are strange unlikely words,' she said. 'I know not how to take them.'

'Truth,' said Vandermast gently, 'was ever a strange wild-fowl.'

'Truth! I that was born and bred in Rialmar, where else then shall I be at home? I that am your Queen, how should I be a fugitive, and from what?'

'To be here before your time is to be homeless. And the necessity you flee from is necessity by this cause only, that yourself (albeit I think you have forgotten) did choose it to make it so.'

The violent blood suffused all her face and neck, and with the suddenness of her half-rising from her seat the rich and costly embroidery slid from her lap and lay crumpled on the ground. She sat back again: 'I see you are but some phantastical sophister who with speaking paradoxically will gain the reputation of wisdom and reach. I'll listen to no more.'

'I am nought else,' answered that aged man, painfully upon one knee retrieving the fallen satins, 'than your highness's creature and servant. You do misprize, moreover, the words I spake, referring unto one particular accident what was meant in a generality more loftily inclusive.' Then, standing again in respectful reverence before her, 'And yet, it fits,' he said, under his breath as to himself only;

but the Queen, with head bowed as before over her needlework, seemed to shrink, as though the words touched her on a wound.

'I have lost my needle,' she said. 'No. Here it is.' Then, after a long pause, still sewing, and as out of a deep unhappiness: 'Will the gull choose to dash herself against the Pharos light? Will a seaman, where the tide runs in the wind's teeth between skerry and skerry, choose to be there in a boat without a rudder? Why should I?'

'How shall any earthly being but your highness's self answer that? Perhaps 'twas in the idle desire to feel your power.'

With that, the Queen's hand stopped dead. 'And you are he they tell me can read a man's destiny in his eyes? Can you not read in mine,' and she raised her head to meet his gaze, 'that I have no power? that I am utterly alone?'

'The King's power is your power.'

She said, resuming her sewing, 'I begin to dread it is not even his.'

'It is yours, will you but use it.'

She said, bending her white neck yet more to hide her face, 'I begin to think I have lost the knack to use it.' Then, scarce to be heard: 'Perhaps even the wish.'

Doctor Vandermast held his peace. His eyes were busied between this woman and this statue: this, more like in its outward, may be, to the unfacing reality, but of itself unreal, a mere mathematic, a superficies: that other real, but yet, save for an inner and outer loveliness, unlike, because wanting self-knowledge; and yet putting on, by virtue of that very privation, a perfection unique and sufficient unto itself albeit not belonging to the divine prototype at the fulness of Her actual; even as the great lamp of day has at sunrise and at sunset perfections of uncompleteness of transience which are consumed or blotted out in the white flame of noon.

'You are a strange secret man,' she said presently, still without looking up, 'that I should have spoke to you thus: things I'd a spoken to no creature else in the world. And, until today, ne'er so much as set eyes on you.' Then, suddenly gathering up her needlework, 'But you give me no help. No more than the other standers by or hinderers.'

He said, 'There is none hath the ability to help your highness, except only your highness's self alone.'

'Here's cold comfort, then. Yet against burning, I suppose, there may be some good in coldness.'

She rose now and walked a turn or two in silence, coming to a stand at last under the statue; looking up at which, and with a face averted from that aged doctor, she said to him, 'True it is, I did send for you in a more weightier matter than this of me. I have a son.'

'Yes.'

'Can you read stars and significations in the heaven?'

'Be it indeed,' he replied, 'that in the university of Miphraz I did seven years apply my youth to study in the Ultramundanes and the Physicals, I have long since learnt that there is no answer in the mouth of these. My study is now of the darkness rather which is hid in the secret places of the heart of man: my office but only to understand, and to watch, and to wait.'

'Well, have you seen the child? What find you in him? Give me in a word your very thought. I must have the truth.' She turned and faced him. 'Even and the truth be evil.'

'If it be truth,' said the doctor, 'it can in no hand be evil; according to the principle of theoric, *Quanta est, tanto bonum*, which is as much as to say that completeness of reality and completeness of goodness are, *sub specie aeternitatis*, the same. I have beheld this child like as were I to behold some small scarce discernible first paling of the skies to tomorrow's dawn, and I say to you: Here is day.'

'To be King in his time?'

'So please the Gods.'

'In Fingiswold, after his father?'

'So, and more. To be the stay of the whole world.'

'This is heavenly music. Shall't be by power, or but by fortune?'

'By power,' answered Vandermast. 'And by worth.'

The Queen caught a deep breath. 'O, you have shown me a sweet morn after terrible dreams. But also a strange noise in my head, makes stale the morning: by what warrant must I believe you?'

'By none. You must believe not me, but the truth. I am but a finger pointing. And the nearest way for your highness (being a mortal) to believe that truth, and the sole only way for it to take body and effect in this world, is that you should act and make it so.'

'You are dark to me as yet.'

'I say that whether this greatness shall be or not be, resteth on your highness alone.'

She turned away and hid her face. When, after a minute, she looked around at him again, she reached out her hand for him to kiss. 'I am not offended with you,' she said. 'There was an instant, in that wild talk of ours, I could have cut your throat. Be my friend. God knows, in the path I tread, uneven, stony, and full of bogs, I need one.'

Vandermast answered her, 'Madam and sweet Mistress, I say to you again, I am yours in all things. And I say but again that your highness's self hath the only power able to help you. Rest faithful to that perfectness which dwelleth within you, and be safe in that.'

III

Nigra Sylva, Where the Devils Dance

THAT night Prince Aktor startled out of his first sleep from an evil dream that had in it nought of reasonable correspondence with things of daily life but, in an immediacy of pure undeterminable fear, horror and loss that beat down all his sense to deadness, as with a thunder of monstrous wings, hurled him from sleep to waking with teeth a-chatter, limbs trembling, and the breath choking in his throat. Soon as his hand would obey him, he struck a light and lay sweating with the bedclothes huddled about his ears, while he watched the candle-flame burn down almost to blueness then up again, and the slow strokes of midnight told twelve. After a tittle, he blew it out and disposed himself to sleep; but sleep, standing iron-eyed in the darkness beside his bed, withstood all wooing. At length he lighted the candle once more; rose; lighted the lamps on their pedestals of steatite and porphyry; and stood for a minute, naked as he was from bed, before the great mirror that was on the wall between the lamps, as if to sure himself of his continuing bodily presence and verity. Nor was there any unsufficientness apparent in the looking-glass image: of a man in his twenty-third year, slender and sinewy of build, well strengthened and of noble bearing, dark-brown hair, somewhat swart of skin, his face well featured, smooth shaved in the Akkama fashion, big-nosed, lips full and pleasant, and having a delicateness and a certain proudness and a certain want of resolution in their curves, well-set ears, bushy eyebrows, blue eyes with dark lashes of an almost feminine curve and longness.

Getting on his nightgown he brimmed himself a goblet of red wine from the flagon on the table at the bed-head, drank it, filled again, and this time drained the cup at one draught. 'Pah!' he said. 'In sleep a man's reason lieth drugged, and these womanish fears and scruples, that our complete mind would laugh and away with, unman us at their pleasure.' He went to the window and threw back the curtains: stood looking out a minute: then, as if night had too many eyes, extinguished the lamps and dressed hastily by moonlight, and so to the window again, pausing in the way to pour out a third cup of wine and, that being quaffed down, a fourth, which being but two parts filled left the flagon empty. Round and above him, as he leaned out now on the sill of the open window, the night listened, warm and still; wall, gable and buttress silver and black under the moonshine, and the sky about the moon suffused with a radiancy of violet light that misted the stars. Aktor said in himself, 'Desire without action is poison. Who said that, he was a wise man.' As though the unseasonable mildness of this calm, unclouded March midnight had breathed suddenly a frozen air about him, he shivered, and in the same instant there dropped into that pool of silence the marvel of a woman's voice singing, light and bodiless, with a wildness in its rhythms and with every syllable clean and sharp like the tinkle of broken icicles falling:

> 'Where, without the region earth,
> Glacier and icefall take their birth,
> Where dead cold congeals at night
> The wind-carv'd cornices diamond-white,
> Till those unnumbered streams whose flood
> To the mountain is instead of blood
> Seal'd in icy bed do lie,
> And still'd is day's artillery,
> Near the frost-star'd midnight's dome
> The oread keeps her untim'd home.
> From which high if she down stray,

On th' world's great stage to sport and play,
There most she maketh her game and glee
To harry mankind's obliquity.'

So singing, she passed directly below him, in the inky shadow of the wall. A lilting, scorning voice it was, with overtones in it of a tragical music as from muted strings, stone-moving but as out of a stone-cold heart: a voice to send tricklings down the spine as when the night-raven calls, or the whistler shrill, whose call is a fore-tasting of doom. And now, coming out into clear moonlight, she turned about and looked up at his window. He saw her eyes, like an animal's eyes, throw back the glitter of the moon. Then she resumed her way, still singing, toward the northerly corner of the courtyard where an archway led to a cloistered walk which went to the Queen's garden. Aktor stood for a short moment as if in doubt; then, his heart beating thicker, undid his door, fumbled his way down the stone staircase swift as he might in the dark, and so out and followed her.

The garden gate stood open, and a few steps within it he overtook her. 'You are a night-walker, it would seem, and in strange places.'

'So much is plain,' said she, and her lynx-like eyes looked at him.

'Know you who this is that do speak to you?'

'O yes. Prince by right in your own land, till your own land put you out; and thereafter prince here, and but by courtesy. Which is much like egg without the meat: fair outsides, but small weight and smaller profit. I've heard some unbitted tongues say: "princox".'

'You are a bold little she-cat,' he said. Again a shivering took him, bred of some bite in the air. 'There is frost in this garden.'

'Is there? Your honour were wiser leave it and go to bed, then.'

'You must first do me this kindness, mistress. Bring me to the old man your grandsire.'

'At this time of night?'

'There is a thing I must ask him.'

'You are a great asker.'

'What do you mean?' he said, as might a boy caught unawares by some uncloaking of his mind he had safely supposed well hid.

Anthea bared her teeth. 'Do you not wish you had my art, to

see in the dark?' Then, with a shrug: 'I heard him tell you, this afternoon, he had no answer to questions of yours.'

'I cannot sleep,' said Aktor, 'for want of his answer.'

'There is always the choice to stay awake.'

'Will you bring me to him.'

'No.'

'Tell me where he sleeps, then, and I will seek him out.'

Anthea laughed at the moon. 'Hearken how these mortals will ask and ask! But I am not your nurse, to weary myself with parroting of *No, no, no,* when a pettish child screams for the nightshade-berry. You shall have it, though it poison you. Wait here till I inform him, if so he may deign to come to you.'

The prince saw her depart. As a silver birch-tree of the mountains, if it might, should walk, so walked she under the moon. And the moon, or she so walking, or the wine that was in his veins, or the thunder of his inward thought, wrought in him to think: 'Why blame myself? Am I untrue to my friend and well-doer and dispenser of all my good, if I seek unturningly the good that seems to my incensed brain main good indeed? She is to him but an engine to breed kings to follow him. With this son bred, why, it hath long been apparent and manifest he is through with her: the pure unadulterate high perfection of all that is or ever shall be, is to him but a commodity unheeded hath served his turn. By God, what cares he for me either? That have held her today, thank the Gods (if any Gods there were, save the grand Devil perhaps in Hell that now, if flesh were or spirit were, which is in great doubt, riveth and rendeth my flesh and spirit), in my arms, albeit but for an instant only, albeit she renegued and rejected me, to know that, flesh by flesh, she must be mine to eternity? God! No, but to necessity: eternity is a trash-name. But this is now; and until my death or hers. And what of him? That, by my soul (damn my soul: for there is no soul, but only the animal spirits; and they unknown, save as the brief substance of a dream or a candle burning, that lives but and dies but in her): what surety have I (God damn me) that he meaneth not to sell me to the supplanter (I loathe him to the gallows) sits in my father's seat? Smooth words and sweet predicaments: I am in a mist. Come sight but for a lightning-flash, 'tis folly and madness to trust aught but sight. Seeing's believing. God or Hell, both unbelievable, 'tis time to believe whichever will show me firm ground indeed.' He was in a muck sweat. And now, looking at that statue as an enemy, and in the ineluctable grip of indignation and love, each with the frenzy of other doubled upon it by desire, he began to say within himself: 'Female Beast! Wisely was that done of men's folly, to fain you a goddess. You, who devour their brains: who ganch them on your hook by their dearest flesh till they are ready to do the abominablest treasons so only they may come at the filthy anodyne you offer them, that is a lesser death in the tasting, that breaks their will and their manhood and, being tasted, leaves them sucked dry of all save shame and emptiness only and sickness of heart. Come to life, now. Move. Turn your false lightless lustful eyes here, that you may see how your method works with me. Would they were right cockatrice's eyes, should look me dead, turn me to a stone, as you are stone: to nothing, as you are nothing.'

Swinging round on his heel, with his back to that image which was but as a reflection in shattered mirrors, least unsufficient in its almost changelessness, of that which is everlastingly changing and yet everlastingly perfect and the same, he came face to face with Doctor Vandermast; whose eyes, under this moonlight which has no half-tones, seemed pits of darkness in the bony sockets of a death's-head. 'Wisdom,' said the doctor, 'is seldom in extremes. And I would wish your noble excellency consider how this mischief of blasphemy operateth not against God nor Goddess, who one while find in it diversion and matter for laughter, and another while pass it by as unworthy their remark; but it operateth against the blasphemer, as an infection wonderfully deadly to the soul.'

Aktor, listening to these words, looked at him aghast, and at the delicate mountain lynx who, with flaming eyes, kept at the doctor's heel. 'You who can prophesy of others,' he said, 'I beseech you deny no longer to prophesy to me of me. The more, since I find your eyes are upon secret thoughts which, afore all things, I'd a supposed mine own and inviolate.'

Vandermast answered and said, 'Prince, albeit I am not wholly untraded in the noble dark science, and maybe could show you marvels should make your hair turn, I have not an art to discern men's thought; save indeed as any prudent man may discern them, which is to say, in their faces (as but even now, in yours). Neither pretend I to fore-knowledge of things to come.'

Aktor said, 'You did prophesy, as many can witness, this very day.'

'Of whom?'

'Of these lords of Rerek.'

'No,' replied he. 'I did but point to probabilities. It belongeth to human kind ever to desire certainties, but it belongeth as well to the world never to satisfy that desire. God, who wrought all things of nought, is doubtless able to know all things: past, present, or to come, to unbound eternity. But it shall not orderly hereupon ensure that He will elect to make actual that knowledge in very deed even in His own unscrutable inmost Mind. Whether he will so or no, is a question philosophers may wisely leave unanswered. Myself therefore, that am a humble scholar in divine wisdom and a humble seeker of truth, attempt no prophesyings of things to come. Only, observing constantly the train of the world and the bent or aptitude of the mind and heart of this man or of that, I do (so far as by conferring of act and word and outward aspect it be possible to reach some near guess or judgement thereon) now and then speak my thought. But such speech, howsoever it be addressed to unwrap the hid causes and events of things, is of likelihoods only: never of certitudes. For what, in this world, to a man or a woman, which be reasonable beasts, seemeth utterly certain and inevitable, is none the less in doubt and a thing contingent: at its highest, no higher than a probability. And this is because mortals, being that they are free movers, do daily by will or act make, transmute, or unmake again, such seeming certainties. And in action there is but one certainty, and that of God.'

'For myself,' said Aktor, 'I tell you with open face and good conscience, I believe not in God. Nor Devil neither. But wisdom and true-heartedness I can embrace when I do see them; and I do embrace them in you. My perplexities are like to turn me into madness, and they are matters it were unsafe to give a hint of, but to mine own heart and liver, under my skin. For pity sake, speak to me. Let me entreat to know what likelihoods attend for me.'

That learned man surveyed him awhile in silence. 'I did constantly refuse this, for the sufficient reason that I could not understand your excellency clearly enough to speak aught save upon conjecture. But I do now understand you more thoroughly, but still I am slow to speak; because I judge your nature to be of that dangerous complexion that, hearing what I should have to tell you, you would like as not misapply it to so high a strain as should soon or late call you to a fearful audit.'

Aktor said, 'I swear to you, you do misjudge me'.

'And yet,' said Vandermast, sitting now on the bench, while the Prince waited for his words as a suitor waits before a judge for judgement, and this lynx sat elegantly on her haunches against the doctor's knee, licking her fur: 'And yet, who am I to set impediments in the path of the strainable force of destiny? To hide from your excellency the matters I see, were (it might with some colour be argued) to deprive you of the chance which They who command the great wheel of things do intend for you: the chance to choose between the worser course and the better not by luck nor by sway of mood, as appetite might egg forward or timorousness hold you back, but by reasoned judgement of right and wrong. And be it that, knowing what hangeth on your choice, you must run the hazard of a wrong choice which would damn you quite and so end you, yet have you it *in potentiâ* (if your choice be noble) to make your name great and honoured among generations yet unborn. A wicked fault therefore it were in me if I should rest silent and thus, intermeddling (albeit but by abstinence) betwixt you and the unlike destinies which contend together to entertain your soul, should leave you but a weak creature uncharactered, such as of whom saith the philosopher that weak natures can attain to greatness in nothing, neither to great good nor to great evil.' He paused. Those upright glowing slits, which, in the lynx's eyes staring at the Prince, were instead of pupils, pulsed with yellow fire. The frost in the garden deepened. 'Know then that I seem to find in you,' said the doctor: 'That you are like to be in such case that, slaying your friend, you should gain a kingdom; and again, that, sparing your enemy, you should slay your only friend. Upon which matters,' he said, and the voice of him was now as very frostbite in the air, 'and upon whether they shall seem fit to you to be embraced and followed or (by contraries) to be eschewed and renounced, resteth (I suppose) your bliss or bale unto everlasting.'

When Doctor Vandermast had so ended, Aktor, standing like a stone, seemed to consider with himself. Then, even in that moonlight, the flush of blood darkened his face, and he, that had held himself but now like a suppliant, stood like a king, his breast mightily broadened and his shoulders squared. Suddenly, glancing over his shoulder as lions do before they charge, he took a step towards the doctor, checked himself, and said, his words coming thick and stumbling like a drunken man's: 'You have spoke better than you know, old man: lanced the imposthume in my breast and freed me for action, and that to the very tune I have these many weeks heard drumming in my head, but till now my fond doubts and scruples used me for their fool and rein'd me back from it. My friend: him, my seeming friend: yes, I'll kill him and be King in his place: who is my vile unshowing enemy, and to spare him were as good as go kill my only very friend in the world; and that is, her. About it, then. But 'cause you know so much, and 'cause I'll take no hazards, I'll first settle you: put you where you shall not blab.'

With that he leapt at the doctor and seized him, whose tall lean body in his clutches seemed fleshless and light as the pitiful frame of a little moulted hen that seems frail as a sparrow under her sparse remnant of feathers; but the lynx bit him cruelly in the leg, that he as swiftly let go his hold upon Vandermast. His hand jumped to his belt for a weapon, but in that haste of coming down from his chamber he had forgot it. He beat her furiously about the head with his fists, but got naught for it but bloody knuckles, for she stuck like a limpet, her fore-claws deep in the fleshy parts of his thigh, her hind-claws scrabbling and gashing his calves and shins like razors. All this in a few brief moments of time, till staggering backwards, heedless of all save the bitter mischief of her teeth and claws and the agony to rid this horror which clung to his flesh like

a plaster of burrowing fire, he tripped upon his heel at the pond's
brink and fell plump in. His head struck the statue's plinth as he
fell, which had well been the end of him, to drown there senseless
in two foot depth of water. But may be the cold ducking brought
him to himself; for scarce had Anthea, letting go as he fell, come
out of her lynx-shape to stand, nymph once more, by the water-side,
than he crawled to land again painfully, drenched and dripping.

That oread lady said to the doctor, 'Shall I rip his belly open
up to the chin?'

But Vandermast, lending him a hand to find his feet again,
answered, 'No.'

Aktor, for all the ache and smart of his wounds, could not
forbear to laugh. 'You are of a better disposition, I see, than this
hot-reined stew-pot of yours, to say nought of that hell-cat you
did set upon me. Where is it?'

Mistress Anthea curled her lip: turned away from him. The
classic beauty of her face, thus sideways, was like an ivory in the
fireless pure glimmer of the moon.

Aktor said, ''Twas never in my heart, learned sir, to a done you
any hurt. 'Twas in a way of taste only: trying your metal.'

'I am glad to hear that,' replied he dryly. 'As for her, 'tis a most
innocent animal, howsoever nature hath armed her most magnifi-
cently: fell to action, it is true, somewhat hastily (like as did your
excellency), and with no setting on by me. As well, perhaps, that
she did; for fighting is an art I am scantly customed to, both by
natural inclination and as being somewhat entered in years. You
did take me, also, a little by surprise, bursting forth into such a
sudden violence; which I hope you will henceforth be less ready
unto, and will wisely bethink you beforehand, using meditations
and weighings of *pro* and *contra*, afore you begin to attack men.
But as for the wounds your excellency did (to consider the matter
honestly), do unto yourself, here is better than any leech to their
speedy healing'; and Anthea, a little impatiently at the doctor's
bidding, using simples that he gave her from his purse, washed,
dressed, and bound up with bandages torn from the gauze of her
skirt, the evidences of her expert science in claw-work.

IV

THE BOLTED DOORS

So ended the twelfth day and last, of that marriage-feast in Rialmar. Upon the morrow, guests took their farewells and departed: a few betimes (and earliest among these that ancient doctor and his questionable she-disciple); but the most part of them, suiting by just anticipation the measure to be set them by bride and bridegroom, lay till past midday. The Lord Emmius tarried but to greet his brother and sister and, for the while, bid them adieu. In mark of singular favour the King and Queen brought him to the gate, and so, parting with them in the greatest esteem and friendship, he rode off with his train by the great south road.

Supervius and his bride, it was given out, would remain yet another week in Rialmar. But when it came to the day for their departure, Marescia said she would stay yet a full week more: let her lord go now with the baggage and stuff, and see all prepared orderly against her home-coming to Laimak. This absurdly, with no further reason assigned; but folk thought it sprung of her insolency and the wish, since she was now wife, to be not only his mistress still (as were right and fitting) but her great master's master. Howe'er that might be, upon that twenty-fifth of March Supervius rode south without her.

He being gone, with the honourable leave-taking as his brother had had, and the King and Queen being now returned up to Teremne, Stateira, with her hand upon her Lord's arm as he came his way to his private chamber, prayed him gently that she might come too. 'I am infinitely full of business, madam,' he said. 'But come if you must.'

In that chamber, which was round and domed and with great windows looking east to the mountains, were tables and heavy chairs old and curiously carved, and, between the pillars of polished marble jet-black with yellow and purple veins in it which ranged at every two paces along the walls, presses with shelves to put books in. Upon a hearth well fifteen foot wide a fire of sweet-scented cedar-wood was crackling and blazing, and the floor was carpeted to within two or three feet of the walls with russet-coloured velvet that the foot sank in, giving warmth in winter and silence all the year. But the King, crossing to the further side, undid with his secret keys the ponderous iron-studded doors, an outer and an inner, of his closet, and, when she had followed him in, locked both behind them. For here was the close work-house of his most deep-laid policies, and to it neither counsellor nor secretary had ever admittance: not Aktor even, to whom men noted he showed, more and more this last year or two, the kindly and dear respect due to a loved kinsman or very son. But the Queen, it was said, was partner to all its secrets; and a light misspeaking it was, that were she invited more oftener to his bed and seldomer to his chancery, there were a custom all the ladies in the court could be envious of, to be owl in such an ivy-bush.

The closet measured but five or six foot-paces either way. Cupboards of black iron with latches of silver lined the walls from ceiling to floor, and here, as in the outer chamber, was the like deep-piled velvet carpet. A long table of green prassius stone, resting on six legs of solid gold in the semblance of hippogriffs with wings spread, was under the window, and a great chair, hard-cushioned (seat, back, and arms) with dark, wine-coloured silk brocade, was set at the table to face the light. Upon that table papers and parchments lay thick as autumn leaves: here an unsteady pile with an armoured glove for paperweight: there another, capped with a hand-mace to keep them together: great maps, some in scrolls, one at the far end of the table, unrolled and held down flat with inkstands at two corners and a heavy ivory ruler at a third. Into which seeming chaos King Mardanus when he had thrown himself down in that chair, began now to dig; and easy it was to see that what to the general eye were confusion was in his capable mind no such matter, but orderly, where whatsoever scrap or manuscript he had need of came instant to his fingers' ends.

'Still Akkama?' said the Queen, after watching him awhile from between table and window.

'What else?' he said, clearing a space before him by pitching a heap of letters on the floor by his chair. 'Do you expect that business to be huddled up in a week or two?'

'It has trickled on for years. I wish it were ended.'

'It moves,' said the King. 'And moves at the pace I mean it shall. There's his latest letters missive (God give him a very mischief): pressing most sweetly for the handing over of Aktor': he tossed it across the table.

She let it lie. 'Well, hand him over.'

King Mardanus, for the first time, looked swiftly up at her; but there was nought in his look beyond such shock as a tutor might betray, having from his chosen pupil a foolish answer.

'Nay, I meant not that,' she said hastily. 'But yet: poor Akkama. 'Tis a pardonable impatience, surely, seeing he broached that demand two years since. Wonder is, he does not drop it.'

'No wonder in that,' said the King. 'I keep it alive: I mean not to let him drop it. Here's reports from two or three sure intelligencers, imports Aktor's faction plus on flesh, grows to admired purchase. Treat with the one and bolster up t'other: these two'll cut each other's throats i' the end. Then I walk in: take what I please.'

The Queen said, 'Yes, I know. That is our policy,' and fell silent as if held in a still, strained eagerness, between the desire to ask a thing and the terror lest, asked, it should be denied, and thus leave the matter in worse posture than before. She said suddenly, 'I wish, dear my Lord, you would send Aktor away.'

The King stared at her.

'I wish you would.'

'What, back to Akkama? That were a dastard's deed I'd be sorry for.'

'Never that. But send him away from Rialmar. Let him go where he will.'

'And fall in all kind of mischief? No, no. Safest here, under my hand. Besides, 'twere pure lunacy: discard the knave of trumps in the middle of the game.'

'He does no good here.'

The King sat back in his chair. 'Why are you so stubborn set of a sudden to be rid of him? What harm does he do to you?'

'None at all,' she paused. He said nothing. 'I advise you,' she said, 'make clean riddance of him.'

Mardanus, as if troubled by some urgence in her voice that he could ill understand, looked hard in her face. But if there were characters writ in it they were in a language he was as little schooled in as was his two-year-old son in the Greek. 'But why?' he said at last.

'Because I ask you.'

'The best of all reasons, madam': (she interrupted, under her breath, 'It used to be'): 'but not a reason of state. Come, come,' he said, still watching her narrowly, and his brows frowned as with some mounting anger at this insisting, without all reason, upon a thing of so small weight or moment to fool away his time withal: 'Woman's nonsense. The boy wants his revenge; wants to be his own again: wants to be king. And all these are appetites make him meat for us. Why, he is the peg my whole design's hung upon. No need for you to be troubled with him; but I will for no sake let him go. Besides,' he said, turning again to his papers, 'I love him well. Were't but to play chess a-nights with, which is a prime merit in him, I'll not forgo his company.'

Queen Stateira bit her lip. He reached for the letter from the King of Akkama, took his goose-quill pen and, slowly and awkwardly as with fingers to which such an instrument comes with less handsomeness than a sword or a spear, yet steadily without pause nor doubt, as one under no necessities to search for words to fit his clear-built purpose, fell to drafting of his reply.

The Queen, noiselessly on that deep carpet, came round behind him: hovered a moment: bent, and kissed his head. He wrote on, without sign that he was any longer ware of her presence. 'I must go,' she said. The King sprang up: undid the doors for her. As she came into the outer chamber, where at a side-table the King's secretary was setting papers in order, the great iron locks clashed home behind her.

Not until she was well shut in the privacy of her own room, did she unmask. There, thrown, as on a bed of snakes, between (like enough) some drunkenness in her blood strained up by Aktor and (like enough, for the moment) a scalding indignation against the King, she let go all and wept.

V

PRINCESS MARESCIA

THE lord Supervius Parry, albeit with pace slowed by a long train of pack-horses laden with wedding gifts and nine-tenths of Marescia's wardrobe, came by great journeys south over the wind-scourged wastes of the Wold, and so down to Megra, and thence by Eldir and Leveringay to Mornagay. Thence, taking the bridle-path over the mountains (which is steep, dirty and dangerous, but shorter and more expeditious than the low road south-about by Hornmere and Owldale), he came, after a three-and-a-half-weeks' journey from Rialmar without stay or mishap, on the afternoon of the seventeenth of April, home to Laimak. Here were preparations already completed for his return, but for the next seven days he set all his household folk to toil and moil as if three-score devils were at their tails, labouring to turn his own private quarters above Hagsby's Entry into a fit place to lodge a bride in, to whom luxurious splendours were but the unremarkable and received frame proper to ordinary polity and civility. And doubtless it would have ill suited his intents, were his great house of Laimak to show in her eyes as little better than a rude soldier's hold, or she to suppose him content that here from hence-forward she should live like a hog. By the week's end, all was altered and nicely ordered to his liking, and the folk about the castle set agog for impatience to welcome home so great and famous a lady as history hath not remembered among those that had been mistress here aforetime.

But as day followed day and yet no word or sign of the Princess, men began to wonder. Nor did they find wholesome nor comfortable their lord's thunderous silences that deepened and darkened as the days passed; nor his sometimes flashings into unforeknowable violence, which, like flashings of lightning, struck with impartial chanceableness and frightening suddenness who or what soever happed in their path at their blasting-time.

Between sunset and dark on the second day of May, it being a clear evening with the stars coming out in a rain-washed sky after a day of down-pour and tempest, Supervius was pacing to and fro in the great courtyard: slow, measured steps with a swift caged-beast turn-about at either end of the walk. Laughably in manner of a farm-lad who approaches an untethered bull of uncertain temper that may suffer him to draw near, then, without gare or beware, rush upon him and destroy him, came the captain of his bodyguard: said there was a lady below at the gate, alone and on horseback, would answer no questions as concerning her name or condition, but demanded to be brought instant before their master.

Supervius glowered at him. 'Hast seen the woman?'

'No, my lord.'

'You lewd misordered villain, why not, then? Why is she not brought to me here, if she asks that?'

'Because of your lordship's command, that no unknown person shall be admitted without your lordship's pleasure first known. 'Twas referred to me by the officer o' the guard for tonight, to learn your will, my lord, what he must do with her.'

'I would the Devil had her, and you to the bargain.'

The captain waited.

Supervius took another turn. 'Well, why is she not fetched up?'

The captain, with a low leg, departed: came again the next minute with the Princess Marescia Parry in pitiful disarray. Supervius looked at her, and the whole poise of his body seemed to stiffen. 'Leave us,' he said, resuming his to's and fro's. When they were alone he came to a halt and stood there, looking at her. Not a muscle in him stirred, save that a quick ear might catch a thickness and a tumultuousness in his breathing and a keen eye note the eyes of him in this half-light, while he watched her as a trained dog points at game. The Princess, for her part, held a like silence and a like stillness. Even in this gathering dusk it was easy to see she was as a very dowdy or slut, dirted and dishevelled with long hard riding, and hard lying may be, in the open field; and, for all she bore herself bravely enough, there was that in her that said, for all her speechlessness and the firmness of her lip, that she held it good her travels were over and she, howsoever miserably, here at last. With bull-like deliberation he began now to move towards her: then, as he came near, seized her in like sort and to like purpose (but with all unlike effect) as Tarquin seized Lucrece. Marescia was a big woman and a strong, but in a twinkling he had her up in his arms and in under the huge shadowy archway of Hagsby's Entry. Thence, without pause for breath, and despite her inarticulate protests and gusts of astonished half-smothered laughter, he carried her up the dark stairs of his own chamber trimmed up on purpose for her with those sumptuous costly furnishings he had brought south with him, and there, without ceremony, and quite unregarding of the pickle she was in, rain-soaked riding-habit and muddied boots, disposed her on the bed.

'Nay, and now tell me, you sweet-breath'd monkey,' said Supervius, upon his elbow, and with his face at near range looking down at hers. She lay there supine: outplayed and tamed for the while: closed eyes, half-closed lips: head turned away, exposing so into view her throat, smooth, sleek, white, like some Titan woman's, and the pulse of blood in it: one hand twining and untwining and straying and losing itself in the curled masses of his great red beard, the other yet straining down on his hand which rested upon her breast.

'Shorn of my train,' she answered presently, in a sleepy voice that seemed to taste pleasure in its own displeasure: 'tooken like a common cut-purse by my own folk: should a been clapt up in prison too, I think, and I'd not given 'em the slip. I hope you deserve me, my lord: so good faithful a wife, and a so quick contriver of means. There's this in you, that you love me impatiently. I'd ne'er stomach you less than greedy.' Then, suddenly springing up: 'In the Devil's name, how much longer must I famish here without my supper?'

'Shall be here in the flick of a cat's tail.'

'Well, but I'll dress first,' said Marescia.

'Meantime, tell me more. So far 'tis the mere chirping of frogs: terrible words I scantly believe and can make no sense of.'

'I'll dress first,' she said, opening a cupboard or two and, with some satisfaction, seeing her clothes hang there that came on before with Supervius. 'Nor not with you for looker-on, neither, my lord. Who suffers her husband in her dressing-chamber, were as good turn him off to go nest with wagtails. Where did I learn that, think you? From my mother's milk, I think. 'Tis native wisdom, certain.'

Supper was in the old banquet-hall, that was built in shape like an L, having a row of great windows in the long north-western wall, a main door, opening on the courtyard, at the far end, and a door going to the buttery and kitchens at the end of the shorter arm of the L. On the inner angle was the hearth, capacious enough to roast a neat, and a fire burning, of mighty logs. The walls were of black obsidian stone, and upon all save that which had windows were huge devilish faces, antic grotesco-work, cut in high relief, thirteen, with their tongues out, and upon each tongue's tip a lamp; and the goggling eyes of them were of looking-glass artificially cut in facets to disperse the beams of the lamplight in bushes of radiance, so that the hall was filled with light that shifted and glittered ever as the beholder moved his head. Long tables ran lengthways down the main hall, one on either side, and here the Lord Supervius's home-men were set at meat.

When the great leaved doors were flung wide and the Lady Marescia Parry, for this her first time, entered in state, gorgeously attired now in her bridal gown of white chamlet and lace of gold and with her yellow hair braided and coiled in bediamonded splendour above her brow, every man leapt from his seat and stood up to honour her and to feast his gaze upon her; while she, not a filly unridden but with the step and carriage of a war-horse and with bold chestnut eyes flashing back the bright lights, passed up between the benches on her lord's arm to take her place with him at the high table, which stood alone upon a dais in the north corner opposite the fire. Here, in sight but out of ear-shot of all other parts of that banquet hall, were covers laid for two.

'And now?' said Supervius, when they were set. He brimmed his goblet with a rough tawny wine from the March lands and drank to her, pottle-deep.

'And now?' said she, pushing her cup towards him. 'Well, pour me out to drink, then. Is these Rerek manners? a man to bib wine while's wife, out of a parched mouth, shall serve him up tittle-tattle?'

He filled. She swallowed it down at a single gulp, first savouring it curiously on her tongue. 'To go to the heart of the matter,' she said, 'as touching mine own particular, I long since took a mislike to that Aktor. The Queen I love well, albeit but cousins by affinity (not german, as I was to the King). And in this pernicious pass, with the whole land in a turmoil, besides fury and sedition of the rude people grown in the late unhappy accident, methought it likely Aktor would use her for his fool: she being caught in a forked stick betwixt doting of him (as I, of my quick sense, have precisely long suspected) and fearing for her son, and thus uncapable of firm action; while this hot-backed devil, under colour of her authority, more and more carrieth the whole sway of the court. So, to cut the Gordian knot and do for her (no leave asked) what, might she but be unbesotted, she must know to be most needful, I fled with the King before a soul could note it, meaning to have him away with me hither into Rerek. But they caught me in two days: took the child back to Rialmar, and would—'

'A burning devil take you!' said Supervius, breaking in upon this: 'what misty Tom-a-Bedlam talk have we here? of Aktor: and the Queen: and you ran with the King's highness to Rerek? Are you out of your wits, woman? Are you drunk?'

Marescia stared as if stupefied at his amazement. Then, clapping down her hand on his where it grasped the table's edge, 'Why, is't possible?' she said, her sight clearing. 'I'm yet here faster than news can travel, then? Faith, I've lost all count of time i' this hugger-mugger, and know not what day it is. Hadn't you not heard, then, of King Mardanus's death: tenth day after our wedding?'

Supervius sat for a moment like a man stricken blind. 'Dead? On what manner? By what means?'

'Good lack, they murdered him up. By a hired rascal from Akkama stol'n into Teremne. So at least 'twas given out. But (in your secret ear) I am apt to think 'twas Aktor did it. Or by Aktor's setting on.'

The Lord Supervius drank deep. She watched him turn colour, pale then red again, and his brow became as a storm-cloud. She said, 'I see't hath troubled you near. Say you: begin you now to think that was an ill cast you threw then, when you married with me?'

'O hold your tongue with such foolishness: I think no such matter.'

'That's as well, then. I gave you credit for that.'

Supervius, as brooding darkly on this new turn, ate and drank without more words said. The Princess followed suit, now and then casting a glance at him to see, if she might, what way the wind was shifting. After a long time he looked at her and their eyes met. Marescia said, 'Yet I'm sorry they got the child Mezentius from me. Better he were here, for his and our most advantage, rather than with's mother, if Aktor must rule the roast there. And yet, 'tis a roast we may yet draw sustainment from, God turning all to the best.'

Her lord looked still at her with an unmoved stare that, from a bullish sullenness, changed by little and little to the stare of a proud ambitious man at a looking-glass that glads him with the express counter-shape of his best-loved self. 'Come sweet heart,' he said then, 'we will closely to these matters. And somewhat we'll presently devise, doubt it not, much to our good. But I'll take my brother Emmius with me, or I move one step on the road I seem to see before me.'

He bade his steward, supper now being done, dismiss all the company. And so, private in that banquet-hall hour by hour, till the lamps began to flicker and go out and only the glow of embers on the hearth showed them each other's faces, he and she sat long into the night, talking and devising.

VI

Prospect North from Argyanna

EMMIUS Parry had sat now more than four years in Argyanna, keeping house there in so high a style as not in all Rerek had its example, but yet to compare with Rialmar in the northlands or Zayana of the south it should have seemed no such great matter. It was thought that, need arising, he could at any time upon three days' notice set forth an army of a thousand men weaponed at all points and trained in all arts of war: this not to reckon two hundred picked men-at-arms whom he maintained under his hand at all seasons, for show of power and to keep order, and in readiness for any work he might assign them.

For three or four generations this lonely out-town, set in strength amid untranspassable fens, had been to the Parry in Laimak as a claw stretched forth southward upon the batable lands watered by the river Zenner: an armed camp, governed by the lords of Laimak through officers who were creatures of theirs and servants but never until now men of their own blood and line, in case, from the great strength of the place, it might grow to be a hand which someday, turning against the body it longed to, might break down the whole in ruin.

From Sleaby and Ketterby on the northern part and thence, west-about by the Scrowmire and east-about by the Saylings, to Scruze and Scrightmirry on the south, the Lows of Argyanna lie ten miles long and as many in breadth. In these Lows is going neither for man nor for beast (be it more than a water-rat or an otter): only the water-fowl inhabit upon that waste of quaking-bogs. The harrier-hawks share out their dominion there by day: the owl (which the house of Laimak have for their badge or cognizance) hunts there by night, when all feathered living beings else are at roost, except the night-jar who preys on night-flying moths that breed in the fen. And through the night hobby-lanterns flicker, hither and thither in the mist and the darkness, above scores of thousands of acres, unpathed, quicksandy, squeltering in moss and slub and sedge.

In the middle of this sea of quagmire is a lone single island of sure footing and solid ground, watered with streams that have their source in a tarn of which no plummet has found the bottom: an unfailing source that puts up pure, cold and sweet from the under-rocks, not surface water from the highlands of old Rerek such as feeds the marsh. The firm land stretches a five miles' length north-west to south-east, with a biggest width of about three and a half: all of rich well-husbanded grazings and ploughlands which train upwards towards the north, but nowhere to rise more than twenty foot at most above the marsh-level; except at the head of the land north-westward near the tarn where the northern scarp comes up gently to a flat of perhaps twice that height, to fall again abruptly in a low cliff on the west; and here, wholly ringed about with walls of great thickness and strength, lies Argyanna. The highway from the north, coming down by Hornmere and Ristby and so south through Susdale, strikes the Lows two miles south of Sleaby, and is carried south across them, straight as a carpenter's rule, to Argyanna and so on south to Scrightmirry, by a ten-mile causeway of granite which rests upon oaken piles through mire and ooze to bed on the rock. This road, where it crosses the tongue of land that lies out westward from the fortress, runs along the moat for several hundred paces, and so close under the walls of the main keep that, granted good natural munition and aptitude and a favouring wind from the east, a man on the battlements might spit on a passer-by. The Lord Emmius, when after his father's death he moved household and came down hither from Sleaby, built gate-houses astride of this road: one where the road comes upon the tongue, and that almost within stone-cast of the town wall, and another somewhat farther off where the road leaves land again for the marsh: this the greater and stronger of the two as a hold against the south should occasion require it. In time of peace the gates stood open, and travellers whether rich or poor had free entertainment there and a night's lodging if they would, and all with the greatest openhandedness and largesse.

Upon the fifth of May, Supervius came with his lady to Argyanna about midday and there had good welcome. When they had eaten, Emmius took them to walk in the sunshine upon the wide paved walk that runs full circle round the top of the keep between the battlements and his private lodging which stood back, full circle, in the midst of it.

'You have a fair prospect southward, lord brother-in-law,' said the Princess, shading her eyes with her hand to look across the Lows to where, between forty and fifty miles away and a little east of south, the Ruyar Pass cuts the mountain spine at the meeting of the Huron range with the peaks of Outer Meszria, carrying the great road over into Meszria itself. 'Where your fancy dallies, they tell me.'

'My wife's home. Should not that be commendation enough?'

The Lady Deïaneira smiled. She was tall: exquisite, whether in movement or at rest, as some fine-limbed shy creature of the woods: high-cheekboned, smooth-skinned and dark, and with eyes dark and lustrous that seemed as by native bent to return always, save when he was watching them, to her lord.

'And yet,' said Marescia, 'you had these tidings from the north, too, two days sooner than I could bring them.'

'I have lived in this world, dear Princess,' said Emmius lightly, 'near five times seven years, and I have learnt the need to have eyes and ears to serve me. Give me, prithee, what you saw with your own eyes. One pinch of fact outweigheth a bushel of hearsay.'

'Ay, tell it as you told it to me,' said Supervius.

Marescia said, ''Twas heard with mine ears first: a cry out of

the King's bedchamber, made the gold cups ring on the shelf above
my bed and the geese scream in the yard under my window.'

'And that was, when?' said Emmius.

'About first light.'

'Ay, and the day?'

'Fifth morning after my lord here was ridden south. Then a
noise of doors flinging open, and the Queen's voice, dreadfully,
'*Marescia, Marescia.*' So, on with my nightgown and scarce get
the door open but her highness's self meets me there into my arms,
trembling like a frightened horse: in her hair: nought but her
sage-green velvet nightgown upon her: moaneth out over and over,
the King's name: bringeth me thither: he on the bed, dead as
doornail, boiled up huge as a neat, blue and grey and liver-colour,
his eyes sticking out like a crab's, and his hair and his beard and
his nails all bursten off him.'

Deïaneira's lips pressed together till they whitened, but no sound
escaped them.

The Lord Emmius had all this while of Marescia's speaking
studied her face, with that gaze of his which commonly seemed,
to those on whom it rested, strangely undisturbing; so free of
concernment it seemed, effortless and intermittent as a star's among
changing clouds, but yet as steadfast too, deep-searching, not to
be eluded, and so, when they considered again of it, strangely
disturbing, as able to touch and finger their privatest inward
thought. He looked away now, past her, to that sun-veiled skyline
in the south. 'Tell me, sister-in-law, if you can: slept she by him
that night?'

'Never. Not these two years.'

'But would your ladyship a known?'

'If so they did, 'twas a thing without precedent since many
months at least.'

'Truth is, we know not. Who was in the chamber when you
came in, besides the Queen?'

'Not a soul. O, a woman or two o' the bedchamber I think.
Then more. And then Aktor.'

'Who's that?'

'Yonder princox.'

'I remember: I caught not the name as you said it. What made he there? Was he sent for?'

The Princess changed glances with Supervius. 'I cannot tell,' she answered. 'Was in a pretty taking: weeping and lamenting: My dearest friend, my King (and so forth); author of all my good: murdered and dead.'

'In those words? Murdered: said he so?'

'A dozen times.'

'Well?'

'But at first sight of the handiwork, shouts out in a kind of fury or terror to the Queen: God grant you ha'nt touched him, madam? Go not you near, nor any person else, till leeches examine it. Here's the vile murderer's doing I sent last night to sup in Hell: woe that I should a squeezed the sting out of him but not afore he'd sown the poison.'

'What meant that gibberish?'

'Telleth us how, afore supper, he'd caught this rascally instrument of the king of Akkama (had been in Rialmar, it seems, under pretext of service in the buttery or the black guard, quite unsuspected, and for weeks biding his happy chance): Aktor caught him skulking in the private room the King and he were wonted to play chess in—'

'Slip we not there into hearsay?'

''Twas out of Aktor's mouth, in my hearing. Tells us (still in tears) how a had wrung a true tale out of this devil's-bawd—'

Here Emmius looked round at her: a comical glint in his eye. 'Is this still the Prince's words? Or is't Princess's gloss?'

'Cry you mercy, 'twas my tongue slipt,' said she. 'Tells us the fellow confessed a was sent a purpose to murder the King's highness (and Aktor too if that might be compassed): says this threw him into so fierce a sweat of anger he killed the man out of hand and, not to mar our evening, huggled the dead carcase into a big box or coffer was there i' the room, to wait till morning. There was an act me thinks smelleth something oddly in this Aktor.'

'What next?'

'Next, Aktor (thinking, belike, enough made of weeping and blubbering) takes charge. Calleth for leeches: shows us the dead vermin stiff and be-bloodied in the box and with Aktor's own dagger sticking in his ribs: (a pretty property for such an interlude, that, me thought).'

'Well?'

'Well, those learned men sat in inquest 'pon what was left: 'pon the dead poison-monger, 'pon the King's highness, and 'pon the chessmen. ('Twas pity Aktor thought not sooner the night before, of those chessmen.)'

'That the King and he wont to play with? Had they played with 'em that night?'

'Yes. Nay, I know not for sure. We left them to it, being bedtime.'

'And what found the leeches, then?'

'Upshot was, some nasty pothecary stuff in the King's finger and thumb: had run all over his body: same stuff on one or two chessmen, but the most of 'em pure and harmless: some more of it on the man's knife: conclusion, knife was to do the business had the chess failed.'

She ceased speaking; and Lord Emmius Parry, a cloud on his brow, looked at her in silence for almost a minute. She, with cool smile and hot chestnut eyes, met his gaze steadily as if minded to out-stare him. But as well should a printed page hope to out-stare the reader, as out-stare that eye that looked forth, cold, meditative, ambiguous, and undisturbed, from the iron yet subtle face of the Parry, and rested without distinction of kind, alike upon the land-scape, or upon the stone coping of the wall, or (as for this, to her, uneasy minute) upon the challenging eye of this woman, young, fierce-blooded, masterful, who, come to a halt close under him where he halted, set the air about him afire with the agitation of all senses mixed and stirred up in the goblet of her bodily nearness and her domineering will, bent to some end as yet unrevealed. Even just as a reader, having read, looks up from his book to ruminate the matter he has read there, Lord Emmius turned now from her and, standing a little apart by the battlements, in the same remote meditation remained awhile, looking south. The Princess,

left so, albeit scarcely victorious, in possession of the field, said apart
to her lord, the hot blood suffusing all her fair face and brow
even to the roots of the shining yellow hair that was drawn with
a smaragdine fillet sleekly up from it and from behind her ears,
'Was it fitly spoken, think you?'

'Beyond admiration well,' he answered, taking his arm about her.

'No case argued, as yet.'

'No, no. It needs not.'

'He is a man I'd rather have before me than against me: your
brother,' she said, and let her voluptuous weight settle closelier in
the assurance of Supervius's strong encircling arm, while still she
watched the Lord Emmius. Deïaneira, with a look in her sweet
secret Meszrian eyes more deeplier composed, more akin to his,
watched him too. A man worth their eyes he seemed, standing
there: towering above them in bodily height, save Supervius, and
above him for settled majesty of bearing: loose-limbed and of so
much reposement of easy power, his left hand, a true Parry hand,
beyond the ordinary in breadth and strength and with broad
spatula-shaped fingers, yet long-fingered as a woman's, resting on
the stone battlement, his right crooked in his jewelled belt. His
bonnet of black velvet sat tilted across his brow: there was a set
lift and downward trend of his eyebrows, betokening thought, and
a breadth and heaviness in the upper lids. His nose, great, high-
bridged and (like the fox's) scenting to all airts, wore a pride and
a keenness of discrimination on every fine-carved surface of it: so
too the lean flats of his cheek-bones and the sternness and strength
of his mouth, partly veiled by a melancholy downward sweep of
dark mustachios. His beard, sedulously brushed and tended,
thinned to a certain sparseness of growth betwixt the mouth's
corners and the chin, undiscovering so a taint of heaviness and
hard implacability in his under lip.

He turned to face them now, his back against the battlement
and the light behind him. 'But why, dear sister-in-law, will you
think Prince Aktor the author of that deed?'

'I never said I thought so,' replied she.

'No. But it peeped from behind most every word you said.'

'Well, truly, I think it not unlikely.'

'Why disbelieve his story?' said Emmius. 'Doth anyone else? What avail to him, thus to bite the hand that fed him?'

Marescia laughed. 'Best avail of all, seeing a loveth the Queen's person to distraction. And she him.'

Emmius paused: raised an eyebrow. 'Be not discontent with me,' he said, 'if I question your ladyship somewhat sharply. The matter is of highest moment. Mean you that he acquainted himself over familiarly and unhonestly with the King's wife?'

'At a word, I do.'

'And that he and she had nothing more in their vows than his serene highness's ruin?'

'O you miss my sense abominably!' she said. 'Kill me dead at your feet if I'd e'er credit Stateira with any such wicked purpose. Him, yes.'

'Then why not her?'

''Cause I have known her since children, like a book. 'Cause it lies not in her good nature.'

'I praise your trusting affection,' said Emmius with a crooked smile. 'But remember, good qualities are easier spoilt than bad ones.'

They began to walk again, in silence till they were come more than full circle round the battlements of the great keep: Emmius with long deliberate stride, hands clasped behind him, eyes moody and lightless under half-lowered moody lids: Supervius (as if policy, counselling attend and wait, strove within him against a wolfish impatience that ill can stomach delays) opening once and again his mouth to speak, and as swiftly shutting it after a sidelong glance at his brother: the Lady Deïaneira walking as some mislaid remnant of a perfumed summer night might miraculously walk here in the face of day, between this rockish imperturbability upon her one side and that hunger for action upon the other: the Lady Marescia tasting and managing, with her bare hand linked in his, Supervius's chafing, the while she studied, all uncertainly as she must and with jealous despiteful eye, weather-signs in Emmius.

When he spoke, it was to shift no clouds. 'It is all misty stories and conjecture,' he said to Supervius. 'The one clear act was when she (as you told me at first) made to steal away the boy. But (no blame to her) that miscarried.'

Supervius said, 'Question is, what to do? And that suddenly. Whether Aktor's hand was in it or not, I account him neither fool nor weakling. He is like to seize kingdom now if we give him time to settle in his seat.'

Marescia covertly gripped his hand: whispered, 'Enough said. Better it come out of his mouth than ours: will love his own brat better than a stepchild.'

'One thing I see,' said Emmius: 'what's best not to do.' His eye, cold and direct, moved from his brother to his brother's wife, and so back again. 'Some would counsel you levy an army and ride north now, with me to back you: proclaim yourself Lord Protector i' the young King's interest: or, proclaim your father-in-law, if he would undertake it. If the Queen send Aktor packing, we join force with her. If, econverse, she join with Aktor, you might look to all Fingiswold to rise and throw them out. In either event, you could hope to attain an estate and power such as you had scarce otherwise dreamed to climb up unto. For all that,' he said, and Marescia's face fell, 'I hold it were a great unwisdom in us to touch the matter.'

Supervius reddened to the ears. 'Go,' he said, 'you might a listened to reason first, I'd think, ere condemn so good an enterprise.'

'Reason? Mine ears are yours, brother.'

'Why, 'tis a thing at the first face so wholly to be desired, it needs no more commendations than you yourself have e'en just now given it. What's against it, we are yet to learn.'

'First of all,' said Emmius, 'we know not whether Aktor bore part in this business or not; neither know we the terms he is upon with the Queen.'

Marescia let go a scoffing laugh. 'As well pretend we know not upon what terms a drunken gallant consorteth with a stewed whore.'

'Well,' said he, viewing her with an ironic crinkling of his under eyelids, as if she were lit by a new light. 'You know your own kinsfolk better than can I, sweet Princess. But, be the case so, it but strengtheneth the possibility her highness may publicly wed with Aktor; and then what surance have you that the King's subjects will cleave to us and not to them?'

'Good hope, at least,' replied she, 'that the better men will follow us. They will behold the Parry of Laimak, wed with a princess of the blood, upholding the King's right against his landless outlander hath beguiled a Queen, not of that blood at all, to's vile purposes; and herself suspect too, though I ne'er heard it voiced till you yourself informed me—'

'Come,' said Emmius, 'you cannot argue it both ways.'

'We speak of how 'twill appear to others. For myself, I said I'd ne'er credit the Queen with such wickedness.'

'And as for Aktor's case by itself, nobody shared your ladyship's suspicions? Is't not so?'

''Tis so, I admit,' said Marescia and added, under her breath, a buggish word.

'And the Prince is not ill looked on by the folk? There is, by your own account, sister-in-law, no evidence against him sufficient to hang a cat?'

Marescia said, very angry, 'O, some can pretend argument as ingenuously as scritch-owls. Thank Gods for a man who will act.'

Whereupon said Supervius, loosing rein on his tongue at last: 'You are a skilful thrower down of other men's designs, brother: a fine miner. But you build nothing. This was my very project, that I came hither thinking to have your friendship in. And you, like some pettifogging lawyer, but cavil at it and pick faults. Truly was that said, that *Bare is back without brother behind it.*'

The Lady Deïaneira's night-curtained eyes rested on Emmius, a little uneasily. But no lineament of his cold inwardly-weighing countenance betrayed his mind, nor no alteration in the long slow rhythm of his walk. Presently he spoke: comfortable equable tones, without all tang of disputation or of sarcasm: rather as a man that would reason with himself. 'States come on with slow advice, quick execution. You, brother, nobly and fortunately allied (and not without help from me there) by marriage with this illustrious lady, have your footing now as of right in the council-chambers of Rialmar. It were a rude folly to waste that vantage by menace of civil battle: foolisher still, because we can never be strong enough to win, much less keep, the victory against Fingiswold; and should besides need to purchase passageway for our army through country subject to Eldir, Kaima, and Bagort, and even so I'd never trust 'em not to break faith and upon us from behind. Our true, far, aim is clear: make friends with the lion-cub against the day he be grown a lion: I mean King Mezentius. And that must be through his mother' (here he looked at Marescia). 'In the meanwhile, prepare quietly. Strengthen us at all points. Have patience, and see.'

The same day, before supper, the Lady Marescia sat in a window of Emmius's great library or study, writing a letter. Supervius, from a deep chair, watched her, stroking his flaming beard. Emmius, arms folded, stood in the window, now turning the leaves of his book, now, as in quiet thought, letting his gaze stray to far distances over the Lows and the wide woods of the Scrowmire, lit with the reddening evening-glow out of a cloudless sky. A serving-man lighted candles in branched candlesticks of mountain gold which stood on the writing-table, and so, upon a sign from Emmius, departed, leaving the rest of the room in dusky obscurity. The windows stood open, yet so calm was the evening that not a flame of the candles wavered.

The Princess signed with a flourish, laid down her pen, and sat back. 'Finished,' she said, looking first to Emmius then to her husband. 'Will it serve, think you?'

Over her shoulders, Emmius upon the right, Supervius on the left, they read the letter. It was superscribed *To the Queenes most Serene and Excellent Highnes of Fingiswold*:

Beloved Soverayne Lady and Queene and verie dere friend and cozen in lawe, my humble dewtie remembred etc. It is to be thocht my departure from yr. highnes Court was something sodene. I am verie certaine I am abused to yr. Highnes

*eare by fables and foolische lyes alledging my bad meaning
toward yr. highness and to the yong King his person. I beseech
you believe not the sclaunders of todes, frogges and other
venemous Wormes which have but a single purpose to rayse
dislyke and discorde betwixte us, but believe rather that my
fault was done in no wicked practise but in the horrable
great coil and affricht wee then all did stagger in, and with
the pure single intente to do Yr. Serene Highnes a service.
For my unseemelie presumptuous attempte in that respecte
I am trewelie penitent, and sufficientlye punisht I hope with
being clapt in goale at commaunde of that lewde fellow*
Bodenaye, *who I am sure dealt not as one of Your aucthorised
people in using of mee thus dishonorable but by order of
some of yr. secretories withoute your privetie, for which his
behaviour hee deserved to have beene putt to death. I saye
no more here but that I will learn wisdome of this folly.
More att large of this when I shall have the felicitie to look
upon yr. face and to kiss yr. hand. My humble suite is that
Your Serene Highness, through the olde gracious bountifull
affectioun wherewith you and Kinge Mardanus upon whom
bee peace did ever honor mee, wilbe plesed to receyve mee
againe and gentlie pardon my fault. Unto which ende it willbe
verye good if of yr. specyall love and kyndnes you sende me
lettres of Safe Conducte, because withoute such I do dread
lest this Bodenay whom I know to be a villain or els some
other of his kynde may out of lewdnesse and malice to
meward finde a waye to do mee the lyke disgrace or a worse.*

*May the Gods move Yr. Highnes hearrte to order thinges
by such a corse as wil stande with yr. Highnes dignitey and
the relief of me yr. highnes pore cozen and verye loving
penitente Servaunte,*

MARESCIA

'Will it serve?' she asked, leaning back to look up into the face
first of one and then the other, when they had read it.

'Most excellent well,' said Supervius, and, bending her head yet farther back, kissed her fiercely in the throat: adding, as he turned away to the window, '—as the sheep-killing dog said when they showed him the noose.'

Emmius held out his hand. The lady laid in it her own right hand, soft, warm, dazzling white, able. He raised it to his lips and kissed it. 'You are a good fighter, dear Marescia. And a generous loser. Care not: you will not often lose.'

The Princess, blushing like an untutored maiden, gave him a smile: not lip-work only, but, rare in her, a smile of her eyes. 'I can bow to reason when I am shown it, lord brother-in-law,' said she, and tightened her grasp on the hand that held hers. 'I bear no grudge. For I see I was wrong.'

Supervius, stiff-necked and haughty, but serene, came from the window. 'Yes,' he said, his gannet eyes staring in Emmius's face: then wrung him by both hands.

Book Two

Uprising of King Mezentius

VII

ZEUS TERPSIKERAUNOS

STATEIRA had by then reigned a full month Queen Regent in Rialmar, wielding at once that dignity and the supreme power on behalf of her infant son, King Mezentius, that was not yet three years old. She was well loved of the folk throughout that country side, nor was any lord or man of mark in all Fingiswold found to speak against her, but every man of them made haste to Rialmar to do her homage and promise her firm upholding and obedience. To all these, she made answer simply and with open countenance, as might a private lady have done to tried friends come to condole her sorrow and renew pledges of friendship; but queenly too, commanding each instantly raise forces and stand ready at time and place appointed. For she meant to let go every lesser business till she should hear reason from the King of Akkama and have of him atonement too, and sure warranty of good behaviour for the future, and punish with death every person who had took hand, were it as deviser or as executer, in this most devilish mischief, that had left her a widow in the high summer-season of her youth, and a great kingdom bereft of the strong hand that had ably ruled it: a child on the throne, and a woman to be over all, and to take order for all, and to answer for all.

Men were the better inclined, in these dark and misty matters, to follow and obey her and have confidence in her judgement and resolution, because well they knew how King Mardanus had made her secretary of his inmost intents and policies, insomuch that no lord of council nor no great officer of state had knowledge of these things so profound as she had; and they thought reasonably that her, whom so deep a politic as the great King had instructed, used, and put his trust in, they might well put their trust in too. Her council she had set up immediately under new letters patents, passing by the names of two or three but keeping all who had shown proof of their powers and weight of authority as counsellors of King Mardanus and whom he had set most store by: in especially, Mendes, the Knight Marshal: Acarnus, High Chancellor of Fingiswold: the High Admiral Psammius: Myntor, Constable in Rialmar: Prince Garman the late King's uncle and father to Marescia. The Constable she had despatched, within a week after the King's murder, upon secret embassage to Akkama with remonstrances and demands aforesaid.

Prince Aktor had throughout the whole time behaved himself with a fitness which many commended and to which none could take exceptions: bearing out a good face after the first dismay and confusion were over, and showing he had the eye of reason common with the best: never a putter forward of himself in counsel, yet, being consulted, not dasht out of countenance by any big looks: ever the first, if disagreements arose, to devise some means of concord: making himself strange always sooner than familiar with the Queen, towards whom he maintained, as well in private as under the general eye, a discreet respectuous reverence as never thinking upon other but to please her.

True it is that in the first hours, when the town was in uproar, and lie and surmise flew thick and noisy as starlings in late autumn, some shouted 'twas Aktor had slain the King in hope to ingross the kingdom to himself. Two or three voices there were that vomited out words of villany even against Queen Stateira: rhymes of *the adulterous Sargus* (which is a sea-fish, Aktor having come first to Fingiswold by sea) *courting the Shee-Goats on the grassie shore*. But a proclamation by the Lord Mendes to 'see these rumourers whipt' was so punctually put in execution by standers by, that the catchpolls running to do it found it done already; and the soundlier, as a labour of love. Since that, slanders miscoupling Aktor's name with the Queen's had no more been heard in Rialmar.

Thus these businesses rested, while the fates of peace or war swung doubtful, waiting on Akkama. But as May now passed into June, perceptive eyes in the court that had delicate discriminative minds behind them began to note, as a gardener will the beginnings of violet-buds under their obscuring leaves, signs of kindness betwixt the Queen and Aktor. The soberer among these lookers began to think they saw, in her as in him, whenever chance or the pleasures of the court or affairs of the realm brought them together, a drawing of curtains: a strained diligence to conceal, and that no less jealously from each other than from the general, and more and more diligently as the weeks passed by, his, and her, secret mind. It was witness to the good opinion the Prince now stood in, and to men's faith in the Queen's wise discretion and loyal and noble nature, that these things, as they grew to common notice, stirred up neither cavil nor envy, but were let alone as matter for her concern and nobody's else.

Upon the fourth of June the Queen, as, since her assumption of the Regency, she was wont once in every week to do, came down from Teremne and so through the town and up to the temple of Zeus upon Mehisbon, in which were the royal tombs and, last of them, the tomb of King Mardanus. Without state she came, on foot, through the wide streets and through the press of the market-place, and thence by the triumphal way that ascends from the market-place in broad sweeping curves, now left now right to ease the slope, up the steep backbone of that, the north-western, horn of Rialmar. Pillars of rose-red marble line that way on either hand, with on every pillar a mighty cresset for lighting on nights of high festival when, viewed from the Teremnene palace or from the town in Mesokerasin, the road shows like the uncurling on the hill of some gigantic fire-drake's serpentine and sinuous body, fringed with lambent flame. It was mid-afternoon, sunny, but with a hot heaviness in the air, and on all sides an up-towering of great cloud-bastions that darkened the horizon southwards but were of

a dazzling and foaming whiteness where they took the sun. Upon
her left, the Queen led with a golden chain a black panther tamed
to hand, his fur smooth and sleek as the gown she wore of black
sendaline edged with gold lace, and upon her right a nurse wheeled
the infant King in his childish hand-carriage of sandalwood inlaid
with gold and silver. Save for an officer walking at a good distance
behind with a half-dozen men of the bodyguard, and save for this
nurse and child, she was alone and unguarded; maintaining in this
the old custom of Kings of Fingiswold, to come and go their ways
in Rialmar on their private occasions much like private folk and
with scarce more ceremony: people but curtseying and capping to
them as they passed. They of the royal seat-town liked well this
custom, as proof ocular (had proof been needed) that the King
thought his subjects at large the right guards of his person, and
that his greatness was not a withered beauty that durst not be
seen without ornaments of state, but rather a freshness and a
youthful halesomeness that can strip all off if it please and be as
beautiful, and majestical.

The temple of Zeus Soter, high over all the lesser temples of
Mehisbon, stands upon an outcrop of wild crag close under the
peak. It is built all of jet-black marble with unpolished surfaces for
the more darkness, and naked of ornament except for the carvings
on the vast pediment and the sculptured frieze above the portico.
Queen Stateira, when she was come to the foot of the threefold
great flights of steps which, where the road ends, go up to that
temple, took the child Mezentius by the hand and went on with
him alone. Between the pillars of the entrance, so huge in girth that
five men standing round the base of one of them might scarce
touch hands, and well sixty-foot high from plinth to capital, she
turned to look back across the saddle of Mesokerasin south-
eastwards to the kingly palace of Teremne.

That way thunder-storms were brewing. A murky darkness of
vapours, thick, leaden-hued, and oily, swoll and shouldered and
mounted and spread upward till that whole quarter of the sky,
east and south-east up to the zenith, was turned to the colour of
black grapes. The King pulled his mother's hand and laughed,

pointing to where against the black clouds the palace on that sudden appeared in an unearthly splendour, lighted by the sun which, through some window rent in the glowering and piling masses to the westward, yet shone.

There was no wind now in the lower air, but a great heat and stillness: and, with the stillness, a silence. It was as though all sound had been emptied out till not even (as in ordinary silences) the unemptiable exiguous residue remained: fall of leaf, or, immeasurably far away, in immeasurably faint echo, the unsleeping welter and surge of the sea, or stir of the market-place below. Even such shadows of sound had drowsed away to nothingness. There was left but that simulacrum of audibility born of the pulsing of living blood in the hearkening ear as it strains to catch the extreme unvoiced voice of the silence.

The Queen, still gazing on that which her son's dancing eyes still returned to, the louring gleam upon Teremne, drew him back a little under the shelter of the portico as the first thunder-drops plashed on the outer paving. Presently she began to say in herself:

Queen of Heaven, Paphian Aphrodite,
Let not me, too easily up-surrend'ring,
Prove i' th'end unnoble, a common woman,
   —Me, of like metal

Cast with Your divinity. Nothing lower
Dare I rate me, since that in all true lovers
You, Who are the ultimate Fire, do burn and,
   Burning, transmew them.

Me Your flame-tongu'd fingers, Your flick'ring lids, Your
Kisses, Your empyreal heats distraining
Soul alike and body with hapless passions,
   Long ago vanquish'd.

Yet, – for Beauty dwelleth as well in action:
Not in flesh alone and the flaming semblant

(World's desire and wonder of earth and Heaven
   Warmed as jewels

'Tween Your breasts, or stars in Your hair's deep
   night-shade),
But besides in mind: and in You the twain are
Undivisible even in thought, an inly
   One everlasting—

Therefore, burn me inwardly: burn my thinking
Mind, as by this lover You sweep Your fires through
This fair body, changing its blood to ichor:
   Fine me, until my

Mortal eyes behold You in very presence,
Not as feeble fantasy do conceive You,
But the truth's self, even as
   You Yourself behold Your own Godhead.

As for answer, the storm broke on Mehisbon. A ball of eye-blinding flame, like a falling sun, went betwixt raging sky and the low land westward from the town; and upon its heels, with great shakings of the air, the thunder crashed and tumbled as if in a casting down about the temple of heavy palpable bodies toppled from some unsighted brink of the upper heavens and falling in a huddle amid darkness and rushing of rain. Stateira, looking down at her child, and tightening her clasp of his hand, had now, and now again, in the momentary livid out-leapings of the lightnings, swift sights of his face. There was one matter only to be read in it: not fear: not concern with her: but delight in the thunder.

Argument with Dates

THE PLOT SYNOPSIS, EDDISON'S 'ARGUMENT WITH DATES', BEGINS WITH THIS CHAPTER AND CONTINUES THROUGH TO CHAPTER XXVII. CHAPTER VIII IS ALSO THE FIRST FOR WHICH WRITINGS UNPUBLISHED IN THE ORIGINAL 1958 EDITION EXIST. IN THIS AND SUBSEQUENT CHAPTERS, I SHALL INCORPORATE THE UNPUBLISHED DRAFTS WITH THE PUBLISHED ARGUMENT ACCORDING TO THE CHRONOLOGY OF THE STORY'S EPISODES.

TO PREVENT CONFUSION WITH EDDISON'S DATES OF COMPOSITION, I HAVE MARKED ALL ZIMIAMVIAN DATES AZC (*ANNO ZAYANAE CONDITAE*, OR 'FROM THE FOUNDING OF THE CITY OF ZAYANA'), AND TO PREVENT CONFUSION WITH EDDISON'S WRITING, MY EDITORIAL COMMENTS HAVE BEEN SET IN THIS SMALLER TYPE.

P. E. THOMAS

ARGUMENT WITH DATES

King Mezentius grows to manhood
Queen Rosma
Tragedy of Aktor
(Chapters VIII–XII)

VIII

THE PRINCE PROTECTOR

CHAPTER VIII BEGINS WITH THE ARGUMENT:

AKTOR, within a few weeks of the death of King Mardanus, utterly
loathes his horrid deed. (It had been in fact not so much deed as
abstention: he deliberately abstained from warning the King that
the chess queens had been poisoned, and taking care not to touch
his own queen, left chance to decide whether the King should
touch his.) As time passes, he begins to think his crime can be
'wished' into nothingness. The Queen, so far as he can judge,
suspects nothing: he begins to live in a new world, almost
convincing himself that his crime never took place: the King is
dead, but not through Aktor's doing or contrivance. Aktor and
the Queen settle down to an Arcadian existence of trust, affection,
and understanding. She, feeling the alteration in him, is touched
to the heart and can hardly refrain in his presence from showing
her affection and passionate desire for him. However, she does
refrain.

Before any reply can be received to the Queen's ultimatum, the
revolution of the Nine takes place in Akkama.

IN CHAPTER VII, EDDISON NARRATES THAT QUEEN STATEIRA
DISPATCHED MYNTOR THE CONSTABLE OF FINGISWOLD TO AKKAMA
WITH AN ULTIMATUM REGARDING THE MURDER OF KING MARDANUS.

ON 9 JANUARY 1944, EDDISON DRAFTED NOTES FOR A SCENE IN WHICH THE QUEEN RECEIVES HIS LETTERS IN LATE JULY OF 726 AZC:

Queen at work in King Mardanus's study (*not* closet). Letters from Constable reporting revolt in Akkama: King and all his family thrown to the pigs (a nasty custom of the country for low-class criminals). Complete confusion, and Myntor is therefore waiting for some responsible power to crystallize with whom he can deal, and would like any new instructions. Is convinced no grave danger to him and members of their mission: Akkamites too uncertain of their position and afraid of what they've done (Aktor winces inwardly at the parallel) to bring Fingiswold into enmity against them.

Queen sends for Aktor and consults him. (Bring out relations between her and him.)

Queen: Here's news from your country. I want your head in it.
Aktor: Is't good or bad?
Queen: Doubtful. I'll read it to you: dated 20th June.
Aktor: That's quick travelling.
Queen: He's been kept waiting for audience – at last given one and an interim answer. Thinks the King is raising forces. But nobles are showing signs of divided counsels. There's a strengthening of your party.

IN ADDITION TO THE NOTES ABOVE, EDDISON COMPOSED PART OF A LETTER FROM THE CONSTABLE TO QUEEN STATEIRA. THIS UNFINISHED LETTER DOES NOT MENTION THE REVOLUTION OF THE NINE, BUT IT DOES TELL OF AKKAMITE HOSPITALITY TOWARD FOREIGN AMBASSADORS:

My whole entertainment from my first arrival till towards the very end, was such as if they had devised meanes of very purpose to shew their utter disliking of the whole Fingiswold nation.

At my arriving at —— there was no man to bid me well coom, not so much as to conduct me up to my lodging. After I had stayed

2 or 3 dayes to see if anie well coom or other message would come from the King or the Lord ——, I sent my interpreter to the said Lord ——, to desir him to be a meanes for audience to the King. My interpreter having attended him 2 or 3 dayes, without speaking to him, was commanded by the Chancellour to coom no more to the Court, nor to the house of the said Lord ——. The Counsell was commanded not to conferr with mee, nor I to send to anie of them.

When I had audience of the King in the verie entrance of my speech I was cavilled withall by the Chancellour . . .

The presents sent by yr. Highness to the King, and delivered to him in his own presence, with all other writings, wear the day following retourned to mee, and very contemptuouslie cast downe before mee.

My articles of petition delivered by woord of mouth, and afterward by writing, with all other writings, wear altered and falsified by the King's interpreter, by meanes of the Chancellour ——; . . . manie things were putt in and manie things strook out, which being complained of and the points noted would not be redressed.

I was placed in a howse verie unhandsoom, unholsoom, of purpose (as it seemed) to doe me disgrace, and to hurt my health, whear I was kept as prisoner, not as an ambassadour.

EDDISON MADE NO MORE NOTES UPON THE EVENTS OF THIS CHAPTER, BUT ON 20 JANUARY 1944, HE MADE SOME NOTES ON THE GEOGRAPHY OF AKKAMA:

Akkama's capital 300 miles from Rialmar WNW as crow flies. 1,200,000 square miles (about 500 miles greatest length and 400 N to S, roughly bean shaped). Southern part, the Waste of Akkama, sandy desert: Northern and central part a high tableland (? 4–5000 feet). Only practical communication with Fingiswold (except by sea) is through passes in comparatively low country 50 miles WNW of Rialmar between Western mountain end of mountain boundary that encloses the fertile lowlands in horseshoe shape, of Fingiswold, and the Bight. This way leads to the Shearbone range.

FEW OF THESE PRECISE DETAILS HAVE A PLACE IN THE ARGUMENT,
WHICH BRIEFLY DESCRIBES AKKAMA AND THEN SUMMARIZES ITS
HISTORY:

Akkama is a vast country lying north-west from Fingiswold:
its southern parts all sandy desert, its north and centre a high
table-land. The country has a wintry climate and is sparsely
inhabited by nomads and woodmen. Five or six generations ago
rebellious nobles from Fingiswold fled to Akkama and there
founded a dynasty, intermarrying with the natives and living like
robber kings on Pis-sempsco, a high rock on which sits the capital
and only city of importance. With this for their hold, they lived
by foray and piracy, throwing criminals to the pigs (their chief
cattle, and very fierce), and worshipping the 'dirty gods' of the
country. They vaunted themselves rightful heirs to the throne of
Fingiswold and the nobles speak the English tongue (which is
common to the three kingdoms), but the natives, a cruel, base
and savage people, have a gibberish of their own. The Nine
represent these noble families who had fallen from power when
the usurping king, Tzucho, expelled Aktor and slew the king his
father. This Tzucho was a bastard of a cadet branch of the ruling
family, his mother a queen of Akkama who was thrown to the
pigs for adultery with a pirate of native birth.

The Nine, having slain Tzucho and set themselves in power as
an oligarchy, now send an embassy to Rialmar offering every
conceivable apology and atonement, short of surrender of their
country. The Queen, dealing with the ambassadors in person,
makes a treaty whereby Akkama promises perpetual friendship
and alliance, and Aktor renounces any claim to the throne of
Akkama.

It is Aktor's conduct during these negotiations that finally decides
Queen Stateira to marry him. With great dignity and finesse and
in a scene which does credit to them both, she in effect proposes
this, and Aktor is almost frightened at the sudden fulfilment of
his dearest hopes. Upon their marriage (September 726), he is
proclaimed Prince Protector, making at the same time public and

solemn renunciation of any higher ambition and swearing fealty to King Mezentius and to Stateira as Queen Regent.

The Queen sends for Doctor Vandermast and gives him the responsibility, under her, for the young King's upbringing. Aktor is at first in a dread lest Vandermast should disclose his secret, and meditates the doctor's destruction. But while he procrastinates he learns to trust the doctor, and soon to revere him.

With the passage of the years, Mezentius learns that he himself is King: learns too, with surprise, that he had a father other than Aktor. He shows an early instinct for command and a delight in danger for its own sake: dangerous dogs, horses, bulls, and Anthea in her lynx dress: dangerous climbing on the walls and cliffs of Rialmar. He is untirable, incredibly generous and open-handed, and in all dispute an upholder, from native inclination, of the losing side.

IX

LADY ROSMA IN ACROZAYANA

IN 732 Emmius's Meszrian policy bears fruit in the marriage of his daughter the Lady Rosma Parry, now eighteen, to King Kallias. Kallias's meaning was by this alliance to re-estate his power in the Meszrian Marches and further to aggrandize himself at the expense of Rerek. But Emmius, a more subtle and no less brutal Machiavellian, had a private understanding with Haliartes, the king's brother and heir presumptive, whereby, in case the king should die and the succession be endangered, Emmius would support Haliartes by force of arms upon condition of his immediately making Rosma his queen.

The lady, taken with a loathing for Kallias (who is forty, a gloomy tyrant, and very dissolute and debauched), murders him on his wedding-night and forthwith weds Haliartes, a weak and easy-mannered prince much more to the taste of the lords of Meszria than his self-willed, hard-driving brother. She easily persuades Haliartes to make her not his queen only but joint sovereign with himself.

X

STIRRING OF THE EUMENIDES

In 736 the Nine secretly offer to Aktor the throne of Akkama. The envoy, seeing Aktor in private, explains that this is upon condition of his first becoming King of Fingiswold. Aktor refuses, and the matter is dropped. He refuses mainly because of his love for the Queen (to whom he never reveals this offer) and because of his oath of renunciation, to break which would ruin him for ever in her esteem. But the refusal is wormwood in his soul. He grows more and more melancholic: begins to ponder whether it were not best to make away with Mezentius who he fears may, as he grows up, find out the true circumstances of his father's taking off: but devotion to Queen Stateira (perhaps the one stable principle in him), seconded by a congenital proneness to put things off, always holds him back from this further crime. Nevertheless, the bloody secret is always a barrier between himself and the Queen.

XI

COMMODITY OF NEPHEWS

QUEEN Rosma, grown weary after five years of the unenterprising water-gruelish Haliartes, in 738 casts her eye on his nephew Lebedes, a villainous young scoundrel five years her junior, to whom she now promises her hand in marriage if he will first kill the king his uncle. Lebedes accordingly raises rebellion and kills Haliartes in battle; but Rosma, alarmed now lest this young man prove too devilish, denies her part of the bargain and, finding ready to hand Beltran, Lebedes's elder brother, invites him to rid her of Lebedes, the consideration of which service is to be, as before, her hand in marriage. Beltran, unscrupulous but attractive, and with many saving graces, and able moreover (as no man she had before encountered) to stir faintly her affections, is madly in love and savagely jealous of his brother. He surprises Lebedes in the queen's chamber and, with a hearty good will and under her very eyes, stabs him to death. In the same hour she takes Beltran as lover, but forthwith upon a revulsion repudiates him, threatens him with death, and drives him with contumely into exile.

Rosma, now aged twenty-four, reigns henceforward as Queen of Meszria in her own right. She is a big powerful woman, dark-haired, black-eyed, dissembling, proud, grasping, perfidious, and cruel. She is handsome, and can be physically extremely alluring: not vicious, but cold: obsessed with the lust of power. In due course, Beroald, her son by Beltran, is born in Zayana. Rosma, being by nature 'of masculine virtue,' hates to be a woman, hates her offspring, and indeed has posed, and continues to pose (with what justification none can tell) as a Virgin Queen. She conceals the birth and orders the child to be exposed on a mountain. Anthea, in her lynx dress, saves it, and, by direction of Doctor Vandermast, substitutes it for the same-aged son of the wife of a gentleman in South Meszria.

XII

ANOTHER FAIR MOONSHINY NIGHT

KING Mezentius, as he approaches manhood, begins to discover justice: begins too to discover that the beauty which is in action is the necessary complement to that physical beauty which he has already learnt to worship. He shows early promise of that supreme gift of a man of action, the power to put from his mind everything except the business in hand, and develops at the same time berserk traits: fits of intense vigour and achievement which alternate with periods of moodiness, silence, lassitude, and retirement into himself. Stateira watches these things with mixed admiration and anxiety. He begins to talk to her about his father, and about Aktor, to whom (without himself knowing why) he begins to take a certain dislike. This troubles him, and his mother. And it troubles Aktor. The closer Aktor draws to the Queen, the more he is tortured with remorse. Yet he realizes that it was in fact that wicked and secret treason that gave him his present happiness and power. His mind is thus in a perpetual conflict, and his melancholy increases upon him. Queen Stateira for her part never ceases to be under his passionate domination and grows more and more fearful lest he should someday confess to her the guilt which she never admits, even to her own secret mind, that she suspects. Deeper and nobler and more Olympian is her clinging to Mezentius's future greatness (foreshadowed by Doctor Vandermast), as her sheet anchor.

In December 740, the King (aged seventeen) has been questioning his step-father about his father's murder. He does not, save in recurring moments of gnawing uneasiness and guesswork that originate in the blood rather than in the brain, suspect Aktor's complicity. Moreover, his rooted dislike for Aktor itself makes him the less ready to suspect; for it is clean against his nature to be unjust, most of all to a man personally repugnant to his sympathies. He questions Aktor now, simply because he is impatient to clear up the mystery and have done with it, and Aktor (having caught and disposed of the actual poisoner) seems to be the one person who may be able to throw any light on the thing.

The outcome of their conversation is indeterminate (as for any advancement of the King's purpose), but to Aktor, devastating. His fears, bred of a bad conscience, tell him the King has divined the secret, or been told by Vandermast. In a like agony of spirit as fourteen years ago, he comes once more at midnight to the Queen's privy garden, expecting solitude but finding Anthea there, as if waiting for him.

It is the real frost this time: the longest night of the year. That oread lady is cold, pitiless, scornful, and unkind. She knows, of course, the truth, and 'harries mankind's obliquity' in the person of the unhappy Prince Protector. Her unmercilessness, terribly seconding his own inward conscience, is in effect a means of illuminating the good (which is not inconsiderable) in Aktor, and so of awakening in an onlooker, had any been there, pity and charity on his behalf.

In this cold and this clarity induced by the scorpion sting of Anthea's scorn, he reviews the choices:

First: Kill Mezentius? But that would kill also the Queen's love for himself. And moreover, how could he hope to escape?

Second: Flee? But where to? Akkama will not have him. Besides, what profit in life without the Queen? They are by this time, it is true, scarcely more lovers than she and Mardanus had been after Mezentius's birth; but this time it is the Queen, not her lover, who has sated her passion and finds it burned out at last. But she is deeply fond of Aktor, and (as he believes in his bones) has never imagined the truth about his hand in Mardanus's murder: and to live with her, even upon terms of brother and sister, has become to him the one reason for continuance upon earth.

Third: Confess all to Mezentius, and hope he will kill him? But that, albeit quieting his conscience, would (again) hurt the Queen. Also Mezentius would tell her all, and that Aktor cannot even in imagination face.

And so, feeling he has miscooked his life (possessed his lady by unlawful means, mixed his love with ambition and, for sake of both, become a traitor, a murderer of his friend and benefactor, and a life-long liar henceforth and fugitive from truth: things which can never be reversed and never confessed but can, maybe, be expiated), and being resolved the Queen shall never know, nor Mezentius (if he does not know, or has not guessed, already), he asks Anthea to do him a single favour: the favour of silence. She scornfully, but (as Aktor by some obscure intimation realizes) with faithful meaning, assents. Aktor throws himself backwards down the eight-hundred-foot cliff that overlooks the harbour.

Anthea keeps her word. The King keeps his thoughts to himself, and refrains, with an almost feminine sympathy and intuition, from letting his mother suspect the truth, or what he guesses to be the truth.

ON 5 DECEMBER 1943, EDDISON RECORDED SOME OF HIS THOUGHTS ABOUT AKTOR'S SUICIDE:

Make Aktor's tragic end not a melodramatic retribution on a villain, but the destined expiation of a crime that demands expiation. 'What's done is done'; and in taking that way out Aktor may be thought to have redeemed himself. He is not a Morville, far less a Derxis; a man of promise, led by passion and ambition into wicked courses but in some sort reconciled at last.

BOOK THREE

THE AFFAIR OF REREK

Book Three

ARGUMENT WITH DATES

Emmius Parry continues his policy: looking north
King Mezentius gains Rerek
(Chapters XIII–XIV)

XIII

THE DEVIL'S QUILTED ANVIL

In 741 the Nine fall from power in Akkama and Melkis becomes king, being by Aktor's death the next in legitimate line of succession. After eighteen months of hesitation and diplomatic interchanges, Melkis moves to unseat King Mezentius. Supervius Parry, aged forty-six, who has now sat in Laimak twenty-one years, sends his younger son, Horius Parry (now aged sixteen) as an officer in attendance upon the general in command of a Rerek contingent in aid of King Mezentius in Fingiswold. This first meeting of Horius with the King results in a mutual interest and subtle equivocal attraction.

In the campaign which follows, the King, aged nineteen, finally repulses Akkama, who is left disgraced and licking his wounds (742).

Supervius's main concern is now to oust Gilmanes (who has succeeded his father Alvard as Prince of Kaimar) from his position of favour in Rialmar. He is jealous of Gilmanes, as of the other princes in the north (Ercles, Keriones's son and successor in Eldir, and Aramond of Bagort). Supervius is no great statesman, and is obsessed with his ambition to see Laimak received as mistress of all Rerek. He is never really loyal to his brother Emmius, as Emmius is to him for family sake and for a kind of love of him. He walks in a net so far as Emmius is concerned, and Emmius, enjoying and frustrating his brother's deep-laid and tortuous disloyalties, constantly uses him as a cat's-paw to further his own more subtle and less parochial policy.

Emmius (aged fifty-two), is preeminently by nature a user of cat's-paws: this explains his never attempting to seize Meszria for himself, but preferring to control it through his daughter Rosma. He is probably already privately toying with the notion of a marriage between her and the King. This he sees might mean the hemming in and even (if the King turns out from these beginnings a very great man) the subjection of Rerek. But if the King turns out so, this will be of little moment; for Rerek, on the doorstep of Fingiswold, could not then in any event hope to stand long against him. If, on the other hand, the King's capacities prove but mean, then the alliance would strengthen the Parry (particularly Emmius's own branch of the family), and would mean an aggrandizement of Meszria and so run with Emmius's policy, since the queen his daughter has not only married into the reigning house in Zayana but now supplanted it.

Openly, Emmius plays for time; refuses to regard Gilmanes seriously (a view justified later by the event); and prepares to use Peridor of Laveringay, his sister Lugia's son, as a thorn in Ercles's side. This project fails, however, Peridor inclining more and more to Ercles.

King Mezentius (now aged twenty), noting the uneasy balance of power in Rerek (the age-long leadership of the house of Parry counter-weighted by the loose alliance of the princes of the north, and the complicated courtship, by both sides, of the free cities), begins to think of extending his influence southwards.

His mother, Queen Stateira, mistrusting the Parry instinctively, now produces in Rialmar Ercles's sister, the Lady Anastasia, a beautiful girl whom the King easily falls in love with and marries (July 732): a further setback for Emmius Parry.

XIV

LORD EMMIUS PARRY

OPEN strife breaks out next year (744) between the Parry and
Ercles in Rerek. Supervius holds Megra, left to Marescia by her
father's will who died a year or two ago. Ercles, feeling that this
threatens his safety in Eldir, disputes the will. He prepares to
besiege Megra, and Supervius, getting wind of this, sends an army
to ravage the lands of Eldir itself. Ercles, thwarted, appeals to
Rialmar for succour. The King refuses, telling Ercles plainly that
he is not disposed to make his policy a family affair. Horius Parry
(aged eighteen), shrewdly diagnosing the King's impartiality,
induces his father (with Emmius's approval) to agree with Ercles
to a joint application to the King to arbitrate. The King establishes
a just peace, confirming the Parry in Megra, but (to save the old
treaty) formally as Lieutenant of the King of Fingiswold, and he
must retire from Lailma pending a free election in that city.

Early in 745 Queen Anastasia dies.

In 746 a renewed attack by Akkama is bloodily thrown back
by the King, demonstrating once more his armed strength in
Fingiswold.

Emmius Parry now judges it the happy moment for a crucial
move to bring the King into Rerek. For this purpose he success-
fully makes Peridor his cat's-paw (who is quite unconscious of
being so used) to provoke Ercles, Gilmanes, and Aramond to
assault Megra in violation of the concordat. After fruitless

negotiations lasting eighteen months, during which Megra stands a siege, Supervius, as injured party, appeals to the King. The King summons a conference in Rialmar, insisting on personal attendance: no ambassadors or legates. Mainly because of stiffness on the part of Supervius and Horius, whom the princes distrust, the conference is stormy; but Emmius's diplomacy brings it at last to a joint request by all unanimously, backed by other lords of Rerek, that the King should assume the crown of Rerek as their overlord, guaranteeing all freedoms. The King accepts this (748).

Henceforth, the King's policy in Rerek is consistently *divide et impera*; and his great weapon a scrupulous fairness. (His habit, all his life, is to look for (and find) the best in people. This does not mean he is never taken in, but he consistently sees the best in them, and gets the most out of them. In Horius Parry, for instance, and (later) in Rosma, he sees many bests (and many worsts). Those that disappoint him (for instance, later, Valero, and Akkama) have been wittingly tested by him, and run risks with.

BOOK FOUR

THE AFFAIR OF MESZRIA

ARGUMENT WITH DATES

The King gains Meszria
Amalie
Rosma in Rialmar
(Chapters XV-XIX)

XV

QUEEN ROSMA

THE king's thoughts have for some years been drawn toward Meszria. This works well with Emmius Parry's long-sighted policy, who, independently and with different (but far from hostile) interests, has been steering towards the same mark: namely a nearer and still more exalted connection between the Parry (this time, of Argyanna) and the royal house of Fingiswold.

In 749 the King sends Jeronimy to ask Rosma to receive a visit from the King in person, since they are now conterminous sovereigns and ought to be friends. In late autumn the King comes to Zayana. Purely as a matter of high policy, he proposes marriage. Posing as an unscrupulous politician after her own pattern, he shows in their preliminary conversations a remarkable and detailed knowledge of her history and her polyandrous proceedings. (He is now aged twenty-six: Rosma thirty-five.)

The queen, reflecting on these conversations, has the sensation of having been saddled and bridled: of having been made drunk with the King's personality and led by that to talk too much. However, it is not her habit to let anything except cold logic govern her actions, and by that test alone his offer is not one to be let go: by it he gains Meszria while she gains Fingiswold and Rerek. She gains, also, what is less to her taste: a master. But this inconvenience may in any case be unavoidable, since the King's overlordship in Rerek brings nearer home the danger of coercion if she is obdurate. Moreover, although their conversations have throughout been upon the explicit terms that marriage is to entail no relations between them beyond the political, she feels vaguely, as with Beltran, but now at a profounder level with King Mezentius, that here is a man for whose sake she might, if ever she should, which is to her inconceivable, make a fool of herself. After a few days' consideration, she answers that, on his present proposal, the scales are too much weighted in the King's favour as against her, since she, as a woman, gives up her independence by marrying. If, however, he will bring Akkama into the dowry, then she will accept.

XVI

LADY OF PRESENCE

MEANWHILE, the King's heart is set upon Amalie, a young lady of the queen's bedchamber, aged sixteen, and passionately beloved by this self-willed and bloody woman. He and Amalie do not so much fall in love as have an intimation, at first looks exchanged between them and without word spoken, that they are lovers, and have been so since the beginning; and this, since not in this present (Zimiamvian) life, therefore presumably in some other world, or worlds. This echoes back to the *Praeludium*: the fifteen years 'in our own house at Nether Wastdale,' and his seeing her 'dead in the Morgue at Paris'. The intimation, sometimes momentary, sometimes longer in duration, is yet fitful and unseizable. Like a perfume, it cannot be revived in memory, but, when present, has the quality of conjuring up in solid actuality of circumstance and detail all that belongs to it. He tells Amalie that he cannot offer her a crown: kings wed for policy, not for love. But he does offer her himself, and on no temporary nor no partial terms. He tells her he is going north on the Akkama business, and that in two years he means to come back, with that accomplished, for her.

In this the King is entirely open with Rosma. He will make Akkama tributary to Fingiswold, and in two years will return to Zayana to claim her hand. Their marriage is to be a purely political relationship: his wife, except in name, will be Amalie. The queen will be free (on sole condition of avoiding public scandal) to console herself as she may please. Rosma laughs. She holds these amusements much over-rated, and is perfectly content with his proposals.

XVII

AKKAMA BROUGHT INTO THE DOWRY

THE king returns north, stopping a few days in Argyanna to confer with his future father-in-law. Preparations last far into the summer of the next year (750). In August, he marches on Akkama with a great army of Fingiswold levies and a powerful contingent from Rerek under command of Supervius Parry, who has with him Horius, his son by Marescia, aged twenty-four, and Hybrastus (Emmius's son, aged thirty-three). Ercles (aged thirty-two), and Aramond (aged twenty-three), and Valero, Prince of Ulba (aged twenty), are also in this expedition. Emmius had pressed personal participation upon Supervius, both in the family interest and not to be outweighed by the Ercles faction.

The campaign of 750 ends with a severe reverse: Supervius Parry killed in battle; Ercles taken prisoner. But the King after a few months retrieves all and, taking Akkama by surprise by a winter campaign (a thing unheard of in that part of the world), crushes all resistance after three or four big battles, the last one about mid-February 751.

Throughout this decisive war, Horius Parry distinguishes himself both as soldier and as counsellor: an old head on young shoulders. He on land and Jeronimy at sea are (after Supervius's death) the King's chief lieutenants. Prince Valero, a protégé of Emmius Parry's, also does brilliant work. Seeds of ill will are sown in Horius's secret heart against Valero.

During four months' intensive work in subdued Akkama a violent quarrel comes to a head between Horius and Hybrastus Parry. Hybrastus palpably in the wrong bids his cousin to the duello and is killed. Horius, with great courage and judgement, obtains leave to go south immediately to make his peace with his uncle Emmius. He comes to Argyanna, outspeeding all rumours, armed with a letter from the King that gives the facts, and in effect offering Emmius 'self-doom'.

Emmius, partly for love of bravery in a man, partly for deep and sound reasons of policy, magnanimously forgives his son's death, but demands from Horius, by way of atonement, material guarantees in the March of Ulba, including possession of the fortress of Kessarey and the personal right to appoint a Lord President of the Marches. He appoints Count Bork. The result is that politically as well as strategically Emmius will now be all-powerful (under the King) in the whole region of the Zenner.

Horius Parry succeeds his father in Laimak. He remains on good terms with his uncle (now aged sixty) but chafes at his power, likely to be greatly increased as the King's father-in-law as well as by this new agreement. As his personal agent and intelligencer at Emmius's court in Argyanna, Horius maintains one Gabriel Flores (aged twenty-two), a low-born adventurer whom he seduced from Ercles's service a year or two back when Ercles had placed Gabriel, as his spy, in Laimak.

With his own elder half-brother, Geleron Parry, who sits like a thorn in Anguring, Horius is on terms of thinly disguised hostility. Geleron (as son to Supervius by his first wife Rhodanthe, whom Supervius put away to marry Marescia) thinks he ought by rights to have Laimak, but Supervius left it by will to Horius.

XVIII

THE SHE-WOLF TAMED TO HAND

THE king returns at midsummer, five months before the date appointed, to Zayana – and to Amalie. He weds Rosma, in great state and with public acclamation and rejoicings, on the terms agreed upon.

The Queen, in spite of her view of such 'amusements,' cannot upon actual experience brook Amalie's position as the King's mistress in Zayana. Her attitude in this is complex, and her grievance not so much that Amalie is her rival in the King's affections (which she at this stage cares nothing for) as that he has taken Amalie away from her. At the Yule feast, December 751, Rosma tries to burn the King and Amalie together; but in this she is thwarted by the King, who also succeeds (almost beyond belief) in keeping the whole affair secret so far as Rosma's share in it is concerned.

After this, he tells the Queen that Meszria is not good for her, nor she for Meszria: to save her face, she had better give out (as her own proposal) that she desires a change of residence, and that the Queen of the Three Kingdoms ought to live in the chief seat-town, namely Rialmar. As underlining the fact that she must play second fiddle (politically), the King says he proposes to install Jeronimy in Meszria as Commissioner Regent.

Rosma is at first mad wroth at all this, and the King with great difficulty prevents her from hurting herself or him. However, he keeps his temper; and the end of it is that she, savouring curiously on her palate a new pleasure (of a man that can master her and also laugh at her), falls in with his plans.

This is the beginning of a closer and deeper relationship, almost of friendship, between the King and Rosma. She now resides permanently in Rialmar, while he divides his time between the three countries in turn.

XIX

THE DUCHESS OF MEMISON

THE Queen Mother, distasting the prospect of continuing in Rialmar, where she must now yield precedence to a daughter-in-law whose reputation and capabilities she reviews with dismay, resolves to leave Fingiswold. In the spring of 752 she moves south to Lornra Zombremar, in a high eastward-facing valley on the far side of the great snow ranges that enclose Meszria from the east. In this mountain retreat at the edge of the world, in a 'house of peace' built for her by art of Doctor Vandermast, she now lives retired from the busy life of courts and the restlessness of great men.

In April 752, Barganax is born in Meszria, and Amalie is made Duchess. On learning of this, the Queen offers divorce; but the King has no intention of making Amalie a queen, nor has she any ambition to be made so. From this arises a strengthening of friendship between King and Queen.

This same year Lessingham is born at Upmire, posthumous son of Romelius, a lord of Rerek who had married in 751 Eleonora, grand-daughter of Sidonius Parry. When in 726 Supervius had put away his wife Rhodanthe (Eleonora's aunt and Geleron's mother) in order to marry the Princess Marescia, this sowed enmity between his uncle Sidonius and the house of Laimak; and in that tradition Eleonora of Upmire now brings up her son.

The next few years are years of peace and consolidation, during which the personal hand of the King is felt everywhere throughout the realm.

The Queen indulges in underground political intrigues with her cousins Horius and Geleron Parry, Valero and others. She tries, more from spite than from policy, to set the King against Horius. None of these practices is hid from the King, who cannot resist teasing her; yet their queer friendship (and his and Horius Parry's) persists and grows. With unseen hand, the King fans the rivalry between the two brothers for his deep purposes.

BOOK FIVE
THE TRIPLE KINGDOM

ARGUMENT WITH DATES

Beltran returns
Birth of Fiorinda
End of Geleron Parry
Barganax and Styllis
Barganax and Heterasmene
Barganax made Duke of Zayana
Prince Valero
King Mezentius and Duchess Amalie visit Queen Stateira
Edward Lessingham and Lady Mary Lessingham
Rebellion in the Marches
Overthrow of Akkama
(Chapters XX–XXVII)

XX

DURA PAPILLA LUPAE

IN August 755, Beltran (now aged forty-three) appears in Rialmar, under an assumed name and in disguise, while the King is in Memison. He discloses himself to the Queen and makes fierce love to her. Rosma, who is now forty-one and in a perilous state of boredom, is at first infuriated but at last, saying she will ne'er consent, consents. Then, in a revulsion as much savager than sixteen years ago it had been in Zayana as her present surrender has been deeper and more passionate, she murders him.

The King, returning, smells out this secret. At length Rosma, knowing herself with child and thoroughly frightened at the King's enigmatical bearing, confesses all. He receives it with so much humour and magnanimity that she is, for the time at least, bound to him as never before. His only condition is secrecy: if ever she suffers her amours to become public, that will be the end of her. Rosma thinks he means, cut her head off. The mere suggestion (of mutilation of a woman) sickens him. No; but he would make her drink a lethal draught.

On midsummer night 756, Fiorinda is born to Queen Rosma in Rialmar. This child she would have killed or exposed, but the King, employing Anthea for the purpose, and with the help of Beroald, places it, without trace of origin, with the same suppositious parents in Meszria as Beroald was foisted upon, sixteen years ago.

XXI

ANGURING COMBUST

ABOUT April 757, Horius Parry's feud with his half-brother Geleron comes to a head (not without fostering by the King's unseen hand). The immediate occasion is Horius's discovery of foul play between his wife and Geleron. He kills his wife and burns Anguring, destroying Geleron, Geleron's wife, and their sons and daughters. This hellish deed both rids away, in Geleron, a turbulent and tiresome vassal and puts Horius under yet closer obligations to the King; for the King by a sudden swoop catches him outside his safe hold of Laimak and by pardoning the fratricide (by law, punishable as parricide) tightens the bonds of allegiance that bind Horius to the throne, impressing him at the same time with the sense of being, as it were, in the hand of God.

Rosma finds the King's handling of this episode after her own heart. It brings her, at this late date, furiously in love with him, partly because of his magnanimity, partly because she is seized with a sudden hankering to give an heir to the Triple Throne, and with the feeling that time is running short if this is to be done. The King, now aged thirty-three, does not trouble himself much about this. If he ever thinks of the succession, his attitude is coloured with the conviction that kings must be kings by competence, not by birth merely, and with an inclination to toy with the idea of Barganax's possible fitness. Constitutionally, the King is but lightly interested in posterity, intent on building his own edifice of power in his own lifetime: fate and his successors must settle what comes after.

Rosma addresses herself to fascinate him. He is at first repelled, then amused, and finally touched. He suddenly looses himself in a fierce passion for this tiger-cat of his: a kind of lustful camaraderie, involving no disloyalty to the Duchess.

In January 758, Styllis is born in Rialmar. The Queen, full of philoprogenitiveness for her first legitimate offspring, is full too of jealousy against Barganax on her son's behalf. As Styllis grows up she neglects no occasion to set him against his half-brother.

Beroald, now aged nineteen, studies law under Count Olpman.

XXII

PAX MEZENTIANA

DURING the next twelve years (758-770) of *Pax Mezentiana*, underground strife still smoulders in Rerek, with constant friction between the Parry and the princes, the free cities putting up their favours by auction to the highest bidder.

In 760, another child, the Princess Antiope, is born to Rosma in Rialmar.

Emmius Parry, looking ahead, in 766 makes Horius his heir. The King, disliking the prospect of so much personal power in one hand (Laimak, Argyanna, Kessarey, and the Marches), also looks ahead. He now declares Megra, Kaima, Kessarey, and Argyanna fiefs royal, but this is not to operate as regards Kaima or Argyanna so long as Gilmanes and Emmius Parry are alive. He puts his own lieutenants in the other fortresses: Arcastus in Megra, Roder in Kessarey. (Arcastus is grandson to Morsilla Parry and her first husband, Caunas, and therefore by tradition opposed to the Pertiscan branch. But Horius Parry captivates his fancy, and he always remains Horius's loyal supporter.) The fact that Emmius accepts without cavil the position as regards Kessarey, is an evidence of the strength of the friendship and understanding between Emmius and the King.

Beroald (aged twenty-seven) takes, thanks to Jeronimy's support and recommendation, a large part in advising on the administrative, diplomatic and legal problems involved in this settlement.

The King, much taken with his character and abilities, makes him lord of Krestenaya, and presently joins him with Jeronimy as Commissioner Regent in Meszria.

Horius Parry is not best pleased about these arrangements; but the King, admiring the way he accepts them, promises him (and confirms it under seal in his favour) inheritance under his uncle's will, except as for Argyanna which on Emmius's death will revert to the crown. Horius, when he succeeds, will thus be all-powerful in the Marches (subject however – a weighty exception – to the key fortress of Argyanna), but is deprived of Megra and (of course) of Kessarey. He (in common with most of the great vassals of Rerek and Meszria) inclines to dislike Beroald and the Admiral and Roder as 'office nobility' and upstarts.

XXIII

THE TWO DUKES

BARGANAX, at fifteen, is as big and as strong and well grown as any young man in the land three years his elder. His first love is Heterasmene, a young widow and lady of honour at the Duchess's court in Memison. Heterasmene for her part greatly enjoys this worship but, when he makes violent love to her, thinks it her duty to inform the Duchess. Amalie, judging it an admirable education for her son and making sure that the lady scoffs at the very thought of marriage with a boy half her age, rejoices that Heterasmene should at once amuse herself and bring up Barganax in the way he should go: an arrangement which works to their mutual benefit and, after a year or two, ends gradually: friendship preserved and no hearts broken. The lady, in return for this kindness, is made Countess in her own right by the King, and soon afterwards weds a lord in Rialmar.

In 770 Barganax, being now eighteen, comes of age. The King creates him Duke of Zayana, the title formerly held by heirs apparent to the old kingdom of Meszria. Rosma dislikes the implication. On Barganax's induction into his dukedom, Doctor Vandermast (hitherto his tutor) assumes the post of secretary. The King assigns to Barganax an apanage with lands extending far beyond the limits of the dukedom. Styllis, incensed at this, nurses his old jealousies and old and new grievances, which the Queen his mother does not neglect to influence.

XXIV

PRINCE VALERO

PRINCE Valero of Ulba, who had thought he deserved one of the key fortresses in 766, has ever since been secretly busy forming a faction and endeavouring to win the confidence and support of Count Bork, Lord President of the Marches. Horius Parry, having secret intelligence of this, fosters and waters it, meaning to destroy the prince in due time and win merit thereby.

The Parry's young cousin, Lessingham, has a finger in this 'secret intelligence'. (In spite of his upbringing, Lessingham at the age of sixteen fell under the spell of Horius and became the means of reconciliation between him and Eleonora of Upmire, who, at her son's request, now allows him to reside in Laimak as page to Horius.)

Valero, now (770) in his fortieth year, is handsome and well liked, but vain, a brilliant rather than an able politician, and fundamentally dishonest. Nobody, except the King, Emmius, and Horius, sees this vital weakness. Beroald, for his part, knows Valero only by hearsay. Emmius, in this single case, suffers his predilections to blindfold his shrewd hard judgement, and is always inclined to forgive Valero and favour him. The King leaves him alone, partly to please Emmius and Rosma (whose pet he is); but he has his eye upon him, and lets Horius Parry know, pretty unmistakably, that he holds him answerable for seeing that the prince does no serious harm.

Horius (now aged forty-four) hates Valero, but pretends friendship and does him various good turns. Valero foolishly underestimates the Parry's subtlety and reach, and is in the end a complete victim to his wiles. Horius has for years maintained a most masterly patience in this business, never involving himself but always and by every means lulling Valero's suspicions, encouraging him in his grievances, flattering him, giving him rope, and pretending not so much as to dream of his having subversive intentions.

XXV

LORNRA ZOMBREMAR

QUEEN Stateira has now for many years lived at Lornra Zombremar. The king has been her guest there more and more often as the years of *Pax Mezentiana* afford more opportunity for such pleasures of quietude; and always Doctor Vandermast is her frequent visitor, as also (of more recent years) is the King's niece Zenianthe, herself a hamadryad and friend and pupil of the learned doctor. All the nymphs, faun-kind, and half-gods, who inhabit these solitudes, are there to do Queen Stateira service. These creatures, with their pure unquestioning sight discerning the Queen Mother for who, under the disguise of wise and lovely old age, She truly is, are as children to her, loving her the more tenderly as they perceive Her inward divinity of which she for her own part is ignorant: an ignorance which is itself a grace; of equal excellence (in Vandermast's philosophic eye) with that far different but no less perfect and essential grace, of self-enjoyment and self-knowledge, that belongs to the fully conscious Godhead. She is now well entered upon her seventy-third year.

In November 770, the King and the Duchess (now aged forty-seven and thirty-seven respectively) come to see his mother in Lorna Zombremar. Amalie has never before made this journey, and it is eighteen years since she met the Queen Mother, who, then on her way from Rialmar to her new home, had been her guest in Memison. During the present visit the King and Amalie experience, in a more vivid and detailed manner than ever before, that assurance of having loved and had each other in another world (the world of the *Praeludium*: that is to say, this nineteenth- and twentieth-century world of ours): this time with the mutual knowledge that his name, there, is *Lessingham*, and hers *Mary*. They think of the Parry's young cousin whose name is Lessingham: a strange coincidence. As on other occasions, the memory (or dream?) fades and vanishes; but this time less completely in the King's mind than in the Duchess's. Even in hers, there remains a teasing sense of a forgotten or unplaceable time, whenever she hears the name 'Lessingham'.

XXVI

REBELLION IN THE MARCHES

CHOOSING the favourable moment when the Wold is impassable in winter and the King safe out of the way in Lornra Zombremar, King Sagartis of Akkama, in contempt of all treaties, attacks Fingiswold and invests Rialmar. Bodenay ably defends it, with the assistance of Romyrus and of Roder, what happens to be in Rialmar for the winter. Queen Rosma, in face of this deadly peril, directs and inspires the defence with politic wisdom and with the courage and fire of an Amazon.

The King, on receiving the news, comes down to Sestola, and thence sails with Jeronimy in mountainous seas (830 miles from Sestola to the nearest port of Fingiswold, fifty miles from Rialmar).

Valero, as it now appears, has been in league with Sagartis, the tributary king of Akkama, who promised secretly his support to Valero's wild scheme to make himself king in Rerek. As soon as the King has sailed to the north, this traitor raises rebellion in the March of Ulba. With foolhardy courage, he has placed himself for this purpose in Argyanna, where he now attempts to seize Emmius Parry's person, his host and benefactor. Emmius, now an old man of seventy-nine, valiantly resists, but is cut down by Valero's men in Valero's presence. His wife, Deïaneira, flinging herself between Emmius and the murderers, is butchered with him. Morville, a distant cousin of the Parry, plays a part here: tries to help Emmius and, after his murder, escapes to inform Horius.

Valero fails to secure Argyanna. Horius Parry, whose agents have kept him remarkably well informed, appears swiftly and in armed strength before the fortress (too late indeed to save his uncle: enemies ask whether he really wanted to), and demands its surrender. Valero escapes by the skin of his teeth.

After several heavy battles, Horius (771) puts down the revolt. He then cleans up the rebels with merciless thoroughness and not without an eye to the interests of persons friendly to his house and supremacy in Rerek. He beheads Count Bork and a dozen other great men: spares, and so binds to his obedience, Olpman and Gilmanes (the latter, as Valero's brother thirteen years his senior, is dangerously under suspicion): punishes many more. Valero himself, fleeing for sanctuary to his brother Gilmanes in Kaima, is by him handed over to the Parry, who puts him to death in a horrible and secret manner in Laimak dungeons. Because of these severities, the Lord Horius Parry comes to be called by his ill-willers (not too loudly, and behind his back) 'the Beast of Laimak'.

Barganax, leading a small force into the Ulba March during the rebellion, wins a brilliant cavalry victory: this to the confusion of many who had until now set him down as no better than a chambering dilettante, a do-little, and a dallier with women.

With a small force the King makes a surprise landing in Akkama, defeats that power at the battle of Elsmo, and cuts the communications of the invading army, which is eventually destroyed before Rialmar, and Sagartis slain.

XXVII

THIRD WAR WITH AKKAMA

LESSINGHAM gains renown at the battle of Elsmo, and in his pursuit of the enemy through the Greenbone ranges. It was upon Horius Parry's recommendation that the King had taken Lessingham with him on this expedition. A mysterious and mutual attraction, as if rooted in some inward tie between them more subtle and more intimate than kinship, is privately felt both by Lessingham and by the King. The King indeed, when he looks at this young man, seems to see as in a mirror the image of his own opening manhood of thirty years ago.

In 772 the King permits Sagartis's young son Derxis (aged sixteen) to succeed his father as tributary king of Akkama, with a Fingiswold Commission of Regency to govern the country in his name, and tutors to guide him. This discontents the Queen and Styllis, who can see nothing but bravado and rashness in such action. But Barganax and the Duchess completely understand the King's settled policy of admitting even the most unhopeful and dangerous of mankind to probation, and deeply delight both in his policy and in him.

Horius Parry, since his quelling of the rising in the Marches, has enjoyed new power and exalted station as Vicar of Rerek.

Beroald is made Chancellor of Fingiswold, but continues to live at Krestenaya.

Roder, in recognition of his share in the defence of Rialmar in 771, is made an Earl.

Bodenay (aged seventy-two) is, on similar grounds, made Knight Marshal of Fingiswold.

Jeronimy, for his service at sea in this third war with Akkama, receives the kingly order of the hippogriff, hitherto conferred only upon persons of the blood royal. He, Beroald, and Roder are now joined in a triumvirate as Commissioners Regent for Meszria, exercising (in like manner as the Vicar in Rerek and Bodenay in Fingiswold) vice-regal powers during the King's absences.

Barganax is well content with his dukedom and apanage, and rules it ably and well. He is much given to women: paints, and composes poems, and is often with his mother in Memison. He becomes more and more the centre of hopes of those Meszrians whose acceptance of the King is not only because they have no choice but because he has won all hearts, and who yet resent the King's power in Meszria as embodied in the Admiral, the Chancellor, and the Earl. Of these three, Beroald is the least unpopular, because a Meszrian by birth; but they are jealous of his power and fearful of his strong hand, his pride and subtlety, and the far-laid nets of his intelligence system.

Lessingham, accompanied by his friend and lieutenant Amaury, goes abroad in 772 (aged twenty) to seek adventure as a soldier of fortune in distant countries of the world. (He does not appear again in person in this book.) After the crushing of Akkama and the putting down of the rebellion in the Marches, the Three Kingdoms enjoy yet another five years of *Pax Mezentiana* (772-6).

BOOK SIX
LA ROSE NOIRE

XXVIII

ANADYOMENE

It was spring of the leaf now: mid-April of that year seven hundred and seventy-one, and these victories new in Rerek and the north. My lord Chancellor Beroald was with the King in Argyanna about the business of bringing in of Stathmar as King's Captain there, the place being devolved, since the death of Lord Emmius Parry, to estate of fief royal under like government with the other key-fortresses.

At home at Zemry Ashery the Chancellor's young sister dwelt still sweetly, quite untraded in court ceremonies or the ways of men, but in the theoric of these matters liberally grounded through daily sage expositions and informations by Doctor Vandermast, who had these four years past been to her for instructor and tutor. To try her paces and put in practice the doctor's principles and her own most will-o'-the-wisp and unexperimental embroiderings upon them, ready means lay to hand in converse with her brother: a merry war, sharping and training up the claws of her wit, and admiredly watering and firming at root the friendship between her and him, who was long become to her both father and mother in one. With the open countryside for nursery, Anthea and Campaspe for playmates, all living creatures of wood and farm and mountain for her familiars, and her fifteenth birthday at hand within a month or two, she was beginning day by day at this season, in tune with the rising of the world's whole sap, to put on herself fresh beauties, fresh intimations and ambiguities of awakening power, while the sun mounted from Aries into Taurus.

In a place of her own, a backwater private beside the river under Zemry Ashery, she was lazing herself today through the soft spring afternoon, upon a kind of hanging bed or hammock woven of daffodil-coloured silken cords and swung by ropes of silk from the boughs of one of the ancient alder-trees that have their roots deep in the marshy banks of that backwater. Overhead, these trees spread their canopy: bare of leaf, but with gold-brown catkins dangling, gold-edged against the unclouded blue, from every mesh of that network of tiny twigs. Ever and again a light zephyr ruffled the stillness and made these tassels swing delicately in the spice-laden, faintly salted, sweetness of the Meszrian spring-time. Here she reclined, with none save the trees and the water and the little living beings of the field to bear her company, and her own maiden thoughts.

A heavy book lay in her lap, bound in quarto in sweet-smelling leather with hasps of gold set with ruby and pearl. Presently she took it up, lazily turned the leaves, and began to read in it at that page of Homer's Hymn to Aphrodite where the Goddess, smitten by Zeus with sweet desire for Anchises, a mortal man, comes to Her own temple in Paphos and, shutting to the shining doors, makes the Graces wash and anoint Her with olive oil,

> Immortal, such as the Gods have upon Them that live forever;
> Ambrosial, fit for Her wear.

And in the fair margin of the page was all this drawn and pictured, in colours of lapis lazuli and lamp-black and vermillion and incarnadine and leaf of gold and silver.

Idly she read on:

> Nicely upon Her skin disposing Her beautiful raiment,
> Herself with gold adorning, laughter-loving Aphrodite
> Swept on Her way toward Troy, leaving sweet-perfum'd
>   Cyprus:

Swift so, high amid clouds, fulfilling Her journey.
Thus came She to Ida, many-fountain'd mother of beast-kind,
And so by straight path thorough the mountain; and here
  about Her
Grey wolves fawning, and lions with eyes glad-glaring,
And bears, and fleet-footed panthers of roe-deer's flesh
  unsatiate,
Went. She at that sight took pleasure, both bowels and
  spirit within Her.
And cast in their breasts desire, till they, of one motion,
Paired and lay with each other in shadowy mountain
  nest-beds.

Fiorinda put down her book and lay back luxuriously, clasping
her hands behind her head. Her hair, not plaited, but tied with a
single gold-lace ribbon and having for its self-colour a jet-like
blackness that held, where the sun caught it, shimmerings and
sparks of heaven's blue, rumpled its dark splendours against the
satin cushion. In a confusion of twists and tendrils it strayed here
over the cushion's crimson, here past ivoried smoothness of neck
and arm; one deep-convoluting tress reaching out, like as a many-
headed hydra, its curling ends to shadow vine-like the white silk
bosom of her gown, under which her ripening breasts gently with
her breathing rose and fell.

After a while, the sun wheeling lower began to strike golden
between the branches, full on the back-strained pure lovely throat
of her: wrought marble to look upon, by the firmness of its
contours, were it not for the fluttering pulse of blood in it. Her
eyes were closed drooping their night-black fringes above high
cheekbones which (and also something estranged and unreinable
in the very lure of her lips, that were lightly parted now to the
quickened coming and going of her breath) brought to mind, but
faintly only and distantly, as things Olympian may things of earth,
the features of her brother. Her nose, for its falcon-like keenness
and mobility of wing and nostril, was her true maternal grandfather's, Emmius's; but delicatelier moulded, and with aphrodisian

seductions ensweetening and ensphering to very heaven the Parry
pride and hardness.

There was a kindling might of summer rising now, against the
common tide of nature at this hour of declining day and at this
young season of the year; an invading heat, that heightened the
musky moist scents of spring to an urgence beyond use and beyond
imagination. In that warmth and that languor, she let her right
hand reach down over the swung hammock's edge. It touched the
new growth of a narcissus: stiff, green, eager fingers, thrusting up
through grass, out of the awakening earth beneath her. With this
for hand-hold to begin with, then letting go and yielding herself
to an almost imperceptible shifting of her weight back and forth
under the gathering rhythm, she began to swing the couch she lay
on: back and forth, without all effort, yet with slowly increasing
power. The heavenly unnatured warmth, and these spring-scents
stung to drunkenness with the summer-strangeness in the air about
her, waxed and grew with the motion of that swinging till they
seemed to swallow up the whole vast universe of sense and thought
and being, dissolving her like a sweet in the goblet in an over-
whelming Elysian languor.

When at last she unclosed her eyelids, the sun was about setting:
a flattened ball of incandescence that suffused the whole arch of
the sky westwards with a blush of tremulous light. Not a breath
stirred. She stood up, aery-delicate in the pallour of her silken
gown, but bearing, in the light lilt and sway of her carriage, patent
of some hitherto unthought-of power new born. The day-birds'
voices were hushed, save for here and there the call of a water-hen
going to bed, or a dabchick's trill of high bubbling notes, sweet
naiad music trembling to silence. The nightingales had not yet
begun their night-song. She looked about her, as to assure herself
that no human presence was here to spy her solitude, then put off
her shoes and stockings. Standing on the verge, her left hand upon
a branch at shoulder-level to steady her, her right kilting her skirt,
she dipped a foot into the darkening water. The cool of it warmed
to the touch, as if some property within her had power to raise

summer heats even in that inert element, home of newt and water-beetle and roach and char. Ripples travelling across the pool from her paddling foot broke the reflections. She stood back, both feet on the bank again. The ooze welled up luscious and warm between her toes through the grass-roots.

The sun being gone now and the after-glow fast fading in the west, a bower of moonrise began to open from behind the hills eastward. In the midst of this presently the virgin-cold moon appeared. Yet still that unearthly warmth, spring-like in its newness, summer-like in its depth and potency, grew and strengthened. Fiorinda, as utterly surrendered up to these influences, surveyed for a while, now up, now down, the moon-drenched obscurities of land and sky, the ground and the sleepy waters at her feet, and night's thousand eyes opening one by one. Then she laughed, in herself, very low, soundlessly. All the adoring earth seemed to laugh and open its arms to her.

For the first time, with only the moon for tiring-maid, she began to put up her hair: braided it, then coiled and piled it high on her head; and finding her hair-ribbon unsufficient to hold it there, took off her girdle of white silk and margery-pearls to bind up the heavy tresses, with two brooches from the bosom of her gown to learn a new office as hair-pins. She leaned her out over the water, to have viewed herself so; but, with the moon behind her, could see nought to her purpose only but dark shadow outlined against a background of dusky blue twig-fretted sky and glimmer of star-images deep below all. Turning again, she saw where there sat, on a birch-tree's limb not a dozen paces from her, the shape of a little owl, erect, clear-outlined against the moon. Suddenly it took wing and lighted without sound, upon her proffered wrist: a being that seemed without weight or substance, and the clasp of its claws upon her tender skin harmless as those sweet smarts that are fireworkers to pleasure. She raised her arm, to look level in its round fierce eyes; but it lowered its gaze. The trembling of it, sitting there, sent little shudders up her arm and through her whole body. With her free hand she stroked its feathers, then brought it near to her lips. Gentle as a turtle-dove with his mate,

it fell to billing her, trembling in the doing of it, like a young
untutored lover at first kiss of his mistress: then suddenly upon
noiseless downy wing departed. In that sudden she was ware of
Mistress Anthea standing beside her, regarding her from eyes
coruscant with yellow fire, and holding up to her a looking-glass
edged about with three rows of moon-stones that shone with their
own light.

Fiorinda abode motionless beholding how, from that mirror
and lighted by that enchantment of stones, her own face looked
out at her: a face new-wakening in a soft self-amazement, and
still, perhaps, half asleep. The eyes, large, almond-shaped, set almost
infinitesimally aslant, and infinitesimally at variance between themselves, altering and altering again in their sea-green deeps yet ever
the same in the sweet level lines of their under-lids, gave to the
slender sweep of black eyebrows and to the lovely open purity of
brow above them and to the proud and immitigable characters in
nose and mouth and cheek, a bewitchment of newness and time-
lessness, and agelessness. Suddenly, even while she looked, the
mirror was gone, and before her no longer her own face but
Anthea's, staring upon her in a kind of awe and wonder. It was
as though, in this creature, there stood before her but a thousandth
part, perhaps, of her own self; and, in Campaspe (who waited too
at hand now, ready to help her on with her cloak), another, all
different, thousandth part. Taking the cloak about her, for the
Meszrian spring was sobered to its natural self again, and the
night-breeze came cool from the river, she said to Anthea, 'There's
more difference between me of yesterday and Me tonight than
between you in your girl-skin, Madam Fuff-cat, and you in your
fur and claws.' At the under-musics in her voice, all the April night
seemed to hold its breath and listen.

But Anthea at these words, all decencies cast aside, fell to
leaping in and out of her lynx-dress, gambolling about her mistress,
fawning upon her, rolling and bowling herself, rubbing her head
against her, hugging and kissing her feet and ankles, till Fiorinda's
hair was fallen down again about her shoulders, and herself fallen
backwards on the couch, weak with laughter. Campaspe, as

betwixt joy and terror at these extremes, took safety in her water-rat shape and, seated in mid-stream upon a lily-leaf, from that secure refuge awaited the riot's ending.

Fiorinda stood up: called them to heel, and then to their true shapes again: bade them, with girdle and brooches where they belonged, bring to rights her dress: last, with the hairband of gold lace, tie her hair. That performed, they soberly accompanied her, on her way homewards at last, through the open field dewy and white with moonshine.

'Men call it the star of Artemis,' Campaspe said after a while, in a whisper, gazing on the moon's face.

Fiorinda threw back her head in a slightly disdainish, half-mocking, half-caressful little motion of silent laughter. 'What is Artemis,' said she, 'but My very Sister? part of Myself: a part of Mine.'

'And Pallas,' said Campaspe as, like an unbodied shadow on air, the owl floated by.

'Her too. Is a kind of engine in my soul too.'

They were come, maybe, another hundred paces in silence when Anthea spoke: very low, and with a glitter of pointed white teeth under the moon, 'And Hekate?'

'Yes. But when that shall be stirring in My blood, it is time for dogs to howl, and even for the gorgons to veil their eyes and cry out for the darkness to cover them.'

The learned doctor was waiting in the castle gate. Kissing her hand, he peered closely in her face, then kissed her hand again. 'I am glad,' he said, 'that your ladyship is safe home.'

In Fiorinda's eyes looking up into his was a conscient merriment, as feasting on some secret knowledge shared by her with no person of this world save with him only and these nymphs. 'But why this new ceremoniousness of "ladyship," reverend sir?' she said.

'I think,' answered Vandermast, 'your ladyship is now awake to your very Self. And wisest now to entreat You as such.'

XXIX

ASTARTE

Pax Mezentiana was begun now to rest deep on the land: a golden age, lulled with airs blown, a man could have believed, from Zayana, or Memison, or Lornra Zombremar. This most of all in Meszria and Rialmar. But even upon the factions in the Middle Kingdom, peace strewed her poppies; under cover of which the Vicar, by firm government, by lavishness in hospitality, and by a set policy of fastening a private hold on each man worthy his attention (laying them under obligations to his person, or holding over them his knowledge of some secret misdoing which they would wish least of all to see brought to light), was, without show but with patience and with thoroughness, consolidating his power in Rerek.

The King, for his part, held by his old wont of progresses, constant so as no corner of the Three Kingdoms but had either the fresh remembrance, or early expectation, or instant taste, of his presence; like as roosting birds should taste, familiar under their feet, the comfort of their tree's perdurable might. His occupation was much with merriments and light pleasures, sauced with philosophical disputations and with princely pastimes, as to see his gyrfalcons fly at the crane, heron, and wild swan, or to hunt wolf and bear; but greatly, amid all these doings, with overseeing of and giving order for the training up of his fighting men in all arts of war and feats of endurance

and might and main. Those nearest in his counsels, well thinking
that lust for great performance grows with full feeding, noted
how he had furnished forth that young Lord Lessingham to find
out distant countries beyond seas and observe and learn their
several powers, riches, and (most of all) any novel and good
ways they might have devised for waging of war, and so at five
years' end to come back and report to him of these matters.
They smelt, though, in his mood at this time something of that
evening-sleepiness which, in skin-changers and berserks, used to
follow the bouts of fury and strength and blood-shedding. But
well they perceived that, spite of all this unaction and sometimes
seeming retirement within his own self, his sudden apprehension
and piercing wits were busy as of old with every eddy and trend
and deep current of the world about him; nor had they mistrust
(or if any had, a word with the King, as the wind and the sun
clear mists, was enough to end it) but that, whatsoever turn-
about might come of these smothering times of peace, a man
might as well eat hot coals as enter upon any perverse and evil
dealings in hope the King should not mark him, or should wink
at his misdemeanour.

Upon a May morning of the year seven hundred and seventy-four,
that Lady Fiorinda being now near upon completing of the eight-
eenth year of her age, the Chancellor and she were ridden forth
before breakfast to take the air along the sea-shore of the Korvish,
south from Zemry Ashery. The tide was out, so that the whole
of this silted-up southern arm of the Bishfirth, two or three miles
wide upon their bridle-hand, lay dry: firm level sand, white as
powdered marble, over which they galloped their horses the full
six miles to the waterhead, then halted and turned homewards.
Before them now, a little to the right in the far distance, the tide
began to come in, with a cross-wind from the east whipping it
to foam. Overhead, feathery trailers of white cloud streaked the
azure: a mistiness of spindrift whitened the sea-line beyond
the expanse of white sands: the slopes landward, above them on the
left, were misty-grey with olive trees: ahead, Zemry Ashery upon

its promontory showed dusky-blue, against the more cerulean and paler hues of the great mountains afar in the north, and with edgings of gold light where the sun took its eastern walls.

They rode leisurely at a walking-pace, the horses' breaths coming in clouds on the cool morning air after that long stretch of speed. Here and there they halted to peer from the saddle into the emerald depths of some great sea-pool, sometimes with an outcrop of jade-like rock at its bottom upon which limpets had their homes, and sea-anemones; some that slept, shiny lumps of sealing-wax, scarlet or dark brown; some that waked, opening flower-like faces in hope of sea-lice and other small deer to be their breakfast. And from chinks in these drowned rocks bosky growths of sea-weed spread fans and streamers, dark green, tan-colour, orange-tawny, and rusty red, from whose shadows little iridescent fishes darted in the sunlit stillness, or a crab crept sidelong. That brother and sister, being now more than half-way home, were pleasing themselves with the contemplation of one such little seaish garden of the nereids, when they were aware of a rider coming down to them through the olive-groves. He had that seat that belongs to a man that cannot remember the first time he bestrode a horse: as though, as in the centaur-kind, man's body and horse's were engrafted and one.

'Good morrow, my Lord Baias,' said the Chancellor, returning his salute. 'I'd a mind these three weeks past to a come to greet you as our next neighbour now, which glads me for long acquaintance sake. But I've been wonderful full of business.'

Fiorinda, looking up from her pool-gazing, turned in the saddle to have sight of him. His great stone-horse, winding her little mare, threw up his head: snorted, whinnied, pawed the ground. Baias struck him with the horn handle of his riding-whip a devilish blow on the jaw, and, but for fine horsemanship, had doubtless been thrown and killed for his pains, but after a short fight brought him to order. 'I am for Krestenaya, my lord Chancellor,' he said, his eyes returning still to the vision of her where she sat, mysterious against the light, "'pon a business with your own

armourer you told me of. Hath my best sword to mend. I hurt
it upon a swashing fellow bade me to the *duello*, weeks since,
ere I came south.'

'You hurt him worse than you hurt the sword?'

'Nay, that's certain. I hear a be dead.'

Beroald said, 'Let's ride on the way together. On a more fitting
occasion you must come and see us in Zemry Ashery.'

'Joyfully,' answered he, bringing his horse up upon Fiorinda's
right as they moved off. 'Have no fear, madam: he knoweth his
master.'

She replied by an almost unperceptible half-scornful little
backward lifting of her head, not looking at him but forward
between the mare's ears. The beauty of her face, lit with morning
and flushed with the wind, seemed to flicker between self-
contrarying extremes: sweets and lovelinesses drawing at their
train diamond-hard unswayables and that pride that binds the
devils: lips whose stillness was a pool where, like lotus-buds
closed under the sun's eye, delicate virginal thoughts and witty
fancies seemed to slumber, but rooted, far below that shining
and tranquil surface, in some elixir of darkness potent to shake
man's blood.

Baias spoke: 'Your lordship has forgot to do me that honour
to present me.'

'Cry you mercy. I'd forgot there was the need. This is my lady
sister.'

'Your sister?' Baias bent to kiss the hand she offered him,
crimson-gloved. There was here, as indeed in his every motion, a
certain taking haughtiness of manner; but easeful: begotten, not
court-bred. 'From what I'd heard tell,' he said to the Chancellor,
'I supposed her but a child yet. And yet, behold. You've kept her
very close, my friend.'

They rode awhile in silence, Baias with eyes still upon her. When
at length, turning her head, she met his gaze, he laughed merrily.
'Is your brother a blood-sucker, a troll-man, to a kept you so long
time closeted up from the world?'

Faintly raising her eyebrows, that seemed of their nature to carry an air of permanent soft surprise, she said, 'I am very well content with my company, thank you.'

'He is a very secret man. I know him of old and his ways. How comes it we are never honoured with a sight of your ladyship at the presences in Zayana?'

'Some day you may live to see such a thing.'

'There is time yet,' said her brother lightly. 'Over-hastiness was never a distemper in our family.'

After another silence, Baias said softly to her, 'Life's not long enough, in my seeming, to slack sail when a fair wind blows. But, for myself, to say true, I am by complexion hasty.' He paused, studying her face, sideways to him. 'I'm in hasty mood now,' he said.

Something not altogether unkind, betwixt comprehension and mockery, glinted at her mouth's corners as she said very equably, 'Then it were wrong in us to delay you further, my lord. Our horses are breathed, and I would not put them to speed again this morning.' She glanced round to her brother, who drew rein.

'Why there,' said Baias, 'spoke a true courtesy, and I'll act upon it.' They halted. In his eyes, meeting hers, sat some swift determination that seemed to stiffen the whole posture of his body and (as by infection) of the great horse's that carried him. 'But since here's parting of our ways, and delays breed loss,' said he, looking from her to Beroald and so again to her, 'I'll first, in great humility, request of your ladyship your hand in marriage.'

Save for the faintest satirical lift of eyebrows she made no response, only with great coolness regarding him.

'Was that over-sudden?' said Baias, noting the manner of her look, which was interested, meditative, removed; even just as she had looked down from above upon fishes and marauding crabs in the sea-pools' transparent deeps. 'Saw you but with my eyes, felt with my blood, you should not think so. Nay, sweet madam, take time, then, I pray you. But I pray you, for my peace sake, not too long time.'

'Your lordship were best ask my brother here, my guardian. I

am not yet of full age. Besides, as he told you but now, we are
not, of our family, rushers into unadvised decisions.'

'You're not offended at me, I hope?'

Fiorinda smiled: a shadowy ambiguous smile of lip and nostril,
her eyes still level upon him in that studious remote intention.

'Offended because you wish to marry her?' said the Chancellor.
''Tis the best compliment he could a paid you, sister.'

'Is it?' Then, to Baias: 'O, not offended. Surprised, perhaps.
Perhaps a little amused. Pity your lordship should have to wait
for your answer to so natural a demand.'

'Admired and uncomparable lady, be not angry with me. I'll
wait. But beseech you, not too long.'

'Depends of the answer. Too long, you may think, if answer be
good; but if t'other way, you'd then have at least the comfort of
delay to thank me for. We meet again?' she said, giving him her
hand.

'If I thought not,' kissing it and holding it longer than need
were in his, 'God for witness, I'd go stab myself.' With that, like
a man unable to hold the lid longer on a boiling pot, Baias struck
spurs into his stallion's flanks and, with great rearings and tossings
of mane and clatter of hooves, departed.

The lady said, after a few minutes' silence as, alone together
once more, they came their way: 'A turn I least looked for in you,
brother. And gives me strangely to think.'

'What do you mean?'

'As good as hold me out like a piece of merchandise to this
friend of yours, by I know not what fair promises made to him
behind my back; and no leave asked of me.'

'You're quite mistook, I'd ne'er made mention of you.'

'Strange. If true.'

'This is the nature of him: ever rash and sudden. But a man of
many and remarkable virtues, and of high place in the land.'

'Does he think I am so agog for a husband, there's nought to do
but whistle on his fist and I'll hop to him?'

'Come, you're too bitter. 'Tis not unpardonable in a man to
know his own worth.'

'Nor in a woman. But I think he hath eyes for no other worth than his own.'

Beroald said, with an ironic twitch of his nostrils, 'You cooled any such hare-brained thought as that in him ere we parted.'

After another silence: 'I still suspect you as of his party, brother. By your talk. By your praises.'

'Well, the man is a friend of mine. And friends are useful.'

'The uses of friendship! And sisters, too, made for use?'

'I shall not answer that.' Their glances countered: a kind of merry hand-fast in the air, while that thing at the corner of Fiorinda's mouth conjured some dim earth-bound shadow of itself on the Chancellor's stony lip. 'Only,' he said, cold, careless, judicial again, 'if there your fancy should chance to light, I confess 't should not displease me.'

'How old is this friend?'

'Of some five years' standing.'

'His age, I meant?'

'O, of my age, I suppose, within a year or two.'

'Old enough to have known, then, I'd have thought, that a girl's hand is to be suited for, not guttishly demanded.' She added, after a pause: 'As call for a pottle of ale in a tavern.'

They rode on, a mile or so: no word spoken, the Lord Beroald watching her. When at length their eyes met there was that in hers that seemed to hold him again at arm's-length as if, upon revolving the matter, she was not to be persuaded but that they now no longer played each other's game, but he his, she hers. Beroald smiled. 'Forget the man.'

'Pew! One needs remember in order to forget.'

'I count him but our instrument. No more but that. Forget him.'

'Alas, poor instrument! He and I have at last some fellow-feeling there, then.'

'I'll not have you think such a thought.'

'No? You are a skilful player at the chess, brother; but when you would use me for your pawn—'

'That's a wicked lie, and you know it. Where were my skill, if

I knew not the difference 'twixt pawn and queen? Both in the
worth and in the manage.'

'Where indeed? But I am not for your political chessboard, in
whichever capacity: to be moved about. I begin to find I have an
appetite,' she said, in a pensiveness now, delicately inclining to
stroke her horse's neck, 'to be my own self-mover.'

That same day at evening, upon bidding goodnight, Beroald said
to her, 'I will make you a promise which, until this unlucky turn
this morning, I'd have thought needless between you and me. It
is this: never to use you, unless of your own free motion or consent,
for a means to ends of mine.'

In Fiorinda's eyes was a twinkle of the mind between sceptic
caution and comical intuition, touched with a kind of love. 'Thanks,
noble brother: let's make this bargain mutual. And hold me not
ungracious that I do fear th' engagement may prove harder for
you to abide by than for me 'twill be.'

'Come, be just to each other. For me, what is't but stick to what
hath become my natural habit since first you could prattle?'

'I think,' said she, playing with his fingers, 'you may find it less
easy now.' Then, looking up, and very demurely and sweetly putting
her arms about his neck: 'We understand each other?'

As a sophister should at need speak smooth words at the Sphinx,
'I think so,' said the Chancellor; and so saying, with an unbelieving
twist of his lean lips, beheld shadows of things past all understanding, unmapped stars of bale and of bliss, come and go in the
profundities of his young sister's eyes.

'Good,' she said, and kissed him. Laughing, they took hands,
and so goodnight. He watched her go up the shining staircase; a
beauty of motion that was intertangled as in counterpoint with
the beams of lamplight and candlelight faintly swaying; then, with
the same unbelieving smile on his lips, betook him to his study.

The Lord Baias's wooing, thus hastily begun and ever the more
furiously urged and with an impatience the angrier and the sharper
set as it became more manifest what dance his mistress meant to

lead him, dragged and tarried through the summer. In the end (more, it was commonly suspicioned, with a mind to humour her brother than for any inordinate liking for her suitor's person), she accepted him. A few days later (early September) they were wed in Krestenaya with circumstance and ceremony befitting their noble station, and so with honour and rejoicing brought home to Masmor.

After the first month guests began to be received, and greatly was Baias envied his fair and lovely bride. Some, with more inquiring eyes and shrewd minds observing the climate, tasted uneasiness in the house, spite of all outward gaiety. It was noted moreover that Baias and his lady seldom accepted invitations in the countryside but kept much to their own society, and that she, for her part, was never seen in Zayana. Some that were very knowing said, wagging their beards, that the Chancellor's hand was in this, contriving, through Baias, to continue still his old policy of seclusion. Howsoever, it was the household folk at Masmor that had best commodiousness to acquaint themselves with these affairs, and with other little things besides. And now, as the season drew on toward mid November, it began to be merrily whispered among them that not only had her ladyship had since some time past her own chamber, but her lord was nowadays not seldom exiled to his own bed for several nights together.

These misspeakings coming at length to Baias's ear, he took marvellous displeasure at them: let seize three of the girls deemed guilty of such tittle-tattle: duck them in the castle pond; then scissors, for well shorting and clipping away of their garments to large show of their naked thighs: for last disgrace, off with their hair; and so, in that dishonest and ugly pickle, pack them home. Whether upon suspicion of this talk's having a higher source than the mouths it had been heard drop from, or whether for a spite fed by deeper springs wholly removed from these, he now upon some slight unclear pretext sent for Anthea and Campaspe. These maidens being come before him he used very roughly, speaking doggery at them: calling them a pair of fleering slavish parasites, whose jibes behind his back (because he was not book-learned) he highly disdained any longer to endure: bade them therefore within one hour void clean out of the castle and no more resort to the same. 'Any she that disobeys, her hair goes off for it. That's blushed your cheeks, ha? And not to be compounded by a minute's perfunctory scissoring such as sufficed this morning. O, no: you ladies would be honoured with very respectful care and tendance: have it close shorn to begin with: then the razor. Fear nothing; you need but dispose yourselves as convenience of shaving may require, and so sit still, gently resigned up to have it taken so, with extreme particular dainty, everywhere all completely off, quite and clean. Ponder on that. If you have no desire for such a needful service to be done unto you, study to meddle with your own business and obey my command. And now begone. Nay then, come you back a moment, you laughing minxes: one more word. Flatter not yourselves with the vain conceit that being gentlewomen exempts you from the barber. Were you never so noble born, upon my honour as a Meszrian lord I swear to you, it should off. Trespass you but once; clipped, soaped, and faithfully shaven you shall be, nesh and smooth as two little sea-pigs. Except your eyelashes, for I'll not be cruel, there's not one hair shall remain upon.'

My Lady Fiorinda took no overt notice of this undecent severity against her domestics nor of the dismissal of her waiting-gentlewomen, as though she would have it supposed that she thought it best to suffer the order of the world to manage her, for this present, without further inquisition. In truth, she herself was put to but very slight inconvenience; for Anthea and Campaspe, unshaping their bodies to their customary disguise of beast or bird, were able at all times of day or night to be present at need in Masmor. It is not to be thought that their nymphish minds misdoubted their lady's inward peace; for how (they might in their innocency question) should She, that holds in Her own self the world everlasting and unbegotten, She for whom all worlds are made, behold or know unhappiness? For all that, they scented trouble. Many a time, as the days grew shorter and the sap sunk and even in these soft sea-lands of South Meszria light ground-frosts sometimes sharpened the breath of night, Mistress Anthea licked her lips and, as frost makes the fire glow brighter in the grate, so the upright slits of her eyes burned with a more fulvid splendour. Many a time too, in her lynx-dress, she frighted her sister, chasing her for her sport. And had Baias been a man of less lion-like metal, having the ordinary aptness to obey the heart-emptying touch of fear, he were like to have been frighted too: beholding from the solitude of his bed, and not once or twice only, during these nights of the dying year in the chill betwixt midnight and dawn, those beast-eyes stare upon him, out of the black and silent darkness. The third time, a little before Yule, he said to Fiorinda at breakfast that albeit she seemed, for reasons of her own, to prefer to sleep a-nights oftener with her mountain cat than with him, himself had no such preference; and unless she would promise to kennel the beast henceforth and to give him her company nightly, as of old, as a wife should, he would without further warning dispatch it with his hunting-knife. The lady listened, her green eyes cold upon him as frozen pebbles on a sea-beach under the moon. She replied: '"First serve, syne suit," I've heard say. But that is no maxim of yours, my lord, as I have found from the beginning, more's the pity.' With that, she left the table.

Late the same afternoon, Baias being ridden abroad upon some business and not expected home before supper-time, my Lady Fiorinda was walking her alone in the borders of those great oak-woods that train southwards along the skirts of the hills from Masmor. Here she was met with the learned doctor. After greetings they stood silent awhile, Vandermast's eyes from beneath their jutting thatch of white eyebrow searching her face in the uncertain and now fast fading light under the trees.

'Your ladyship walks alone?' he said presently. 'Where be my little disciples?'

'You must not ask me questions to which you already know the answer.'

'Nay, I worded it amiss, my mind being wholly taken up with

your ladyship's affairs and forgetting that sometimes it is right and needful we attend to matters contingent. I know they are in Lornra Zombremar, having myself, by means of a certain crystal, beheld them there this morning. But I would have asked why.'

'I sent them away after breakfast, with order to dwell for a while in their true shapes, sometimes there, sometimes in Memison, and not to return, in whatever dress, until I shall send for them.'

'You are all alone, then?'

'All alone, with my lord. The time has come when it is best for us to be alone.'

Doctor Vandermast regarded her narrowly. Then he said: '*Res nullo modo neque alio ordine a Deo produci potuerunt, quam productae sunt*: Things were not able to be brought to being by God in any other manner, nor in any other order, than as they have in fact been brought. And yet this thing is, to my confined and but part-conceiving intellects, absurd: an irrational uncogitable. I mean, your ladyship's having art or part in this Baias.'

'Indeed it is certain,' she said, turning her colour and with a curl of the lip, 'he is, albeit a man of great birth and courage, very smally sensed; save in one particular and there he is a mere commonplace fellow and little deserving of so sanctified a gift: an enslaver of women, hapt in a most unlucky hour upon one he hath not the art to enslave. The nearer known, the more unsufferable he is, I think.'

'Beloved and honoured Mistress,' said the doctor, 'being yours while life swayeth within me, and knowing your ladyship, may be, better than sometimes you do know yourself, I consider not of this. For to you there is nought uneasy to achieve. But when I consider of these honest humble harmless children, the great offences and misbehavings he hath done against them as lambs voiceless before their shearer, and abominably purposeth the like against my pretty nymphs—'

'Mew!' said she, breaking in upon him: 'these are light occasions of small moment. But if you must know, no harm's done. My lord Chancellor, by my request, harboureth them in Zemry Ashery: when fit to be seen again, will be ta'en into his household there.

There are other privacies committed to my charge more trouble-
some and of far weightier import than these. As by proof will
appear. And if you think not, reverend sir, your love towards me
is not such as our watchful friendship towards you hath deserved.'

Vandermast held his peace. For a minute in silence now, that
lady steadily beheld him. The hueless cold light of the winter sun
setting unseen behind thick cloud-banks was yet strong enough
for his eyes, gazing into hers and upon her countenance, to see,
for that minute, the truth of her: her eyes tender as a dove's: in
the bird's-wing curve of her eyebrows a timeless question that
seemed to attend no answer: in her nose, a critical outward-regarding
superbity that judged without appeal, and an all-transcending
power dwelling serene in each exquisite line (carved by Him who
carved the lily's purity) of bridge and tip and wing and thought-
disclosing nostril. Her lips were lightly pursed together, as in a
divine demur between doubt and unrelenting will: their sudden
up-turns at the corners held, through these strained moments, a
gravity of annealed barbed hooks forged from a half-regretful
gentleness: turtle's breast changed to adamant by infection of
some unturnable spirit that informed the strength of her underlip,
clear-cut and level above the slender firmness of her chin. Worlds'
wonder and heaven's uncloying commonplace seemed, on these
lips, to lie stilled in immortal meditation; wherein, as things
partly asleep, love and scorn, and a high Olympian quintessence
of inward laughter, and those hearts of pity and ineffable sadness
that throb unseen beneath all glory and honour and beauty and
beyond all worlds' endings, seemed to rest, and, as Gods may
grieve, to grieve.

'Is it not the way of Them that keep the wide heaven,' she said,
and her voice was gentle as falling shadows of night, 'to give scope
to whomsoever shall require it of Them, that none may needlessly
perish? But there cometh always an hour of decision. Lest eternity
itself be parcelled out in too unprofitable leases.'

'The ways of Her are unscrutable,' said that old man, slowly
and softly, after a long pause.

'Your deep discerning wisdom,' she answered, 'has never

disappointed me.' She was wearing, against the wintry weather, a great cloak of rich black sables fastened at the throat with clasps of hammered silver. She opened it: flashes, under his eyes for a timeless instant, Her beauty that can by its glory darken heaven and consume to ashes all worlds: then, muffling her cloak again about her, was gone: through the trees, back to Masmor.

Left so, the aged doctor stood fixed: blinded for the while, uncertain of his direction, as a man whose light has been suddenly blown out stands lost in pitch darkness; but Vandermast, for all his darkness, stood rapt in that vision that never until today (he said to the self within himself) was vouchsafed to mortal eye.

Ten days later, upon New Year's Eve in Masmor, supper done and the guests departed, her ladyship was sat idly reading before a fire of cedar-wood in her own bower that opened off the main hall. To her left, upon a three-legged table of walnut inlaid with ivory and mother-of-pearl and arabesques of silver, nine candles in a great crystal candlestick gave a gentle and companiable light, pleasant for reading. These, and the lamplight, and the firelight, and the transmuted splendours, begotten of all three, which glowed in the inwards of the twin escarbuncles, big as gold-crest's eggs, at her ears and sparkled from the facets of the pendant of the same blood-dark stone that slumbered above her breasts, seemed to be things without substance save as part of her: part of her body's grace: visible emanations of the spirit that informed that body so that it held within itself (mixed and made one, as stillness and the extreme of ruinous power unite at a great whirlpool's centre) the ruin of worlds and the untarnishable eternity of every world's desire.

Baias, in a seeming discontent and irresolution, paced the room, his eyes returning to her as moth to candle-flame. 'What were you and Melates discoursing of?' he said, coming to a stand at last over against her, his back to the fire.

'Pleasant nothings,' she answered, without looking up.

He came and sat on the arm of her chair. 'Talk some to me.'

'I pray you begin, then,' she said, continuing her reading.

"Twill be a pleasant change when you do as I wish, for once in a while,' said he: then noting the little mocking lift of her head, snatched her book and threw it on the floor. 'We might agree better that way.'

Fiorinda rose, saying under her breath, 'Oh how long? how long? It is half a death to me, this.'

'What do you mean, "this"?'

'If you would be answered, let go of my skirt.'

'Sit down, then,' he said, letting go, and sitting himself in her chair. 'Here.'

She remained standing, looking him steadily in the eyes.

'Very well,' he said, and stood up again: thrust his face close to hers. 'You like to stand, 'cause you are more than common tall? Beware, though, how you look down on me.'

'Don't touch me, you were best.'

'I haven't, for a fortnight. That were a pleasant change, too.'

'To you, maybe. We have our several tastes in these matters.'

Upon that he seized her: mouth kissing her fiercely, her throat, her eyes, her lips, and between her breasts: hands greedy upon her: while she like a very dead thing abode in his arms, suffering all, inert, hard, and without response. After a while he desisted: swung round from her and, under the sting and fury of that flesh-enraging madness, kicked the table over.

Fiorinda, standing where he had left her, hair fallen down, dress disordered, yet in an imperial immobility, looked on. 'Poor table. What had that done to be kicked? Have you hurt your toe?'

'Pick up those candles. Would you have us all burn?'

She remained without stirring. Baias, halting on his right foot, set in order table and candles again: then stood glaring upon her. 'Fut, I cannot fathom you: this strained modesty: counterfeit coyness. Or is it some prank, some new fantasticness of whorism? What end do you look of it? Are you a woman? Or a tormenting Fury, sent to make me kill you and then myself? Were we wed for that?'

'Perhaps we were. You know better than I.'

Sitting him down again in her chair, 'Get you to bed, madam,' he said, avoiding her gaze. 'I'll give you ten minutes for unreadying of yourself. Then I'll follow and make my peace; and an end so, I hope, of these jars and bickerings.'

That lady, looking down on him, searched his face for a moment, but still his eyes avoided hers. She turned and, with head bowed, walked very slowly to the door: paused there, and with head erect looked on him again. Their eyes met. 'You desire me,' she said, 'but you do not know, nor desire to know, how to make love to me.' He glowered upon her in silence, the sweat shining on his brow, the great veins standing out thick and hard on his temples. 'And,' she said, her hand behind her on the door-latch, 'so it has been from the beginning: a disableness in you, I suppose, to understand what things, and when, please me, and what displease.' She opened the door: then, turning her again to face him: 'In brief, you are a gluttonous and malignant fool.'

With that, she was gone.

Baias sat still as death. His hands, that had a sheen on the backs of them of delicate golden hair, were clamped upon the chair's arms. His eyes were on the clock. When it was a little past eleven he stood up and with firm but noiseless tread went from the room and so upstairs, and, being come to his lady's bedchamber, tried the door. It was bolted on the inside. Smoothing the accents of his voice, albeit like a hot proud horse his high blood quivered in them, 'Open,' he said, 'my love, my dew-pear, my earth's delight. Open, and I will you the order of all that I have. Let me in. I love you.'

He stood listening: not a sound from within. So still it was, he might hear the clock ticking in the hall below. He shook the door. She said, from inside, 'No opening of doors to you tonight, my lord.' And, upon his shaking it again: 'If you look for any more love-liking, in your life, betwixt you and me, importune me no more tonight'

Baias made as if to charge against the door with his shoulder: break the bolt if he might; but, ruling himself, went away.

My Lady Fiorinda listened until the sound of her lord's foot-steps, of his going downstairs and across the hall, ceased and everything was still. Then, smiling, she set to to disapparel herself and, suddenly serious, stood awhile betwixt fire and mirror to

contemplate with cool appraising eye, like as that morning seven
months ago she had examined from horseback the sun-lit sea-
pools of the Korvish, the wonder of her own face and of all her
naked beauties. Even as thought against thought, passion against
passion, and all against each, made up the ever-changing bewitchments of her face: even as, throughout this other enchanted
queendom, of her body, from throat to toe, from shoulder to
finger-tip, some deep harmony between conflicting superlatives
issued in a divine perfection: so between these two several queen-
doms was utter diversity in kind swept up to unity. In the face,
her soul sat free: now bared, now all or in part disguised or veiled.
In body's loveliness, through lively and breathing balance of form
with form and of her three fair colours (white, red, and that
blackness whose outbraidings are but one mode, of many divine
and coequal, of the pure empyreal fire), shone the peace of Her
beauty that to its eternal substance subsumes both earth and
heaven. Each queendom by itself, face alone (incarnate soul) or
body alone (incarnate spirit), were a thing abstracted: soul without
platform or warmth or stature: spirit without understanding and
without truth. But that were an impossible. Spirit, within and
without, suggested this soul; and this soul spirit. Soul's beauty
and spirit's were in an untimed ecstasy so steeped in each other,
and by each other interpenetrated, that, without question of the
outward hierarchy, each feature and lineament of her face and
each particular treasure of her body, each flicker of an eyelid,
each moving or stillness of swan-smooth surface, each filigree
delicacy of jet-black hair, was inwardly of equal honour and
worth, as implicate with all the remain and, wholly as each of
these, postulating and ensphering both them and Her. So that
here stood She in very presence; self-exiled (doubtlessly for some
such Olympian purpose as she had foreshown to Vandermast) to
this house of Masmor. With a narrowing of eyes that seemed
snake-like now, and with a deadly twist of some quality never,
may be, noted until now even by herself, of some tigerishness and
pride and unmercilessness in the contours of her lips, she smiled
again. In a whisper that, to hear, should have struck chill to a

man's veins and sent the blood fleeing to the heart, she said: 'Not a commodity. Not to be had by choosing or by slices, as eat a chicken. Not that, whether for man or God. And the reward of inveterate transgression, death.'

In her bower below, meanwhile, Baias threw logs on the dying fire, then sat in her chair, fidging and musing. Her book lay on the floor beside him, where he had thrown it. He picked it up. It opened at Anchises's second speech in the *Hymn to Aphrodite*:

> If mortal, then, thou beest, and woman the mother that
>   bare thee;
> Otreus of name renown'd thy father, as thou averrest;
> If thou through grace of the deathless Guide be hither-
>   ward comen,
> Thro' Hermes, and wife of mine must be call'd to
>   everlasting:
> Then shall none, were't whether of Gods or of men mortal,
> Me constrain nor hold, till mixt in love I have thee,
> Instant now: not were Far-darting very Apollo
> Launch from 's bow of silver the arrows that worketh
>   groanings.
> Wittingly I thereafter, O woman Goddess-seeming,
> So but first I mount thy bed, would sink to the House of
>   Hades.

'Yes,' said Baias, closing the book and with shaking hand putting it by: 'so that's the trash she reads. And he had, at that time, but his own imaginings to light that hot fire in him. How much more I, that have proved and know?'

Wine and goblets stood on a side-table. He walked over to it; poured a cup; drank; returned to her chair. Quarter by quarter and hour by hour, the clock's chimes led on the watches of the night. At two o'clock, after nigh upon three hours of sitting so, he drank a second cup of wine and went upstairs again to listen. There was not a sound, save only of her breath taken peacefully in sleep. Her sleep, by native habit and suited to her years, was quiet and profound. It was dark in the passage. A faint glow of firelight showed under her door and in the chink between door and door-jamb. Baias went to his own room, a few paces along the passage, shut the door silently, and leaned out of the window nearest hers. The night was moonless, but clear and starry. From sheer hunger for her and from hard staring to make sure that her casement stood open, as even in these winter nights was her custom so to have it, his eyes watered and smarted. He leaned out: measured the distance with his eye, window-ledge to window-ledge: said in his mind, "Tis the road her cat-a-mountain took. Where that can go, there can I': stood now erect on the broad outer sill, steadying himself by hand-grip on the roll-moulded top edge of the stone architrave above his head. It was as if some unvoiced menace spoke out of the night's star-lit stillness to the proud will of him standing there: as to say, *Leap not*. He took a mighty leap sideways, face to the wall: landed with both hands clutching upon her window-sill with a jerk enough to have broken the finger-joints or dislocated the shoulders of another man, but by main strength hung on, and by the might of his arms and with scrabbling of toes against the wall pulled himself up till, half in half out of the window, he could rest at last: a thirty-foot drop below him on the outer side; but inside, the slumbrous glow from embers on the hearth; the assurance of her presence; the undisturbed sound of her sleeping, peaceful as a child's.

Next morning she rode into Zemry Ashery, gave her horse to the grooms, went up usherless to the Chancellor's study, and there found him but just finishing his breakfast. She sat her down at the far side of the table, facing him, her back to the window and the sunrise.

'An unlooked-for pleasure to begin my day with. You have breakfasted?'

She shook her head and, when he would have risen to pull the bell, prevented him with a look. He took a bit of marmalade and waited.

'I'm come home,' she said at last, looking down with the

question in her eyebrows, while with one jewelled finger she moved a plate in circles before her on the sandalwood table.

'But why?'

'Decided that I do not care any longer for married life.'

A sardonic smile flickered across the granite features of the Chancellor. 'Why?' he said, and she shrugged and looked at him: a strange look. The look of a lily that has been rudely handled: but no entreaty in it, no asking for pity.

He poured out two cups of white hippocras: pushed one across the board for her. She left it untouched. He finished his breakfast in silence, as it to let her take her time. When she looked at him again her eyes were stone-hard, like a snake's eyes, but, for all that, piercingly piteous now; as though here were some proud implacable thing, armed with a merciless power, come to him in its unhappiness as a hurt child to its mother.

'Is't there the wind sits?' said Beroald. 'Anchises begins to show the defects of a mortal man? A rough herdsman, albeit a prince?'

'Let's not talk Greek. There was Roman ways rather. A rape of the Sabines last night.' She gave him a steady look, then suddenly rose up and went across to the fireplace to stand there with her back to him. The curve of her neck as she looked down into the flames: back hair sitting exquisitely in the nape of it, gleaming, smooth-wound, pear-shaped, voluptuously coiling down upon itself, a black leopard, a sleeping danger: the pure and stately lines of her body, amphora-like, giving nobility to every hanging fold of her pleated skirt: as the Chancellor looked and beheld these things, his lean lips and clipped mustachios and the lines of his shaven jaw and chin seemed changed to iron.

He began a stalking up and down the room, hands clasped behind his back, and so after a turn or two placed himself to front her, a little on her right, his shoulders against the mantelpiece. 'One should not strike a woman,' he said, 'even with a flower.'

'He did not strike me.'

The Chancellor studied her face. In this shadow cross-lit with the leaping fire-flames, it was like the Sphinx's. 'Shall I talk to him?' he said.

Fiorinda smoothed her dress. Very softly nodding, still looking wide-eyed into the fire, she answered in a low voice, clear and dispassionate: 'If you think it talking matter.' She looked up swiftly in his face with eyes that from their sphinxian coldness were suddenly become those of a frightened child: then bent her head for him to kiss her on the forehead. 'I was asleep,' she whispered close to his ear. 'In my own chamber, very well secured, to be from him for a while. Let himself in by the window, I suppose, without waking me. By some goatish trick, in my sleep, upon me: no help: the enemy in the gate.' She buried her face on her brother's shoulder, arms tight about his neck, sobbing and shuddering. 'I hate him. Dear Father in heaven, how I hate him.'

The next morning, not so unseasonable early as yesterday his lady, the Lord Baias came to see the Chancellor. He opened the matter with an easy frankness as between friends and brothers-in-law: a wretched inconvenience, not worth the time of day, save that it concerned her that was very dear to both of them. Main necessity was to clear with the business and stop report; and were it even for that sake alone (though he was most desirous not to hurry her) he earnestly wished her speedy return to Masmor. In this he doubted not he should have her brother's wise help, who knew as well as she did in what dear respect and love he held her. Maybe himself had been at fault too. Be that as might be, 'twere worst thing in the world were she, by tarrying over long time in Zemry Ashery, to set foolish tongues a-wagging; which, to say true, they had to his own knowledge already begun to do weeks ago, but he thought he had so far scotched that. There was nought behind it, save lovers' humours. And remember, 'twas yet but honeymoon.

At this last the Chancellor, who had listened in silence without stir of a muscle, smiled somewhat scornfully. 'For myself,' he said, 'I have never yet adventured me in the toils of wedlock, but I am enough otherwheres experienced to tell you that when a four-month honeymoon ends as this hath, 'tis time to end all. I'm sorry, my lord, but since as between kinsmen-in-law you seek my help and counsel, I can but counsel you to agree to a divorce, and that without pother or delay. Indeed, there's no choice else': here he gave him an ill look, and added, 'unless a worser.' So saying, chill and formal again, he rose from the table.

Baias rose too: his face scarlet, but his tongue well curbed. 'This is scarce the help I looked for,' he said, 'when I came hither to you. I must take time to think on't.'

'I will give your lordship twenty-four hours,' said Beroald, 'to accept my decision.'

'You speak high, my lord Chancellor.'

'It is my custom,' replied he with great coolness, 'when the occasion demands it. Fare you well. And consider with thoughtful care what I have said to you.'

'It shall not fail. Fare you well.'

With that went Baias forth from the room, and so down the wheel-stairs in the west turret, and so through the main hall. Thence in his way out, he chanced upon his lady as she came in from the garden. She turned ashy white: checked in her walk and seemed to hesitate how she might pass him, but the passage was narrow and he blocked up the way. He unbonneted: 'I came to ask forgiveness.'

'To make your peace? I' the fashion of Wednesday night?'

Baias, as letting this pass unnoted, said, 'There's no living soul I'd accept it from but you: much less ask it. For God sake, some place with closed doors. We cannot talk here.'

'Closed doors. Upon you and me!'

'The garden, then: care not for eyes, so there be no eavesdroppers. I entreat you. I am tame. But I cannot away afore this be some way mended.'

They went, whence she had come, into the garden. After a score of paces she halted. 'This is far enough. It is past mending.'

'God forbid.'

'I have made my brother my attorney. You must talk to him.'

Lord Baias set his jaw. 'Is your pride so devilish that you cannot be high-minded enough not to tread down mine, when like some humble miserable suitor to his sovereign lord I come to prostrate it before you?'

'My pride, God save the mark! When you've used me with such outrage as I'd a supposed a scullion, perfumed with grease, would have spared his meanest punk.'

'Must you cut my heart out? My fault was but my love for you.'

'I owe you thanks for that admission. Bear with my ignorance: I ne'er knew man till you. And truly this half-year's testing hath killed my appetite for more, if you be a right example.'

'By God's lid!' said Baias, as a man whose will is seldom wonted to be gainsaid, letting loose his passion, ''tis a perilous game you play, mistress, and a foolish. What aim you at? Are you levying faction against me? What have I done? Because your brother is the great Chancellor and grows here to great abominable purchase, think you by running to him with lies against me—'

'What needed lies? Truth was enough.'

'You're an ill wife. Yet hearken, for a last word: come you home with me.'

'I will die sooner.'

'Nay, then, I have a deeper vengeance is preparing for you. Filthy beauty. There's a man in this: men, more like. Well, 'tis Friday morn. If by Monday you be not come back, I counsel you keep yourself mewed in Zemry Ashery for the rest of your life. For I swear to you by my honour, if you prove loose in the hilts I'll take you to my fury. And I am a man that never missed of nothing yet that I took in hand. If, being your husband, I may not have you, I'll so deal with you as none else shall desire you. I'll slit your nose. Best cure, as most lasting, for such as you.'

Without more for goodbye, he left her: took horse and departed.

But my Lady Fiorinda stood a full minute motionless there, gazing after him. Upon her brow some dreadful ghastliness of old night seemed, frowning, to rise into its throne and to shed its garment as a veil over her slanting eyes' worm-glance darting, and cover her lips, changing them for the moment to things carved out of frozen blood. In the same hour she recounted to her brother, word by word, these things said to her by Baias. While Beroald listened, his lean countenance, flat in the cheekbones, wide between the eyes, clean cut about the jaw, close shaven save for the bristly mustachios, remained moveless as a stone. When she had done, 'Forget it,' he said, in a toneless voice, as cold and stately and as unreadable as his face. 'And forget him.' Their eyes met, and rested a moment together, as brother's and sister's who well understand each other.

Next day, in the afternoon, was news brought to the Chancellor in Zemry Ashery of a horrible fact committed in Krestenaya market-place: of the Lord Baias, coming down the piazza steps there in open sight of the people and the sun shining in full splendency, set upon at unawares and stabbed in by six men with daggers: his speech and senses taken suddenly away from him, yet lived awhile, 'but the surgeons told me,' said the messenger, 'it should not be long.' Of this, some hours later, the Chancellor informed his sister; saying besides that by latest assured intelligence Baias was dead. The murderers, it seemed, were persons unknown. Except two, whom Baias had killed outright in the scuffle, they seemed to have gotten clean away, 'An act of God or the King's enemies,' said the Chancellor, looking her straight in the eye.

'An act of God,' said the lady soberly, with a like steady, uncommunicative, understanding look. 'It were wicked to be unthankful.'

ARGUMENT WITH DATES

Barganax and Fiorinda
The King and the Vicar
(Chapters XXX-XXXIII)

XXX

Laughter-loving Aphrodite

I THINK EDDISON FINISHED CHAPTERS XXVIII AND XXIX IN JANUARY 1945 BECAUSE ALL THE NOTES AND DRAFTS WRITTEN BETWEEN JANUARY AND AUGUST 1945, EDDISON'S LAST EIGHT MONTHS OF LIFE, SHOW HIS WORKING UPON CHAPTERS XXX–XXXIII. HERE IS HIS DRAFT FOR THE OPENING OF CHAPTER XXX:

FEW shed tears for Baias's sake. There ran a rumour that his slaying was in revenge of the strange heathenly excess of legs exposed up to mid-thigh and heads unhaired employed by him to the correction of his chamber maids; but friends and kinsfolk of these, being had before the justicier were, for want of even ocular proof, one and all pronounced guiltless. No man made so bold as alledge openly that persons in the Chancellor's service had done the thing, or by his or his sister's setting on. Any that said so, said it with circumspection, and behind closed doors. Indeed, in Meszria such idle report and surmise soon died down. In the middle kingdom however it found kindlier soil and was speedily brought by busybodies expectant of reward, to Prince Gilmanes's ear in Kaima. The Prince, vailing his eyelids close, heard them out: then seeming extraordinary indifferent to his nephew's unhappy ending, dashed their hopes by asking how durst they come to him: 'What a mischief mean you, to come unto me and tumble out as brainless and passionate fooleries as ever I heard tell? Albeit in these lean times

I be thought to hold out but small territories and little authority in respect to the whole land, or to what my fathers held aforetime, you shall see I'll not be played withal; nor made to swallow idle report and surmise what they are or how untrue. I am not justly possessed, [. . .] that joining great names to such black villainy standeth little with the interest of the realm or the dignity of our lord the King.' With that, he gave order that they be well flogged in the market-place and then clapt up in prison: directed a writ to his chief officers, charging them see to the punishment of any that should repeat the like slanderous lies: last with his own hand wrote privately to acquaint my lord Chancellor of these proceedings. This letter, ending with much similitude of love and good inclination, Beroald perused with a vinegar-tart smile upon his lips: then filed it in a secret box along with copies of certain two or three letters he had of recent months intercepted on their way between Baias and Gilmanes: letters having a far different importment.

The third week of January the King came down from Kessarey, where he had spent Yule-tide, to Sestola, and there held council. Business done and the council risen, he took the Chancellor apart into his closet: said he would learn more of this matter of Baias. The Chancellor recounted it at large, saying in fine, 'There, Lord, it resteth. We have, I am to confess, failed to trace the guilty persons.'

'Such a confession we have not yet learnt to expect from you, Beroald.'

'I hope your serenity will not think 'tis a failure likely to recur.'

'I think not,' said the King, steadily regarding him. 'And that is why I think now we will not let it rest.' There was a mock in this King's eye.' The Chancellor abode it without a blench.

'I thank your serene Highness,' he said at last, 'for your trust in me.'

'You have yourself to thank for that. If I trust you, 'tis because you are trustworthy.'

'You have copies of the letters came into my hands.'

'Yes. Fits well with certain other informations I have for your secret eye. But we will leave that affair untouched till it be nearer looked.'

'I have not mentioned aught of these things to any person else than your serene highness.'

'You have done as I would have you do. Keep it betwixt me and you alone. You have seen no sign, otherwhere, of its spreading into Meszria?'

'No sign; albeit my eyes have been busy for that.'

They sat silent for awhile in the easy and comfortable freedom of a mutuality where each can, the better for the other's presence and unvoiced comprehensions, follow his own unimpeded. Then suddenly the Chancellor was aware of his great master's eye gaze turned upon him and studying his face as it had been an open page on which some quaint matter was characterized.

'You are complained of,' said the King.

'To your highness?'

'Not directly so. But on all hands I hear you blamed.'

'Not groundably, it is to be hoped.'

'Until the other day, it is ten years since I had seen your sister. They tell me it is your fault she is never set eyes on in Zayana.'

The Chancellor gave a silent laugh. 'My fault? She is no longer *in statu pupae.*' But (for I know your highness would not have me hide my mind from you), is it not come to be a by-word now-a-days that if any woman worth notice (unless she be wed already) shall go in there it must be to the tune of "Let in the maid that out a maid departed never more"?'

'What? And will you, whom rumour hath so oft maligned, be a believer of that jade?'

'Not I, Lord. I have my own means to sieve idle report from fact.'

'And how much sticks after the sieving?'

'Not too much for my taste.'

'Nor for his duchess?'

At that, Beroald's face was again unreadable. Only a momentary stiffening of his hand where it rested on the table did not escape the eye of the King. 'I do not look so high,' he cried after a pause.

'Well, you and I have this habit in common, dear Beroald: viewing the world, to stand rather with the reals than with the nominals.'

The Chancellor bent his head in a graceful assent. 'Since your serenity hath done me the honour, and her, to touch on the matter, I must remember you that, there, ladies are fashions: one commonly lasts him but a two or three months at most. There's another thing too, if the Devil must draw the tongue out of my mouth.'

'Out with it, for I've guessed it already.'

'I well believe you, for your serene highness knows me. I am an ambitious man.'

'True.'

'Ambitious as respects my sister.'

'O yes. Sisters can be ladders.'

'I think not of that. Or not only.'

'I know you are not: not beyond reason. Confess: you are yourself in honorable sort, a little in love with her?'

From betwixt half-closed eyelids, Beroald gave him a shrewd look.

''Tis no bad thing,' the king said, ''twixt brother and sister.' He paused. 'To say true, having beheld and spoke with her this morning, first time since ten years, I think, and then she was but a child, I can savour and appraise in my own self some whiff or draught of this penetrating humour strained brotherly affection: its very scent: something past that of friendships yet by native notion obedient to the mind's rein. Myself, I ne'er had a sister. But neither have you, I think, a daughter.'

The Chancellor's finger of his right hand had made a slow dance on the table-top before him. 'I can subtilize you points of law,' he said. 'But here your serene highness hath me out of my depth.'

'I think I know where the shoe pinches,' said the King. 'Instance of a Queen.'

The Chancellor looked swiftly at him, then lowered his eyes again. 'There be great examples,' he said very soberly, 'not necessary for everyone to follow.'

'Well, enough said for the while.' King Mezentius rose.

'A notable honour: to her and to me,' Beroald said, rising with him. Then, looking him in the eye, 'May I add this, Lord? After a sharp frost, on the heels of over-early spring, the damage comes of too sudden sun.'

'Content you,' said the King. 'I do not forget it.'

THE PASSAGE ABOVE ALLUDES TO A SCENE IN WHICH THE KING CONVERSES WITH FIORINDA. EDDISON NEVER WROTE THIS SCENE, BUT HE DESCRIBED IT IN NOTES WRITTEN ON JANUARY 26 AND 29, 1945:

The King and Fiorinda: The King of course knows (secretly – no one else knows) the parentage of Beroald and Fiorinda. He is deeply impressed with her. In this scene concentrate on her wit, incalculableness, and gaiety of heart. The King laughingly asks whether she would like him to get her a new husband. She is much honoured, but would prefer, after this first experience, to take her time and look round a little.

EDDISON PLANNED FOR KING MEZENTIUS TO RETURN TO THE DUCHESS AMALIE IN MEMISON AFTER CONVERSING WITH BEROALD AND FIORINDA IN SESTOLA. SOMETIME IN EARLY MAY 1945, EDDISON JOTTED DOWN SIMPLE EXPRESSIONS FOR A CONVERSATION ABOUT FIORINDA BETWEEN THE DUCHESS AND THE KING:

Duchess: I'm sorry to hear it.

King: Come: that's not very reasonable – just an hearsay and fancy.

Duchess: (shrugs her shoulders)

King: I should like you to have a look at her.

Duchess: Why?

King: Because I've as good as told the Chancellor I would be glad to see her Duchess of Zayana.

Duchess: That was cruel of you, never to consult me.

King: Don't jump to conclusions: nothing's settled. He may not like her. You have a look and make up your mind.

Duchess: (angry) It's made up already.
(later) I'm sorry I was so horrid. I'll see her.

PROBABLY USING THE SIMPLE CONVERSATIONAL NOTES ABOVE,
EDDISON COMPOSED, BETWEEN 15 AND 17 MAY 1945, A MORE
DETAILED SCENE BETWEEN MEZENTIUS AND AMALIE:

A night or two later, the King being in Memison, Amalie asked
whether he had a true tale, among the many tales that flew:
concerning Baias's taking off. He answered he had talked with the
Chancellor and that clear as day it was that the Chancellor had
himself procured it; but this were best not spoken of.

'She hath made a fair beginning, the she-scorpion,' said the
Duchess.

The King laughed. ''Tis not to be denied it was somewhat highly
handled. Yet fitted so well with greater matters I have in view, I
had not the heart to blame him.'

The Duchess sat pensive. 'Barganax will be home from the west
in three weeks. God be thanked, not to such a wife.'

'You have seen her?'

'Never that I remember. Beroald keepeth her as formerly he
did, close boxed. So Baias did while he had her. Wisely so, I should
say. Stibium disguised with honey. Best kept out of reach.'

'Nay, be not so unlike your dear self as fall into injustice. She
was ill-served of her husband.'

'And ill rid of him, though a vile fellow indeed. Both vile together.
Her reputation stinks to heaven.'

'What have you to work upon ne'er having spoke unto her,
save what's prated or libelled by sluttish pamphleteers?'

'But strongly persistent. It is easy to tell by the smoke and the
sparkles that there is a fire in the chimney.'

'See and speak with her before you judge.'

'Well, I'll bottle up judgment, then: I'll not judge. She concerns
not me; and truly indeed, dear my lord, I've no desire to look
upon her.' Amalie's fair and lovely face wore, as she spoke, its
little-maid look: half-timorous, half-humorous, all self-resolved:
like as when, over the pure deeps of a tarn open to the sky at
evening or morn, a light breath of wind, or a stirring here and
there of the glass-smooth surface stillness with the momentary

alighting, immaterial as air, of some tiny winged creature, wakes ripples that seem to react, through the starred remoteness of the moment upon that profundity, to scarce-heard echoes of the innumerable laughter of the waves of ocean: a look only not to be kissed, lest that fresh enchantment break, for the while, the reign of the present.

'I'm sorry, then,' said the King. Then, answering the question in Amalie's eyes: 'Because I myself have seen her, t'other day.'

'So, indeed?'

'I liked her at first word; first glance.'

'Very strange.'

'You may think so, if you send for her. You may feel as though you were viewing your own image in that strange artificial the learned doctor fashioned and set up in Acrozayana, which mirrors, but by contrary colors. And yet, this, a greater wonder, seeing the very forms are changed. As though my Rosa Mundi should behold in this girl her own self, looking at herself, as La Rose Noire.'

The Duchess sat silent. Presently he was aware of her hand finding his. 'Will you look, and tell me?' he said.

'Well,' answered she, after a moment, and her hand trembled: 'I'll consider of it; sleep on it.'

IN FEBRUARY OF 775 AZC, A MONTH AFTER THE SLAYING OF BAIAS, SUITORS SEEK OUT FIORINDA IN ZEMRY ASHERY. ON 26 JANUARY 1945, EDDISON MADE SOME NOTES ON THE MEN WHO PURSUE HER AND THE TREATMENT THEY RECEIVED:

Wooers begin to line up – Barrian, Zapheles, Morville. Barrian, huffed at her rejection of him, damns her with faint praise to the Duke (a great friend of his), and is thus the means of postponing for some time any interest in her on the Duke's part.

The Zapheles episode is pointed by the fact that Zapheles is a professed misogynist and confirmed bachelor: Fiorinda very delicately and humorously pulls his leg about this, and (in spite of his cynical and embittered, backbiting, habit of mind) achieves the triumph of sending him away as her devoted and – so far as in him lies – loyal friend.

AS APRIL TURNED TO MAY IN 1945, EDDISON MADE MORE DETAILED
NOTES ABOUT FIORINDA AND ZAPHELES:

Fiorinda and Zapheles: Zapheles comes across Fiorinda alone in the countryside about Zemry Ashery. She is in her contemplation. They know each other slightly – well enough to excuse his stopping to talk with her.

He says Barrian is much upset by her rejection of his addresses: she has done a good job there: turned him into a misogynist (of Zapheles's own kidney). She mockingly questions the truth of this: Zapheles says it is obvious; therefore, the Duke, who had shown some curiosity about her and her affairs, is quite put off by Barrian's damning her with faint praise. Moreover, Bellafront holds the fort.

She plays with Zapheles: makes further assignations with him; finally, after a few weeks, driving him to a recantation of his cynical attitude and having him at her feet with a proposal of marriage. (Make it clear that she is completely heart-free in all of this: merely enjoys the exercise of her power to twirl and turn Zapheles to her will.)

Fiorinda's attitude toward Zapheles is consistently this: any approach on his part to the role of lover sets her at arm's length. They are friends on the basis of mocking and scorning mankind (the side of her nature that lives its incarnate purity in Anthea). Zapheles soon learns to accept this, and is – on that basis – her devoted friend and admirer. (Loyal too? Well, yes – as far as in him lies!)

BETWEEN 19 AND 22 MAY 1945, EDDISON DRAFTED THE FIRST
MEETING BETWEEN FIORINDA AND THE DUCHESS AMALIE:

The next Tuesday sennight the Duchess gave out that she would go down (for a week or two's tarriance and tasting of the salt breezes) to Rojuna, a little pavillion of hers beside the sea, and take but one lady along with her. Servants were sent before to open up the house and have all in a readiness; and upon the Thursday she, with Bellafront and but a groom and two serving maids to attend them, rode for Acrozayana. There they were joyfully welcomed and entertained by Medor, who for the three months of the Duke's absence was in charge there; and so next morning, took their way south eastward toward Krestenaya, meaning to cross the sands of the Korvish at ebb tide and found themselves an hour before noon under Zemry Ashery. The Duchess said, 'It is Valentine's Day, and twenty miles yet to Rojuna. We will make surprise upon my lord Chancellor: bear him a morning visit.'

The Lord Beroald was sat at meat in his privy dining-chamber with his sister. Besides Anthea and Campaspe, they had no company save Zapheles only, who, having concluded some business with the Chancellor this morning, had remained a-talking with the Lady Fiorinda till dinner time. Word being brought that the Duchess of Memison was below, the Chancellor left table and went down himself to bring her in. 'Had we but had notice of your grace's intending hither,' he said, 'there should a been entertainment to offer you better fitting this happy occasion. But if you will excuse the want of preparation and partake our simple family fare (there's but Lord Zapheles here: chanced upon us like as thus, fortunately, your noble excellence hath done) 'twill be a joy to us indeed.'

'Nay, 'twas but the thought took me, passing so near your gates, to greet your lordship for friendship's sake. I am for Rojuna, and must not miss the tide for crossing of the sands. I ne'er expected to have interrupted you at dinner.'

'I pray your grace do us that honour to come in. We are now but set: our usual hour for dinner is eleven of the clock. You are already behind time for the crossing: the tide runneth in sudden and to great height, with the wind in this quarter: 'tis much too hazardous you should attempt it, and but five miles further round by land. I cannot quit you, dear madam, disappoint us not.'

Amalie smiled. 'I see you are a powerful persuader, as ever. Very well: we are persuaded.' Delicately she gave him her hand, to be helped down from her horse.

As they began to mount the stairs, a murmur of talking and laughing sounded from the dining-parlour above: now a ripple of laughter that the Duchess might know for Campaspe's: now Zapheles's known accent as that clatter of tin cans, precise, bantering, uninviting: then a burst of merriment and, as the laughter died down, one laugh that out-stayed the rest. Low-toned it was, shot with colours borrowed from the feather-soft descending cloud-gates of downiest slumber, and sun-warmed in its luxuriousness as the slow honey-dropping of those streams that have their well-spring in Mount Helicon. And yet it was a light laugh, disdainful, self-enjoying, gay, fancy-free; but with harmonies in it, sudden and fleeting, that opened upon wonder, as night opens to summer-lightnings and, with the flash's passing, shuts down again upon a mystery deeper and darker than before. The Duchess, her foot on the stair, stayed herself for the instant as if, having come so far, she would yet change her mind for some panical terror bred in her by that laughter. This for the merest instant only: nobody marked it. Mistress of herself again, she, with Bellafront, followed the Chancellor.

'Please your grace that I present to you my lady sister,' said Beroald as, upon their entering the room, all rose from their seats. Fiorinda, coming from her place at the foot of the table, nearest the door, bent into a lily-like courtesy to salute the Duchess's hand. This done, and the lady standing again at her full stature, Amalie's eyes surveyed her over as though she knew not how to frame her look: a gaze so ambiguous that Fiorinda, a sudden flush over-spreading the pallour of her cheek and neck, said, 'I fear your grace taketh some little dislike to see me so thus in tissue of yellow, 'stead of in widow's weeds? But truly I have a distaste for mourning colours, and especially with spring-time soon beginning.'

'Think not I'd such a thought,' said the Duchess. 'Remember we have not looked on one another till now. I was seeking for the likeness.'

'With my brother?'

'Yes, with your brother, I mean.' She added, as if to herself: 'There is not, after all, much likeness.'

To that, Fiorinda, glancing at Beroald: 'Not much likeness in looks. But more, perhaps, in likings.'

The Duchess remained for a moment in the same uneasy contemplation, which took up its rest at last on Fiorinda's sea-green eyes that now looked level into hers. Those eyes seemed to still their sea-fires, under this searching inspection, to a sweet and grave respect; but in the most imperceptible slant of them, and in the curves of the underlids, an intimation seemed to tremble on some edge of disclosure, untellable whether of fanged monsters stirring in their sleep in those green pools' deeps, or of a star that danced there unseen. Then, as if started out of dreaming, the Duchess turned to the Chancellor who had let place a chair for her on his own right, Zapheles moving down to sit by Fiorinda. Upon the other side of the table Campaspe moved closer to her sister, to let Bellafront have her seat at the Chancellor's left.

'The King's highness (Gods send he live forever) guesteth with Lord Stathmar, I learn, in Argyanna,' said Beroald. 'The Admiral showed me letters he had from him yesterday.'

'I had letters too,' said the Duchess, 'the day before, in Memison: by the same courier, doubtless.'

'Your grace means to go a-fishing at Rojuna?' said Zapheles.

'No, I love not the sport: go but to taste the spring coming in that way.'

'My lord Duke is at his fishing, 'tis said, for giant sea-pike off Quedanzar: never content but with dangerous occupation.'

'His grace told me,' said Bellafront, 'they will charge a big boat if the humour take them, supposing it to be a fish. And that human flesh they distaste, but will yet rush upon a swimmer in the water if he stir a muscle, supposing, from the motion, 'tis fish. This when they be hungry. And can at one snap take his leg off at the thigh. But I think he invented this to fright me.'

'Ay, believe not all he tells you,' Amalie said; and Bellafront reddened to the roots of her hair that, caught in a shaft of sunlight from the window, became a live fire in its heavy splendour, thick, long, close-braided on her head, and red-hot Titian colour, near the like of her mistress's own.

The Duchess saw, while they talked and jested, how Zapheles's sallow hatchet-face was at every while returning toward my Lady Fiorinda in an admiration undisguised: a strange trick in him, who was of all men noted for a soured bachelor wedded to simple life, and an inveterate back-biter of women.

'I love the comedy,' she said, laying her hand on the Chancellor's sleeve, 'of Zapheles behaving himself so unlike himself in the enemy's camp.'

Beroald shrugged. 'It is but one more pair of wings at the candle-flame,' he said under his breath. 'They come and go till they be singed.'

The Duchess's words, chancing upon a pause in the general talk, were not unheard by Zapheles. He whispered behind his hand to Fiorinda, 'She means, I have no eye for those others. Well, if it be, may I not study in what books I will?'

Fiorinda caught the Duchess's eye and said in her most langue-fied tones, plainly, for all to hear, 'My lord Zapheles says this behaviour is but his ordinary: that, should it appear otherwise, 'tis but that he finds me to be (as, to his thinking, all sane beings ought to be) altogether unwomanly. And therefore he would deign to take notice only of me alone. I have had left-handed compliments ere now, but this I think the curiousest.' Upon which outrageous speech, spoken with so much elegance and forced innocency of idle and lazy grace, the Duchess could not but fall a-laughing.

Zapheles, stroking his beard and putting on as good a face as he might, found no better rejoinder than say lamely to the Duchess, 'I said no such thing.'

'But you think it,' said Fiorinda.

There was a deep seduction in her voice but when he turned to her, a bed of snakes in the mockery of her lips. 'True,' replied he, 'I did think it (does that wring your withers?): until your lady-ship said it. But, by your saying it (though I grant you're too deep skilled in manners to roll your eye at me), I perceive that underneath you're but as the rest.'

'Very prettily complimented. I, too, am disappointed. I had even begun to think you a remarkable man.'

'You would not find yourself alone in that opinion.'

'I was even so silly as begin to be almost persuaded there might be found in you that singularity, not to be wholly eat up with your own self-conceit.'

'Will you not speak louder? Let 'em hear how fishwifely you can rail.'

'But it was foolish in me to imagine so unnatural a monstrosity,' she said, and the same honeyedness, overlying bee-stings of silent laughter, was on every smoothly spoken word. Then, a little louder: *'Quelle est la difference, monsieur, entre un elephant et une puce?'*

He looked at her in silence, half angry, half at a loss, as a fox should look, ears down, toward some undefinable and teasing presence the menace of which is felt but hid far from view.

'Un elephant peut avoir des puces; mais une puce ne peut pas avoir des elephants. I sometimes question whether I be not myself an exceptional puce.'

Amalie's cheek dimpled to the shadow of a smile. It passed, and her eyes still rested, sweet and dubious and searching, on Fiorinda. Zapheles said sulkily, 'I'll talk with your ladyship more on these matters when you have not an audience to use against me.'

'Pray do my lord,' said she lightly. 'I shall heartily look forward to it.'

Dinner being done, Zapheles took his leave. The others walked awhile in the garden. Amalie, when she had Fiorinda to herself, said to her suddenly, 'Do you like Lord Zapheles? Is he a friend of yours?'

'Does your grace? Is he by chance a friend of your grace's?'

The Duchess, set then at a non plus, looked round upon her. Fiorinda was bended down as she spoke, to pluck a purple blossom of lenten rose from a great bunch which grew beside the path. She stood up again, holding the flower to her nostrils to take the scent, looking the while in the Duchess's eye with so unruffled a demeanour and into so much sweetness of pensivity on her lips that the Duchess, if she were disposed to take offence, changed her mind and but said, 'I think you are well suited to one another.'

'I am honoured by your grace's kindly interest in my affairs. 'Las it hath no scent, or I no sense of it.' She made as if to have dropped the flower: as upon second thoughts, fastened it in her bosom.

'I would not be so uncivil,' said the Duchess, 'as claim any particular interest.'

'I think he is a man. Howe'er that be, he amuses me.'

'Is that what men are made for?'

'I think probably so.'

'An illuminating answer.'

'I hope, madam, it does not scandalize you?'

'Not in the smallest. Only I understand you, and myself, better than I did.'

Fiorinda very slowly smiled. There was that in her eyes now that made Amalie, after a moment's wrestling with them, avert her own. 'If I may be permitted to speak my thought, I would guess that your noble excellence views them mainly as I do,' said she, 'And (to do justice to your beauty and other high qualities besides) with precisely as much justification.'

'I think it a hateful doctrine.'

'I am glad you should think so. Even and it be pure error, it enhances your grace's charm.'

BARGANAX'S FISHING TRIP LASTS FROM DECEMBER 774 TO MID-MARCH 775 AZC. BEFORE THE DUKE'S HOMECOMING, BEROALD AND MORVILLE MEET IN ZAVANA, AND AFTER THIS MEETING MORVILLE LEARNS OF FIORINDA IN AN IDLE CONVERSATION WITH BARRIAN, ZAPHELES, AND MELATES:

The Chancellor: (Long talk with Morville in Zayana upon some question arising out of Emmius Parry's will. Some property of Deïaneira's which has been claimed by the Chancellor for the crown but the Vicar wants it to revert to him. It is complicated by being mixed up with some claims of the Duke's (the name of Alzulma?). The Chancellor is impressed with Morville's modesty and intelligent firm handling of the business.) 'Fact is, until the

Duke is back, my hands are full: Medor brings me dozens of difficulties unwilling to settle them uncovered. The Duke was not expected home from the West till Wednesday March 18th: but here's letters this morning saying he's advanced it to a week earlier, that's day after tomorrow, so as to hold his presence on Friday 13th. If you can divert yourself here for a while, come and see me in Zemry Ashery today fortnight. I think I can give you an answer then to take back to the Vicar: nothing official and binding, but enough to help him judge how the land lies.'

Morville, coming out from the Chancellor, meets Barrian, Melates, Zapheles.

Barrian: Well, what speed, my Lord Morville?

Morville: I took your advice, my Lord. The Chancellor used me very honourable: I never spoke so long with his excellence before. He is a hard man to deal with?

Zapheles: A man of iron body and mind [. . .] as full with [. . .] as a spider with poison. The devil speaks in him.

Morville: Well, I'm to see him again when he's studied the thing: Sunday March 22, in his own home.

Zapheles: Oho? Look out you be not catched there by his charmer.

Morville: What's that?

Zapheles: Barrian can tell you best.

Barrian: Pah, that's an old story. I've forgotten it.

Morville: (with self-engrossed curiosity) I ought to know.

Melates: Enough if you remember; keep away from his treasure chamber. And be not dazzled with that diamond he keeps there. 'Twill cut you if you touch it. His (Barrian's) cut is raw yet, howso a try to pretend otherwise.

Barrian: Well, I must bid you good morning: I have an appointment.

Zapheles: But not in Zemry Ashery I hope? (exit Barrian)

Morville: I've heard the tales. But I'm not a fisher in those waters.

Zapheles: A woman-hater? I could kiss you for it!
Morville: O, no hate. I'll wed one day, for the good of the
            family: 'tis common practice. But women are women,
            and I never had sleepless nights for any woman, nor
            will neither.
Melates: Barrian was badly bit. Would've hung up his hat
            there, but puss scratched him properly and sent him
            away with his tail between his legs.
Zapheles: Keep off, sweet youth. Be caught by her and live
            withal? Why I'd as lief go a courting of [. . .] wife.
Morville: Who's that?
Zapheles: [. . .] A beast that eateth patient husbands.

AT THE END OF FEBRUARY 775 AZC, DUKE BARGANAX COMMUNICATES
WITH HIS OFFICERS:

The month ended, and the Duke of Zayana, putting off at every
few days the date of his return, still tarried in the west at his sea-
fishing. In the first days of March came Barrian from the west:
brought commands to Medor from his Grace that they must expect
him about three weeks hence, and in the meanwhile prepare
[masques] and revels in Acrozayana against his homecoming.

ON 30 MAY 1945, EDDISON DRAFTED AN INCOMPLETE CONVERSATION
IN WHICH FIORINDA TELLS DOCTOR VANDERMAST OF HER INTENTION
TO ATTEND THE MASQUERADE BALL THAT MEDOR HAS PLANNED
FOR BARGANAX'S HOMECOMING. CONSIDERING FIORINDA'S
HABITUALLY RECLUSIVE LIFE IN ZEMRY ASHERY, HER DESIRE TO GO
IS A CURIOUS INCLINATION:

Fiorinda with Doctor Vandermast in Zemry Ashery—
Fiorinda: Indeed my Lord Zapheles told me of these
                 intended revels, and pestereth me still to go meet
                 him there and look upon them. Ladies all to go
                 masked. It would amuse me. I gather you are to
                 be the master of the revels?

Vandermast:	Yes, I have framed up some fantasticoes.
Fiorinda:	I'll go, but not tell my brother. I've heard so much of what's done in the palace and been so thwarted when I would see for myself, I'm resolved I'll go. Do you advise me to?
Vandermast:	I always advise your ladyship to follow your own inclinations. I can't always understand them, but [sic]

ON 25 MAY 1945, EDDISON PLANNED THE PAIRINGS FOR CONVERSATIONS AT THE MASQUERADE BALL THAT MEDOR PREPARES FOR 17 MARCH 775 AZC:

Fiorinda goes to masked ball in Zayana

Overhears Barrian reporting to Barganax about her ('faint praise').

—[Barrian says to the Duke: 'O no: not the mysterious lady mewed up in Zemry Ashery. I saw her when you were away: a very commonplace person. Handsome? O yes, but so so. Affected: full of herself: spiteful. No presence, like that. Voice quite different, too.']

Duke making love to Bellafront—

Bellafront – 'I like you better in this mood.'

Duke – 'I'm like a hunting leopard: better in my mood when starved. Starved now.'

Bellafront – (bring out her mindlessness, and sensual charms: a nice good girl, but after all only one of the 'dishes of hers' served up by the Marchioness of Monferrato).

Pantasilia – (very episodic, this): huffed by Duke's attentions to Bellafront: Melates rises on her horizon.

Masked Ball: very unusual: a conceit of the Duke's.

Every guest must bring a lady with him. She is to be masked and no inquiries made as to her identity.

Zapheles brings Fiorinda.

Melates brings Pantasilia.

Medor brings Rosalura.

Perantor brings some light-o-love of his own, who deserts him for the Duke at one stage, and causes much rage to Bellafront.

?Vandermast there with Anthea.

ON THE SAME DAY THAT HE MADE THE OUTLINE ABOVE, EDDISON REVISED SOME NOTES, FIRST WRITTEN ON 30 APRIL 1945, ABOUT BARGANAX'S RELATIONSHIPS WITH BELLAFRONT AND PANTASILIA:

Barganax's education by Heterasmene had made him have 'such a way' with women that they always fell in love with him. This in a fair way to spoil him: also to bore him with such easy preys.

Bellafront (who was in her ascendant March–June 775 [AZC]) quite unintelligent but indefatigably sensual. She is indeed the subject of the 129th Sonnet. Barganax always 'past reason' hates her *ex post facto*, and always returns like moth to flame. She is stupid, tactless, unrestrained: a lovely animal, and Barganax comes back to her as the drunkard to the bottle. But her lack of artistry and her excessive 'forth comingness' grate upon him increasingly (if only intermittently and subconsciously).

Pantasilia also his mistress, but she is a restful βοῶπις πότνια. Also, their affairs are less passionate, more sleepy and lazy. In March or (?) April he notices Melates is falling under the spell of this quiet luxurious peony-like beauty, and unobtrusively resigns in Melates's favour. (This shows his principle – never violated till the case of Morville arrives – of never hunting in another man's preserves.)

BETWEEN 25 MAY AND 1 JUNE 1945, EDDISON DRAFTED MORE DETAILED NOTES FOR THE MASQUERADE BALL:

Evening of the Masque in Zayana.

Torchlight procession through the town up to the citadel, after supper. Masque is by the lady guests and Dr Vandermast (as 'an ambassador from beyond the Hyperborean Mountains') 'presents' it. Enter to a slow music, grotescoes playing their lutes: jewels: candle-holders. Dr Vandermast craves leave for 'their ladies to come in'.

(Guests and 25 ladies) – They come in, all masked. One by one the ladies play die with the Duke: he wins in turn and gets all their money: and in turn each lady plays then against one of the guests, and wins: after which she is his partner for the evening. Bellafront at last plays and wins all his money from the Duke: he pours it out before her on the table from a golden goblet: then a little boy (as Cupid) shoots at her and then unmasks her: Bellafront is enthroned beside the Duke as Queen of the revels.

After she has won his money at dice and is seated by him as Queen of the revels, Bellafront (according to the rules) still wears her mask.

Bellafront:	Are you glad it is me?
Duke:	I knew you, before you spoke, spite of your visard.
Bellafront:	By my lips?
Duke:	Never have a painter for your lover if you mean to cheat him. He can see through taffeta as you through clear glass.
Bellafront:	And you're glad of me?
Duke:	Part of me is.
Bellafront:	Only part?
Duke:	Care not: 'tis the part your heart is on.
Bellafront:	Your grace seems a little short and cynical. I hope you love me as you swore you did.
Duke:	Loving goes by haps.
Bellafront:	So cold as that? I'd as well a stayed in Memison. Better, with all the work I had to persuade her noble excellence give me leave for tonight.
Duke:	O foolish girl. How should I know whether I love you? Give me that mouth to try (she does so). Hath that answered you?
Bellafront:	Yes (much stirred). But you talk so strange.
Duke:	'Tis t'other part talks.
Bellafront:	What's true then?
Duke:	That you are, in all my former misled life, the sweetest card-conny-catcher that ever turned up ace.
Bellafront:	That's better. But how says t'other part?

Duke:	That here is the great bur again, commonly more known than commended.
Bellafront:	I hate it: and you, for so cruel a lie.
Duke:	Kiss again, then, and unsay it.
Bellafront:	No, I hate you for it. Unsay it first.
Duke:	(laughing) Come, come. If such a thing I did utter out of my distractions, 'tis easy unsaid. But your lips must help mine to unsay it. (Kisses her again.)
(Barrian comes to them)	I see your Grace is merrily disposed and sets us good example.
Duke:	Ay, Barrian!

All rise now and tables removed. Series of dances, in which all take part: first the lords in a line and the masked ladies facing them: then each with his lady. Dances for a time, then two by two sitting out in alcoves and lights lowered: stars of various colours wandering about in the hollow roof, like tame comets. Barganax and Bellafront: her mindlessness and sensual charms.

Pantasilia and Melates.

Perantor and lady (who deserts him to talk to the Duke, to Bellafront's annoyance).

Then Car of Night enters: great crystal, colour of a black diamond: throned on it, in dusky cloak and hood, and with black mask like the rest – Night. Drawn by four beasts – unicorn, water-horse, flying bull, owl-headed tigress.

Car halts before the Duke: the lady casts off her hood and cloak as the wandering stars descend and circle about her head in an aureole. She is masked with a mask of moleskin, and the green light of her eyes burns in the eyeholes. She is in a flowing gown from waist downward made all of raven's feathers and black cock's feathers, some with stag beetles' wings and spangles of ebony and jet, and a girdle of filigree silver set thick with black diamonds and black pearls. From hip to throat and from throat to finger-joints she was clad in a skin-tight garment made of the skins of black adders: her throat and neck and the lower part of her face were bared to view, of a dazzling fairness against this black and the black of her hair, that was piled high on her head and bound with enchanter's nightshade.

Beside this, the tips of her fingers alone were bared, armed with claws of gold like a lioness's claws expansed.

Fiorinda insists on going home early – before the fun becomes too fast and furious. On the way home, Zapheles proposes again, and they make their platonic pact: [She makes terms with him as cynic with cynic: he is right about women, and she too (upon her experience with Baias) right about men. 'Come then, let's be friends and mock the world together, keeping ourselves uninfested by this madness. I hate you when you begin to show signs of this common disease: as yourself – i.e. when you scorn mankind and womankind both – I delight in you.']

Beroald knows all about her going to Zayana: waits up for her return (not that he ever went to bed early) and cross examines her. Fiorinda gives impressions that she has had enough of this 'nightclub' atmosphere and considers the Duke a mere philanderer. Beroald decides she should marry Morville.

BEROALD'S THOUGHTS HAD BEEN IN EDDISON'S IMAGINATION FOR MONTHS BECAUSE ON 13 FEBRUARY 1945, EDDISON JOTTED DOWN THIS NOTE:

The Chancellor begins to incline to a connexion with the Parry – for political reasons: his thoughts turn to Morville.

ON 30 APRIL AND 1 MAY 1945, EDDISON MADE MORE NOTES ABOUT BEROALD'S ATTITUDE TOWARD MORVILLE, STRESSING THAT BEROALD SEES MORVILLE AS A MORE ADVANTAGEOUS MATCH THAN DUKE BARGANAX FOR HIS SISTER, PARTLY BECAUSE OF THE DUCHESS'S ATTITUDE TOWARD FIORINDA:

The Duchess is prejudiced against Fiorinda (on Lewisian and Geraldian grounds) at their first (and, until her appointment at the King's instance, to be a lady of honour at Memison, only) meeting, scents the atmosphere affecting every conceivable outrageousness of opinion and behaviour.

This interview confirms the Duchess in her feeling that Fiorinda is likely to bring disaster to any man that has to do with her, and finding the King shows signs of favouring Fiorinda as a wife for Barganax, makes it perfectly clear that she will have nothing to do with such a woman, much less accept her as a daughter-in-law. Beroald, learning (direct from the Duchess?) this attitude, dismisses any ambitions that may have formed in his mind in that direction.

Beroald thinks Morville, as a kinsman of the Parry, may be useful to him: also thinks his sister had better be married (instead of a centre of such a buzz of flies and perhaps one day a cast-off mistress of the Duke's): thus he urges the Morville connection.

MORVILLE'S FIRST GLIMPSE OF FIORINDA OCCURS WHEN SHE GOES SWIMMING IN A SECLUDED LAKE WITH ANTHEA AND CAMPASPE:

Bathing in a little mountain tarn they have just discovered: she does it rather to the scandalizing of Campaspe and enjoyment of Anthea. Morville, by chance, looks on undetected. Thinks he has, Actaeon like, surprised Artemis at her bath. [Anthea volunteers to slip into her lynx dress and deal with (Morville). Fiorinda decides, wait. After all, what harm?] He goes to Zemry Ashery (whither he is bound) and is introduced. Recognizes her at once and immediately falls in love.

ON 29 AND 30 APRIL 1945, EDDISON WROTE THAT FIORINDA TAKES ZAPHELES WITH HER TO DINNER ON THE EVENING OF MORVILLE'S ARRIVAL IN ZEMRY ASHERY, AND, PRESUMABLY, THIS DINNER FOLLOWS HER SECRET BATHING WITH ANTHEA AND CAMPASPE:

Takes him [Zapheles] with her to Zemry Ashery for dinner: there they find Morville, come on business to see the Chancellor. This is Morville's first sight of Fiorinda: Morville secretly falls in love at first sight: (Zapheles's presence gives Morville his first pangs of fatal disease – jealousy). She divines (as does Beroald too) that he has the same 'bias' – though a far different temperment and without the self-pleasing tyrannical violence and passion – as Baias.

Fiorinda, though in no way moved by Morville as a wooer, is touched by the gentleness of his methods, by contrast with Baias. She is also amused by her brother's subtle but (to her) transparent effort to steer this new boat of his into harbour. Half out of kindness, half for fun, and half because she is tired of the 'buzz' (and of the four or five with whom she has condescended to experiment up to the hilt but with small satisfaction though doubtless with great gain to her knowledge of masculine nature and her expertise and perfection in *ars amoris*), Fiorinda betrothes herself to Morville.

AT THIS POINT, EDDISON'S DRAFTS AND NOTES CATCH UP TO THE ARGUMENT FOR CHAPTER XXX. FIORINDA AND MORVILLE MARRY ON 20 APRIL 775 AZC:

In April, barely three months after the violent death of her first husband, she (once more, to please her brother) marries Morville, a distant cousin of the Parry. The King, seeing and talking to her for the first time in May and having Barganax in mind, confers on Morville the lieutenancy of Reisma and persuades the Duchess to give Fiorinda a place at court in Memison and, later, in June, to make her lady of the bedchamber.

ON 25 MAY 1945, EDDISON WROTE A DRAFT NARRATING THE DUCHESS'S AND MEDOR'S REACTIONS TO THIS MARRIAGE AND THESE OFFICIAL APPOINTMENTS:

When the Duchess heard of this wedding she said to Medor (dining with her upon his way to Mavia about some affairs of the Duke's): 'These news are altogether good; I shall send her as my wedding gift, in token of the joy they bring me, the best white mare I have in my stables. 'Tis a match will please Lord Beroald, who is a good friend of mine. I know nought of Morville but by repute:

so if he be eat up in the fashion of the former one, I need waste no tears upon it. Best of all, she will away to Rerek: a joyful departure for all concerned.'

Three weeks later, Medor bethought him of the Duchess's words. For it was in every man's mouth, and soon confirmed beyond question, that Morville was by royal letters patent appointed to the lieutenancy of Reisma, and would shortly move household and take up his abode there upon the lake, at but a short two miles distance from Memison Castle. This too, which made Medor laugh in himself: that the Duchess (yielding, it was thought, to repeated suasions from the King) had offered Fiorinda a place as one of her own ladies at the ducal court of Memison.

High summer began to draw on now in Meszria, with a great settledness of warm sunshine weather, and all quiet. It went among those that lived in the court, and more able so to note the haviour of those nearest about the Duchess, that her grace seemed some-what better content than at first she had been with the Lady Fiorinda; but many judged that she still regarded her not without afterings of aversion and distrust. The lady for her part bore herself very demure and very respective of her honest name, and (scenting, it was supposed, her grace's mislike of any meeting or acquaint-anceship prospective between her new lady of honour and Barganax) absented her always from Memison if the Duke were there or expected.

IT IS FIORINDA'S 'VERY DEMURE AND VERY RESPECTIVE' BEHAVIOUR THAT CHANGES THE DUCHESS'S ATTITUDE TOWARD HER, AS THE ARGUMENT TELLS:

Upon this nearer acquaintance the Duchess now changes her mind: thinks less about the reputation which, bruited by idle tongues, follows Fiorinda as a train of fire some red disastrous comet: in fine, surrenders wholly to the spell of this Dark Lady, in whose scintillating, unanalysable, and perilous perfections she seems to see (as a rose might see its own image mirrored but changed to incandescence in the surface of a pool of molten metal) a counter-image of her own inmost self: *Rosa alba incarnata* looking upon *La Rose Noire*.

MEANWHILE, THE LOVE BETWEEN FIORINDA AND MORVILLE DOES NOT STAY SWEET FOR LONG. EDDISON ANALYSES THEIR PROBLEMS IN NOTES WRITTEN ON 30 APRIL, 1 MAY, AND 25 MAY 1945:

Make it abundantly clear that she is honest and whole hearted in her efforts to make their marriage a 'marriage of true minds' (and bodies). She has, through experience and the maturity of her self knowledge, far greater power (and also, doubtless, far greater will) to do this than she had when Baias was the partner: but Morville's selfishness (in its peculiar form of weakness, self-distrust, gratuitous jealousy, fear of her beauty, of her wit, of her incalculableness, and of her abandonments) defeats her power: even Hers.

Baias had defeated her (and defeated his own ends) by selfishness in the shape of too unadulterated a masculinity: seeking to enslave her, crudely avid of his own greedy lusts, crudely obtuse to the instinctive subtleties of her innate and divine beauty, which offended Him – as pearls before a swine – the perfection and acme of all unspeakable excesses.

Morville, to the contrary, defeats her by his unmanlike inability to take the lead: his timidity, self-pity, mistrustful puritanism, and self-absorption, and these at every return make him retire into his shell to brood and hatch out unworthy discontents and suspicions.

Condense all this into one great scene between them—? *al fresco*, on a perfect summer's evening (? 1st June) not far from Reisma.

1st June (see last preceding sentence): Have in mind, in writing this, the 'awakening' scene between Barganax and Fiorinda (end of Chapter XXXIII and of Book VI); and point, by juxtaposition not by disquisition, the tragic contrast – tragic because this present scene (Chapter XXX) seals Morville's fate. (It is at the end of this scene that, in fact, Fiorinda for the first time realized Morville's inescapable character and destiny that she had in mind later in

Memison [*A Fish Dinner in Memison*, 'Queen of Hearts and Queen
of Spades'] when she said to the Duchess that Morville was 'the
kind of a bull-calf that is likely to sprout horns etc., within the
first year.')

Fiorinda is, for the first time in her life, in that deep content
and receptiveness that (had Morville been the man to divine it and
make himself part of it) might have been the unshakeable founda-
tion (as it was later, on July 22 in Reisma, between her and
Barganax) of eternal true love. In an outward-seeming idleness, but
inward contemplation, she exercises her divine power of (a) making
the moment stand still and be sucked like an orange, and of (b)
packing the moment full of pasts and futures which thereby become
presents: i.e., of tasting eternity in the interludes of time. (Some
faint foretaste or instinct of this was I think in HLE's* habit of
living happy times and episodes over again in memory: treating
her memories as present possession, for present enjoyment, the past
not dead, but a thing to be preserved, watered, and treasured. This
must surely be part of the nature of divine Θεωρία.)

Morville breaks the spell by some discordant remark, which
reveals his 'commonness' and unworthiness and the impassable
gulf of self-centred timorous doubts and discordants which divide
him from his wife.

AS THE STAR OF MORVILLE WANES, THAT OF BARGANAX WAXES. THE
ARGUMENT FOR CHAPTER XXX CLOSES WITH THIS SENTENCE:

Fiorinda is passionately adored at first sight by Barganax on
midsummer night, 775 [AZC], at a ball given by his mother in
Memison.

---

* Helen Louisa Eddison, the author's mother'.

XXXI

THE BEAST OF LAIMAK

THIS CHAPTER ENVELOPS CHAPTERS II, V, AND VII OF *A FISH DINNER IN MEMISON*, AND IT SHOULD BE READ WITH THEM IN MIND. ON PAGE 33 THE KING SPEAKS OF VISITING THE VICAR IN LAIMAK TWO WEEKS BEFORE MIDSUMMER, AND EDDISON PLANNED FOR THIS CHAPTER TO BEGIN WITH THAT EPISODE. ON 27 JANUARY 1945 HE WROTE NOTES FOR THIS:

THE King's visit to the Vicar in Laimak – three nights (June 9–11, 775 [AZC]).

The Vicar hastily makes Gabriel go and meet Gilmanes (who is expected to come for secret discussions on 8th) postponing his visit: he does not trust Gabriel to play a discreet part in the King's presence, and fears his presence may be suspected too by the King.

AFTER NARRATING THE EPISODE BETWEEN THE KING AND THE VICAR, EDDISON PLANNED TO TELL MORE OF THE KING'S ACTIVITIES DURING HIS DAYS IN MEMISON THAN HE TELLS IN CHAPTERS II AND V OF *A FISH DINNER IN MEMISON*. HOWEVER, EDDISON NEVER DRAFTED THESE NOTES, AND THE OUTLINE FOR THIS SECTION OF THE CHAPTER ONLY SAYS: 'THE KING IN MEMISON.' THE ARGUMENT FOR THIS CHAPTER DESCRIBES THE GROWTH OF THE VICAR'S CONSPIRACY IN REREK AND TELLS THE KING'S RESPONSE TO IT:

The Vicar (whose policy, as Beroald once said, 'is that of the duck: above water, idle and scarce seen to stir; but under water, secretly and speedily swimming towards his purpose') has ever since the rebellion been unobtrusively but with patience and thoroughness consolidating his power in Rerek. By firm government, lavishness in both promise and performance, good-fellowship, princely hospitality, a certain directness that tempts many to trust him where they had wiselier been ware of him, and by a set policy of fastening a private hold on each man worthy his attention (laying men under obligations to his person, or holding over them his knowledge of some secret misdoing which they would least of all wish to see brought to light), he has in the four years of his vicariate used the royal commission (as Beroald said) 'to grapple to his private allegiance the whole mid kingdom 'twixt Megra and the Zenner'.

The King, who has for years understood, as from inside, this 'most wolvy and most foxy sergeant major general of all the Devil's engineers,' and loves him dearly, partly for the very danger of him and for the zest of feeling his own powers stretched to their uttermost in controlling himn, is well alive to these proceedings, but cannot be moved by those nearest in his counsel (Beroald, Jeronimy, Roder, Barganax) to take overt action to coerce him.

At last, this summer of 775, the King has secret intelligence (which he partly discloses to the Chancellor and to the Duchess but to no person else) of a conspiracy to seize Rerek and set it up as a realm to itself, with the Vicar for king. The conspirators have appointed to meet one night in Middlemead, a lonely ruined farmstead on the upper waters of the Zenner; and here the King means to surprise them in person: 'wherein if I bring not the rest to destruction and him to his obedience, at least I'll die attempting it.' At the last moment he makes the Chancellor wait behind, a few miles short of Middlemead, and himself goes on, completely alone.

This incredible act of daring succeeds. The Parry, already misdoubting him of the sufficiency of these men he has assembled to be his instruments, and (which the King had with unerring insight gambled upon) coming himself to heel when faced with the King in person, accepts the King's whispered diagnosis of the situation: namely, that the Vicar has lighted by chance upon a wasps' nest which the King has come himself to take. The five rebel lords, suddenly surprised, are overcome by the King and the Vicar after a bloody fight, and their three survivors (Gilmanes, Arquez, and Clavius) are, upon the King's direction, then and there beheaded by Gabriel Flores.

TO THIS POINT, THE ARGUMENT HAS NOT REALLY EXPRESSED ANYTHING THAT HAS NOT ALREADY BEEN NARRATED IN *A FISH DINNER IN MEMISON*, BUT THE CONCLUDING SECTION SHOWS HOW EDDISON PLANNED TO GIVE NEW TREATMENT TO THE EPISODE OF MIDDLEMEAD:

This episode, treated in detail in *A Fish Dinner in Memison*, is in this present book not narrated directly but disclosed in a private and secret conversation, after the event, between the Vicar and his mother Marescia, now aged seventy-three. He has always been her favourite child, and so far as he ever opens his mind to anybody it is to her. But even from her sympathetic ear the greater part (for example, the true extent of his implication in this conspiracy) is forever hidden.

The Vicar's personal attachment to the King not even this treason can break: in fact the outcome is an immeasurable strengthening of it. The savage dog has, for the first time, snapped at his master. But he knows he ought not to have done it, and is sorry. He will never snap at King Mezentius again; but all the more is he inwardly resolved to brook no overlordship in Rerek (were the King to die) from a young quat such as Styllis, or, for that matter, from Barganax.

Bad feeling has been growing between the Vicar and Styllis to an extent that gives Rosma real anxiety. For the first time she comes to be ranged in a definite hostility against her cousin the Vicar, and tries, in sober earnest not in half earnest as of old, to set the King against him. But her efforts merely harden the King in his curious affection for this untameable unforeseeable ravening wild beast of his, grown now so big that by no power on earth can he be safely handled but by the King's personal ascendancy alone.

IN JANUARY 1945, EDDISON DRAFTED NOTES FOR THE CONVERSATION BETWEEN THE VICAR AND HIS MOTHER, AND THESE NOTES FOCUS UPON ROSMA'S ENMITY TOWARD THE VICAR:

The Vicar and Marescia. Bring out in this conversation that fact – shrewdly suspected, and (?) revealed by some indiscretion of the questions which has come to his ear, by the Vicar – that Rosma is now definitely his enemy on account of the bad blood between him and Styllis. Also bring out fact that the Vicar (before Middlemead) began to believe that Rosma's influences had in fact turned the King against him, but the episode had now convinced him he was mistaken, and his whole mind is now cleared of that suspicion and concentrated on effecting a long-term reinsurance policy against the event of Styllis's succession to the throne.

ON MAY 25, 1945, EDDISON WROTE MORE NOTES FOR THIS CONVERSATION:

Laimak: the Vicar and Marescia.
  Steer round the rocks by
  a) making the Vicar not reveal too much and
  b) making it clear (and this can partly be done in the earlier chapters) that his relationship with his mother is strangely confidential, and that is why he can say as much as he does. Make clear at end of scene that he has not told the whole truth – not even to her (and the reader ought to realise what the whole truth is: also that the King had astutely guessed true).

XXXII

Then, Gentle Cheater

THE ARGUMENT FOR THIS CHAPTER BEGINS THUS:

THE STROKE at Middlemead (publicly understood, with the King's connivance, to have been a signal service to the crown on the part of the Vicar) was on 26 June 775 [AZC]. During the following few weeks, Barganax's frequenting of Fiorinda's company has become matter for every scandalous breath in both Memison and Zayana.

ON 27 JANUARY 1945, EDDISON MADE NOTES FOR THE EARLY DAYS OF THE RELATIONSHIP BETWEEN BARGANAX AND FIORINDA:

Barganax, except for purposes of his weekly presences in Zayana, is now always in Memison. On polite (but never friendly) terms with Morville: paints Fiorinda's portrait (the El Greco). This arranged on the Thursday, June 25 – first sitting to be Sunday, June 28. This portrait painting is his very transparent stalking-horse. Morville is generally present and conversation is discreet.

June 28 – Barganax begins by talking about the portrait and the difficulties. Fiorinda is very knowledgeable about this, which delights him. She also talks about his management of his dukedom, and is in her turn delighted: he is evidently not disposed to let any affair interfere with that (or with his art).

After a few days Barganax gets a private interview – in Memison,

on the out-terraces, in the heat of the day (Date: Wednesday July
1st) Fiorinda very subtly and delicately begins asking him about
his views on love. This talk is interrupted by Morville. He is correct
in his behavior but clearly angry to find them together.

ON THE SAME DAY THAT HE MADE THE NOTES ABOVE, EDDISON
DRAFTED A WORKING VERSION FOR THE PRIVATE INTERVIEW OF
WEDNESDAY 1 JULY 775 AZC ON THE OUT-TERRACES:

Barganax:	The art of love is the art of pleasing women.
Fiorinda:	But your grace has never been married.
Barganax:	That is true, but true also, what I said.
Fiorinda:	I daresay it is true. Does it mean we are harder to please?
Barganax:	I think so. When you're worth pleasing: and most of you are for a time.
Fiorinda:	I think if I were a man I should not bother my head – or my heart – much about the temporary cases. After all, love is a bird easily caught, if one has the right bait and nets, but to keep it is what needs art.
Barganax:	The art of keeping it: a new idea to me. I wonder where it came from? What's the secret of that, do you think?
Fiorinda:	For men or for women?
Barganax:	For both.
Fiorinda:	That one should find every morning and every night something span-new in the same person.
Barganax:	A profound saying. Is it permissible to ask whether it is spoken from experience or merely from theorizing?
Fiorinda:	Permissible to ask? Yes. But also permissible not to answer. I think it rather an impertinent question.

Morville clearly angry to find them together, and Fiorinda looking
particularly lovely and 'wrought up' in a way he instinctively

recognises but has never noted so strongly before, and the sight of her, so stirred, lights his jealousy in a terrible manner. He conceals it as well as he can, but becomes boorish and unpleasant. The Duke finally departs and they go home together in silence: Morville surly and melancholy, Fiorinda singing and 'walking on flowers'.

THE ARGUMENT SUMMARIZES THE BEHAVIOUR OF FIORINDA, MORVILLE, AND BARGANAX DURING THE FIRST THREE WEEKS OF JULY 775 AZC:

The lady, with every exasperation of mockery, elusiveness, and unbearable provocation, holds him on a string, but at arm's length. Morville, a simple and stupid man fatally conjoined to a wife whom he can neither win nor hold nor satisfy nor understand nor be worthy of, is wrung with jealousy, while Barganax is almost driven out of his wits by a love which he can neither fulfill nor yet tear himself away from.

HIS MANUSCRIPT SHEETS ARE UNDATED, BUT EDDISON WROTE DETAILED NOTES ABOUT THE ACTIONS OF THESE THREE CHARACTERS DURING THE FIRST THREE WEEKS OF JULY 775 AZC:

After this (from Wednesday July 1 onwards), the Duke is daily with Fiorinda in Reisma or in Memison or meeting on rides, etc. (except only that on Fridays he has to be – and always is – in Zayana).

Scandal begins to grow. Fiorinda more and more, as she feels her power on him (and his on her), torments and plays with him, never of course to make a fool of him, but in a way that on the whole draws him daily deeper in her enchantments: so that now he has the heavenly certainty that she will let him have her; now again is dashed from such hopes; and the bitterness cured by some adorable new turn which draws him once more. Sometimes he is angry beyond controlling. In one of these moments he composes (and sends her) his poem (Dorine's in fact) 'The Dampe'. (But even in these extreme moments of resentment and half despair his nobleness of heart keeps him from any blasphemy or grossness – such as Baias or Morville are betrayed into at times of similar exasperation.)

Morville, after about a fortnight (i.e., by July 13th or 14th) is stung into a violent scene with Fiorinda. Neither of them mentions Barganax, but Morville lets out in a spate of recriminations all his self-pity, etc., all these distresses he, of the μικροψυχία of his nature, blames on her – trying by bitterness and injustice and railing to reduce her to tears which will enable him to regain some degree of ascendency in his own eyes, and make (as he thinks) a reconciliation and new start possible. But Fiorinda is not readily to be bullied into tears: she retires into her hard shell. Finally, when Morville instances his own single-eyed faithfulness, she retorts that an unfaithful husband is infinitely more tolerable than a jealous. He leaves her in a fury.

On Monday July 20 (Barganax having on the previous day been a little too possessive in his attitude, and having sent her the next morning – i.e. this Monday morning – his insolent poem 'The Dampe'), Fiorinda keeps him waiting nearly an hour attending her leisure in a gallery, then has him shown in – only to find it is a three-cornered party with Morville! Barganax behaves unexceptionally – very nice to Morville, in strong contrast to Morville's surliness and veiled hostility. Without a single sign in all the interview giving a clue to either of them what is on her mind, Fiorinda does in her heart, definitely and irrevocably this evening at last, fall in love with Barganax and resolve to take him as her lover – i.e., recognises Him with Her Olympian insight through his Zimiamvian dress, for who in truth He is. On saying goodnight She says privately to Barganax, no use coming tomorrow evening – she is going away – doesn't know for how long. Well, may be back in a week: provisional appointment for Saturday August 1. But Barganax himself goes home in despair (in the Ninfea di Nerezza mood – *A Fish Dinner in Memison*, Chapter IX), determined to be off to Zayana next day and break with her or good and be no longer dragged, an unsatisfied spaniel-dog, at her apron strings, but have his freedom again. She is an enchantress, he thinks, and high time to be out of her toils. Morville, in a boorish way, refuses to [. . .] her and they retire to bed in their respective rooms, unreconciled. She for the first time realizes the nonentity of Morville. It is Astarte, or [? . . . Hecate . . .] (not yet – not until 10 or 11 a.m. on the morrow – 21 July, Tuesday, after Morville's final blow and 'salt bitch' outburst – seated in her throne) that is tossing and turning in Fiorinda's bed in Reisma that night.

XXXIII

Aphrodite Helikoblepharos

IN ZIMIAMVIAN TIME, THE OPENING OF THIS CHAPTER FOLLOWS
BY MOMENTS ONLY THE CONCLUSION OF CHAPTER X OF *A FISH
DINNER IN MEMISON*. ON 28 JANUARY 1945, EDDISON DRAFTED A
WORKING VERSION FOR THE CONVERSATIONS OCCURRING IN REISMA
ON THE MORNING OF MORVILLE'S STRIKING OF FIORINDA:

ANTHEA and Campaspe (a little after 11.00 a.m., Tuesday, July
21st, 775 [AZC])

Anthea:	Had you not better go up to her ladyship? She will want you to do her hair.
Campaspe:	She has not rung yet.
Anthea:	No. It is late. The more need to go. I liked not the look of the bull-fly when he flung out of the house just now.
Campaspe:	Thank god he's away from home tonight.
Anthea:	Yes. The Admiral sent for him to ride north, meet the King in Rumala, and tomorrow south again. His serene highness is for Sestola. I hope Morville will break his neck. There's the bell: run you little flitterjack.

(Campaspe goes upstairs: finds Fiorinda sitting, in her hair and
in one underfrock without sleeves, before the mirror. Campaspe

is frightened at the expression of her face – Terror Antiquus – in the looking glass: sees the mark of Morville's glove stroke on her flushed face. Seeing Campaspe, her expression changes: she is her Olympian Aphrodisian self again – reaches out her hand. Campaspe kneels and kisses it, and buries her face a moment in her mistress's lap.)

Fiorinda: Put up my hair, little warbler of mine.

Campaspe: (doing so) His lordship is gone, madam. (Fiorinda says nothing, but her whole posture is like an opening rose after a storm.)

Campaspe: What will your ladyship do today?

Fiorinda: Wait. (Rings for Anthea) Anthea, go you to Memison. Find out what the Duke is about and bring me word at once.

    (Exit Anthea)

        (The mark has faded now as Campaspe shows her the back view with a hand-mirror.) No. I've changed my mind. Low on my neck, as it was this morning before breakfast. (Stretches her arms and leans back: the flashes of 'black lightning') And see you put out for tonight my new dress of red sendaline: the one I've never worn. I've been keeping it for a purpose.

Campaspe: (wide eyed) Yes, beloved madam.

Fiorinda: The clock has struck.

Campaspe: Will your ladyship wear with it the new silk cutwork undergarments I made?

Fiorinda: 'Twill be hot today. I'll wear no undergarment.

Campaspe: No, madam.

    (Re-enter Anthea)

Anthea: His grace is set forth, baggage and all, for Zayana.

Fiorinda: 'Las, has he taken me at my word then, when I told him to go this morning? How strangely will men mistake one. Saw you him set forth?

Anthea: Yes.

Fiorinda: In what fashion went he, then? At a herd's gallop?

	He is a hasty man in all he undertakes. Galloped
	he, then?
Anthea:	At a walking pace. And to the tune, methought,
	of 'Loth to depart'.
Fiorinda:	You must overtake him: fetch him back again.
Anthea:	What must we say to him?
Fiorinda:	That I request his company at supper tonight, here
	in Reisma. And inform him – not as from me, but
	in kindness as from yourselves: lightly, as upon an
	afterthought: that her ladyship sleeps alone tonight,
	the lieutenant being from home.

THE ARGUMENT FOR THIS CHAPTER GIVES FACTS WHICH ARE FULLY
NARRATED IN CHAPTERS XI AND XII OF *A FISH DINNER IN MEMISON*:

On 21 JULY, foully insulted and struck across the mouth by Morville
upon the false (or at least, premature) accusation of being the
Duke's mistress, she takes the Duke for her lover indeed. Morville,
guilty of further threats and outrage, is destroyed by Anthea in
her lynx dress.

EDDISON INTENDED TO NARRATE THE KILLING OF MORVILLE IN
THIS CHAPTER. ON 30 JANUARY 1945, HE DRAFTED THE SCENE:

Morville walking distraught in the woods near Reisma, raging in
himself: 'Yes, I'll kill them both . . .'

Anthea (in her own shape appearing from behind a tree) 'Good
morrow, for the second time today, my lord Morville. Is it safe
for you, think you, to wander in these woods alone and unarmed?
You are a great striker of women. I know. You struck my Lady
yesterday morning, an act that requires your death. And you struck
me betwixt midnight and dawn with your riding-whip. So, upon
that great count and this small one (yet to me of itself sufficient)
I have tracked you forth and mean now to rid you of your life.'

Morville becomes numb and with clumsy fingers draws forth
his dagger.

Anthea: 'You have not the power to murder me (the dagger drops from his fingers), but the will to do it so courts, if the cup of your iniquities were not already full. You have been tried and found wanting. I hate such horrified cattle as you should walk upon middle earth: but there's one thing yet you can do: your flesh shall make me a breakfast.'

Morville: 'Witch, deviless, I'll slay you with my hands, and then your mistress, and then her vile leman. Then at last I'll die happy.'

Leaps upon her. She, suddenly in her lynx-dress, fastens her teeth in the great veins of his throat: tears him bloodily in pieces, eats her fill, takes her shape again and, beautiful and virginal, returns to Reisma.

AFTER DUELLING WITH MORVILLE (A SCENE NARRATED IN CHAPTER XII OF *A FISH DINNER IN MEMISON*), BARGANAX RETURNS WITH FIORINDA TO THE SECRET CHAMBER WHOSE DOOR CAN BE REVEALED ONLY THROUGH DOCTOR VANDERMAST'S MAGIC. ON 29 JANUARY 1945, EDDISON MADE NOTES ABOUT THE EVENTS OF 22 JULY 775 AZC:

Barganax and Fiorinda waking (for 2nd time) about 9–10 a.m., in Reisma on Wednesday morning July 22:

Barganax wakes and sees her asleep. The 'peace of her beauty'. The soul asleep in her face, but in the beauty of her naked body (the clothes thrown off and piled on the floor) the sleepless spirit awake, argus-eyed, as if returning her lover's gaze. She had fallen asleep in the crook of her arm, her cheek resting upon his heart. The black hair in deep confusion all over the pillows and bed: the white line of the parting, under his eye as he looks down on her, straight and undeviating as the right road of true love. He softly kisses it: her eyes open and she puts up her lips as though there had never been since world's beginning an awakening upon which these two had not so kissed good-morning.

That same afternoon Duke Barganax rode south to Zayana in preparation for certain knotty questions to be dealt with on Friday at his weekly presence, then, with promise to be back by Saturday.

For upon Saturday his mother had appointed to give a fish dinner in the King's honour in Memison to but eight guests besides: the Vicar, the Admiral, the Chancellor, and the Duke, and for ladies, besides Fiorinda, the Princess Zenianthe, Anthea, and Campaspe. As he rode southward, he found men's mouths full of talk: how that the Lord Morville had been eat up with wild beasts in the woods near Reisma: but no word of another truth which might have tasted yet saucier to some of these blabbers, namely that a duel had been fought in Reisma in the midnight hours betwixt Morville and the Duke: neither hurt, but Morville worsted: spared by the Duke, but departed unreconciled and loudly menacing murder against both the Duke and my lady Fiorinda. Of her the Duke was not spared the hearing of much dishonest talk that day: as that she rustled in unpaid-for silks, lived very disorderly, married but to unmarry herself by running away or, the better to unencumber herself of a husband, take a resolution to have him murdered. Such talk, uttered in Barganax's presence, mixed so ill with memories in his mind and veins of the forenight, that not two but three men's blood was shed by him in that journey in [. . .] for such slander talk: two in duels; the third but seized and flung against a wall, to so good effect as dash his brains out, so that he never again spoke word.

THE REST OF THE ARGUMENT FOR THIS CHAPTER SUMMARIZES THE GROWING RELATIONSHIP BETWEEN FIORINDA AND BARGANAX:

The course of true love for Barganax and Fiorinda never runs smooth: their natures are too fierce, hazardous, and passion-ridden, for that. But it runs always deeper and stronger and with mounting superlatives, and always morning-new. He repeatedly urges her to become Duchess of Zayana, but she as steadfastly refuses; knowing, by an insight which (in common with all her qualities) reaches perhaps beyond the strain of mortality, that it is in the core of his nature to set supreme store by unsafeties and uncertainties, dangerous elysiums, the bittersweet: γλυκύπικρος ἔρως. And these things she gives him, unfailably, often almost unbearably, and with both hands.

THE FISH DINNER AND ITS AFTERMATH

NOTE ON TRANSITION TO CHAPTER XXXIV AND ON CHAPTER XXXV
AS YET UNWRITTEN.

ON 25 July, the Duchess entertains privately at a fish dinner in
Memison the King, the Vicar, Barganax, Jeronimy, Beroald,
Fiorinda, Anthea, Campaspe, and the King's niece Zenianthe.

The talk turns to divine philosophy, and so to questions of Time
and Creation: *If we were Gods, what manner of world would we
choose to make?* To this question, raised by the King, most of the
company answer, in effect: This actual world (that is to say, of
course, Zimiamvia). But my Lady Fiorinda, in a dangerously irre-
sponsible and contrary mood tonight, and speaking as if the King
were in sober truth the Almighty and she herself Aphrodite Herself,
for whom this and all conceivable worlds are made, asks him to
make for her a strange mechanical hitherto undreamed-of world
which she describes at large.

What followed, upon this request, probably none of the company
but the two pairs of lovers (the King and Amalie, Barganax and
Fiorinda) fully understood. Certainly, all present, the King and
Fiorinda alone excepted, had forgotten by next morning.

The fact was this: Speculation merged into action: the King,
sitting there at supper, did in very truth create, to her specification,
this world we ourselves live in and belong to, so that they saw it

evolve, a large teeming bubble, as this whole material universe might present itself under the eyes of the Gods, its miniature aeons passing beneath Their immortal gaze, as millions of years condensed into, say, half an hour. More than this: the King and the Duchess, Barganax and Fiorinda, in a desire to *know* this new world from within, entered it and so lived out a life-time here (in our own century), while to the other guests they merely seemed to sit gazing in a rapt attention for a few minutes on a monstrous bubble poised before them on the supper-table. Then the company, returning to reality, began to break up for bed. Fiorinda, in her most languefied luxuriousness lazying on Barganax's arm, having understandably had more than enough of this not very admirable world, snuffed it out for ever as though it had never existed, by idly pricking the bubble with a bediamonded hair-pin idly drawn from her hair as she passed. In that moment the Duke, looking in Her face, which is the beginning and the ending, from all unbegun eternities, of all conceivable worlds, knew perhaps (momentarily, and with as much certainty as is good for him) Who in very truth She was.

(This theme [of our present world as a misconceived and, were it not for its nightmarish unreality and transience, unfortunate episode in the real life of the Gods] is the subject of another book, *A Fish Dinner in Memison*. In *The Mezentian Gate* that ground is not gone over again, but sufficient indications are allowed to appear of the nature and outcome of the proceedings at supper-table to enable a reader to realize the cosmic repercussions of Aphrodite's sudden 'unfledged fancy' and to be prepared for their effect upon the mind of the King. It is to be noted, that he and Fiorinda alone remember next morning (and thereafter) what took place at the fish dinner after talk had passed over into action.)

This brings us to August 775. Chapter XXXIV (*The Fish Dinner: First Digestion*), dealing with the effect of the fish dinner upon the minds of the Duchess and of Barganax, is already written. The as yet unwritten Chapter XXXV (*Diet a Cause*), covering the next six months or so, deals with the effects upon the King and the Vicar.

The effect on the King, of this taste in Himself of omniscience combined with omnipotence in practice, is partly disclosed in a scene between him and Vandermast.

On the Vicar, who smells a subtle change in his great master which he is at an utter loss to define or understand but which he finds profoundly disturbing, the effect is to determine him to take all further precautions against the possibility that the King may die and he himself be left to fight for his place in the sun. By all covert means the Vicar begins to build up his armed strength in Rerek to such a pitch that, if it should come to a trial of mastery between himself and Styllis, he shall prevail, even though the united forces of Fingiswold and Meszria be brought to bear against him.

The grand finale of the book (Chapters XXXVI–XXXIX: *Rosa Mundorum*, *Testament of Energeia*, *Call of the Night-Raven*, and *Omega and Alpha in Sestola*) is already written.

E. R. E.

BOOK SEVEN

TO KNOW OR NOT TO KNOW

XXXIV

The Fish Dinner: First Digestion

UPON a morning of late August the Duchess of Memison was
abroad before breakfast upon the out-terraces above the western
moat. The year was turning golden to all ripenesses, of late flowers,
and fruit, and (albeit yet far off) fall of the leaf. In this light of
early morning the yew hedges that run beside the terraces were
covered with spiders' webs wet with dew-drops, a shimmering of
jewels on mantles of white lace: a beauty ever changing, and with
a hint of things altogether strengthless and ephemeral. No bird-voice
sounded, except twitterings of swallows in the sky or exclamations
from the Duchess's white peacocks, whose plumage was like woven
moonbeams, and the eyes in their tail-feathers like iridescent moons
when they displayed in the slant rays of the sun.

At the far end of the terrace southwards, she was met with
Duke Barganax, picking his way among the peacocks and bending,
as he came towards her, to stroke now this one, now that. They
drooped tails, and with an elegant, crawling, swimming, undulating
gait, in its extremity of submission too abject to be called pavane,
passed under his hand for the caress. 'You are up early, my lady
Mother,' he said.

'Well, and what of you? And besides, is it not a virtue?'

'Depends of the occasion. For my part, I never (provided I lie
alone) insult a fair morning by lying a-bed.'

'A very needful proviso. But tell me,' said she, 'while I think on't: was not that a misreckoning of mine, at our fish dinner here a month ago, not to bid you bring the learned doctor with you, 'stead of leave him to stew in his most metaphysical juices in Zayana?'

'I had not thought so. Why?'

'Might have told us now what in sober truth happened that night.'

'I can tell you that,' said the Duke. 'Noble feasting. Good discourse.'

'No more?'

'Come, you remember as well as I.'

The Duchess shook her head. 'If so, we are in one ridiculous self-same plight of forgetfulness. I remember nought past the ordinary, as you have summed it. But even next morning I woke to a discomfortable and teasing certainty that there was much forgot; and amongst it, the heart and argument of our whole proceeding.'

'What if 'twere so indeed?' said the Duke. ''Twas but pleasant talk. If unremembered, as like as not worth the remembering.'

They walked slowly on, back along the terrace, in the way of the summer palace, peacocks following them at heel. She said presently, 'More I consider of it, more am I suspicious that 'twas not talk only, but something we did. Could I call it back to mind, might give me the key to unlock certain perplexities.'

'Did you not ask the King my Father?'

'Yes. But no light there. Did but laugh at me: fub me up with quips and riddles and double meanings: made me worse.'

'Or my lord Chancellor? Or the Admiral (heaven be kind to him)? No light there? As for the Vicar—'

''Las,' said she, 'what a red lion, and what a red fox, is that! Disputations in divine philosophy are but dry hard biscuit to him.'

'And to mend the dryness, did drink drunk or the true main act of our masque were led on. And that, as myself have noted in him afore this, needeth an unconscionable, unimaginable, deal of wine.'

'The true main act: what was that?'

'Why,' said he, 'I meant when, after the rest of us (you remember this, surely?) had spoken our minds 'pon the question: What world would we choose to dwell in for ever, say we were Gods, and thus able to have our desire fulfilled into our hand soon as thought on? I meant when, after that, she, under pressure from you and from my Father, began to speak of the world which, had she that absolute sovereignty of choice, she would choose.'

'And it was—?'

Barganax had come to a stand: his gaze across the dew-drenched grass. Here, seen in the pathway of the sun, hundreds of starry lights glowed and sparkled: topaz, emerald, fire-opal, ruby, sapphire, diamond; always changing place and colour, kindling, flashing, disappearing and appearing again in least expected places, as some shift of the eye of the beholder called them into being or laid them by; tiny unsure elysiums, here and away, unreachable; and yet perfect, yet never wholly extinguished: spawned or conceived by this unsightable golden splendour of the risen sun. 'Strange. 'Tis a thing I had not thought on,' he said; 'my mind being bent on things nearer my concern. But true it is, when I try now to recall that latter part of our discourse, I am in your case: 'tis gone from me.'

'Perhaps the night put it from our minds?'

'The night?' said the Duke: no more. But when he looked round at her it was as with eyes dimmed after gazing too near at hand into a naked flame.

He began to walk up and down, the Duchess in silence watching him. Suddenly he turned heel, came straight to her where she stood, took her in his arms and kissed her. He said, still holding her, looking down into her eyes: 'Who made you such a queen-rose, my Mother?'

'I don't know,' she said, and hid her face on his shoulder, her right hand coming up to his cheek. 'I don't know. I don't know.' When she looked up, her eyes were smiling.

Taking her hands in his, 'What is this?' he said. 'You're not unhappy?'

'Something has changed since that night.' She was looking down now, playing with his fingers.

'Come, sweet Mother. You have not changed. I have not changed.'

'God be thanked, no. But – well, weather has changed.'

'Nonsense. It is set fair.'

'It is changed,' said she, 'and changing. I have a disliking for changes.'

He said, after a pause, 'I think I should die of the tediousness without them.'

The Duchess smiled. 'Everybody has a different weather, I suppose. You and I certainly. May be that is why we love each other.'

Barganax kissed her hand. She caught his and, under laughing protest, kissed it.

'My Father, then?'

She said, 'I can feel the change in him. It frightens me. I would have him never change.'

'And he you.'

'That is true, I know.'

Barganax's brow was clouded. He walked over to the parapet's edge, upon their left, and stood there silent a minute, looking over. The Duchess followed him. 'I have not seen him since then,' he said, after a while. 'So I cannot tell.' A clump of belladonna lilies were in flower there beside them: thick strong stems, sleek and columnar, and great trumpets of a silvery rose-colour, smooth-skinned as a woman's throat, cool, bedewed, exhaling a heavy sweetness. The Duke picked one. Suddenly he spoke: 'Can you remember what she said that night, when you and my Father pressed her to answer? About her world she would have?'

'Yes. That came before the things I have forgotten. She said: "The choice is easy. I choose *That which is*."'

'True. And the King took exceptions: saith, what could that be but the ultimate Two alone? They, and the lesser Gods and Goddesses who keep the wide heaven, of a lower reality, may be, than His and Hers, yet themselves more real than such summer-worms as men? And he bade her picture it to him that he might perceive it: all this and the golden mansions of the Father – I liked not that. I saw she was angry with him, thinking he mocked. She was in a strange contrary temper that evening. Answered him, "No. Like as her grace, I also will change my mind too: look lower." You remember that *Look lower?*'

The Duchess covered her face with her hands. 'When I would remember, I seem to walk on a swaying rope between darkness and darkness. What happened in truth that night?' she said, looking up again. 'Had we drunk too much wine, will you think?'

'A love-draught?' said Barganax. ''Tis not impossible.' He clasped his strong hand about his mother's shoulder and drew her to him: then, in her ear: 'Those words, *Look lower*. And with them a look in her eye I'll swear, Mother, no eye but mine hath seen or shall ever; to be seen, it needs to be loved. An unplacable look: a serpent-look.'

'The dream comes back to me,' said the Duchess, turning her fingers in his, of his hand that rested on her shoulder. '"I have thought of a world," she said. "Will your highness create it indeed for me?"'

'Be careful,' the Duke said, in a kind of fierceness. 'It was no dream. You have brought it back alive to me, and not the words only, neither. You have caught the very accents of her voice beyond all elysiums.' Then, loosing his hold and stepping back to have full view of her: 'You remember my Father's reply? "I'll do my endeavour"?'

The Duchess was trembling. 'Since when have you, my son, had this art to speak to me, out of your own mouth, with his voice?'

'She lifted her head,' said the Duke, as if locked up alone with his inward vision, 'as a she-panther that takes the wind. By heavens!' he said, as the Duchess lifted hers; 'you have the motion. Continue, if you love me. Continue. Her eyes were on me, though she spoke as if to him. Rehearse it: act it for me, to prove it more than a dream of mine.'

And the Duchess, looking at this son of hers as it were to look through a perspective that should show her his father, her lover, began to speak: as a sleep-walker might, not her words but the Lady Fiorinda's.

When she had ended, her son abode motionless against the

parapet, staring at her. Then she, as if by mere silence startled out of her sleep-walking: 'What have I said? It is gone from me: I cannot remember.'

He leaned towards her. 'For all sakes, remember. Think of me as the King my Father. He made it, that thing, that massy glistering bubble, even as she required it of him: made and fashioned it, there on the table before us, growing between his hands. What was it? Did we not behold it put on substance, mature to an inconceivable intricacy in obedience to her unbitted fancy? As though all Gods and Powers had been but ministers to her least desires (as, by my soul, they ought to be). But a clockwork only it was: a make-believe: a dead world.'

'His words,' said the Duchess, and trembled: 'his voice yet again. "A dead world. A dead soul." And she desired him then give it life: "Let it teem with life," she said; "and that horribly." So, and in that humour. Her laws for the living beings in that world: you remember? "I will tease them a little with my laws."'

Barganax narrowed his eyelids, looking at his mother; and yet (it may be thought) not at his mother but, in her, at his Dark Lady. 'That they should seem to have freedom,' he said; 'and yet we, who look on, should know 'tis no such matter. And her law of death: "Every one that knoweth life in my world shall know also death. The little simplicities, indeed, shall not die. But the living creatures shall." Well, was she not right? "A just and equal choice: either be a little senseless lump of jelly or of dead matter, and subsist till world's ending; or else—"'

'"Or else be a bird, a fish, a rose,"' said the Duchess, as if unburying a new fragment from amongst the chaos of broken memories of that strange supper-entertainment: '"or men and women as we be—"'

'"Upon condition to fade, wax old, waste at last to carrion and corruption" – Well? Is it so much unlike this loved world of ours?'

''Tis too much like,' the Duchess replied. 'It is the same as this world: but crooked: but spoilt.'

'Your grace needs not to tell me,' said the Duke: '*et ego in Arcadiâ*,' and he laughed, '– but that scarce fits. "Men and women as we be." And then she said, sitting at your table here, before your summer palace, while her world-destroying beauty, pensive and stilled, shone down upon that misconceived master-work of self-thwarting perfections: "As we be? How were that possible, out of this? Is there mind in this? – Unless, indeed" (you remember), "unless We Ourselves go in and enter it. Know it so, go down –" And then my Father said: "Undergrope it from within. For a moment, We might. To know."'

'No more, I beseech you,' said the Duchess. 'What are we about?'

But Barganax had her by the hand. 'Think of me constantly now, as the King my Father. Let's try it again. You and I, this time. I begin to remember things I, too, had forgot; and I know not who I am, nor who you are. Come, we will. I will know again whether there be truth in it or but make-believe.'

'Stop!' she said, 'I cannot bear it: not a second time.'

But he, still straining her by the hand, overbore her. For a minute they stood, here in lovely Memison, as two unfleshed souls might aboard Charon's ferry, waiting to be put from shore. But nothing came about: no expected half-remembered translation out of their native substantiality of life and being into a more dimmer and crippled world, in detail so like, in sum so alien: unimaginable now: a prison-life which had been, or could be, theirs, but now well forgotten; and yet half tasted in remembrances which, slight, smudged, fleeting, were now blessedly lost again, blotted out in a wreathing of mists and fog and billowing darkness. Then, as with the going of a shadow from across the sun's face, was this real world back again true and perfect: smells of wet earth and wood-smoke, the snail on the path, the wren scolding from the yews: on the glassy waters of Reisma Mere afar a rippling here and there where the morning breeze touched them: great sulphur-coloured lilies seen against the yews' darkness, distilling on the air their voluptuous sweet scent: morning light upon Memison; and breakfast-time.

The same day, Duke Barganax rode south, having appointed the day after to hold his weekly presence: receive petitions, hear suits if any there were of enough matter and moment to be pleaded before him in person, treat with men in their quarrels and set them at one, or, where that would not speed, deliver judgement and give order for its execution.

It was past supper-time when he rode up into Acrozayana. He delayed but to eat some cold collation: smoked salmon, caviar, boar's head spiced and dressed with hippocras sauce, with a flagon of Reisma wine to wash it down; then, retiring himself to the western balcony of his own privy lodging that looks on Zayana lake and Ambremerine, summoned Doctor Vandermast. 'I would have your head in a matter, honoured sir: not as my secretary, but as of old, master and teacher in the noble dark science. How came this world, think you, and other worlds if other there be?'

Vandermast answered and said, 'By God alone, that made all.'

'Good. *Ergo*, made also Himself?'

'Undoubtedly so. Your grace hath not forgotten the definitio: *Per causam sui intelligo id, cujus essentia involvit existentiam: sive id, cujus natura non potest concipi nisi existens?* Nought else save God alone is able to be cause of itself, since nought else hath such a nature as is not able to be conceived save as existing. In none else doth the Essence thereof inescapably involve also the Existence.'

The Duke sat gazing before him, as rapt with some picture in his mind. Then leaning forward to look in the doctor's eyes (as well as a man were able, under their shadowing eaves and but starlight to see by): 'But there is a Twoness,' he said, 'in the ultimate Onehead of Godhead?'

'There is a Darkness. If indeed by God we understand a Being absolutely infinite, that is to say, a Substance made up and compounded of infinite attributes, every particular one of which expresseth an Essence infinite and eternal.'

'And you yourself,' said the Duke, leaning nearer, eyeing him yet closelier, 'when I was but of years sixteen and did first dally with the Metaphysicals, you did ground me in that principle you name lode-star and cynosure of divine philosophy: *Per realitatem et perfectionem idem intelligo*: "Reality," that is, "and perfection are the same thing."'

'Through the monster-teeming seas of thought, ay, and in action, assaying those topless spires whence in highest majesty God looks down, that,' replied Vandermast, 'is indeed man's cynosure: the alonely certain star to steer by.'

Barganax sat back in his chair. The sky was of a soft violet-colour and full of stars whose beams showed, in those windless upper airs, a strange constancy, but the mirrored stars in Zayana lake swayed and broke in pieces and ran together again as quicksilver: a changefulness and a restlessness like as that of the dew-lights that morning in Memison. A like unrestful secretness stirred under the deep harmonies of his voice as he said, as if examining some strange unheard-of novelty in his own hidden mind: '*Realitatem: Perfectionem*. Well, I have found perfection.'

Doctor Vandermast held his peace.

The Duke said, still as to himself, almost with a tang of mockery in his accents, yet in the same slow wonder: 'Am not I therefore beyond example fortunate? What need I further, having possessed me of Perfect and Real in One?' He stretched his arms as one waking from sleep, and laughed. 'Come, you are silent. Will you envy me, old man, to have found, and in my young years, this true philosopher's stone?'

'How shall any man but yourself tell whether you are to be envied or commiserated? Satiety is death. Desire is life.'

'And is not the mere quality of Perfection, this,' said the Duke, leaping to his feet to stand against the balustrade, his back to the night sky, his face in deep shadow looking down on Vandermast: 'to be infinite? Infinitely desirable, and infinitely unsupportable: explored without and within, yet ever the more terrible and the more appassionately sought in its unknowable secrets. In fiercest beauties, in supremest *deliciis*, absent, yet absent unsparable. And so, elysium beyond elysiums: here and away, yet so as a man would joyfully cut his hand off to buy off change, and when change is come, cut off t' other sooner than go back to *status quo ante*.'

'*Laetitia*,' said that ancient doctor slowly, as to weigh each word, '*est hominis transitio a minore ad majorem perfectionem*: Joy is the passing of a man from the smaller to the greater perfection.'

'And (corollarium) the greater oft-times becometh greater by bringing back the smaller. Infinite change; yet infinite self-same bewitchment.' There was a grandeur of line, beyond the use of human kind, in the lithe frame of him outlined there against stars. Vandermast watched him in silence, then spoke: 'I observed this in your grace, even at my first coming into your noble service, that alike by soul and body you are of apt temper to understand the depth of that wisdom: *Nous connaissons la vérité non seulement par la ration, mais encore par le coeur; c'est de cette dernière sorte, que nous connaissons les premières principes.*'

'That is wisdom,' said Barganax. 'That is truth.' He settled himself on the stone of the balcony that was warm yet after a day of unclouded sun, and, sitting there against the sky, said: 'Our talk hath wandered somewhat beside my purpose, which concerned the making of worlds. Were I to tell you I saw one such devised and created, under my nose, a month ago, at supper-table, would you credit that?'

Doctor Vandermast paused. 'As coming from your grace, known to me for a man of keen judgement and not given to profane jesting, I should impartially examine it.'

'I have not told you I saw it. The more I consider of it, the less know I whether I truly beheld that marvel or 'twere but legerdemain.'

'If it pleased your grace open it to me more at large—'

'Better not. I have indeed almost clean forgotten it, save the circumstances. But this I will tell you, that I seemed, when 'twas over, to have lived myself (and yet something more than myself: mixed of myself and his serene highness my Father, and, in the mixture, may be a less than him and something less too than me, as impurer; like as orange-colour hath not the pureness of red neither of yellow, being compound of both) – in that mixed self, I seemed to have lived a life-time in that world. Well,' he said, after a moment: 'I sucked its orange. But a cheap frippery of a world it was, take it for all in all: made tolerable, as I bethink me now, but by rumours and fore-savourings of this. And I seemed, besides, to have looked on from without, while untold ages passed there: first the mere ball of incandescence: then the cooling: the millennial ages through which a kind of life was brewing, in enormous wastefulness and painfulness and ever-growing interweaving of tangle, until human kind began there: slow generations, ever changing and never (on the whole) bettering, of human kind, such as we be. Ay, and I was stood by, viewing it thus from withoutward, even at the golden moment for which that defaced, gelded, exiled creation, so like the real world, yet so unlike, had from its first beginnings waited and thirsted: its dissolution. And that was when she, to pleasure whose chanceable idle soon-changed fantasy it was made, took from the braided blackness of her hair a pin starred with anachite diamonds, and as idly with it touched the bubble. And at that prick – puff! 'twas gone: nought left but the little wet mark on the table to witness it ever existed.'

Vandermast said: 'With one breath They create: with one breath uncreate.'

'I have forgot, almost,' said the Duke. Then, 'Indeed since I spoke to you even this instant moment gone, old sir, all is fled from me, like as dreams are scattered and broken at the very words we wake with on our lips to recount them. This remains (O the unsounded seas of women's bloods), that that night she wore glow-worms in her hair.'

'There is danger for a man,' said Vandermast, after a silence, 'in knowing over-much.'

'Or for a God?'

'To be able to answer that with certainty,' said Vandermast, 'were, for a mortal, to know over-much.'

XXXV

DIET A CAUSE

EDDISON WROTE NO ARGUMENT FOR THIS CHAPTER, AND THERE
ARE NO EXTANT DRAFTS FOR IT. HE DISCUSSES IT BRIEFLY IN 'THE
FISH DINNER AND ITS AFTERMATH'.

XXXVI

Rosa Mundorum

VELVRAZ Sebarm stands upon the lake, among orange trees and pomegranates and almonds and peaches of the south, a mile north-west over the water from Zayana town, and two miles by land: an old castle built of honey-coloured marble at the tip of a long sickle-shaped ness that sweeps round southwards, with wild gardens running down in the rocks to the water's edge, and behind the castle a wood of holm-oaks making a windbreak against the north. Here my Lady Fiorinda was keeping household in June of that next year, some few months later than these things last told of, the Duke having put it at her disposition for such times as she should not be resident in Memison or his guest in Acrozayana.

It was midsummer morning, at the half-light before the break of day. For the heat of the night, the curtains were left undrawn in the great bedchamber that looks three ways across the water: south, towards Zayana, whose towers, spires, and gables seemed in this twilight to be of no solider substance than the sky against which they rose, the reflections of them barely set moving by a ripple on the lake's placid surface: west, to the isle of Ambremerine, wooded with oak and cedar and cypress and strawberry-tree, and all misted with the radiance behind it of the setting silver moon: east, across low vineyard-clad country, to the sea at Bishfirthhead. Within that chamber the colourless luminosity of the summer

night, beginning to obey at this hour some influence of the unrisen
sun, partly obscured, partly revealed, shapes and presences: lustrous
balls of moon-stone and fire-opal like a valance of strange fruits
fringing the canopy of the great bed, which was built to the Duke's
designing and by art of Doctor Vandermast, and with posts of
solid gold: lamps and sconces and branched hanging candlesticks
of gold and silver and crystal: pictures let into the panels of the
doors of tall wardrobe presses: bookshelves filled with books
between the windows: two scented lamps, filigree-work of orichalc,
burning for night-lights at the bed's head, one upon either side,
whose beams dimly lighted a frieze, of eagles, phoenixes, chimaeras,
satyrs, gorgons, winged bulls, sea-goats with fish-tailed bodies,
water-horses, butterfly-ladies, carved out of rose-coloured marble
in high relief on a background of peacock green. And with the
incense of the lamps was mingled a perfume more elemental and
of a sweeter and more disturbing luxury: of that lady's breath and
her sleeping presence.

She lay there prone, in an innocency of beauty asleep, face
turned aside and pillowed in the curve of her right elbow, her left
hand inshrining its smoothness between smooth right arm and
cheek. All naked she slept, sheet and bed-clothes thrown off to lie
in a heap upon the floor at the bedside for warmness of the night.
Anthea, too, was asleep on the bed, curled up in her lynx shape
at her mistress's feet.

From the gardens below the western window, the first bird-song
sounded: bodiless little madrigal of a peggy-whitethroat, ending
upon that falling cadence. So, and again. A third time; and the
dividing notes took to themselves the articulation of human speech:
Campaspe singing her morning hymn to Her that is mistress both
of night and of day:

> 'Our Lady, awake!
> Darkness is breaking.
> Bat wings are folded:
> Crop-full the owl.

Night-flowers close,
Their sweetness withhold:
The east pales and quickens to gold:
Night-raven and ghoul
Flee to their make.

A breath of morning stirs on the lake.
Colours disclose:
Carnation, rose.
The Worlds are waking—
Thou, Onemost, awake!'

At the sound of that singing and at a touch of the lynx's cold
nose against her foot, Fiorinda, with a little unarticulate slumbrous
utterance still betwixt sleeping and waking, turned on her back.
In a more slowed voluptuousness than of python uncoiling, she
stretched her sleep-loosened limbs to the wide ambiency of self-
oblation, and, with that, her whole body was become a source of
light: sea-glitter between her opening eyelids: a Praxitelean purity,
swan-white fined to tinctures of old ivory, in breast, throat, thigh,
and in all the supple rondure of her hips: panther-black livery of
the darkness that burned as consuming fires, blackness shining
down blackness to the out-splendouring of all earthly suns. Her
youth, with the lithe wild-beast strength and dove-like languor of
these perfections, shadowless now, faintly incandescent, was trans-
figured to that ache and surquedry of beauty which great poets
and great lovers, uncontented by earth's counterfeits, have strained
inward eye and sense to draw down from Olympus, those things'
true home; where they subsist unsmirched by times or allegiances
unsubject to their sovereignty, and are not exiles bound servant
to ends not theirs. Thus for a while (which whether it were of
minutes or of ages, were a question barren of all result or answer)
she lay: She of Herself: the verities of Her waking presence manifest, convenable to sight, touch, hearing, scent, and taste: here, in
Velvraz Sebarm.

Rising at last from the golden bed, She stood to contemplate awhile, in the tall looking-glass by the growing light, the counter-image of Her own face and, at their plenilune upon which not even the eyes of a God can long bear to rest, Her ultimate beauties, from unbegun eternity lode-star, despair, and under-song, of all hearts' desires. And now, with Her standing so in deific self-knowing, everything that was not Her went out like the flame of a blown-out candle: the room, the familiarities of that Meszrian countryside, the softness of velvet carpet under Her feet, fallen to the formless ruin of oblivion.

Beneath Her, presently, some unfading dawn uncovered itself: morning of life, ancienter than worlds: saffron-hued, touching cliff and glacier to pale gold, and throwing into gullies and across snow-fields shadows of an azured transparency, chill as the winds that sprang up with day. From behind Her mountain-top where She stood, the sun lept up, throwing the shadow of the mountain mile upon mile across lesser heights to the west-ward that were gilded with the first beams, their nearer summits bathing in primrose radiancy, their more distant in more paler, more air-softened, hues; range succeeding range to where, over the furthermost crest, day was breaking on the sea-strand and sea-foams of Paphos. Long and level in the mid distance far below Her, grey-houndish clouds drove past, trailing ever-changing shadows across the landscape of ridges and hill-tops and deep-cleft dales. Against that dawn-illumined background the great cast shadow of Olympus rested, a wide-flung wine-dark mantle of obscurity, wearing on its outermost edge a smoulder of crimson fire. Anthea and Campaspe, in their nymphish true outwards, knelt at Her feet in virgin snow. In the depths, but far above the habitations of men (if men were yet, or yet continued), a gyr-falcon, queen of the air, took her morning flight.

But She, eternal Aphrodite of the flickering eyelids and the violet-sweet breast, laughter-loving, honey-sweet, child of Zeus, She for whom all is made, spoke and said:

'Rise you worlds, made and unmade, and worship Me.

'Worship Me, women of all worlds, dresses of mine, shadows of Me in turbid water. I am the truth of you. Without those glints or keepsakes that are in you of Me, you are nothing.

'O men, kings and lords of the ages, heroes, lovers of wisdom, great strikers, adventurers upon perilous seas, makers and doers, minds and bodies framed in His image that made you, and made Himself, and because without Me Godhead were but a trash-name, therefore, to have Me beside Him from the beginning, made Me: Rise, and worship Me. Rise and, who dares, love Me. But he that would love Me, be it God Himself, shall first kiss My feet.'

Unnumbered as motes in a sunbeam, or as the unnumbered laughter of the waves of ocean, eyes were upon Her from all remoteness of earth and sky and sea, and the rumour of them was as the rumour and rustle of starlings' wings flying in flocks of unnumbered thousands.

She said: 'Look (if your sight can face the nakedness of your hidden mind) into the sea-fire of My eyes. Look: My lips, blood-red, that can at one imperial kiss drain out the rendered soul from your body, and give it back so dyed with the taste of Me as from that now unto your death you shall seek Me ever, never finding yet never altogether losing. These jewels for snares in My hair's darkness are sleet and scourge of wild-fire. The moth-like bare touch of My hand can do away worlds or raise up the dead. In Me is the Bitter-sweet; grave, cradle, and marriage-bed of all contrairs: Rose of the Worlds: Black Lily, Black Flame, that but with the glance do stab, sear, and violently stir to one essence, spirit and sense. In all noble enterprise, in all your most fantastical desires, behold here your cynosure: this centre where all lines meet. I am She that changeth, yet changeth not. Many countenances I have, many dresses, bringing to My lover the black or the red, spade or heart, or pureness of golden flowers or a gold of waning moons at morning; and maidenhead always new. Of all that was, is, or is to come, I, even I of Myself, am end, reason, last elixir. He that loveth, and he love not Me, loveth Death. Love Me who dares. He shall be Mine, I his, for ever; and if it were possible for more than ever, then for ever more.'

She ended: terrible, lifted up above all worlds, shining down all other lights, even to the sun's.

From behind Her, eastwards, the other side from Paphos, came a roaring of avalanche and rockfall. Mists blowing upwards swallowed the mountain-top in a freezing tempest of sleet and lightnings and thundering darkness. In that void where duration can have no hour-glass, time stood still, or ceased.

Then the mists, falling apart, opened a sudden window upon Ambremerine and clear morning. Fiorinda had taken about Her lovely shoulders a robe of diaphanous black silk figured with-flower-work of gold and crimson and margery-pearls. Beside her the two nymphs, looking upon her in fearful adoration, were still kneeling.

Some three hours later, about seven o'clock, the Chancellor, riding up the Memison road a mile or so north from Zayana, had sight of her above him in the high open downland: white jennet, french hood, grass-green riding-habit, merlin on fist. She saw him and began to come down leisurely by the directest way, a steep rocky slope, slacking rein for the little mare, clever as a cat, to choose her steps amid the tangle of creeping rhododendron and daphne with boulders and stumps and old scree hidden beneath it. 'Blessings of the morning upon you, my lady sister,' said he, when they were within talking-distance. 'I am from Sestola: a message from the King's highness (Gods send he live for ever), for the Duke. You and he are commanded to supper tonight, at Sestola.'

'Excellent. Have you told his grace?'

'Not yet. I intended for Velvraz Sebarm, supposing to find him there.'

'That was a strange unlikely guess. Dwells he not in Zayana?'

'A new custom, then, when your ladyship lies in Velvraz Sebarm.'

'Have you breakfasted?'

'A bite and a sup.'

'I too. Let us breakfast together ere you go back to Acrozayana.'

They turned off from the road at a walking-pace by the path that goes to Velvraz Sebarm. Their morning shadows, still long, went before them. A heat-mist was rising from Zayana lake, and all the soft landscape westward was golden with morning. 'I would counsel you, brother,' she said, 'to stick to your politics: not pry into my domestical affairs. I too have my policies: have long ago learned, like as my Lord Barganax (as you, I thought, had likely observed), that prime article of wisdom of the learned doctor: μηδὲν ἄγαν: nothing over-much.'

They rode awhile in silence.

'How like you of my little falcon? Is she not a jewel?'

The Lord Beroald perfunctorily gave it a look. 'Good for flying at vermin.'

Upon that, sourly said, she glanced sidelong at him out of her slanting green eyes. 'Clouds in your face? And so fair a morning?'

'Clouds from Rerek, may be.'

'Are but smoke-balls. Blow them away.'

'The council will sit today. By latest secret advertisements I have had, he still draweth forces to Laimak.'

'And what else indeed, then, would you look for?'

'Nought else; save now for the sequel. 'Tis time to end it.'

A satirical sumptuosity of suppressed laughter stirred at the corners of that lady's mouth. 'Heaven shield me from a condition where you and your friends swayed all. I think you would leave us no great eminent thing extant might you but avail to end it, lest by some far-fetched possibility it grow to danger perhaps your little finger.'

'I am a man of common prudence.'

'God for witness, were you that and no more, I think I'd hate you for it.'

'A quality uncommon in some quarters today.'

'Some quarters? O lawyers' equivocations! Which then?'

'Even the highest.'

'Yes, I know,' said she. 'Some safety there for unsafety, by favour of heaven.'

'Trouble not your sweet perverse heart as for that. The wolf will run: you shall see.'

'I shall see good sport, then.'

The Chancellor eyed her with a sardonic smile. 'Your ladyship was not always so chary in ending an inconvenience.'

'You think not?'

'What of your first husband? What of your second?'

'Foh!' she said. 'That was far another matter, and where there was cause why. Small nastiness, of a sort as plenty as blackberries, and thus rightly (with help of your gentle kindness, dear brother) made away.'

He laughed. 'Praise where praise is due, madam. You asked no help from me when you did up Morville.'

They were come now to the gardens, where the path leads round by the waterside to the castle gate between drifts of stately golden-eyed daisies with black-curling petals of a deep wine-purple and, at their feet, pink-coloured stonecrops on whose platter-like heads scores of butterflies sipped honey and sunned their wings. Fiorinda said, 'Because a dog grins his teeth, that means not necessarily he means to bite his master, I have known my ban-dog growl at things I could not myself neither see nor hear, much less smell. And, 'cause my dog's a good dog, and I a good mistress, let him growl. Like enough, hath his reasons.'

'Very well argued. But when, being bid stop growling, yet he growleth, that is not so good.'

'O,' said she, with a little scornful backward movement of her head, 'I follow not these subtleties. Why be so unlike your most deep discerning self, brother? When have you known the King miss in aught he set out to perform? Am I to tell you he hath power to crush him we speak on, soon as crush an importunate flea, were he so minded?'

'I dearly wish he would do it,' said the Chancellor.

'Go then, tell him to. I think you shall have the flea in your ear for your pains. As good crush me!'

As they rode up, they beheld now before them Duke Barganax, upon a marble bench without the gate under an arbour of climbing roses. The involutions of their petals held every indeterminate fair colour that lies between primrose and incarnadine: the scent of them, the mere perfume of love. He sat there like a man altogether given over to the influences of the time and the place, fondling the lynx beneath the chin and sipping hippocras from a goblet of silver. There was a merry glow in his eyes as he stood up, unbonneting, to bid her good-morrow. Helping her down from the saddle he seized occasion to salute her with a kiss, which she, as in a studied provokement and naughtiness, took upon a cold cheek and, when at second attempt he would have had her lips, dexterously withheld them.

The Chancellor, dismounting, noted this by-play with ironic unconcern. 'Fortunately met, my lord Duke,' he said, as the grooms led away their horses. 'I was to speak with your grace, by his serene highness's command, that you sup with him tonight in Sestola: a farewell banquet ere they begin their progress north again to Rialmar. You are for the council, doubtless, this afternoon?'

'I fear not, my lord.'

'I'm sorry. We need our ablest wits upon't, if aught's to come of this business.'

'I have opened all my mind to the King, and have his leave to sit out. Truth is, there's matters on hand must detain me otherwheres today. But as for supper, pray you say, with my duty, I kiss his highness's hands and joyfully obey his summons.'

'I shall.'

'Strange,' said Fiorinda, 'I am bidden too.' She sat down, shedding, as some exquisite lily sheds waft by waft its luxury abroad, a fresh master-work of seducing and sense-ensearching elegancy from every lazy feline grace of her settling herself upon the bench: eye-wages for the Duke.

'Is that so strange?' said he, his eyes upon her. 'I took't for granted.'

'What brings your grace hither in this hour of the morning?'

'Idleness,' answered he with a shrug of the shoulder. 'Want of a more reasonable employment. O, and now I remember me, I had these letters for your ladyship, to wish you well of your twentieth birthday.' With that, turning to the table before the bench where he had sat, he took a parchment: gave it into her hand.

She unrolled it. While she scanned it curiously, a delicate warmth of colour slowly imbued the proud pallor of her cheek. 'A dear bounty of your grace,' she said. 'I am deeply beholden. But indeed I cannot accept of it.'

'You will not be so uncivil as hand me back my gift.'

'Nay, indeed and indeed, I'll not have it. Mind you not the poet?—

> Nor he that still his Mistress payes,
> For she is thrall'd therefore.'

Beroald continued—

> 'Nor he that payes not, for he sayes
> Within, shee's worth no more.'

Barganax reddened to the ears. 'To the devil with your firked-up rhymes,' he said. 'Come, I give it to you freely, out of pure love and friendship. You must take it so.'

She put it into her brother's hand, who read the docket: '*Deede of feoffment to behoof of the Ladie Fiorinda by liverie of seisin to holde in fee simple the castell of Velvraz Sebarrm and the maines therof scituate in the Roiall Appannage and Dukedome of Zayana.* Why, this is princely bounty indeed.'

'Well,' said the lady, drawing down a blossom of the rose to smell to, and watching the Duke from under the drooped coal-black curtain of her eyelashes. 'Not to displeasure your grace, I'll take it. Give it me, brother: so. And now,' (to the Duke) 'hereby I give it you back, i' the like truth and kindness, and for token of my devotion to your grace's person.'

'No, you anger me,' he said, snatching the parchment and flinging it, violently crumpled, on the ground. ''Tis an unheard-of thing if I may not bestow a present upon a noble lady but 'tis spat back in my face as so much muck or dirt.'

'Dear my lord, you strain too far: I intended it far otherwise. Be not angry with me, not today of all days. And before breakfast, seems in especially unkind.'

He loured upon her for a moment; then suddenly fell a-laughing.

'Nor I'll not be laughed at, neither. Come,' she said, rising and, in a divine largesse which at once sought pardon and as sweetly dispensed it, putting her arm in his, 'let's walk apart awhile while the board's a-setting.'

When they were private, 'I think,' she began to say, looking down to the jewelled fingers of her hand where it rested, a drowsed white lily for its beauty, a sleeping danger for its capacities, upon his sleeve; as hands will oftest betray in their outward some habit or essence of the soul that informs them from within: 'I think I have a kind of mistrustful jealousy against great and out-sparkling gifts. Not little gifts, of a jewel, a horse, a gown, a book: that's but innocent gew-gaws, adornments of love. But, as for greater things—'

'O madonna mia,' said Barganax, 'you have the pride of arch-angel ruined. What care I? For I think if God should offer you fief seignoral of Heaven itself, you'd not stoop to pick it up.'

'But surely, you and I,' she said, and the accents of her voice, summer-laden, lazy, languorous, trod measure now with his foot-fall and with hers as they paced in a cool of pomegranate-trees, 'we surely gave all? Body and inward sprite, yours to me, mine to you, almost a full year ago?'

'With all my heart (though I doubt 'tis not wholesome meat for you to be told so), I say ay to that.'

'To speak naked as my nail (and 'tis time, may be, to do it),

I dwell in this house, have use of these lands and pleasaunces, joyfully and with a quiet mind; and why, my friend? Because they are yours, and, being yours, mine so far as need. For is not this wide world, and Heaven's mansions besides (if there be), not yours indeed, nor yet mine, but ours? Is it not graved in this ring you gave me – HMETEPA – Ours? Feminine singular, I that am ours: neuter plural, all else whatsoever, ours. And Velvraz Sebarm, being yours, is therefore the dearer to me, who am yet more entirely yours than it. Am not I yours by blood and breathing, glued infinitely closer than had we two one body, one spirit, to make us undistinctly one? Surely a cribbed lone self-being self were no possession, no wealth, no curious mutual engine of pleasure and of love. 'Twere prison sooner.'

The Duke spoke no word: a silence that seemed to enjoin silence to itself, lest a spell break.

'But what was given already,' she said, 'and given (as it ought to be) with that reckless, unthought, uncalculated freedom as a kiss should be given – to wish now to give that again by bond and sealed instrument, 'tis unbelievable between you and me. As though you should a bethought you: "Someday, by hap she shall be another's. Or by hap I may find (being myself too in the hot hey-day of my youth, and long wedded to variety) another mistress." And—'

'No more of these blasphemies,' said the Duke, his voice ruled, yet as holding down some wolf within him: 'lest you be blasted.'

'Nay, you shall hear it out: "And 'cause I yet love her past remedy," you might say, "I'll give her this rich demesne: and more if need be: make my munificencies play the pander, to drug her for me, and so bind her to my bed." Heaven spare us, will you think to ensure us together by investment?'

'No more,' he said, 'for God sake. 'Tis a filthy imagination, a horrible lie; and in your secret veins you know it. Why will you torture me?' But, even in the setting of his teeth, he clapped down his right hand upon hers where it lay, the pledge of her all-pervading presence quivering within it, along his sleeve: as not to let it go.

They walked slowly on for a while, without word spoken, unless in the unsounded commerce of minds, that can work through touch of hand on hand. Then Fiorinda said, 'We must turn back. My respected brother will think strange we should leave him so long with none but the waiting breakfast-covers for company.'

As they turned, their eyes met as in some mutual half-embraced, half-repudiate, pact of restored agreement: as if the minds behind their eyes were ware each of other's watchfulness and found there matter for hidden laughter. The Duke said, 'You spoke a while since of a token of your regard for me. I know a readier token, if your ladyship had honestly a mind to prove that.'

'O, let's not be chafferers of proofs.'

'It comes o'er my memory, my coming hither was to ask the honour of your company at supper.'

'Tonight?'

'Tonight, madam, I had dearly wished.'

'See then, how fortune makes good your wish before the asking. We sup together in Sestola.'

'Not entirely as I would, though.'

'Your grace is hard to please.'

'Is there aught new in that? 'Tis another likeness between us.'

The lady's head bent now in lazy contemplation of her own lilied hand, where it yet lay out, sunning like an adder in warm beams, along his fore-arm. Her eyes veiled themselves. Her lips, seeming to brood upon some unavowed, perhaps unconfirmed, assent, were honeyed gall. Under the coat-hardy, which from hip to throat fitted as glove fits hand, the Grecian splendours of her breasts rose and fell: restful unrestfulness of summer sea, or of two pigeons closed together on a roof. The Duke said: 'Is it permitted to ask where your ladyship means to lie tonight?'

'Truly I hope, abed. And your grace, where?'

'In heaven, I had a longing hope. It rests not with me to decide.'

The fingers of the hand on his arm began to stir: a sylph-like immateriality of touch: almost imperceptible.

'Well?' he said.

'You must not tease me. I am not in the mood to decide.'

He said, softly in her ear, 'All's hell that is not heaven, tonight. Would you have me lie in hell?'

Some seducing and mocking spirit sat up and looked at him from the corners of her mouth. 'A most furious and unreasonable observation. Nay, I am not in a mood for ayes and noes. I do entreat your favour, ask me no more.'

He stopped, and stood facing her. 'I think your ladyship is own daughter to the Devil in hell. No help for it, then: I take my leave.'

'Not in anger, I hope?' she held out her hand.

'Anger? Your body and beauty have for so long bewitched me, I am no longer capable even of the satisfaction of being angry with you.'

'Well, let's bear out a sober face 'fore the world: before my brother there. Some show of kindness. Pray your grace, kiss my hand, or he'll wonder at it.'

'You are unsupportable,' he said. He raised her hand, hot in his, to his lips: it drew a finger against his palm: then lay still. From her mouth's corner that thing eyed him, a limb-loosening equivocation of mockery, intoxicating all senses to swimmings of the brain. He kissed the hand again. 'Unsupportable,' he said: looked in her eyes, wide open suddenly now, strained to his in an unsmiling stilled intention, eyelids of the morning: beheld, in unceasing birth and rebirth through interkindling and gendering of contrarious perfects, the sea-strange unseizable beauty of her face: the power enchantment and dark extremity of her allurement now plainly spread in the brightness of the sun. He said: 'O abominable and fatal woman, why must I love you?'

'Is it, perhaps,' she replied, and the indolent muted music of her voice, distilling with the sweets of her breath on the air about him, wrought on the raging sense to upsurgings of subterranean fire: 'Is it, perhaps, because to your grace, unto whom all others your best desires, spaniel-like, do come to heel, this loving of me is the one only thing you are not able to command?'

XXXVII

TESTAMENT OF ENERGEIA

IN Sestola that same day toward evening, the Chancellor and Earl Roder, being come to council a little before the due time, were waiting the King's pleasure in the great stone gallery that served there as antechamber.

'Mean you by that, she has been forbid the council?' said the Earl.

'That's too rough a word.'

'Pray you amend it.'

'A bird peeped in mine ear that his serene highness graciously excuseth her from attendance today, and at her own asking.'

'Is that help to us or hindrance?'

The Lord Beroald shrugged his shoulders.

'You think unlucky?' said Roder.

'I think it of small consequence whether her highness be there or no. Yet I would she'd stayed in the north. We'd then a been spending our time in Zayana 'stead of this stony den of Sestola: fitter for a grave than for living men to dwell in.' He cast a distasteful look up at the high lancet-shaped windows whose embrasures, spacious and wide enough here withinward, narrowed to slits in the outer face of the huge main wall: slits to shoot through at assaulters from without, rather than windows to light the gallery.

'We grow customed to strange choices this twelve-month past,' Roder said.

Beroald's nostrils tightened, with a thinning of lips below close-clipped mustachios.

Roder said, 'Know you for certain what way she inclineth now, i' this thing we have in hand?'

'No. Nor much care. Strange your lordship should ask me this, who are far more in her counsels than ever I have been.'

'She is too unnatural with me of late,' said the Earl: 'too kind. Smiles at me: gives me honeyed words. Makes me afeared may be his serene highness listeneth to her more readily than he will listen to us.'

'No need to fear that.'

'No? Well, be that as may, I'm glad she cometh not to this meeting. God shield us from women on our councils of war, I never could argue with a woman. Besides, I mistrust Parry wolvishness. And bitch-wolf was ever more fell than dog-wolf, as the more uncorrigible and unforeseeable in action. Your lordship frowns? Said I not well, then?'

'Too loud. Walls have ears.'

'True. But it's commonly thought those ears are yours, my lord Chancellor.' The Earl stretched his arms with clenched fists above his head, strained wide the fingers and yawned. 'My sword is rusting in its scabbard. I hate that. What latest smelling by your blood-hounds?'

Beroald patted a bundle of dispatches under his arm. 'You shall hear all in good time, my lord.'

'Nay, I seek no favours. So it be there, well. Let it wait due audit.' He stole a look at the Chancellor's face. 'You and I are still agreed? O' the main point, I mean?'

'Surely.'

'The Admiral is with us, think you?'

'We have but the one arm,' answered Beroald: 'all three of us.'

'Ay, but 'tis readiness counts. What's aim, if blow hang i' the air?' Then, after a pause: 'I dearly wish the Duke were expected now.'

Beroald curled his lip. 'Which Duke?'

'Not Zayana.'

'I thought not,' he said dryly.

'Well, I have told your lordship at large of my talkings with Duke Styllis in April in Rialmar. It somewhat did stomach the boy to be left behind there, and this cauldron a-bubbling in the south.'

'It hath long been apparent,' said the Chancellor, 'those two agree best when farthest apart. Howsoever, no Dukes today. Lord Barganax hath leave of absence from the King.'

'I'm glad to hear it.'

'My lady Duchess,' said Beroald lightly, 'arrived today, in Zayana.'

'So. Then the King lies there tonight?'

'Like enough.'

'And cut short so our potting after supper, ha?' said the Earl, and ground his teeth. 'Women. And what comes of women. Were 't not for that, our cares were the lighter.'

'*Mala necessaria.*'

'O, if you speak law-terms, I'm a stone.'

'I but meant, my lord, where were you and I without women had bred us?'

Upon noise of a footstep, Roder looked behind him. 'Here's the great lord Admiral.'

They turned to greet him, walking towards them the length of the gallery with head bent as deep in thought. 'God give you good den,' he said as they met, his eyes, candid as the day's, searching first the Chancellor's then the Earl's. 'We are to reach tonight at last, it is to be hoped, the solutions of a ticklish and tangled business. Have your lordships thought of any new mean to the unravelling of it?'

'So we be at one as for the end,' replied Beroald, 'it should be no unexampled difficulty to find out the means. Has your lordship held more talk with the King's highness in these matters?'

'None since I saw you both last night. I have been afloat all day 'pon business of the fleet. All's ship-shapen now, what-e'er be required of us in that regard. And you, Earl?'

'My folk are so well readied,' answered he, 'we are like to fall apart in rottenness, like over-ripe cheese, if we be not swiftly given the occasion to prove our worth upon't.'

'You will open the matter before the King, I take it, my lord Admiral,' said the Chancellor, 'on our behalf? His serene highness will take it kindliest from your mouth. Besides, among us three, you are *primus inter pares*. And I hope you will stand resolute for action. 'Tis most needful this nettle be rooted up or it prove too late.'

'Yes, yes,' said Jeronimy, fingering his beard. ''Tis a business worth all our wits. We must not be fools, neither, to forget it toucheth the King's set policy of a lifetime's standing. Peradventure, as for this one time, he is wrong: if so be, then is it our mere duty to say so to his face. But before now, and in as weighty matters, when wise men deemed him mistook he hath turned the cat in the pan and, by the event, showed 'em fools for their pains. Well, we must ferret out the true way. And by King in council is the good stablished method so to do.'

The Earl's neck, as he listened, was swelled up red as a turkey cock's and his face, where frizz of black beard and hair disguised it not, of the like rebellious hue. The proud weather-bitten lineaments of the Lord Beroald's face wore a yet colder unpenetrable calm than before. Their eyes met. In that instant, as the Admiral ceased speaking, the door was thrown open upon his right, and the Queen, all but as red as Roder but with countenance uncipherable as the Chancellor's, came forth from the council-chamber.

Even now, when for her the winds of old age had set in, with no deadly force as yet, but enough to make her take in sail and tack against wind and tide, which with slow gathering of power drive back tall ship and feeble coracle without distinction to that hateful and treeless shore whence, against that tide and that wind, none did ever again put back to sea: even in that Novemberish raw weather of her years, some strength of lost youth, some glory, unlosable, uncrushable, indestructible, lived on. Almost might a man have believed, beholding her stand thus in the dazzle, from the open doorway behind her, of warm afternoon sun, that in these few weeks, after twenty-five years of exile, she had renewed

her very body with great draughts of the fecund and lovely magic
of the Meszrian highlands, over which she had so long ago, by
exercise and right of her own most masculine will, made herself
Queen. Here she stood: the argument of her father's dreams and
policies made flesh in the daughter of his desires; and the same
badge of cold ungainsayable relentlessness, more unadulterate and
more openly self-proclaimed than on Emmius Parry's underlip, sat
at this moment upon hers.

She looked upon the Earl's face, whose smoulder of thwarted
anger mirrored, weakly may be, some locked-up passion within
herself: upon the Chancellor's, that carried in its stoniness at this
moment deep-seated likenesses to her own: last, upon the high
Admiral's, which gave back (of any quality of hers) no reflection
at all. They did obeisance to her; Roder, with a low leg, kissing
her hand. 'The King is ready,' she said to them, as if speaking not
to lords but to cur-dogs. 'You may go in.'

King Mezentius sat to receive them in a large chamber fairly
hung with arras, the light streaming in through open western
windows behind him. At this other side of the table the lords
commissioners, at a sign from his hand, took their seats facing
him: Jeronimy in the midst, Beroald on his right, Roder on his
left. They laid out their papers. No person else was present. The
table was empty before the King, neither pen, ink nor paper. 'I
have commanded this council at your request,' he said. 'Speak
without fear, all your mind. Gloze nothing: hold nothing back.
The business, I understand, is of Rerek.'

The Admiral cleared his throat. 'My Lord the King, it needs
not to say that there worketh in us but one thought and purpose,
and that is to behave ourselves, waking and sleeping, as constant
loyal faithful servants unto your serenity's person and, under your
ordination and pleasure expressed and laid upon us, to perform
(within the measure of our capacities) all that should enure to the
safety of this Triple Kingdom and of the common weal thereof.'

'True, it needs not to say,' said the King. 'I know it. Proceed
you therefore, my good lord Admiral, to the matter. What of
Rerek?'

The Admiral paused, as a swimmer might pause upon a high bank before the plunge. His fingers toyed with the jewel of the kingly order of the hippogriff that hung by a crimson ribbon about his neck. 'For me, Lord,' he said at last, 'it is by so much the harder to urge, in a manner, this matter upon your serene highness's gracious attention (even although I hold it most crying needful), by how much it hath been my happiness to have served you and followed your fortunes since your earliest years: seen your unexampled uprising by wisdom and by might and main to this triple throne you have for yourself erected, as history remembereth not the like, so as it is become a common saying upon men's lips in these latter years, *Pax Mezentiana*. And it hath befallen me, through accident of birth and upbringing, to have longer enjoyed the high honour of your inward counsels than any here of mine equals now extant, albeit they be, I am very certain (save in this prime advantage of intimate acquaintance with your settled policy and the roots thereof) more abler men than I. Therefore I speak with due reservation' – here the Chancellor shifted slightly in his chair, and Roder, as if to shade the glare of the sun, leaned over his papers, his hand across his eyes – 'I speak, in a manner, with reservation, and most of all in this business that concerneth—'

The King smiled. 'Come, noble Jeronimy: we are friends. I am not to eat you. You mean the Vicar is my not distant kinsman, and that I have, with eyes open and for reasons not perhaps beyond the guessing of those inmost in my counsels, ridden him on what you begin to think too rashly light a rein. That's common ground. You came not here to tell me (nor to learn of me) that. What of it, then?'

'I thank your highness. Well, to cut short the argument, my lord Chancellor hath here informations and reports, from divers independent intelligencers, throughly tried and not to be doubted, that (despite your plain warning to him to disband his army) he yet draweth strength to it about Laimak. Please your serenity peruse the evidences.' He turned to the Chancellor, who, rising, spread on the table before the King a sheaf of writings.

But the King put them aside. 'I know it. If they reported otherwise,

it were an untruth. What then? You would put me in mind we may
have to enforce our command?'

'By showing the whip: that at least, and at all events.'

The King glanced his eye over the papers, then, pushing them
slowly and thoughtfully across the table to Beroald, shook his
head. 'He will never attack me. These preparations are not against
me.'

'Saving your serenity's presence,' said Roder: 'against whom,
then?'

'Against the future. Which, being unknown, he prudently hath
fear of. He can look round and conclude he hath many and
powerful enemies.'

'Truly, my Lord the King,' said Beroald, 'I would not, for my
part, gainsay him as for that. Some would say your serene highness alone standeth 'twixt him and the uniting of 'em to rid the
world of him. Indeed there be some malignant grumblers –' He
paused. 'Is it your pleasure I speak plain, Lord?'

'More than that: I command you.'

'With deep respect, then. There be some who murmur that your
highness do play with fire may blaze out i' the end to burn their
houses: think you ought to protect them, 'stead of suffer this man
to grow big, run loose, and in his own time devour us all. They
forget not the hellish cruelties used by him upon both small and
great, and innocent persons amongst 'em ('tis not denied), upon
pretext of putting down the rebellion in the Marches five years
ago.'

'Was not that well done, then,' said the King, 'to put it down?
Was it not his duty? You are not a child, Beroald. You were there.
You need not me to tell you this realm stood never in your life-
time in so fearful danger as when (I and the Admiral being held,
with the main of my strength, in deadly and doubtful conflict with
Akkama in the far north) Valero, following the Devil's enticements
and his own wicked will and ambitious desires, raised rebellion
most formidable to my great empire and obedience. By what strong
hand was it if not by the Parry's alone, that the stirrers-up of those
unnatural and treasonable commotions were put to the worst?

And this to the evil example of all such as would hereafter attempt the like villany. And victory is not unbloody. Are you so hardy as question my rewarding him therefore?'

'My Lord the King, you do know my whole mind in this matter,' replied the Chancellor, 'and my love and obedience.'

'But you thought I'd ne'er come back from Middlemead, a year ago?'

'I thought neither your highness nor I should ever come back. Yet must I remember you, it was bitterly against my will you enforced me to stay behind while yourself did enter that cockatrice's den single-handed and alone.'

'Yet that worked?'

'It worked. And for this sole reason, because (under favour of heaven) your serene highness was there to handle it. Another than yourself, were he a man of our own day or the greatest you could choose out of times past since history began: it had been the death of him. And that you do know, Lord, in your heart, better than I.'

'To speak soberly, that is simple truth, dear Beroald,' said the King. 'And thinking upon that, you may wisely trust me in this much lesser danger now.'

There fell a silence. Jeronimy caught the King's eye. 'I would add but this,' he said. 'There is not a man in the Three Kingdoms would trust him an inch were your highness out of the way.'

'However, I am here,' answered the King. 'You may securely leave him to me.'

Again there fell a silence. The Admiral broke it, his eyes in a dog-like fidelity fastening on his great master's and taking assurance, may be, from the half-humorous glints, sun-blink on still water, that came and went across the depths of all-swaying all-tolerant all-sufficient certitude which then looked forth upon him. 'God redeem us from omens: but we were great failers of our love and duty to your highness if we sat speechless, for want of courage to come to the kernel of the thing.'

'Which is?'

'That all men are mortal.'

The King laughed: Olympian laughter, that the whole air in that room was made heady and fresh with it. 'Why, you talk,' he said, 'as if there were no provision made. You three here in the south: Bodenay and a dozen more, seasoned captains and counsellors, to uphold the young King in Rialmar: Ercles and Aramond in north Rerek: Barganax in Zayana. Shall all these appear i' the testing-time bodgers and bunglers, at odds among themselves? Will you tell me the fleet is helpless? Or the army, Roder?'

'A prentice hand upon the tiller,' said the Admiral, 'and a storm toward, 'tis a perilous prospect, like to try all our seamanship.'

'Let me not leave your minds in doubt,' said the King. 'When I farewell, it shall not be to commit the Kingdom to a bunch of ninnies and do-littles, but to men. The Duke of Achery, as legitimate heir, must look to it. He will need all his wits, and yours. I have instructed him fully, in every principle and its particular bearings, this summer, ere I came south now.'

Jeronimy said, 'The Duke of Zayana is also in question.'

'He hath his apanage. He hath no thought of claiming more than his own. You may trust him, as were he mine own younger self, to be loyal and true to's young brother (so the boy have the wisdom and common generousness to play his part), and, were Styllis to die, to be as loyal and as true to's young sister, as Queen. Let me remember you, too: his kingdom is over far other things than lands, rivers, lakes, and the bodies of men. In the camp and the council-chamber I have nurtured him up to be expert in all that a prince should be master of; but, in heart, he is poet and painter. What to Emmius Parry was second subject in the symphony, is to Barganax first subject. He is of Meszria, born and bred. If let live, he will let live. But,' said King Mezentius, his eyes upon them, 'he is my son: therefore not a man to be mocked or teased. If forced to it, a hath that in him will make him able, and he be once set forth upon that path, to overthrow any person whatsoever who should pretend to usurp upon his right. – Well?' he said, watching them sit as men who in imagination see a load presented for them which they begin to think shall prove heavier than their powers may avail to carry. 'Tell me not you are not the men I have known you.'

The Chancellor broadened his chest and looked with resolute eye from the King to his colleagues, then again to the King. 'With deep humility,' he said, 'and I think I speak for these lords as well as for myself: your highness hath told us no new thing, but all lendeth force to the argument that 'twere prudent something be done to contain the power of the Vicar. If (which God forbid) it should someday fall to us, bereft of your serene highness, to shoulder this sackful of contending interests, that were a heavy task indeed, yet not so heavy as we should shrink from, nor doubt our ability (under heaven) to perform it as your highness would have desired and expected of us. But if the Vicar must sit by in embattled strength straddling over the middle kingdom, aspying when we were deepliest otherwhere embroiled and ready then to take us, then were we as good as—' He broke off, meeting the King's eye, keen, weighing, meditative, upon him: lifted his head like a war-horse, and set his jaw. 'What skills it to reason further?' he said, in his most chilling iron-hard voice. 'I have followed your serene highness into the mouth of destruction too many times to boggle at this.'

The King, listening, tranquil and remote, utterly at ease, made no sign. Only when his speckled grey eyes, as though by chance, came back to Beroald's, their glance was friendly.

'If it be permissible to ask,' said the Admiral; 'hath all this that your highness hath been pleased to express to us as touching his grace of Zayana been made plain to Duke Styllis?'

The King answered, 'Yes. And he is content. Hath moreover sworn oath to me to respect his brother's rights, and my will and policy.'

'Did the Duke of Zayana,' asked Roder, 'swear too?'

'It did not need.'

The commissioners began to gather up their papers. 'And we are to understand it is your highness's considered decision,' said Beroald, 'to move in no way against Rerek?'

'He keeps his vicariate,' replied the King. 'No more. No less. I may need to handle him myself in this manner of his maintaining of an army afoot by secret means. My lords Jeronimy and Roder, prepare me proposals tomorrow (and be ready to put 'em in act 'pon shortest notice) for making some show of power about Kessarey and the Marches.'

With that, he rose, liker to a man in the high summer of his youth than to one in his fifty-fourth year: 'On the far view,' he said, turning to dismiss them, 'I mean, when my day shall be over, I see no deadly danger from him, so but North and South stand firm in support of the succession. If they stand not so, that will not be my affair; but the affair of him that shall be man enough to deal with it. And now, you to your charge, I to mine.'

'What think you of this, my lord Chancellor?' said the Admiral, as they took their way across the great open quadrangel of the fortress.

Lord Beroald answered: 'I think the tide is now at high flood that began to run a year ago. And were it an ordinary man, and not our Lord the King, I should think he was fey.'

'We have entered with him between the clashing rocks ere now,' said the Admiral, 'and at every tack found his dangerous courses safer than our own fears. I see no wisdom but to do so again.'

'There is no choice. And you, my Lord Roder?'

'We have no choice,' answered he in a sullen growl. 'But there's nought but ill to come of it.'

XXXVIII

CALL OF THE NIGHT-RAVEN

QUEEN Rosma, observing from her window the occasion of those lords coming from the council, went to find the King. She found him alone in the empty council-chamber, seated not in his chair of state but sideways on the stone of the window-seat, seemingly wrapped in his thoughts. He showed neither by movement nor by look that he heard the opening or shutting of the door, or was aware of her waiting presence. After a while she came nearer: 'Lord, if it be your will, I would desire to speak with you in privity between us two. If this be not a fit time, I pray you appoint another.'

King Mezentius turned his eyes upon her and regarded her for a minute as a man lost in the profundities of his meditation might regard some object, table or chair or shadow thrown by the sun, which should chance within his vision.

'Let it be for another time,' she said, 'if that be better. I had thought your highness's mind being full with matters of the council, which this concerns, the occasion might be good. The thing can wait. Only I hope it must not wait too long.'

Still gazing upon her, he seemed to come back to earth. His brows cleared. 'Let it be now, madam. I am, to times, as a barber's chair that fits all buttocks. Albeit,' and he gave her a laughing look, yet as out of a louring heart, 'I think I am for the while unfit company for honest civil ladies.' He stood up and with a scenical, histrionical, elegance of courtliness, kissed her hand. 'But not here. I'll breathe fresh air 'twixt this and supper or burst else. Come, I'll row you on the firth: seek variety i' the open face of the sea, since pinched earth affordeth none. Get on your cloak, dear faithful help-fellow of an outworn office. When we be launched on the deep, and but the sea-larks to overhear us, speak your fill: I shall not drown you. I see you are come prepared. Nay, not for drowning: I mean for plain speech. You're painted against betrayals.'

'Truly, dear my Lord, I know not what you mean. Betrayals of what?'

'Of another kind of red very good for the cheeks. Of blushing.'

When they were come down to the water-gate, the firth lay under the cool of the evening at the slack-water of full sea, smooth and still as a duck-pool. Eastward and south-eastward the cliffs of the many isles and skerries, and of the headlands that reach down into Sestola Firth from the low-ranging jagged hills in the Neck of Bish, were walls of gold facing the splendour of the declining sun; and upon every sand-spit of the shore-line of Daish, under an immense peacefulness of unclouded heaven, thousands of gulls and curlew and sea-larks and sea-pies with scarlet bills awaited the turn of the tide. The King's boatmen held the boat against the jetty while the Queen took her place in the stern upon a cushion of cloth of silver. The King, facing her on the thwart amidships, took the oars, pushed off, and with a few powerful strokes was clear of the great shadow of the fortress. Presently, warmed with the exercise, he put off his doublet, threw it in the bows behind him, tucked up his shirt-sleeves of white cambric, and, settling to a slow steady stroke, held southwards down the firth. His eyes were on Rosrna, hers on him.

For a long time neither uttered word. Then the Queen broke silence: 'Why must your highness stare upon me so strangely?'

He pulled his right, so that the sun shone full in her eyes, then, resting on his oars, leaned forward to watch her, a kind of mockery on his face. The water talked under the bows: a silvery babble, voluble at first from the way given by that stroke, then dying down to silence as the last water-drops fell from his oar-blades. 'I was wishing,' he said, 'that you were capable to do something of your own motion, undirected and uncontrolled by me: something I had not foreseen in you.'

'I think,' she said, 'there is some distemper working in your highness of late; making you brood vanities: making you, when I ask you any question, answer without sense or reason.'

'Perhaps I am thought-sick. Who knows? But are you indeed so ignorant as know not that you are my thing, my poppet, my creature? Whatsoever you do or enterprise, it is because I will it. You act and think because I cause you so to do: not because you wish to. Tell me,' he said, after a pause, 'do you not find it tedious?'

'Tedious indeed, this manner of speech of your highness's which I suppose proceeded from melancholy and filthy blood. No answer upon any matter, but only put-offs.'

'Try, dear Rosma, to do something. I care not what, so but it be something that shall surprise me: hurt me or pleasure me, 'tis all a matter: do something of your own. To open my heart to you, as wedded lovers ought to do, I am sick unto weariness of for ever climbing mountains safed with a dozen ropes held by a dozen safe men: sick and weary of the remembrance that, venture how I may, I can never fall.'

He pulled a stroke or two: then let her drift. The sun was now touching the hill-tops in the north-west, a flattened red ball of incandescence. The tide had turned, and from every shore came faintly the noise of birds quarrelling and feeding on the ebb. A cool wind sprang up to blow down the firth. The Queen muffled her cormorant-feather cloak about her. She spoke: 'Was this the language your highness held to the lords in council this afternoon? Must a troubled them as it troubleth me.'

'A foolish question,' he replied, backing water, turning, and beginning to pull slowly home against wind and tide. 'I told you beforehand of my decision. And I told it to them in the like terms.'

'Comfortable words indeed. This blind drifting on the rocks in the matter of Rerek: this devilish folly in the treatment of your son.'

'My son? Which one?'

'Your son, I said. There are other names for bastards.'

'I have always admired the refinedness of your language,' said the King. ''Tis a great charm in you. Pity, though, that you are so prone to repeating of yourself. You never give me the pleasures of disappointment: even as, set a fowl's egg under a goose or a turkey, the same chick hatcheth out. Will you not modulate, merely for change sake? Find some new word of opprobriousness for (shall I say?) your stepson?'

'Why would you not suffer Styllis come south with us, 'stead of leave him mewed up in Rialmar? Would a been the fitting, kingly, natural course: most of all in these days when my bloody cousin do threaten, and ('cause of your strange enduring of his packing underboard) scarce troubleth to hide the threat. You forbade me the council: shameful usage of me that am yet, by mine own right, Queen in Meszria. And that was 'cause you were stubborn-set to hold by your pernicious purpose and cram it down their throats who durst not dispute with you to question it; for you knew, had I been there, I'd not a swallowed it thus tamely. Have your heir at your side, one would a thought, ready to take the reins if by evil hap (which kind Heaven pray forfend) aught untoward should befall your highness's person.'

The King, while she so spoke, seemed sunk again into his study, watching while he rowed, as a God might watch from remote heaven, the red glory overspread the spaces of the sky from the going down of the sun. Coming now out of that contemplation, he said in mockery: 'This is your country. If there should need a successor to my throne, why might it not be you? You are hampered by no sexly weakness: as fit as any man living to undertake it. Think you not so? Better than any man, I think: except perhaps—'

As if in that unfinished sentence her mind had supplied a loathed name, the features of Rosma's face, channelled and passion-worn with the years but yet wearing uncorroded their harsh Tartarean beauty, took on now, in the red sunset light, a menace and a malevolence as it had been the face of the Queen of hell.

'Styllis,' said King Mezentius, still playing with her, idly, as a man might with some splendid and dangerous beast over whom he delights to feel his mastery: 'Styllis (I will say crudely to you, in case you be a little blinded by your motherly affections towards him) is as yet somewhat raw. It is a great spot to his good esti- mation (and I think you taught him this trick) to despise and scorn any man other than himself: an unhappy habit of mind in a king. Your Meszrian lords are proud: jealous upholders of privilege. Set him, unfledged and unexperienced, amongst 'em, and—'

Here she broke in upon him, her accents cold and level. 'Well, why delay to cut him off from the succession? One more ill deed would scarcely be noted, I should think.'

'How if I postpone his succession till he be come of years twenty-five? Make you, in that interim, Queen. Regent? All's one to me. As for the world, *Post me diluvium.*'

'I know,' said the Queen, 'what underlieth this mockery and mummery. You are resolved in very deed, though you dare not do it by open means, to leave all to your bastard. But,' she said, the voice of her speech quivering now as with slow-burning anger, 'beware of me. Twenty-five years you have used me for your tool and chattel. But of all things there cometh an end at last.'

The King laughed in his beard. 'An end? That is vulgar, but questionable, doctrine. Howsoever,' he said, suddenly serious, so that Rosma's baleful eyes lowered their lashes and she turned aside her face. 'I will promise you this. When I die, the best man shall have the Kingdom. If that be Styllis, by proof of his abil- ities, good. But upon no other condition. I made this Triple Kingdom: alone, I made it: and out of worse confusion and unhandsomeness than of civil wars. It is mine to order and to dispose of how I will. And I will dispose of it into the hand of no man save into his only who shall be able to take it, and wield it, and govern it.'

'I marvel what madness or devil hath so distract your mind,' she said, slowly, looking him in the face again. 'You are likely to do a thing the whole world must weep for.'

'Care not you for that, madam. It sits awkwardly on you (I could a said unbecomingly) to pretend tenderness for the misfortunes of others. You have acted too many murders in your day, for that to ring true. And devised as many more that I have prevented your performing. Better than you, I know what I am about.'

'And I know what your bastard is about: the sole occupation he is fit for. Wallowing in his strumpet's bed in Velvraz Sebarm.'

'His private concerns are his own. Not yours. Not mine, even,' replied the King, narrowing his eyes upon her. 'But if it shall comfort you to know, I heartily commend all that he is doing. In truth, as a good Father ought, I prepared the opportunity for him myself.' He added, after a pause: 'Tonight he and my Lady Fiorinda are to sup with us in Sestola.'

Rosma drew back her head with the indignation of an adder about to strike. 'Then I keep my chamber. I have an objection to sitting at table with a whore.'

He rowed on in silence. On his left, and behind him over Sestola, night was rising fast. To larboard the sun had set in an up-piled magnificence of blood-red and iron clouds. Astern, above the Queen's head as she sat facing the rise of night, her face no longer to be discerned in this growing dusk, Antares began to open a red eye flashing with green sparkles in a rift of clear sky in the south. The wind was fallen again. The King, with eyes on that star of bale, rested on his oars: seemed to listen to the stillness.

Queen Rosma began to speak again: soberly, reining up her displeasure. 'You are wrong in many matters besides this. For example (to go back to that immediate matter which, from what you have said to me, you so lightly and so headily disposed of at the council this evening), you are deadly wrong about Rerek.'

She paused, waiting. The King made no reply, sitting motionless watching the raging lights of the Scorpion's heart.

'But sure, all's effectless when I speak to you of this,' she said. 'You never heed me.'

He began to row: meditatively, a stroke or two, to keep a

little way on her against the strengthening ebbtide: then rest
on the oars again: then another few strokes, and so on. They
were by this time but a mile short of Sestola. 'But I am all ears,'
he said, again in his baiting, scorning, humour. 'This is a business you have at least some knowledge of. He is your cousin
german, and you have, in the days before I took you in hand,
shown a pretty thoroughness in dealing with your kinsfolk:
Lebedes: Beltran. 'Tis confessed, they were but nephews by
affinity, and he of your own blood, a Parry: not a mere instrument of yours, a lover, as they were. Come, speak freely: you
would have me murder him? Or, better, commission you for the
kindly office? But I am not minded to let him go the way of
your lesser ruffians. Me he will never bite at again. And I enjoy
him. Much as, dear Rosma, I enjoy you. Or have enjoyed,' he
added, with a strange unaccustomed note of sadness or longing
in his voice.

'But you are mortal,' said Rosma. 'And when you shall be dead,
he will bite at Styllis.'

'We are all mortal. A most profound and novel maxim.'

'I think,' she replied quietly, 'your highness is perhaps an exception. Were you of right flesh and blood, you would take some
respect to the welfare or illfare of your son.'

'Do not trouble your head with the business. All is provided.'

'You are unsupportable,' she said, her anger again bursting its
bonds. 'You are took with my father's disease: Meszria.'

'Well? And was it not you, madam, brought me that rich dowry?'

'Yes. But hardly foreseeing you would bestow it, and all besides,
upon your bastard.'

'It was got by you with blood and horror,' said the King. 'Be
reasonable. I have kept my bargain with you. I have set you in a
state and in a majesty you had not before dreamed of, upon the
throne of the Three Kingdoms in Rialmar. Do not fall into
ingratitude.'

'O monstrous perversion. You have made me your instrument,
your commodity, your beast. What profit to me though my chains
be of gold, when I am kept kennelled and tied like a ban-dog?'

'You forget the benefits I have done you. I have kept your hands, these twenty-one years now, clean of blood: ever since your slaying of your lover Beltran, who begat two children upon you. This also you shall know: that them, too, I saved alive, when, being an unmerciless dam, you would a devoured them at birth.'

This he said resting on his oars. In the hush, Rosma caught her breath: then, in a shaken voice, 'You never told me this. It is a lie. They are dead.'

'They are alive, my Queen. And famous. You have spoke with them. But, like the unnatural mother you are, you know not your own whelps.'

'It is a lie.'

'When did I ever lie to you?' said the King. 'And, my dearly loved she-wolf, you have (to do you plain justice) never in all your life lied to me.'

As by tacit consent, no further word went betwixt them till they were come to land. It was almost night now. A row of cressets burning on the edge of the jetty threw a smoky glare over the welter of restless waters and up the dark face of the sea-wall of Sestola, against whose cyclopean foundations those waters, piling up with the down-come of the tide, swarmed and gurgled, surged and fell, without violence on this calm summer night, but as if in tranquil rumination of what, and they please, seas can do and wall and rock stand against. The King leapt ashore: his men steadied the boat while he reached hand to the Queen. The uncertain and palpitating glare, save where its constant shooting forth and retracting again of tongues of light touched face or form or stone or black gleaming water, made trebly dark the darkness. She stepped lightly and easily up, and stood for a minute statue-like and remote, gazing seaward, not at her Lord. Whether for the altering light, or for some cause within herself, she seemed strangely moved, for all she stood so calm and majestical: seemed, almost, a little softened of mood: as it were Persephone in dark contemplation, without regrets or hopes, overlooking her sad domain and that bitter tree of hell. The King might see, in her eye, as he came closer and stood unnoted at her side, something very like the leavings of tears. 'The setting is a good foil for the jewel,' he said in her ear. 'Is this the hithermore bank of Styx? Or stand we already o' the farther side?'

Rosma silently put her arm in his and, with a dozen torches, behind and before, to light their footsteps, they took their way up the rock-hewn stairs: so to the keep and the King's privy lodging. 'I am coming in,' she said, as he paused in the entrance. The King shot a glance at her, then stepped back to let her pass. Without sound on the rich woven carpet she crossed the room and stopped, her back to him, surveying herself in the mirror by the light of two branched candlesticks that stood on the table at her either hand. 'It is near suppertime,' she said. 'We must change our clothes;' and still abode there without moving.

The King said, 'We have understood each other. Twenty-five years. A demi-jubilee. Few wedded lovers can say that, as we can. Was it because we have wisely and frugally held to our alliance as princes, and not been lovers?'

Rosma, very still and proud in her posture before the looking-glass, answered in tones startlingly gentle: almost tender: 'I do not think so.'

'No?' He was seated in a chair now, behind her, taking off his boots.

'I', said she, 'have been a lover.'

'Well, Beltran you loved, I readily believe. None other, I think.'

'"None other" is not true.'

'Your first child by him,' said the King, 'was (to speak home) the child of your lust. The second, sixteen years later, child again of your lust, but also of your love. And, as that, the unsightable wonder of the world: of more worlds than this, could your wolf-eyes avail to look upon such glories.'

The Queen bit her lip till it slowly began to bleed.

'And there was like a diversity of conception,' he said, 'between these two children of you and me.'

With that, a great catch of her breath: then silence. The King looked up. But her back was towards him and, from where he sat, he could not see her face in the mirror. She said, in a choking voice, 'Beltran loved me. That second time, I knew it. He loved me.'

'Yes. Unluckily for him. For you devoured him. I am not for your devouring.'

The Queen, turning without a word, was on that sudden on her knees at his feet, her face hidden in his lap. 'I have loved you,' she said, 'immovable and unreachable, since that first hour of our meeting in Zayana: a more wasteful, more unfortunate, love than ever I had for Beltran. Why could you not have let me be? You ravished me of all: kingdom, freedom, Amalie, the one living being in all the world I tendered above myself. And this I have known: that Styllis was child of your policy, or call it your more hated pity: Antiope the child of your transitory, unaccountable, late-born, soon ended, love.' She burst forth into a horrible tempestuous rage of weeping: terrible cries like a beast's, trapped and in mortal pain. The King sat like a stone, looking down upon her, there, under his hand; her bowed neck, still fair, still untouched with contagion of the hungry years: her hair still black above it as the night-raven, and throwing back gleaming lights from its heavy braided and deep-wound coils: the unwithered lovely strength of back and shoulders, strained now and shaken amid gusts of sobbing and crying. When he lifted his gaze to the spaces of the roof-timbers beyond reach of the candle-light, all the shadowy room seemed as filled with the flowering of her mind into thoughts not yet come to birth: thoughts shawled as yet, may be, from her own inmost knowledge by the unshaping shawl of doubt and terror.

She stood up: dried her eyes: with a touch or two before the mirror brought her hair to rights, then faced him. He was risen too, at his full stature (so tall she was) barely looking down into her eyes. 'You have lied to me at last,' he said. 'How dare you speak so to me of love, who do discern your secret mind, know you far better than you do know yourself, and know that you are innocent of the great name of love as is an unweaned child of wine? Nay, Rosma, I do love and delight in you for what you abidingly are: not for farding of your face with confections of love: which, in you, is a thing that is not.'

She replied upon him in a whisper scarce to be heard, as he, in their old way as between friends and allies, took her by the hand: 'I did not lie.' Then, as if the quality of that touch thrilled some poison quite to her heart, she snatched away her hand and said violently: 'And I will tell you, which you well know, that this bastard of yours is the only child of your lasting love. And for that, spite of my love and longing, which like some stinking weed spreads the ranker underground for all my digging of it up – for that, I hate and abominate you; and Amalie, your whore; and Barganax, that filthy spawn whom (to your shame and mine and hers) you regard far more than your own life and honour. My curse upon you for this. And upon her. And upon him.'

XXXIX

OMEGA AND ALPHA IN SESTOLA

NIGHT was up now over Sestola: midsummer night, but estranged with a sensible power ominously surpassing that July night's of last year, when the Duchess had entertained with a fish dinner in Memison guests select and few. The stars, by two hours further advanced than then, shone with a wind-troubled radiance dimmed by the spreading upwards of veiling obscurities between it and middle earth. The moon, riding at her full in the eastern sky, gave forth spent, doubtful, and waterish rays. On the lower air hung a gathering of laid-up thunder.

Queen Rosma, being come to her own chamber, made her women bestir them to such purpose that she was dressed and waiting some while before the due time appointed for supper. Her lodgings opened upon the westernmost end of the portico which ranges, a hundred and fifty paces and more in length, above the sheer face of the fortress on its southern, oceanward, side. She dismissed her girls and the Countess Heterasmene (now lady of the bedchamber), and, hankering perhaps for fresh air after the closeness of her room and of the King's, went forth to take a turn or two on the paven way under the portico. Square pillars bear up the roof of it on either hand, both against the inner wall and upon the seaward side: at every third pace a pillar. This western half was lit only by the lamps which, hanging betwixt each pair of outer pillars, gave barely sufficient light for a man to pick his steps by. But midway along, from the open doors of the banqueting-chamber, there spread outwards like a fan a brilliant patch of light, and beyond it the uncurtained windows of the hall shed on the pavement bands of brightness, evenly spaced with darkness. With moody, deliberate tread the Queen came towards the light, sometimes halting, then moving onwards again. She was come within a few paces of the doors when, at sound of footsteps approaching from the farther end, she withdrew herself under thick shadow between wall and pillar and there waited. The Duke of Zayana and his lady, new landed and in a readiness for supper together in Sestola, were walking from the east, now in full illumination, now lost again in shadow between windows.

My Lady Fiorinda wore, over all, a hooded mantle of smoke-black silk which, billowing as she walked, took to itself at each step new folds, new mysteries, fire-winged with beauties and graces that were themselves unseen. The Duke, as with every faculty strained up to this fugato, came a pace or so behind her. In the full pool of light before the doorway she stopped, not ten feet from where Rosma stood hid. 'Well?' she said, and her lily-honeyed voice, potent as some unavouched caress, roused whirlpools in the blood-warm lampless sources of sense and being. 'Are you content, now that you have driven me like a tame beast as far as this empty banquet-hall and empty deserted gallery? We're too early. What means your grace to do now?'

'Look upon you,' said Barganax laughing. 'Talk to you. 'Tis the only place I shall get the chance in private.'

'Well, here I am. And here are my ears to talk to.' So saying, she threw back her hood, giving him, by turns of her head, the side-view, either way the same. Her hair was put up in like fashion as eleven months ago it had been, at Reisma: strained evenly back from the parting and from those border-line fledgings, finer than unspun silk, at the temples and at the smooth of her neck behind her ears. And at the back of her head the great tresses were gathered and bound down, doubled and folded in themselves like snakes lying together: a feelable stypticness of night: thunder unshapen to silence and, as by miracle, turned visible. These bewitchments, sitting close and exquisite in the nape of her white neck, she thus manifested: then gave him her eyes.

Surely, thus to mingle eyes with that lady was to be drowned under by a cataclysm that hurled out of their place the sea-gates which divide heaven from earth, flesh from spirit, and to be swept up so into Her oneness: into the storm and night of Her peace, who is mistress, deviser, giver of all. Who, all being given, gives yet the unfillable desire for more, and gives, too, eternally, that overplus to fill it: gives in that divine giving, infinite in contradiction and variety, Her many-coloured divine self, proud with his pride which, ever as brought down by Hers, is as everlastingly, through that unsatisfiable satiety of giving, re-estated. As a God might stand incarnate in fire-hot stone, so, while Barganax stared into those sea-strange intolerable Olympian eyes, the deep-throned majesty of his will rose and, as lode-stone points to lode-star, pointed out her. Like a man who gropes for words in a dream, he said: 'And, under that cloak?'

The falcon-flight of her beauty, stooping earthwards again, answered from her mouth: 'You are very inquisitive upon my affairs. See, then, how obliging I have been.' She let fall her cloak and stood before him in skin-close bodice with skirt flowing wide from the hips down, of red corn-rose sendaline: the dress she had worn for him that first night in Reisma.

'Then I am answered,' he said, surveying her slowly down from throat to emerald-spangled shoe, and thence slowly up by the same road, and so once more to her face.

Fiorinda's eyes, that were a-dance with the scents of earth again, came suddenly to rest, in a wide-open stillness of intention, on his. Her lips, bitter-sweet scarlet ministers of mockery, were grave now: lips of the Knidian Aphrodite. Then, some untameable star rising in her eyes, 'Indeed,' she said, 'it hath a happy commodity, this gown: like as your grace's jests. Remember you not so?'

'As my jests?'

'Come they not off, well and excellent?'

He bent down, one knee on the pavement, to pick up for her the fallen cloak. Being they were alone and unobserved, he locked suddenly his arms about her, his empery, his new-found-land, and for a minute abode so, crushing his shut eyes, that called in aid now a sense both more piercing and more fierier than their own particular of seeing, blindly into the pleats of her skirt. In this she remained motionless: only trembling a little, yielding a little. When the Duke was on his feet again, she had covered her face with her hands, leaving to be seen of her but these hands and arms in their immaculation of whiteness: the jet-black of her hair: this dress, sheathing her like a flame. 'O madonna, why will you look at me through your fingers?' he said, opening his arms.

As a lily leans to its reflection in still water, she came nearer: an opening of the windows of heaven to pour down blessings: nearer, till her breasts touched him about the heart, and her face was hidden on his shoulder. 'Are you still to learn that I never promise? Most of all, never to you. And this, I suppose,' she said between his kisses on her neck and hair, 'for two very ridiculous reasons: ten times more ridiculous and unreasonable when taken together. The first, because I do know you, within and without. And the second,' here, with a sudden intake of her breath, turning her head on his shoulder she gave him her lips, nectar-tongued: not without letting him taste in the end, upon a more melting, then more impetuous, closeness of insinuation of her immortal sweet body to his, a light remembrancer, between play and fierceness, of her teeth: 'And the second, because I am sometimes almost persuaded there may be no help, but you shall begin, someday, in very truth, to make me in love with you.'

Rosma, having employed her advantage to hear and narrowly observe these two lovers, and what way in their loveship they went to work, said in herself: 'So you never promise? But I promise. And most of all, to him.' With slow unsteady gait she returned privately to her chamber.

A hundred feet in length is that banquet-room in Sestola, by forty wide, and the height of it twenty foot good to the cornice and, from thence to the huge ridge-beams of the roof, of oak curiously carved and blackened with age, twenty-five foot more.

Upon the walls of old red sandstone, rough-hewn, gritty to the touch, and of the deep cold purple colour of leaf-shadows on brick in hot sunshine, hung all kind of war-gear: spears and swords and daggers and twirl-spears, maces, battleaxes, morning-stars: byrnies of linked mail, helms and shields, corslets and iron gloves: some from the antique time, some new: all of them pieces of proof wrought by noted armourers, and graved or damascened with gold and silver. From the western end, under the music gallery, lofty doors open south upon the portico. These, and the tall windows spaced six foot apart along the south wall, stood wide now to the June night. Under that gallery lesser doors lead to kitchens, buttery, stillroom, larders and sculleries, and the servants' quarters. The dais, at the eastern end, was carpeted with a weave of mixed wool and silk, having a glitter of silver threads in web and woof. From the middle of it two high-seats faced down the hall, having each a table before it for eating and drinking; and outward from these in a half circle, five to the right, five to the left, stood lesser chairs of state with their tables before them. On the rush-strewn pavement of the floor below the dais a dozen long tables were set lengthways in two double rows of three and three, leaving a broad space up the body of the hall between the double rows. At the higher tables (save upon the dais, where the seats yet stood empty) the company were already assembled, lords, ladies, and gentlemen, all in holiday attire: they of most account at the four tables next below the dais and, at the next four, gentry and officers of lower estate. At the lowest tables, nearest the doors, were places set for the remainder: here (the better to assure decorum) the men on the outward, southward, side, and womenkind on the northward.

Great was the sparkle of jewels and great the splendour of rich silks and velvets of many colours under a hundred hanging lamps which, depending in four rows by long chains of bronze from the high timbers of the roof, wove with their beams between the upward gaze and those high dark empty spaces a tented canopy of air, radiant, demi-translucent, beneath which all was light and clarity of vision. These lamps, shining downward, mixed their rays with the nearer, warmer and more tendering glow of hundreds of candles set orderly in branched candlesticks of cut and polished crystal, eight candlesticks on every table.

The musicians tuned their instruments, preluded and, when the murmur of talk was stilled and the guests rising in their places turned all to face westward toward the doors, struck up a cavatina of old Meszria. A lovely, houseless, land-remembering air was this: rising, falling, returning on itself as loth to depart: even just as a linnet's child, perched with its mother on a fence, quivers its wings to be fed, then leaps fluttering over her head to perch at her other side and in quivering eagerness creeps near to her again, and so and again continually. And ever as that air hovered to full close, always it by some exquisite involution refused and rose circling again, as if end were but foil or frame to some never-ending being and unfolding, of which even the beginning was impregnate with a prophetic sadness of farewells, and the expected end held ever, and at every approach and putting-off, the more of earth-deep promise in it of renewal and spring to be. This music, bodied forth on the plangorous caressful singing of the viols, smoothed the sense of Anthea's and Campaspe's nymphish ears, as they stood listening near the head of that high table under the window close below the dais, with echoes and overtones of a more diviner music: of my Lady Fiorinda's remembered voice, Olympian, all-beguiling, beyond all passion appassionate, yet immaculate, yet fancy-free. And beneath the ever-changing flow and wonder of that melody, plucked notes throbbed, of bass viol and theorbo, in an unchanging rhythm: deep under-march of eternity.

Now, in one tenor with that slow-throbbing plucking of strings, came a clanking of iron-shod boots from without the great doors, and a company of the King's bodyguard marched two by two up the hall. Picked men they were, deep-chested, hard, fierce of aspect, veterans of the wars in Akkama: helmed and byrnied with black iron, and in their plated gorgets and their sword-belts of black bulls-hide were studs and rivets of flashing brass. They halted in two lines, spears at salute, their backs to the tables, leaving wide clear passage-way between the lines, through which ten trumpeters resplendent in cloth of silver, each man of them with his shining trumpet at his hip, passed up now in single file and, mounting the dais, took station, five upon this side, five upon that, against the walls north and south of the great seats. Following the trumpeters came a score of waiting-maids, all in white and garlanded on their unbound hair some with bryony, some with ivyberries, some with flower of honeysuckle. Of these, some strewed rose-leaves on the scented rushes of the pavement: the rest, bearing each her little silver basin, dipped their fingers as they walked and, at every step, sprinkled on this side and on that sweet-smelling perfumes. The rose-leaf-scatterers when they were come up upon the dais shed petals no more, but disposed themselves orderly along either wall, their faces to the tables, their backs to the trumpeters. The sprinklers of perfume, ere joining their fellows, went twice about the whole floor of the dais, meeting and crossing, back and forth, in a sway and intricacy of movement that took time from the interlacing notes of the viols, until all the woven carpet, and, most of all, that which lay in the half-moon space before the tables, exhaled sweetness, as beds of thyme or camomile, being trod upon, send up wafts of their sharp delicate scent. And now, as the King entered in his majesty, those trumpets of silver, pointing upward to the unseen spaces of the roof, sent flight after flight of silver notes showering like meteors, riding like valkyries of the Father of Ages, through over beneath and amidst of the fine-drawn moon-stilled cloud-processions of the cavatina, which by these fanfares was neither interrupted, out-moded, nor cast in shade but, taking them into itself, was by them hardened, masculated, made to tower in climax.

His doublet was of a rich velvet of a most fine texture, revealing, as it had been his very skin, the ripple and play of the great muscles as he moved: the hue of it, warm brown of peat-water where it runs deepest between moss-hags in full sun: slashed with blue satin (wave-reflections of blue heaven on such waters), and the lips of the slashes close-broidered with wire of silver. The ruff about his neck and the lesser ruffs at his wrists were stiffened with saffron: his shoes of velveted brown leather overwrought with gold and silver thread, and their buckles set with yellow diamonds. The linked collar which he wore between neck and shoulder had every link broad as a man's hand, all in filigree of pure gold and ablaze with precious stones: sapphire and topaz, smaragd and ruby and opal, diamond and orient pearl. The belt about his middle was of black cobra-skin, studded with great diamonds in figure of stars and thunderbolts, and fastened by a clasp of pale gold carved in the image of two hippogriffs, nose to nose, wings erect, cabochon rubies for the eyes of them, and hundreds of tiny stones, topaz and burnt topaz and brown zircon and every kind of tourmaline, tracing the convolutions of their manes. Upon his head shone the crown of old Meszria, wrought with artificial semblances, in gold and jasper and pink quartz and sardonyx and jet, of poppies, flower and seed-cod of dittany, mandrake leaves, strawberry leaves, and the thorn-apple's prickled fruit.

For all this array, it was the majesty of the King's countenance and of his bearing that went to the marrow of folks' backbones, of those lords and ladies as they beheld him come up the hall: a majesty that seemed, tonight, no longer of this earth: holding its seat and glory chiefliest in his eyes, that showed hollow now like the eyes of lions, and terrible more for the calm that underlay the glare of them than for that all-mastering glare itself: more, even, than for the slow and consuming heat that seared the eyeballs of each person meeting his regard, as though the glance of this King were able to unclothe the soul of man or woman looked upon: have it out, stripped and freezing, for him to examine, before, behind, above, below, between, in the cold betwixt the worlds.

The men of his bodyguard, two by two as he passed them, fell in and followed him with spears at salute. Upon the dais he halted and turned to overlook the hall, while these soldiers, doing obeisance before him two by two upon the steps, divided and went up past him, these to the left, those to the right, to take their stand along the east wall behind the high-seats. Earl Roder, as captain of the guard, armoured to the throat and with the ties of his sword-hilt hanging loose from the scabbard, took his stand behind the King.

Next entered the Queen, crowned and wearing a robe of black figured satin purfled with gold and lined with watermails, the train of it borne by four little blackamoors in green caps and long coats of cloth of silver. The King took her by the hand: set her in the high-seat upon his left; while two by two the guests of honour came up the mid hall, mounted the dais, did their obeisance, and took their seats in order.

The Duke sat at the King's right hand. In him, when he spoke or when he smiled, the conscience-born gaiety of a bridegroom stirred darkly tonight, fire shut in fickle-force; infusing with a kind of morning splendour both his countenance and his lithe body's strength, lovely, whether at rest or in motion, as the Hermes of Praxiteles. Next to him was that old Lord Bekmar, white-haired, twi-bearded, each half of his beard falling in a diminishing spiral of twisted curls: on Bekmar's right, my lord Chancellor Beroald: then Count Medor: then, at the last of the tables on this side, the Lord Perantor. Upon him as often as Rosma's eye fell and met his gaze constant on her as on some anchorage of his prime, she looked hastily away, as from an unseasonable memento of time's iniquity gravid upon her: that this man, grown fat now, and bald, and with dewlaps on the jawy part of his face, should be, by mockery, that self-same smooth courtier and oiled-tongued suing servant whom, in the latter years of her lone queenship, by this twenty-five, thirty, years ago, she had had for lord chamberlain in Zayana.

Anthea and Campaspe, oread arm wreathed in a most unwonted protective assurance about dryad waist, watched the proceedings from their places at the highest table on the Queen's side below the dais.

'Sister, quiet this leaping thing I find here, under your left breast. Else I'll be sadly tempted to eat you up.'

'It will not quiet, sister, when changes are toward.'

'Little fool. Great and small can alter and change: come and go. But we alter not. Neither can any of these shakings, that shake nations, shake us.'

Campaspe huggled herself closer, her eyes fixed, as by fascination, upon the Queen. 'I do abhor her from my heart,' she said in a whisper. 'As if my flesh were her meat.'

'It is her day: day of darkness and shrouded dawn. Are you afeared, little mouse, little sparrow? We have known such days ere now.'

'Yes. Many time, since the beginning. I fear not, dear sister. 'Tis but only that I cannot but puff up my weak furs and feathers and quake with the cold a little, these nights of dread.'

'They are of our Mother's milk, I think,' said that oread lady, and snarled with her teeth. 'Fix your eye, here, where it belongeth: upon Our Lady. Doth not She fill heaven and earth?' Their pure eyes (hunting-beast eyes of the oread: eyes of the dryad wide and soft as a startled hind's) turned from Rosma, as from void darkness, to that thunder-laced windrush of darkness which is the heat and unpicturable secret centre of light's and beauty's self, the rending of heavens, the coming down: where that Dark Lady sat, last but one on the Queen's side, between Roder and Selmanes of Bish; and in the trust of Her presence found their unrestful rest.

Upon the Earl's right the Countess Heterasmene had her place: upon her right, next to the Queen, the lord Admiral Jeronimy.

With the first service brought in, and all kind of wine in great flagons and gallipots of silver and crystal and gold, merry waxed the talk both upon the dais and in the body of the hall. Queen Rosma, strangely affable and amiable, said: 'You have not been to see me of late, lord Admiral. I miss your company. And now, tomorrow, we must bid you farewell: progress towards the north.'

'All will lament your highness's departure.'

'Not all. Myself, I shall be glad on't. I envy no man that must inhabit in Meszria these days: least of all, foreign-born. Too many hates and cloaked rivalries.'

'Home is good,' he said in his simplicity. 'But duty is best.'

Rosma's regard wandered from his face to rest on that Lady Fiorinda, so that the Admiral had freedom for a minute to study her countenance, himself unobserved. Viewing her thus, a man might have supposed twenty years had been lifted from her natural burden: as though the safe candlelight held an alchemy, transforming as lovers' eyes, to charm away and make effectless that false time which heretofore had carried her past the age of loving and being beloved. 'I laugh sometimes,' she said, an unwonted tender sadness stirring in her voice, 'to think on these turnagains we live in. Born and nursed in Sleaby: Argyanna for my salad-days: then queened here in Zayana, and for so long time wielding powers of life and death here as to mix blood with it. And yet now, no sooner come back hither, but homesick in turn for where's least my home: Rialmar.'

''Tis there your highness's state and stead. Little marvel you should desire it.'

The Queen took a sip from her goblet, set it down and sat silent a minute, gazing into the blood-dark darkness of the wine as though memories floated there; or foreshadowings. Then, turning to him with a smile: 'I think you are homesick too, for the north.'

He made no reply, toying with the dish of prawns before him.

She laid down her fork and looked at him. 'It is not hid from his serene highness nor from me,' she said, leaning sideways over the arm of her great chair, a little nearer him, to speak more privately, 'the weight of the charge we do lay on you three who now have the vogue here. To you yourself, albeit so many years set in government here in Meszria, the land's but a step-dance, and hard it is for you to contend against the jealousies that beset you.'

The Admiral shook his head thoughtfully, then looked in the Queen's face. 'Live and let live. The only way.'

'This late-discovered conspiracy against your own person, for example. We are not ignorant whence such mischiefs draw their sustainment.'

'Nay,' said the Admiral, lowering his eyes under her look, 'if your highness aim at last week's chance, of this rakehelly dissembling scrub who, being brought to my presence, would a sticked me with a dagger, 'twas no conspiracy there. No great hand behind that.'

'Judge you so indeed? I hope you are not miscast in your arithmetic.'

'Only the private discontent of a certain lord who shall be nameless. We shall make friends with him too, ere long. Mean time, the instrument i' the attempt was took and hanged.'

'Well, so far,' said the Queen, 'But you are to remember, my lord High Commissioner, there's hands behind hands in all these things. I that do, from long use, almost to the manner born know the ways of this land, would wish you have an eye to a person I bear ever in mind but will not name. Who (in your ear) may justly think a hath cause (not from you, but from your near friends),' here she cast a covert look, not unnoted by the Admiral, on Earl Roder, 'to fear a knife or a Spanish fig from near about you.'

'In humble honesty,' said he slowly, after a pause, 'I am troubled at your highness's gracious words. And the more, in a manner, that I take not their meaning.'

Without looking at him, but speaking low beside his ear: 'Come to me ere we depart tomorrow,' she said, 'and I'll speak more openly than here were convenient. I have observed in you three, whiles I have sojourned here, a strange carelessness touching ever-present threats to your proper safety, and these from a high quarter not ten miles from here I think you do least suspect. The King's highness would not for all sakes, as I would not, see aught ill befall you. Enough. Let's be merry. But,' said she, looking past the King to Duke Barganax and quickly, as from some undecent sight, withdrawing her gaze to meet the troubled eyes of Jeronimy fixed questioningly upon her: 'come to me tomorrow.'

Madam Anthea, using that *lingua franca* which half-gods and nymphs have amongst themselves, but to human kind it is unlearnable and unintelligible, like the crackling of ice, or soughing of wind among leaves, or cat-talk or bird-talk or all voices else of wood and water and mountain solitudes, spoke saying: 'She is ill at ease, behind all this outward talk, when she looks on my Lady.'

'Will you think,' said Campaspe, in the same safe tongue, 'it cometh her in mind of the nestling she spurned out of the nest for dead and you bore it hither to the southlands in your mouth; by her reckonings, twenty years ago?'

'You can read as well as I.'

'But I cannot endure to look upon her. Or if I look, thought quite forsakes me. Lynx eyes are searchinger too, than water-rats'.'

Anthea drew back her lips, in a stealth watching the Queen.

Her left hand, slipping privily down from Campaspe's flower-soft waist, gave her a nip where least, may be, such liberties were looked for: made her shut together her knees with a little smothered scream. 'She knows in her bones,' Anthea said, 'that 'tis here the very child of her body she looks upon. Which knowledge is wormwood to her, beholding in Her her own lost (nay, never had) youth as might have been; but she, of her own excess, fooled away the winning hand fortune and her father dealt her, and, having misplayed all, is left naked now and penniless, save for her hate against everyone. Seeth my Lady's beauty: the height, the might, and the glory of it, fed to its starriest with desire. Tasteth my Lady: almost even as he tasteth, beside whom much better men than yonder o'er-petted swaggering Styllis of hers should suffer eclipse, meteors beside the sun. And for that eclipse, and because of his blessed condition, as being love-drunk – from my Lady's nice teasing and wantoning and prouding of him up this morning – and as having (as I smell this Queen do foggily sense in their eye-casts and in the under-music of their voices tonight) the world, all worlds, all Olympus, in his having of Her: because of these things, she sits crammed with stinking hellebore. Mark you, my flindermouse: we shall see the vomit ere supper well done.'

So sped the time with eating and drinking, gross meats first and finer meats afterward, and with discourse grave and gay. Bekmar, cheered by good wine and by his exalted place at table, which was above both Chancellor and Earl (this as well for respect of his white hairs as out of policy, the Queen being present, to honour especially the ancient houses of Meszria), was full of instances and remembrances of forty or fifty years' standing: better banquets then in Sestola, when Kallias was King: not a woman let come into the hall here then, save the dancing-girls. As though the memory fanned dead embers within him, a kind of corpse-light stirred in his pale eyes. 'Well,' he said, 'other times, other manners: King Haliartes put an end to those spectacles when he took kingdom in Zayana. 'Twas thought,' he said mournfully, 'that was by the Queen's setting on.'

'In that,' coldly said the Chancellor, 'I have ever thought her highness showed herself more Meszrian than our own folk of those times, Meszrians by birth. 'Tis symptom of decay in a great people nursed in civility and high gifts of learning, when they begin to make so much vulgarness of mankind's noblest pleasure as to have their courtesans dance before them stript to the buff, and so glutton on all in public.'

'I am an old man,' Bekmar replied, 'I account old things best.'

'Measure is best, my lord: ruleth all in the end.' The Chancellor, as if his own word spoken had minded him where his disquiet lay, turned his eyes, uneasy behind their mask of steely irony, on the King. In him, as he talked now with his son, burned (yet hotter and gayer than then, a year ago) that same recklessness and superfluity which, when he sent Beroald back and went on, alone with his self-sufficiency, into known instant peril of death at Middlemead, had outcountenanced the great lamp of heaven. The Lord Jeronimy, watching him, too, was remembered, like enough, of that all-mastering mood the King had set out in, rashly through mountainous seas in the dead of winter, to put down Akkama. And, soon as put down, had, against all prudence and human reason, set it up again.

As the waiting storm-gatherer should speak to the lightning pent up and struggling for birth, so spoke the King now to Rosma, under his breath: 'Remember you my word. Do something. What, I care not, so it be your own.'

She became ghastly white: then red again: then, slowly turning her eyes to meet his, lowered her gaze: answered slowly in a whisper: 'Is it not a prayer commonly made to God; *Tempt me not who am mortal?*'

'But what God were that?' replied the King deep and low, as it had been the houseless mockery of old Night speaking not in her ear but unescapably in her soul: 'What God were that, that should hearken to any prayer of yours?'

The Queen put her hands under the table, in her lap, out of sight. She said, calm and equable again and with a gentleness in her voice: 'Beseech you, dear Lord, spoil not this last night's pleasure for me in mine own land. Suffer me to have good memories to carry north. Torment me no more with riddles I can neither answer nor see the sense of. Remember, if you can, that I love you.'

King Mezentius looked in her black eyes: almost a lover's look, with shadows of laughter in it but purged of all mockery: almost as a God should look, contented, upon the creature of His mind. With grave eyes she met it: then bent her head. In full view of that great company assembled, he kissed her on the forehead. 'I have told him,' he said to her, pointing, by a backward, sideways motion of his head, to Barganax, 'that I am content with him. Content that he is learning to walk without me behind him to direct his steps. I find in him wisdom.'

'I am glad,' said she, her hands still beneath the table. 'Forget, dear my Lord, what I mis-said, afore supper. I think I was sea-sick. In truth I know not what snappish devil drew out my tongue. There was no truth in it.'

'I will forget it all, my Rosma. Have forgot already. Come, now: to make game: let's read thoughts, you and I. Begin with his,' and he looked round upon Barganax, whose face was at this moment partly turned from them in courteous attention to Bekmar telling his tedious old dotterels' tales. 'Where be his thoughts tonight, think you?'

The Queen looked too, this time schooling herself not to look away: saw the Duke, while he listened, change a merry feasting glance with Fiorinda: answered, with a curl of her lip: 'Upon Monte Nero.'

Fruit was borne in now on golden dishes: peaches, dates, raisins of the sun, pomegranates, orange-apples of Zayana, and, in great bowls of gold, little wood-strawberries mixed with cream-cheeses and smothered in cream. The King spoke: 'What sweet voice have we to sing to us, for crowning of the feast? Mistress Campaspe, will you do us that delight, if madam give you leave?'

My Lady Fiorinda, the imperial lazy echoes in whose voice trained on the air perfume-laden leavings of a breeze strayed from Paphos, answered and said: 'Your serene highness's will, in little things as in great, is ours. And indeed I take a delicate pleasure to hear my gentlewoman sing.'

'What song then? You shall choose it.'

'By your serenity's gracious leave, I would have the Duke of Zayana be chooser for, me tonight.'

'Then sing us,' said the Duke to Campaspe, but his eyes, darkly bright, were on her they belonged to, 'that song of *Deare love, for nothing lesse than thee.* Be it mine to choose, I'll have none other tonight.'

Campaspe, standing up in her place now like some little fieldish creature that is here and, whip, gone again in the twilight of nightfall or of dawn, but very lovely and sylph-like of posture in the faintly-moving upward glow of the candles, took her lute and began to sing. Light and immaterial was her singing as the last breath falling asleep with the falling shadows of a May evening without cloud. As the colour of red roses folding their petals as sunset ends, was the colour that softly mounted to her cheek while she sang:

'Deare love, for nothing lesse than thee
Would I have broke this happy dreame,
   It was a theame
For reason, much too strong for phantasie.
Therefore thou wakd'st me wisely; yet
My Dreame thou brok'st not, but continued'st it,
Thou art so truth, that thoughts of thee suffice
To make dreames truths; and fables histories;
Enter these armes, for since thou thought'st it best,
Not to dreame all my dreame, let's act the rest.
As lightning, or a Taper's light,
Thine eyes and not thy noise wak'd mee;
   Yet I thought thee
(For thou lovest truth) an Angell, at first sight,
But when I saw thou sawest my heart,
And knew'st my thoughts, beyond an Angel's art,
When thou knew'st what I dreamt, when thou knew'st when

Excesse of joy would wake me, and cam'st then,
I must confesse, it could not chuse but bee
Prophane, to thinke thee any thing but thee.

Comming and staying show'd thee, thee,
But rising makes me doubt, that now,
   Thou art not thou.
That love is weake, where feare's as strong as hee;
'Tis not all spirit, pure, and brave,
If mixture it of Feare, Shame, Honor, have.
Perchance as torches which must ready bee,
Men light and put out, so thou deal'st with mee,
Thou cam'st to kindle, goest to come; Then I
Will dreame that hope againe, but else would die.'

There was no sound besides in that great hall while she sang.
Eyes for the most part, rested not on the singer but on the lights,
or in high dusky spaces beyond those lights, where nought was
to see but moth-winged memories or wishes, conjured up in myriads
by that unworldly singing: moments uncatchable as the beetle's
droning on the air at the half-light, or as dart of a fieldmouse
amid tufted grass: now here, now gone: lift of skirt above a known
ankle, comfort of known hand, rustle of silks under the promise-
laden starriness of a summer's night, or sound of a known breath
taken gently in sleep: for each listener his own, her own. And each
several one of these innumerable, infinitely little, treasures of hearts'
desire, in this coming and departing and changing as smoke-wreaths
change or eddies in water, seemed yet, at every come and go,
contented: save perhaps for a fear, abysmal under all, lest such
deep-contenting changes should, by some mischieving power
beyond them, ever have end. The Duke, listening, had eyes for
none of these shadows: only for Her, in whom all that beauty
comes home.

She, listening, was leant now a little forward over her table,
her right hand propping her chin. Her left arm rested in a largesse
of lazy grace across the table sideways, its hand playing with her

untasted goblet of golden wine, and on its ring-finger the great eye-refecting alexandrite-stone that changes colour from light to light, of Barganax's ring winking and blazing. Very still was her face: the sheen on her hair a tremble of stars on black sea at midnight. The low-cut bosom of her dress partly gave forth to view, as she so leaned forward, globed twin moons, plenilune at half eclipse, lovelier in their high Grecian pride than the moon of heaven, and holding in their warmed interspace (by patent of every Olympian untamed contour in her countenance above them) all sweets, all stings, all terrors, sense-furying over-weenings, doves, fire-worms, blindings, mandragoras, velvet-sheathed claws, lionesses' teeth: all beguilings: all incorruptibles: all keepings and waterings, returnings and reconcilements, performance and renewal of strength: all raging powers, from everlasting, of beauty and passion of love. And, for seeing eyes to see, between Her brows was the morning star.

Her gaze was, for this while, not upon Her lover but upon the great King, and His on Hers: an eye-parley swift beyond stretch of mortal sense, as though, accommodating Their large leisure to a brief moment of time, as the wide landscape and vault of the sky will lie mirrored in a dewdrop, God should speak with God. As if He should say: Daughter and Sister and Mother and Lover of Mine: Kythereia, brought up with Me from everlasting in the beginning of My way before My works of old: what is this You have done, almost a year ago? Why did you beguile Me to make You that false world?

And awful, gold-crowned, beautiful Aphrodite, answered and said: Because it flattered My mood that night. But I changed My mind. Give it not a thought, My Father. It is abolished: forgot: no, lost beyond forgetting: for how forget what never indeed existed?

He said: It is not the thing create was the mischief, but My creating of it. In that creation I came to know what theretofore I had blessedly (here at least, where to be is to do) not known. What profit to be Me, when action and the springs and issues of action, in Me, in You, in this wide world We live in, are tainted:

known and foreknown to last tittle? This world, this heavenly mansion, is wasted and spoilt.

She said: Not for Me. I am well served. For I (through You, there where, in what I begin to think a more wiser dress of Yours, You do sit at Your own right hand) still find this true world a world apt to My nature. And to Yours.

The 'Why?' in his eyes was a doubt more freezing cold than the grave.

She said, to answer it: Because, I suppose, I can be content to embrace this world's all: can contemplate all; desire all; possess and receive into My being, all; and see that it is good. For I (even when I pleasure Myself to behold Myself in the mirror of My Lover's eyes, and so behold that which is without spot, without bridle, and without bourne) do still, in that all-seeing, limit Me to perfection: to the perfect sum of all perfects which in Me do have their eternity. I limit Me so to All which Is. Eschewing so (through Our common wisdom, which do not You and I possess from the beginning?) that More than all: which is Not; and which (seeing that all which Is, is Good; and all which is Good, Is) is therefore Not Good.

He said: But We went down, into that misconceived misfortuned world of Your passing fantasy. For a moment. To know.

She said: For a life-time's moment. Yes. It was enough.

He said: Since that night in Memison when first I tasted Mine own infinite power: since that unchaining then in Me of this unextinguishable lust of knowing: 'enough' is become to Me a noise without meaning.

She said: Our Father which watchest out of Ida, most glorious, most great, what is this You have spoken? A dangerous saying; and not Your own, I think. Certainly not Mine. What turn next, then?

He said: My creation-old instrument, Death.

She said: No more than so? O, You have turned up the lights again. Your talk had put a strange thing in Me I could not give a name to, without it were Fear.

He said: Be You not too certain sure. This lust that devours

Me, of knowing and doing, burns fiercelier than can be put out with what mortals call Death. I could, before, by that common gate, cross Lethe: even as have not I and You, time unto time and without time, crossing it drunk oblivion? And so, with Our mind as a white paper unwritten, have refreshed Us for life and action in new mansions of this Olympus. In which are many mansions. But what soul-heal is there in that, to redeem this all-knowing knowing? Whereby they are all, here and now, present to Me already: as good go here as there, do this as that: alike it is idleness and vanity.

She said: Do not I, O My Father and My Lover, know them too? Yet there is in My knowing, no stain of this fever, of this unpeace.

He said: Who knoweth better than I, that You know All? But You are of so blest a nature as can be content to know and look on: enjoy, and not meddle: be adored, be had, rest in Your peace: the peace of that which is All, and Enough. But I, by some necessity of My nature, will to go further.

The song had ended. In the moment's silence, while folk yet sat held with the passion of it and the language and the vision, King Mezentius looked still (as Barganax too looked, but he, for his comfort, with a gaze that sounded not, as his Father's, the uttermost deeps) on that Dark Lady.

In the sea-fire eyes of laughter-loving Aphrodite, grown gentler now than a dove's eyes, seeming now to the King to be Amalie's eyes new-unmaidened in Acrozayana five and twenty years ago, but to Barganax Fiorinda's, knowledge sat, detached, tolerant, and merciful; and, by reason of its reach beyond infinitude, begat in the secret places behind the all-wielding all-seeing eyes of the King, infinite pity. Pity for Rosma, who could hate well, but not truly love: for Roder, sitting there, a man of common clay destined within a year or two for a bad end: for Styllis, foredoomed, of his rashness and stiff-necked arrogance, never to seize and hold the shining moment to be given him: for the Admiral, good faithful dog whose loyalties and self-misdoubting irresolution in action must yet withhold him from detachment alike and peace of mind;

for Beroald, blinded by his own sceptic humours and intellectual
ironies to the inmost natures both of Her, his sister in blood, and
of the King, his master: for Heterasmene, left now with but
memories of her governesship to warm her commonplace marriage:
for Emmius Parry, whose greatness could as little reck of other
men's pity as waste his on them: for the great Vicar of Rerek
himself, not because of any warring or unhappiness in his self-
perfect nature (where there was neither), but because, whereas
the King and She understand from within by very feeling what
it were to be this man, who all his life must, but for the master-
hand upon him, have mischieved all middle earth, yet should the
Vicar never understand and contain Their loves as They in a
manner do his: pity for the nothings, rests and pauses and unre-
solved discords necessary in the symphony of this brave world,
as for Fiorinda's ill-starred unsufficient husbands, as well for
Valero, for Aktor, for the tragic nothings of Middlemead: for His
Amalie, who must tonight be widowed and left to her motherhood and her Memisonian peace: for Queen Stateira, now to lose
(except in memory) her very motherhood, and with no memories
of true love and perfect, only of Mardanus's perfunctory transient
love, and of her own restless, consuming, never wholly satisfied
passion for Aktor: for Vandermast, albeit a contemplative that
walked with God, yet exiled (unless through kindly sympathy and
back-returns of the mind) from the joys and fevers of youth: for
Antiope, fated, as the rock-rose's queenly blossom, to a tragic
ephemeral perfection and tragic death: for Barganax even, and
Lessingham, because of the limitations of their beings, not to be
wholly Himself: for these nymphkind, dwelling in the superficies
and so coming short of Godhead: for every man, woman, child, and
living creature in Zimiamvia, because instruments, means, and ingredients to His and Her perfection in action and beatitude: even
for Her, as to all eternity unable to be, were it but for a moment,
He. Last, pity for that which sat conscient in Her eyes: for His
love and Hers, troubled now for sake of God Himself, that He
should be choked with His own omniscience and omnipotence
here terribly loosed in self-emptying collision within Him: for

sake of His loneliness, here where should be His home: that here, through dull privation of that doubt which alone can bring zest to omnipotency in action, He, knowing overmuch, fails of his way.

And, darkly unspoken in that commerce of eyes, a horror moved; horror not of the unknown, but of the unknowable, the impossible, the unconceivable.

King Mezentius gave command now (for ending of the revels) to bring in the Cup of Memory. A great goblet it was, of rock-crystal, egg-shaped, resting in the grasp of three feet upraised to contain between them the belly of it: feet of pure gold, one in the likeness of the pounces and talon of an eagle, another a lion's paw with claws expansed, and the third a hippogriff's hoof, all rising from a nine-sided base of hammered gold bossed with rubies and chrysoprases and hyacinth-stones and pearls. This, being brought in, went round, first at the lowest tables and so in order upwards, until every person in the body of the hall below the dais had drunk of it, each a sip. And each in turn, having drunk, bowed low toward the King. The cup-bearer now, brimming it anew with ruby-dark wine of the Rian, bore it to Earl Roder, who, as captain of the guard, tasted it and with his own hand bore it to King Mezentius. Upon that, all the company below the dais stood up in their places, while the Earl returned him to his chair of state. The King, raising the cup, looked into the wine against the light, savoured it with his nostrils, and so, looking towards the company, drank deep: then said in a great voice, for all in that great banquet-chamber to hear: ''Tis time to say goodnight. Rest well, my friends. Our banquet is sweetly ended.' Upon which word all, save only the company on the dais, bowed low toward the King and so, with that for goodnight, departed. The King meanwhile, wiping the lip of the cup with his handkercher, set it down, yet three parts full, upon the Queen's table before her.

She, for her turn, lifted it in both hands: drank (as next in order of nobility) to Duke Barganax: wiped, and reached across the King's table on her right, to have passed it to the Duke. But the King, intercepting it, said lightly, 'Nay, I will break custom tonight. For good luck, since these be farewell revels, I'll pledge him too.'

Rosma laid a hand on his arm. 'Pray you, dear my Lord,' she said, smiling, but her face suddenly gone grey as ashes: 'that bringeth bad luck, not good, to drink twice ere the cup be gone round.'

King Mezentius but shifted the cup from his left hand to his right. 'Fear nothing, madam. Luck, long as I remember me, hath been my servant still. I'll go my gait, as in great things so here in little, and spite all omens.'

His eyes, while he so spoke, were met with my Lady Fiorinda's, chilling as snakes' eyes now or as stones a-glitter with heatless green fire, and saying to Him: What terrible unlawful unimagined lust is this? You are putting Us, both You and Me, and all that proceedeth from Us (or hath, or shall proceed) into deadly danger. Whither do You mean to go? What do You mean to do?

He was at the point to drink. Rosma made a movement so slight as none but his own most eagle eyes might note it, as if ready, in the open sight of the court, to have knocked the cup from his lips; but his great left hand shut, gentle but unresistable, upon her hand, pinning it to the table. He set down the goblet once more, out of her reach. 'Let's finish the evening in private. Earl, clear the hall. Let the maids and the music be gone. Set guards without all the doors, and to keep folk from the portico.'

While this was doing, those lords of Meszria and the Lady Heterasmene, in obedience to eye-signs from the King and Queen, bade goodnight, took their leaves, and departed. They being gone, Rosma said to the King: 'Lord, I beseech you, for all sakes' sakes, bear with my foolish fears. 'Tis the one boon I ask of you tonight and surely 'tis a light nothing for you to grant. There's a curse in a twice-drunk Memory-Cup. However silly I seem, to take a small matter too heavily, O, tempt no fates tonight. For my sake, Lord. And if not for mine,' she checked: then finished, looking at Barganax, 'for his.'

It was grown very close in the hall now, for all that the windows stood open. The long-gathering storm began: a great flash in dry sultry air, near overhead, and deafening peals of thunder: then pitch darkness without, as the thunder rolled away to silence. Barganax looked swiftly from Rosma to the King: from him to Fiorinda, sitting motionless as Aphrodite's statua: so to the King again. 'Lord and Father,' he said, 'pray you drink it not. The Queen's highness feareth some practice, I think. 'Twere well send for fresh wine. Let this be ta'en away and examined'; and he took hold on the goblet.

'Lay off your hand,' said the King, 'I command you,'

Barganax met his eyes: seemed to hover an instant betwixt unclear contrarious duties: then obeyed. He sat back, eyes flaming, face red as blood. Bringing his fist down upon the table before him with a blow set the plates a-leap and a-clatter, 'Yet would I give my dukedom,' he said violently, 'that your serene highness taste not this again.'

'I do not care whether you would or no. But you, as all man else i' the kingdoms, shall do my bidding.' So saying, the King, taking the great goblet betwixt his hands and looking down into the wine, swirled it about: a whirlpool in little. Presently, laughing in his black beard, 'Moonshine in water,' he said to the Duke. 'Have not she and I drunken o' this same pottle already? Were aught amiss with 't, we were both of us sped ere now.'

Queen Rosma said, and her voice shook: 'Nay then, myself, I do seem now to find, I know not what, but an after-taste in it: something sluggish in its working, may be. By heavens,' she said suddenly, 'I accuse this Roder. A meant it for Lord Barganax.'

The Earl stared at her like a startled bull.

'Come,' said the King, 'this is fits of the mother. A most strange, most unmerited, brainless accusation against a true, tried servant of ours,' he said, with a glance at Roder, whose eyes were now boiling out of his face: then turned him once more to Rosma. 'No more fooleries. A curse in a twice-drunk cup? You are much mistook, madam. This, I pledge you my kingly word for 't, is nectar.' While she sat unpowered to move or speak under the tyranny of his eyes upon her, he drank. 'To your deepest wishes, my Rosma. Which have, e'en at such times as least you dreamed it, galloped in harness with mine.'

He wiped the brim: set the half-empty cup on his table within her reach: then, his eyes meaningly and steadfastly on hers but without all note of menace or blame or resentment in them, held his handkercher to the candleflame. Being well alight, he dropped it to burn out on the table-top: of panteron stone, in some part black, in other part green, in other part purple, which is said to bolden a man, and make him invincible. The Queen, those words echoing in her ears, those things done before her eyes, that understanding in the King's eyes upon her, sat stone still.

At last, sweeping her gaze round upon Barganax, Beroald, Fiorinda, Roder, Jeronimy, to end upon the King again, 'Yes. Well,' she said, 'it is true. It is nectar': then thrust aside her table, rose to her feet and, facing him, seized the cup. 'But I meant it for that whoreson, that calleth himself Duke of Zayana.' Standing so before them, she drained it, no trickle left: turned again with a hideous cry: fell with a crash in the half-moon space before the tables, without a struggle, stone dead.

Barganax spoke silence: 'God's precious Lady be thanked then, your highness swallowed it not.'

King Mezentius gave him his eyes for an instant, undisturbed, resolute, but, save for their good will, unreadable: then, turning to the Admiral and Lord Roder, 'Take up the Queen's body,' he said. 'Sit it in her chair of state.'

When they, in a maze and rather in manner of contrived automatons than of waking men, had done his bidding, he stood up, somewhat slowly, from his high-seat and, taking from his own head the crown of Meszria, set it on hers. 'I'll view it again thus, where it belonged when first I had sight of it. Who loveth me, remember her greatness, and her father's. Put out of mind aught you may think she did amiss. She has paid for that, and as no skulking cheater, neither, nor in no false coin. Sorely tried she was, and, i' the end, no unnoble daughter of the Parry. Few there be that I shall gladlier shake by the hand, beyond the hateful river.'

He looked at Fiorinda: saw how her eyes rested constant on Barganax.

'You may see,' said the King, seated again and surveying Rosma's face, undisfigured and wearing a peace and a majesty not known there in her life-days, 'that here's no villainous discountenancing poison, to mar that which God Himself hath made, and send us aboard of Charon's ferry as puff-balls swol'n up and bursten. 'Tis a clean death, and worthy of royal Princes.'

Outside, now, a gale was raging from the west: rushings of rain, and the huge belly of darkness continually a-rumbling with near and distant thunders. The windows of the hall flickered blue with the ceaseless lightning.

'Beroald,' the King said, 'you are a brave man and a discreet, and a friend of mine. You are instantly to take boat, then saddle and ride your swiftest to Zayana. This ring,' here he took the great Worm-ring from his thumb; 'give it to her grace. She'll know the token. Say to her I have yet a few hours to live, but I am dog-weary, and it is no more in my power to turn this destiny.'

As if the forked lightning-flame had with these words leapt among them, all, save only the King and my Lady Fiorinda, sprang to their feet. The Duke said, out of a deformed silence:

'But the counterpoisons your highness hath alway taken?'

'Without 'em, I were gone, her way, at first sip. Look to the ring on her finger: undo the bezel: so: it is empty, but for specks of this greenish dust. This was her aunt's first wedding-gift, Lugia Parry's; and 'gainst that masterpiece, wetted or ta'en by the mouth, all counterpoisons in the world are naught: save to delay. She had it in her handkercher.'

'Send for leeches.'

'They can do nothing. Begone, Chancellor: your speediest.'

'Shall I bring her noble excellence back with me?'

'No. Though my salvation hung on't, I would not hazard her safety in such a storm. But it were a hell to me to die and no word from her to speed me. Begone, Beroald, and swiftly back. Haste, haste, post haste. Worketh already, dull in my feet.

'Earl,' he said, as the Chancellor, with face like a stone, strode swiftly down the hall, 'fetch me my armour; and the triple crown; and my robes of state. Kings ought not to die lying on their backs.'

'And fetch leeches, for God sake, quick,' said Barganax swiftly in the Earl's ear. 'All blame's mine, if 's highness mislike it.'

Within five minutes, the Chancellor put out upon the firth in the fury and height of the storm: himself at the tiller, and two boatmen to take turns at oars and bailing. There was but a mile to go, but they were not gotten half way when a tremendous sea breaking over the stern swamped the boat and left them to swim or drown. By strength and by heart, but most (it seemed) by some over-riding fate of necessity, they made land, but on a lee shore, much east beyond the right landing-place and set about with sharp rocks and skerries. On the teeth of these one of the boatmen being dashed by a wave was knocked senseless and, taken by the undertow, no more seen. His fellow won to safety, but with 's leg broke. The Lord Beroald, bruised and cut, came aland a little farther east and, with but a tatter of soaked rags left to cover his nakedness, part walked, part ran, till he was come to the little township and fishing-harbour of Leshmar. Here the Admiral's bailiff found him dry clothes and a horse: sent, by his bidding, to bring in the wounded boatman: and so, scarce more than an hour from his leaving of the banquet-chamber, the Chancellor rode up into Acrozayana.

'Dying, and past hope of mending?' said the Duchess when he told his tale. 'God's precious Dear take mercy then of this land of Meszria, mercy of our dear son, mercy of us all. You have spoke to me killing words, noble Beroald. O, I am very sick.' And throwing herself face downward upon the great brocaded couch between the windows she fell into an unmasterable great passion of tears. The Chancellor, that had never seen her weep, turned him away and, with folded arms and iron-lipped, unmoving as stone, stood looking on her picture above the mantel, a master-work of Barganax's painted five years ago, and so waited till this tempest should blow itself out.

Presently she stood up and dried her eyes.

He turned. 'I was to take word back from your beauteous excellency.'

'Word? You are to take me, my lord. Have you not yet given order for my horses?'

'There is a dangerous sea running in the firth tonight. The King's highness did expressly command you must not adventure it.'

'Pray you, pull me that bell-rope.'

Beroald looked at her. Something glinting in his cold eye, he went to the window, drew back the curtain, threw open the case-ment. The wind had dropped. Westward, over Zayana lake, was clear weather and moonlight. He came back to her beside the fire-place, reached hand to the twisted rope of honey-coloured silk and gave it a jerk. 'The Duchess intends for Sestola tonight,' he said to the waiting-woman: 'taketh but one maid and a portman-teau. Her grace's horses are at the Kremasmian gate already, waiting with mine.'

Amalie gave him her hand.

'To be great-hearted,' he said, kissing it, 'is a lovely virtue. And loveliest in woman; 'cause least of course.'

When the Duchess, with the Chancellor carrying her cloak, was come into the banquet-chamber, King Mezentius sat yet in his high-seat, clad now in all his royal habiliments and ornaments of majesty. Above him were seated the Admiral, Earl Roder, Duke Barganax, and my Lady Fiorinda. The body of the Queen had been taken away to lie in state. The Duchess, very white and with eyes only for the King, came up that great empty hall almost as a woman walks in her sleep, but noble of mien and carriage as a tall ship dropping silently down the tideway at evening before a light breeze. So, mounting the dais, she stood before him.

'So, Amalie, you are come to me? and spite of my strait forbidding?'

'How could I choose?'

'Do not kiss me, sweetheart, or I shall poison you. Sit where I can see you. The sands are running out. You, Beroald: thanks, and fare you well. Leave us now: you have had my commands, and you too, Jeronimy and Roder. May the Gods lead you by the hand. You too, my son: yes, but stay you. And stay you too, dear Lady of Sakes.'

When those were sorrowfully departed, the Duke set a chair for his mother and on her right another for Fiorinda, and himself took seat on his mother's left, facing the King.

The Duchess leaned forward. 'Do not kiss you?' she said. 'O yes, that you may take me with you. How can I, after so many years, bear the darkness here alone?'

'I,' said the King, 'am entering upon a darkness that was, until late ago, unthought on: darkness uncompanionable: may be, unreturnable. If there be throughway, my darling dear (and there's no man nor, I think, no God, to tell us whether), you shall find my doing was but to prepare new kingdoms for you. I' the long mean time, comfort you that My choice it was. No will but Mine could force me this gate, open it upon triumph such as eye hath not seen nor heart imagined. Or else,' he paused, and while he looked on her a film seemed to be drawn over his eyes: 'or else: upon Nothing.'

The Duchess listening, from her chair between Barganax and Fiorinda, as if to some terrible commination, seemed to miss the sense but yet to be touched, as fire touches the shrinking flesh, with the deadly import. 'I do not understand,' she said, trembling. 'Your choice? I can never forget you were my lover. I never thought you, of all people in the world, would choose to hurt me.'

He bore her look a minute in silence. Then, 'O turn your eyes away, Amalie,' he said; 'or for your dear sake I shall, at this last, fail of Myself: become less than, of My true whole nature, I must be.'

'How could you do it? O,' she cried, 'how could you do it?' and she covered her mouth with her hand, biting, for silence, at the palm.

'Remove her away for God sake,' said the King. 'I can grapple the great death, but not with My hands tied.'

None stirred.

The Duchess, pale, but collecting herself to sit now in a

self-warranting superbity erect in her chair, said, 'I'm sorry, dear my Lord. It is brought under. I'll not, i' the last turning, become a foot-gin in your way.'

But that Dark Lady, Her eyes like the eyes of a lioness that gives bay to her adversaries, said to the King: 'Is she not Me, albeit she know it not? And think You I do not know Myself and, through Myself, You? It is child's play to You and Me, this world-making; and child's play to abolish and do away a world, or a million worlds. But to abolish (as You seem now, of Your furious self-feeding folly, resolved to hazard it) the very stuff of Being, which is Me and You: this seemeth to Me a greatness which, like overblown bubbles, is of its own extreme become littler than littleness.'

'Be silent, lest I strike You in pieces first with My thunderstone. We will yet see whether God be able to die.'

'Questionless, He is able. To Him is not even the impossible possible? But questionless, He will not.'

'Why not?'

'For sake of Her.'

The Duchess buried her face between Fiorinda's breasts, as if the heart-beats unquieting that violet-sweet enchanted valley were her own eternized: last core and safeguard unsure of an unbottomed world. The King, shutting his eyes not to behold her, said: 'We will see.'

'If You do Your intent, and the throw fail You,' said that Lady, 'then We shall not see. For there will be nought to see, nor eye to see it. By that unexperimented leap, in peril and blasphemy both of Yourself and Me, You may (since there be no chains to chain omnipotency run mad), at a stroke end All. End it so as not so much as a dead universe nor a dead God be left to be remembered or forgotten, but only a Nothing not to be named or thought; because in it is nor existence nor unexistence, hope nor fear nor time nor life nor God nor eternity (not even that eternity of nothing), nor truth nor untruth nor remembering nor unremembering any more: not even such last little wet mark or burnt-out ember as might rest for the uncipherable cipher: *I am not: I never was; I never shall be.*' In the honey-dropping dying music of Her voice, time, space, fate, beauty, seemed let fall as a tale told, and all stings of death desirable before this horror of the void.

'Which is to deny itself,' said the Duchess, turning her head. 'Evil, which is the ultimate Nothing, so shattered at last and broken in its nothingness, as not be able even to be nothing.' She shuddered violently and, sitting up and resting a hand on Barganax's knee, 'Your way is mine,' she said to the King, in a whisper. 'The truth is, love is not able to kill love.'

'To God,' said the King, 'all things are easy. And, save one thing alone, all are accomplished.'

'You say well, my lady Mother,' said the Duke, with his hand on hers. 'But as for truth, I know not. And care not. For what's this but tilling of the sand, to talk so and question so about truth? I have small inclination for this, when this infinite which is beauty's self' (his eyes now upon Fiorinda) 'lieth open for my tilling: the only truth I know the name of, the only truth I would purchase at a flea's worth. And if God be (as I know not nor reck not whether), He is no God of mine when he ceaseth to love where I love.'

There was a long silence. Barganax, with the grace upon him of some hunting-leopard in a muse 'twixt sleeping and waking, gazed between half-shut lids now on his Father, now on Fiorinda. In her face, seen thus sideways, warring insolubles, of heart-break and heart-heal and things yet deeper in grain, not in reason adorable yet past reason adored, seemed to flicker and change with their own self-light. He saw now, like as in Memison almost a year ago but not yet seen tonight, glow-worms in her hair. Her eyes were on the King's. He, bolt upright in his high-seat, crowned and robed and armed, looked now in them; now upon Amalie's tender neck and, smoothly drawn up from it with a high comb of tortoise-shell and inwoven to a voluptuosity of shining twists and coils on the crown of her head, the red-gold glory of her hair (her face was by this time hiding again on Fiorinda's breast); now upon the night-piece of the two of them: Queen of Spades: Queen of Hearts. Presently, as in a mirror, his speckled grey eyes, their eagle gaze unblunted yet and undimmed, met his son's.

'I leave you and the others a tangled business,' he said, 'where I could if I would have left all pat. But you'd have smally thanked me, I think: to do all beforehand and leave my after-comers with occupation gone.'

'Be you thanked as I thank you, O my Father,' said the Duke. With a catch of his breath he made as if to say more; but no words came.

Albeit midsummer, it was now turned bitter cold, in this dead time of night when the tide of man's blood runs lowest: the hour when oftenest men die. Here, under the bright lights and in the large emptiness of this banquet-chamber, scarce was a sound heard, save that of the sea with the storm-swell not yet stilled in it lapping the seawalls: this, and the breathing of those four, and the ticking of the clock. These breaths and these tickings measured out the ingredients of the stillness: hollownesses within, dulling of the spirits from sleeplessness, dulling of the brain: hands and feet grown powerless, fingers all turned to thumbs, eyelids hot and heavy. So they waited, as if for something that itself, too, held back and waited in the night without.

At length the King said, the third time: 'We will see.' Then, as in a secret gaiety which held under-stirrings of that power that moves the sun and the other stars, and which brought the Duchess on the sudden wide awake again, her name: 'Amalie.'

Upon that, Duke Barganax, looking first at his Father and then where his Father looked, beheld a great wonder. My Lady Fiorinda was stood up to her full stature: the red corn-rose dress, fallen down about Her knees, seemed water-green laced with white, sea-waves of the heavenly Paphos; and upon Her brow and cheek, and upon all Her divine body thus unveiled, was the beauty that blinds the Gods. In that great banquet-hall in Sestola was nothing now visible but that beauty, all else, for a timeless moment, put out by it as the risen sun puts out the stars. Barganax, so beholding Her, knew he beheld what his Father beheld: save only that this eternal morning wore, for his Father's eyes, an aurora of red fire, but for his own eyes that sable aurora of night: which, for him, all perfects else excels. And the face of Her, while they looked (as a finger held up before the eyes can seem now to stand against this tree in the far landscape now against that, and so alternately, as alternately right eye or left takes power) seemed now Fiorinda's, now Amalie's.

Then time and space resumed their vicegerency in Sestola; even as when the eyes, leaving to look upon the landscape and converging upon the raised finger, see it its own known self again, familiar and near again, of like flesh with the looker. That Dark Lady sat palpable and exquisite here in her chair, wearing her gown of scarlet sendaline; and on the sweet unrest of her bosom the Duchess of Memison yet laid her cheek, as if in slumber.

Barganax rising softly, came to the King's side: viewed him narrowly. Then he turned to those two. The Duchess raised her head: stood up: looked first at the King, then, as in a sudden fear at her son: saw in his eyes a new depth of power and sufficiency: new, yet far beyond all remembrance old. 'I have thought it, I think,' she said, very low, 'from the beginning: that there have been four of us. Perhaps, more than four. And yet always a twoness in that many. And that twoness so near unite to oneness as sense to spirit, yet so as not to confound to unity the very heart and being of God; who is Two in One and One in Two.'

Barganax took her hand and kissed it. 'Even and we were Gods: (my Father, upon whom be peace, said it, you remember at your fish dinner last July): Even and we were Gods, best not to know. Well: thank God, I know not. Only,' he said to Fiorinda, standing within handreach, 'I believe your ladyship knows.'

In her eyes, unsounded heavens of green fire, and in the gravity that overlay the smoulder of her uncomparable lips, sweet-suggesting inviters, forcible setters-on, to the lime-bushes and labyrinthine ways of love, sat the Bitter-sweet. 'Yes,' she said. 'I know: or almost all. And indeed I suppose I have a bent of mind is able to bear with the knowledge of some matters which even to you, who are a glad man of your nature, should hardly I think be bearable.'

'Promise me this,' he said, watching her eyes, that mouth, the glow-worms in her hair: 'never to tell me.'

'It is,' answered that lady, and there was that in her voice that fetched down for him, from heaven, both the morning and the evening star, 'the one sole promise that I will ever make to your grace. And from my heart. And for love.' And she added, unspoken but read darkly, like enough, by Barganax in the comet-caging deeps of those Olympian eyes: 'for My servant, love, whose triumph We see tonight.'

GENEALOGICAL TABLES

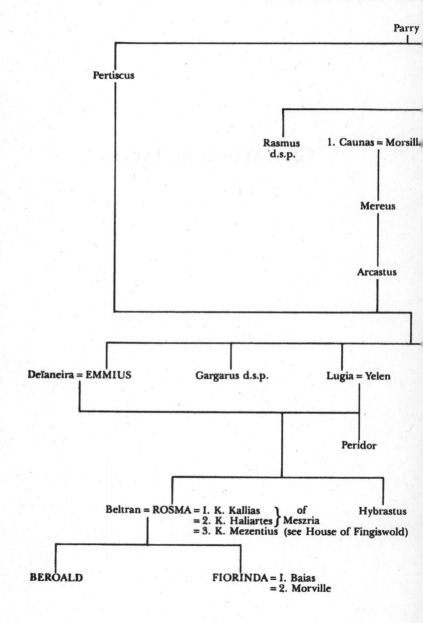

Parry

Pertiscus

Rasmus
d.s.p.

1. Caunas = Morsill.

Mereus

Arcastus

Deïaneira = EMMIUS   Gargarus d.s.p.   Lugia = Yelen

Peridor

Beltran = ROSMA = I. K. Kallias ⎫ of   Hybrastus
         = 2. K. Haliartes ⎬ Meszria
         = 3. K. Mezentius (see House of Fingiswold)

BEROALD   FIORINDA = I. Baias
                     = 2. Morville

RRY FAMILY

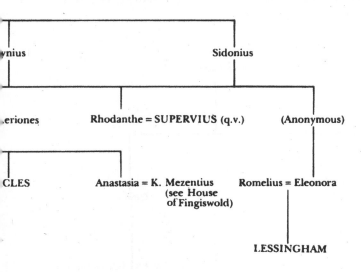

ynius   Sidonius

eriones   Rhodanthe = SUPERVIUS (q.v.)   (Anonymous)

CLES   Anastasia = K. Mezentius   Romelius = Eleonora
                     (see House
                     of Fingiswold)

LESSINGHAM

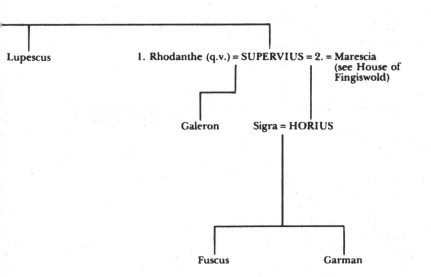

Lupescus   1. Rhodanthe (q.v.) = SUPERVIUS = 2. = Marescia
                                         (see House of
                                         Fingiswold)

Galeron   Sigra = HORIUS

Fuscus   Garman

THE ROYAL HOUSE OF FINGISWOLD

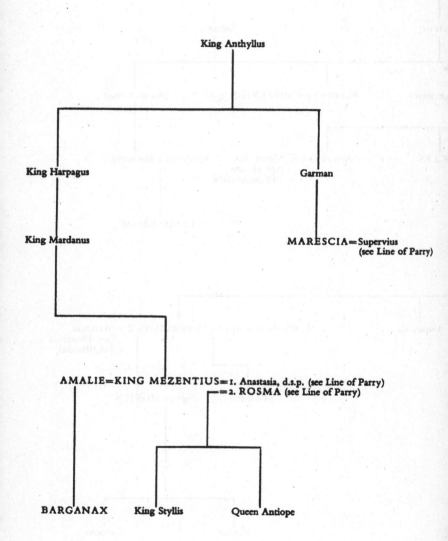

MAP OF THE THREE KINGDOMS

FINGISSWOLD

Rialmar
Ihee Midland
The Sea
Wold

Continuation
Northwards
on a reduced scale
Scale of Miles

Solitudines vasta

Megra

Veiring

Abaraima o

Eldis

Kaima

Mornagay

The Horn

Hornmere
Laimak
Owldale
Ristby

Anyyanna

Ulba
Kutarmish
Zennt
Rumala
Hvewey
Salima
Peraz
Mizulma
Memison
Reisma
Mere

Daish
Jyyana
Sestola
Armash

Sprind

Fashoda

Scale of Miles

THE THREE
KINGDOMS

www.ingramcontent.com/pod-product-compliance
Ingram Content Group UK Ltd.
Pitfield, Milton Keynes, MK11 3LW, UK
UKHW020208190625
459827UK00005BB/577

9 780007 578177